S0-BOG-933

Prince Elmo's Fire

Prince Elmo's Fire

ERNEST LOCKRIDGE

SD

STEIN AND DAY/*Publishers*/New York

First published in 1974

Library of Congress Catalog Card No. 73–82112

Designed by David Miller
Printed in the United States of America
Stein and Day/*Publishers*/Scarborough House, Briarcliff Manor, N.Y. 10510
ISBN 0–8128–1640–4

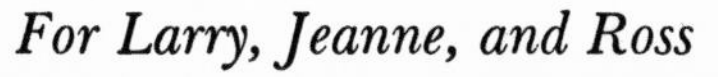

For Larry, Jeanne, and Ross

I want to express my deep appreciation to the Center for Advanced Study, Graduate College, University of Illinois, where I wrote the first draft of this novel, and to its former director, Dr. David Pines.

E.L.

Contents

. . . I grow aware of that eternal flickering of forms which we are now too worldly wise to label progress, and whose meaning forever escapes us.

—Loren Eiseley

Breeding

LET ME reconstruct my first whole memory: the night my father lost himself and I lost him.

"There ain't no justice," Big Dick wailed. "How's a man supposed to concentrate on a chivaree with this draft notice hanging over his head? Who in hell they think they are, telling me I have to pick up ass and go?"

"They're thuh-uh U.S. govermint. They can make you do any goddamn thing they want." Grampa hunched over in the rocker and fanned his crotch. For twenty-five years, his shoulder and right side had spasmodically twitched up and down, because one early morning in June 1918 a hunk of Hun artillery had landed in his trench and vaporized two men, deprived several of limbs, eyes, fingers, and other decorations, but left Grampa's body untouched— shock driving him so wild that he somehow crossed a hundred yards of battlefield, including two six-foot coils of barbed wire, and bayoneted five drooling Hun in their trench. "Thuh-uh goddamn thing blew me through the air like one of them spaceships in thuh-uh movies," Grampa would say, "But nobody believes a goddamn thing I tell 'em." Helen, my mother, would reply, "Grampa, if just once you'd stop drilling for oil, folks wouldn't think you was such a old crazy."

"It ain't as if they really need me," my father went on. "It ain't as if they don't have a million Frenchies and A-rabs left to use up. It ain't even the fact I'm a family man, with a wife and three kids to support, and if that wasn't enough, my old man and old lady—six hungry mouths to feed, not even thinking about my own—it ain't that. It's that for the first time in my whole life, I got my boat coming in. Maybe only one week from today old Tarze Roberts'll come through with that money, and me and him together'll open the Garden of Roses—"

"As for feeding mouths," my older brother Duke interrupted, "if me and Prince Elmo wasn't out stealing, and Cissy here wasn't just plain out all over the place, who'd be eating?"

Cissy was my older sister, Cerulia, twelve then, though she looked much older.

"When you get over there," Grampa said, "watch out for thuh-uh Frenchies. They're thuh-uh goddamn filthiest-minded people in the world."

"Next to you, huh, Grampa? Hey, Granny," Helen asked, "you ever know a time when Grampa here wasn't digging up his garden? Grampa, you old dirty man, you."

"I don't remember of it," Granma replied from her corner.

"I fought next to one of the Frenchies named Row-bear," Grampa said. "And one day me and Row-bear went into this little town together on pass, and Row-bear went into this house, and I come along, and after we come out, I asked him, 'Rowbear, how many of them Frenchwomen in your country'd kiss a peter?' And Row-bear said, there wasn't a Frenchwoman he ever knowed that wouldn't kiss a peter and like it. And then I asked him, 'Row-bear, how many Frenchies'd kiss a pussy?' And Row-bear said all Frenchies'd rather do that than eat dinner. There ain't a goddamn filthy thing in this world that a Frenchie wouldn't do—"

"That you wouldn't do yourself, huh, Grampa?" Helen said. "Hey, Grampa, let's doctor up your face a little, and give you Dick's letter, and you go to Indianapolis and say your name ain't old Elmo, it's Dick Hatcher. Maybe they'll ship you back to that little house, so all them Frenchwomen can turn you ever which way again, you old raunchy thing."

"Well, forevermore," Granma murmured.

Duke looked up from his whittling. "What's all this filthy talk with kids present?" He was nine, and I was four years younger. "Elmo's such a stupid innocent little runt."

"Smartass kid," Dick said. "Make your mother sorry she ever bore children."

"How much cash you be sending back, honey?" Helen asked.

"I ain't letting the biggest opportunity of my life turn to shit," Dick said. "Look, there's a time when a man just has to plow ahead and do what he has to. I simply ain't got no choice."

"Ain't there something about insurance policies if you get killed?" Helen asked.

"Ten thousand dollars," Cerulia said. "And we'll ship back his carcass and plant it in the Garden of Roses."

"But there ain't a thing half-assed about this deal," Dick insisted. "If old Tarze'll put up only five hundred dollars—I mean, sooner or later everybody's got to die, and right now these young guys is dying so fast they're running out of places to plant 'em. In town, hell, ever two feet, you step on a mound, and they don't even bother to keep the place up. It's nothing but a crop of goddamn well-fertilized weeds. But if I open up a new one, on this piece of land only I know about, with a little brook, and all them gentle rolling slopes, and trees, just the right amount of shade so people can feel private, and enough room to keep it in business maybe two hundred years—these kids could feed their grandkids off a place like that. And now some sneaky son of a bitch pulls my name out of the hat. Well, they got me if they can catch me."

"Faw! I'd give out where you was hiding for a half buck," Duke said.

"Ain't no respect," Grampa grumbled. "Before thuh-uh Hun got rolling again this time, I'd like to know one other man-jack in this county that'd ever got across thuh-uh Atlantic Ocean to France."

"Don't worry, Grampa," Helen said. "We'll take up a collection. Them French girls gonna get another chance. They're gonna blow the wax right out of your old ears."

"By God, I'd love to get another crack at thuh-uh goddamn Hun, don't think I wouldn't. Like some old animal just come up out of the slime, them Huns. It ain't no Frenchie whorehouse I dream about at night, it's thuh-uh goddamn Hun trenches, where a boy went in a boy, and if he come out at all, he come out a man, holding up his piece in front of him for more blood. Girlie, this here's a pretty poor old chunk of flesh waving its hand around because of thuh-uh goddamn Hun," Grampa said, looking dead-on at Helen, "but by Jesus, if you don't think it's still all man—"

"I never said that, Grampa," Helen murmured. "I never said you wasn't."

Grampa was a man, all right, and he was teaching me how to shoot, though I could scarcely keep the Winchester bolt-action single-shot twenty-two, with its long, octagonal barrel, to my shoulder without a prop. Ammo was scarce; Duke and I had to wander into the sporting goods in town five miles off, and steal a box from behind the glass counter. When he took a turn shooting, Grampa would suddenly stop quaking, draw a breath, and become stone. He could drill a bottlecap at one hundred feet. "That was thuh-uh goddamn eye of a rich man," he said once.

Duke squatted near the door, on the planking, whittling a stick to a sharp point. I sat on the floor, on my sleeping pad. Nobody paid me any attention. Big Dick paced the shack. Helen and Cerulia sat on one bed, dangling bare legs over its side. Grampa breathed in his rocker. In her corner, on a rickety chair, Granma bent over a blue-and-gold fragment of quilt. Two lanterns flung our only light. I listened for animals in the darkness outside. My bladder hurt, but I didn't dare walk down to the woods alone. When the flickering lights were killed, and the big people grunted in the dark like happy pigs, I would crawl to the corner with the hole that went clear through and ease out my little stream. Spokes of cold air circulated through the shack; outside an April wind blew, and I thought of my twin brother down the hill, in the Gorge, an abandoned limestone quarry, deep in the icy black water, sleeping with open eyes like a fish, naked among minnows, turtles, and frogs. I feld glad Duke had saved my life, instead of my twin's.

"Hey, Dick honey!" Helen called, as if my father were way outside in the darkness, "how come you think Tarze is gonna give you any money?"

"Cause I sold him whiskey," Big Dick said. "Cause I'm a man with something inside his head, and no goddamn idiot like those rich sons of bitches in town."

"That ain't the reason, Mamma," Cerulia crowed. "It's cause we been selling old Tarze other things."

"I was just asking Big Dick what *he* thought the reason was," Helen went on. "By the way, Dick, what did you say Polly's married name was gonna be? I mean, it looks to me like sooner or later all the women in your life feel the need for another man."

"I'm gonna kill somebody," Dick muttered, standing with clenched fists and staring at the floor. "In just about two seconds."

"Dick, you always was all shirt and no pants," Helen said. "That's how come you ain't able to satisfy a woman."

"Grampa, where's the gun?"

"Ain't a bullet in the house," Duke lied. "Me and Prince Elmo ain't been out shopping lately."

"You ain't shooting no family tonight, boy," Grampa said.

Dick grabbed Cerulia, flung her off the bed, and sent her whirling against the door. Leaves in a wind, Cerulia's rags billowed above her naked thighs, then settled. She slammed against the wood.

"Don't damage the merchandise," she gasped. "I better not have no bruises."

"Cool down, sonny," Grampa warned.

Dick rared his fist back to punch Helen.

"Save that for the Japs," Helen said, looking him in the eyes. "You wouldn't know what it was like to hit a man."

"A man"—Dick's tongue choked him—"can take only so much." His eyes shifted around. On the stove sat the skillet, gray inside with an inch of grease; my father lifted it above his head like an ax and banged it against the floor near the bed. Cold globs splattered onto Helen's legs.

"You know, Dick, after the govermint men haul your ass off, I'm gonna pile every man in the county into this bed."

Dick hoisted the skillet again, but it slipped his hand and bounced off his foot.

"I'm gonna get me ten men that's twice your size," Helen kept going, "twice the man you ever were, with pretty faces like Errol Flynn and Rudolph Stayne, and I'm gonna take them out into the woods and do it in the leaves and splat up against the trunks of trees, everwhere, till sap's running out my throat."

Dick clutched his hurt toes and hopped one-footed behind our potbellied stove, where the rifle jutted against the kindling pile.

"Like a bitch on all fours!" Helen wailed. "Front and back, men that work for a living, that fight men instead of women!"

Dick yanked the breech open. "Duke, where's them bullets?"

"*You* know why you think that old filth Tarze Roberts might pour money down your rathole!" Helen cried.

Dick reached in front of Granma for a red-and-black box resting on our dirt-brown windowsill. "Whores and liars," he said. Still stitching furiously, Granma stayed bent over a square of cloth. In her clothes, she weighed maybe seventy pounds. A cardboard banana box sat on the floor beside her, piled above the brim with scraps, a tangled colorful chaos of material. Neat squares, each an identically patterned maze of colors, formed inch-high stacks in a cigar box at her feet. Granma had invented the pattern: an organism in plane geometry, a bird in flight, a maple leaf, or the phoenix in flames. Each square demanded hundreds of stitches, and the whole brilliant field of quilt would hold a thousand squares. Colors changed according to what scraps Granma gathered. Big Dick complained that Granma robbed the patches off his jeans. Once in the middle of a field, I'd seen Granma harvest a scrap of red cloth from a stalk of Queen Anne's lace. "Well, forevermore," Granma had sung out. "Looky here." The woman from Welfare, two tons gasping and wheezing sideways like a crab through our door, had once brought a brown sack full of clothes for me. Granma had stroked and fondled in silent reverence a pair of azure trousers whose legs even my small feet wouldn't penetrate. Helen finally said, "For Christ's sake, Granny, go ahead and shred them up." Granma's eyes in her skinny, wrinkled old face had looked like those of a starving dog with meat in its mouth.

Now Dick poked a gold-colored bullet into the breech. "If I got to die, may as well die happy in the 'lectric chair."

Shuffling from his rocker, shaking violently, Grampa crushed Dick's arms to his sides with a bear hug. Dick's breath went "Rahhhhh!" and the gun went off into the floor, sending up a cloud of dust. Grampa's thick hair fell over his ears. "Cool down, hey, sonny." The old man's shoulders jutted out a half foot on either side of Dick.

"Shove the son of a bitch head first down a well," Helen said. "Feed his peter to the dogs."

"Prince Elmo, get thuh-uh rifle, so it don't get broke."

I took the rifle by its stock, and my father let it go. But he stared hard at the room's one shelf, where his heavy straight razor lay beside Grampa's old Gillette.

"Grampa, you old goat, you can park your shoes under my bed anytime you like," Helen said. "If Dick was half as much man as his daddy, we'd be a happy home."

"Shut up," Grampa said.

"I'm going out," said Dick, "and you all see if I come back. I got me a thing or two on tonight."

"It's thuh-uh rich," Grampa said, breath laboring. "It's that shithead rich man you and Helen got yourselves mixed up with. Put schemes into a poor man's head to make a monkey out of him."

"Let him go," Helen said. "Dick ain't capable of hurting nobody full grown."

"Ain't no pleasure at home," Dick said, pulling loose as soon as Grampa released his grip. "Man schemes and slaves thirty-two years and don't have a goddamn thing in his pockets, has a right to what pleasure he can get. You slobber over pictures in movie magazines and pile my bed fifty men high, and Grampa here gets his head blowed off all night dreaming about French whores, and Granny sits there all day and night stitching herself to the floor. Prince Elmo just eats and smiles and sleeps like a happy little baby, and these two damn older kids shoot any sort of crap they feel like at me, and what do I get? Just a goddamn letter telling me I ain't got no choice but haul ass up to Indianapolis and get my balls shot off by Jews, Japs, and A-rabs. Look around." His gesture took in the builders' scrapboards placed upright and out of plumb, grease and gunpowder and dirtstench, one small room's shelter against chaos. "I ain't got the pleasure of a hound shaking a peachpit loose out of his asshole."

"Well, Mister Bigmouth," Helen flung back, "it's all your own goddamn fault. You throwed that fit on purpose, just to get kicked free of the house." Helen started crying. "I'm a pretty woman. I bore all these children, dead ones and live ones, and I'm still pretty. God knows I tried, Dick. And two months after we married, me knocked up with a big bellyful of Cerulia, you take off to Fort Wayne with a three-hundred-pound whore that said she'd buy you a new Plymouth. Well, you found out that three hundred pounds of lard don't make a woman, and I found out that a long peter all by itself don't make no man."

"Who you talking about now?" Dick asked quietly.

"I'm talking about *you,* you goddamned idiot!" Helen shouted.

"You damn well better be." Dick stroked the front of his jeans with both hands and puffed out his chest.

"Dick, you don't even *hear,*" Helen sobbed.

"Prince Elmo, come along with me," Dick said.

"He ain't going nowhere. It's dark out, and cold."

"How come you want to take thuh-uh boy?"

"Just to spite me, Grampa. He wants me worried to death. Prince Elmo's just a baby, Dick. He should of been asleep now, but you been banging skillets on the floor and shooting off guns."

"You started it, woman," Dick argued, "making out I wasn't a man."

"And now you going out to prove it, taking that poor little boy for audience. Shit, Dick, who you chasing now? Ain't Polly just got married because you wasn't even man enough for her?"

"I'm gonna give a goddamn party for Polly Shiflet and that pretty boy she married," Dick yelled. "Prince Elmo here's the only one that don't give me no shit." He hoisted me under his arm.

"He's only five years old!" Helen shouted. "Hey, Duke, get away from that door! You ain't going nowhere!"

"Sometimes us men stick together." Dick bent for the rifle.

"Aw, let 'em go, Mamma," Cerulia said. "I got to get my beauty rest."

Helen bounded off the bed, small and pretty, shiny grease streaks reaching down her ankles. "At least put him in this wrap."

"What about me?" Duke asked.

"Get your own coat," Helen replied. "You're big enough."

Grampa groaned, "I'm tard!"

"Don't let them two little boys cramp your style none, Dick!" Helen cried. "I'm gonna make a wax doll out of your toenails and crud and stick it with a pin!"

Under Dick's arm, I plunged outside into darkness, just as Granma dropped a square of quilt, crimson, and azure and cornstalk green into her cigar box.

"Fucking worthless bastard!" Helen shouted from the shack's open door. "Tell Polly that Shiflet's a cross between shiftless and horseshit!"

We passed two shadowy hulks of automobiles, a Model A Ford and a 1930 Dodge. While the Ford still ran, Big Dick had bought a pal's Dodge for a song; it wasn't running, his good buddy said, because the points had corroded and the plugs were gucked up and the petcock in the oil pan was gone. From town, Big Dick towed the Dodge behind his Model A by chain; nobody had come along to steer and brake the Dodge, so by the time he hauled it up the hill in front of our shack, the Dodge had butted the Ford's rear end into scrap. Big Dick replaced the Dodge's eight plugs with eight brand-new plugs which he bought ("If you do a thing, do it right," he said), filed the points, robbed a two-bit petcock from a junkyard at midnight, and poured in six quarts of new store-bought oil. He made two trips down to the Gorge for water to fill the radiator, then pulled the dipstick to check the oil. It shimmered like a rainbow. A generous oil slick eyed him from the radiator. "Goddamn," Dick said, " I must of busted the block towing it in from town."

Now Big Dick yanked open the driver's side of our Chevy coupe and threw me into the foot-and-a-half-wide space in back. The rifle followed. Breath steaming, I adjusted my body among the springs and stuffing. In the distance, dogs barked.

We coasted bouncing and jolting downhill; then the engine started. A coat slapped over me. "Better cover up, you precious thing." Duke looked down over the front seat.

"Hoo-wee, boys! We are going to have a party and show these women a thing or two!" Dick cried. "They'll see that the good old U.S. of A. is a man's country."

"Got to piss real bad, Dick," I said.

"Hokay, little man." We halted abruptly in the county road at our hill's bottom. Dick left the engine idling and hauled me out. "Let's go piss out that moon," he said.

Leafless branches twisted against the full moon. We beat a trail through fifty feet of woods, to the wide stone shelf and the Gorge. Across a shimmering football field of water loomed the abandoned stonemill, corrugated iron sheets peeling from its sides.

Dick planted the balls of his feet at the dropoff. "I'm gonna throw out my line and catch me a whopper. There's the biggest fish in the world down there at the bottom of that hole." Big Dick had once told me that the Gorge was a thousand feet deep, and that on its bottom lived a fish big as a man. As a minnow, it had entered through a fissure from the underground river which fed fresh water to the quarry, but soon it grew so large it couldn't squeeze back into the cave. The fish was albino, blind, and free.

Teetering for balance, I cleared the edge with my stream, which disintegrated to droplets, sprinkling the surface. But I felt too afraid of falling in and cut myself short, insides still half full. Big Dick's Icarian spurt jetted upward in a puff of smoke, catching fire in the moonlight.

"Can't nobody else in the county throw his stream so far," Big Dick boasted.

"What in hell," Duke snarled. "We drink that water."

Bending over the water, I saw my twin approach the rippling surface.

Back in the car, our father said, "We got to gas up and run a couple of errands. You boys, this here's going to top settlers and Indians."

"This way's Goldengrove. We know any townfolks?" Duke asked.

We doused our lights beside a car parked near a mailbox. Leaving the engine on idle, Dick jumped out holding a yard's length of hose. But after fussing around between the cars' rear ends, he piled back in and roared off. "Dry's a dead whore."

"Should of saved your pee," Duke said.

The next car kept Dick longer. "Paydirt," he chortled, returning. "Goddamn rich college student's car. Don't need no ration stamps when you got a oil rig."

I brought the chill hose near my face and sniffed. Looking back, Dick said, "That's kid stuff, Prince Elmo. I'm gonna let you and Duke partake of man's treat tonight."

We penetrated a wilderness. Branches scraped the car on both sides. A drooping limb raked the roof. Level with the windshield a root-clasped boulder menaced, then disappeared as we right-angled over rock and potholes. I smelled something sweet and rotten.

"Boys, this here's my old place of business," Dick announced, stopping the car and shutting off the headlights.

Naked shapes crowded around.

"Halloween was last October," Duke said. "How come these guys is dressed like Indians in April? Shit, that one guy ain't even wearing no pants."

I remembered Grampa talking about the tribe of Shawnees camped around Goldengrove two hundred years before, and wondered if these were the "damn halfbreeds" he sometimes spoke of.

"Ain't you ever been to a costume party?" Dick asked, climbing from the car. "That's a fine smell, boys."

A stock man in overalls and T-shirt demanded, "Chip in your dollar, Dick."

"Who's in charge here?" Dick asked. "Shit fire, I need to warm up me and my boys' innards with some of that good corn."

"Pay up, Dick. There's not much juice left. New crop's just now going into the ground, but you wouldn't know about that."

"When I helped run this place," Dick said, "You never had a better worker in your life."

"You never helped run no place," snorted the man in overalls.

Duke and I stood in a clearing, beneath a field of moon-

and star-filled sky. Other cars nosed into the bordering trees and brush. Hounds whimpered. Polished and gold-gleaming, coil worming up and around, an enormous pot rested on a monumental base of rock. A flung-back tarp revealed several wooden barrels. Savages hunkered around a bucket and drank from a metal cup which they passed hand to hand.

Shucking shirt and jeans, Big Dick walked naked to the circle, received the cup, and drank. "Hweeeee hahhhhh!" He seized a burnt stick and slashed black across his face. "Duke and Prince Elmo, get over here."

"Shit on that," Duke said.

Dick pulled off all my clothes beneath the pot's golden sun and blackened me, too.

"I'm cold."

"Give the boy to drink this. He'll warm up."

"Just a slurp, Prince Elmo," Dick said. "Spread them little lips."

I fell double on the cold dirt, maw a river of fire.

"We ain't had a chivaree in ages," a savage said.

"There ain't been a known whore like Polly Shiflet get married in ages, either," Big Dick said.

"I never did get none of it."

"She was Big Dick's exclusive snatch."

"Like hell she was," Big Dick snorted. "Polly Shiflet would of swallered up a stud horse."

"Hope Bud Deckard didn't bring back his army rifle with him, or there may be a few dead Injuns."

"Which leg was it he got shot off?"

"Hear it was his middle leg," Big Dick said. "He's fooling old Polly with a ear of corn."

"Only one ear?"

"I mean a goddamn silo he keeps greased with lard. Shit, I can see it now, old Polly hollering and thrashing around like she's a virgin, and Bud Deckard wishing he'd tied his only ankle to the bedpost to keep from falling in."

"What's Helen say?"

"Helen don't say a damn thing. She complained just once, she wouldn't get another inch."

"Now, Dick, that Helen's a lot of woman."

"Yeah, buddies, but I'm just too much man. Hoooo haaaaa!" Dick cried. "That stuff sure jacks up the boy in you. Somebody go drag Duke over here and get off his clothes."

"Get your dirty paws off my body!" Duke yelled.

The golden pot flamed more brightly. "That must be the last car coming in now," Dick said. "Where's my feather at?"

"Give me back my pants, you old queerbait!" Duke yelled. "Naw, I won't drink that down in a million years! Urrk!"

"That boy's one peck of trouble," Dick said. "If he come along tonight, that's his own fault, nobody asked him. Sometimes all I want to do is kick his ass a few times. But deep down he's all right. He loves his old man."

The three men holding Duke let go. He thrashed and moaned naked on the ground.

"Hey, Tommy, glad you brung them hounds along like I said!" Dick crowed. "Gonna give 'em a old rag of Polly's to sniff and turn 'em loose."

"What old rag, Dick?" asked a fat, shirtless man.

"Trophy won the hard way, haw haw!"

Reaching high, I caught a wet stream of light in my hand. "Watch out for that kid!" a savage cried. "He's pissing at the barrel."

"Hoo hoo hoo hoo." Dick chanted. "C'mon, boys, let's dance roun' the fire!"

I seemed to sprout wings and flew up, straddling my daddy's neck. Men like elephants charged around in a circle, while a fish flopped inside my mouth.

Tossed into a car seat of hot flesh, I twisted and groaned. Wind blasted my face, engines roared, and Dick cried, "Death to Japs! Death to A-rabs, cripples, and heroes! Rip old Polly Shiflet open to her neck. Hell, she'd *like* that!"

"Ain't she Polly Deckard?"

"Hope that damn hound's starving!"

"Bud Deckard's a good man. Didn't he git cripple holding ground against a enemy attack?"

"Bud Deckard got himself the million-dollar wound."

"Since when is a leg shot off a million-dollar wound?"

"Hell, I got me a pipeline to the all-knowing and all-seeing. Ain't no justice. Where's Duke at?"

"Come along in Tommy's car."

"How many of us is there?"

"Baker's dozen. Enough to handle any cripple on his wedding night."

Engine noise died. Car trunks opened, shotguns and axes bristled, hounds bayed. We charged panting and stumbling and bumping each other, between trees, through brush that raked legs and loins, and erupted raggedly at the edge of a three-acre new-plowed field of rich loam. Sweaty blood oiled my legs.

Moonlight marked the furrows. Deep gouges, thick, regular, reeking with dung, led to the field's far end and the swaybacked barn, and the one-floor frame house with a tiny door centered between two small black windows.

"Disability money bought this spread."

"Shit, it's my taxes that bought it," Big Dick snarled, and from his rifle hand produced a crumpled scrap of cloth. "Let them hounds smell of this. Make 'em all horny."

Naked now, Tommy rubbed the V-shaped scrap over the rubber-ball noses of his two hounds, who strained their leashes and whimpered.

"Let go the dogs," Dick commanded.

Baying, noses lowered, the beasts scrambled, dragging leashes through the trenched loam. One black window in the house yellowed. Dick puffed out his hairless bare chest and hefted a gasoline tin by its wire handle.

"Time we moved out, big chief," Tommy said. "That son of a bitch might shoot my dogs, if he don't know this here's just a friendly joke."

On hands and knees, tongue hanging between his lips, Duke rolled his head back and forth. We scrambled after the hounds. I fell on my stomach, face buried in dirt.

"What you fellers want?" a man cried out.

"Just come on a friendly call," Dick shouted back.

A circle of naked savages, pot bellies jogging up and down, war-danced around the house. Hounds whimpered and scratched and mounted the door. Holding his weapons, tall and so lean his ribs showed, Big Dick moved toward the window. The light went out.

"Dick, go away!" a woman shouted from inside.

"Come to see old Bud. Bud? What sort of seed you been planting on this here farm?"

"Damn you, Dick, you take your trash and get on hell out of here and leave us alone!" the woman cried.

"Hi, Polly. Just come to see if old Bud was up to your high standards, or if maybe he needed a little help planting his crop." Savages stood listening about the cabin.

"It's Polly *Deckard.* Me and Bud's a *family,* joined together, and I'm asking you to please take these people away from here and leave me and my husband alone."

"Move on back, honey," a man said. "It's not a fit sight."

"Bud? Wondered if old Polly was in there all by herself, without a good strong plowman to loosen up her dirt."

"I'm in here, Dick. State your business."

"Hell, we been drinking up last year's crop. Tribe's feeling its oats. Come on out, Bud, and have a swig, and bring Polly, too. Let's have a good old friendly chivaree."

"That don't look like corn liquor," Bud Deckard said.

"This ain't no Daisy airgun neither. Hey, Polly, looky here, you sweet virgin, you. Bet you never seen a naked man before in your life."

"If she ain't she sure has left a lot of 'em!" one of the savages shouted. "Plowing up her field in the black of night!"

"Friends, better move on," Bud Deckard said. "These two innocent little boys on the ground yours, Dick? Better put them to bed. All you children, just sing your song and go on home and we'll forget the whole thing."

"Gonna make us, big hero? Got your army gun in there?"

"Don't have truck with guns any more. I wouldn't use one against another man."

"By God, I would!" Polly shouted. "I'm holding a two-barrel shotgun, and I'll blow every last one of you bastards into field dung if you don't leave my husband alone! I don't want him hurt no more than he already has been."

"Come out alone," Dick said. "Hell, Polly, look at all you're giving up," he pointed at himself. "It could be entirely yours, plow and shaft, just the way it always used to be."

"Honey, it's all right," the man said. "Don't get upset over trash."

"They ain't got any gun," Tommy said. "Let's show him who's trash."

"If you ain't coming out—" Dick moseyed to the house and sloshed gasoline against its base. "Sure hate to damage a virgin."

"Don't harm them hounds, Dick," Tommy pleaded.

The door opened, and a man in a candy-striped nightshirt hopped through. I rested on all fours, facing the housefront. Whining and wriggling, the hounds buffeted him. Duke lay vomiting stretched out near me on the ground. The man braced himself inside the doorjamb, blocking the dogs while they slammed blindly against his torso, then found space beneath his left knee and charged under.

"Honey!" the man shouted.

One of the dogs yelped, and Polly crowed, "One filthy dog down!"

Bud Deckard was a short man, wide, powerfully built. The moon made sweat streaks on his face gleam. When Tommy tried to butt through the door, Bud dropped his fist like a sledgehammer onto the back of Tommy's head. Balancing on his right foot, Bud topped the rippling ball of fat onto its back.

"C'mere, Dick," Bud Deckard said. "Let go that rifle and fight like a man."

"Hoo boy," Dick responded in a small voice, tossing the can behind him. A gasoline tail followed its short flight. "Pretty tough you are."

Bud Deckard hopped toward my father, who backed a few steps, ran a quick half-circle around the man's side, and gun-butted his shoulder. Bud Deckard fell, and his nightgown rode up. An elastic sock covered the left leg, whacked off an inch below the knee. When he tried to stand, Dick's savages kicked him back down.

"Mister, you are one stinking host," Big Dick said. "Me and the boys come here for a little old-fashioned fun, and you and that whore in there treat us like dirt, and now we don't have no choice except nastiness. If I had a good piece of land like this, I'd be damned grateful and make a point to treat other folk like friends. Shit, Bud, you're set for life. You don't even have to worry about going off to war like the rest of us." Bud Deckard made a grab for my father's leg, but Dick clunked him with the rifle butt. "And now to top everything else, you run off with my woman."

"Law'll get you if I don't," Bud Deckard gasped. "Keep on with this thing, you'll pay the price."

"Ain't no laws out here," Dick snarled. "There's only justice. You pushed me, Bud, and now I ain't got no choice except to push back."

"Do what you want with me," Bud Deckard said, "I can't stop you in my condition. But leave Polly go."

A hound leaped through an open window, crying piteously. He raced spattering blood and foam through the savage circle and out into the field, where he whirled sniffing at a sagging, jagged wound in his side. Through a door, in a white froth of rags and tatters, her bare flesh gnawed and bloody, a tall woman stumbled, whirling a sickle whose wetness mirrored the moon. Breasts jogged in the momentum of her charge; thighs rippled. She yelled, "You bastards leave that man be!" and rushed directly at Dick.

A shotgun boomed. The house ignited like a flashbulb. My brain felt split apart. Legs raced behind the flaming house. An arm rose and fell, naked shoulders converged around it, the arm disappeared. "Don't let her! Throw her in the fire!" "Not me, by God, let's get out of here!"

"Help *meeee*!" Who called? Too hoarse for a woman. Spitting dirt, I hugged the field, afraid the earth might spin upside down and dump me into the sky. Black smoke boiled across the moon. Nobody stood. Person or hound, something moaned in agony.

Across the field from where Dick's tribe had charged, two men moved slowly. Shifting and fiery shadows illuminated them. One, except for his shoes, was naked. The other, prodding the naked man ahead with the barrel of his six-shooter, wore the neat Roy Rogers cowboy uniform of our county sheriff, and I recognized his face from posters fading and peeling on fenceposts, phone poles, barns. "We didn't—I mean, it wasn't our fault," the naked man pleaded. "Hell, they knew they had no business taking their wedding night around here. They must of wanted it to happen. I mean, if you knew it was possible a crowd of men might show up, would you—"

"Shut your mouth," the sheriff commanded, standing over me. Through cellophane fastened in place by a rubber band, his flashlight shone a red beam. "Stand up. What's your name, son? You're mighty small to be out this late."

"Prince Elmo Hatcher."

"Prince Elmo, who's that other little boy?"

Duke lay on the ground near the sickle. "My brother," I replied.

"Is that your daddy?"

I shook my head at the naked man.

"No, pardner, I mean over there." He corrected my gaze with his flashlight to where a skinny person, all caved in and small, lay moaning, footsoles in a trampled furrow, raised knees pressed together, crossed hands clamped on his crotch like a dressing over the million-dollar wound—the worst wound in the world.

Holes

•1•

ONE DAY the sheriff returned the rifle, but the Chevy, like Dick, had vanished. Dodge and Model A rotted in the space before our shack, whose tarpaper-brick siding hung flabbily from the wood. Granma's flaming patches overflowed one cigar box into a second. A tall, phthisic, gasping bastard with red hair, whose armpit sweat stains in the gray cloth of his uniform, like tree rings, composed a natural record of Indiana weather, began footing it to the hilltop, delivering fresh bread at our door three mornings a week. Sliced and cellophane-wrapped, the loaves fluffed so fresh and weightless that I could compress them like a sponge between my hands. When the breadman called on sunny days, Helen shooed the family out, even Granma, and received his loaf in private.

Grampa shook his head over Dick's fate, threatened the Hun and the rich, and dug up his garden. "Thuh-uh last I heard of thuh-uh boy, he agreed to join thuh-uh army. So they ain't gonna bring him up for trial." But Grampa no longer took me out to shoot the rifle. I don't know all the damage we caused that night—except nobody died. Though the two-ton woman from Welfare made weekly visits with food and clothes, wheezing sideways through our door, Duke and I still walked to Goldengrove with a toy wagon and filched canned food from Kroger, the A&P, and smaller markets, rotating our meager strikes for safety—and yet I felt hungry day and night, and even after a meal of cold beans or unthinned, uncooked concentrated soup, the walls of my stomach still ground together angrily.

That summer after Dick plunged into an ambulance's rear, Cerulia turned thirteen; I remember her full thighs, streaked with dirt, as she lounged in her tattered dress about our shack, shrugging off Helen's badgering:

"Cissy, get off your butt. How did I deserve such a worthless daughter?"

"Oh, Mamma, I thought you come by me naturally."

And two or three evenings a week, a horn would blare from the hill bottom, and Cerulia would stir, murmuring, "Well, folks, that must be the old sugar himself."

"You ain't going out tonight, Cissy," Helen muttered.

"Mamma, he's already twitching with impatience. I hear the coins jingling in his trouser pockets. Don't worry, at midnight my coach turns back into a punkin." And off she went, down the hill, into a car whose engine purred with the sound of silver.

"That daughter of mine's coming to no good," Helen grumbled.

Granma's hand darted through her rag box. I smeared lard onto another slice of fluffy-soft bread and gobbled it in a bite. Down in the Gorge, the blind white fish sniffed patiently for one of his infrequent bonanzas of fresh meat. I wanted something else; I wanted *more*, but I didn't know what.

I started first grade, walking with Duke to a two-room frame building, swing set and two smelly crap shacks outside. One afternoon when Duke and I returned, Helen hugged me and said, "Oh, Prince Elmo, you're my gorgeous child, my golden little boy. You're gonna be the biggest, strongest, handsomest man in the world, *my* man, cause I ain't got none."

"Hey, Helen, what about me?" Duke asked.

"You're old already," Helen replied. "Your juices's all dried up. Prince Elmo's got dew all over him like a little flower. I'll have to pluck him up before all the other girls get him."

"Then it's a good thing there ain't two of him any more," Duke said. "If there was, all the little girls'd go nuts from too much pleasure."

"How come we always go bathroom in the woods, Helen?" I suddenly asked.

"What's wrong with that?"

"Gets cold out there," I replied. "Sometimes it's raining. Sometimes it's out in the derned snow, and there's no leaves for shelter, and maybe strangers from the road watch you do your business. And sometimes you step in other people's stuff. I mean, there's my duty and Duke's and yours and Cissy's and Granma's and Grampa's—and some of Dick's probably still left. Why don't somebody build a outhouse?"

"School's given Prince Elmo fancy tastes," Duke said, looking at me strangely.

Helen said, "Nobody ever felt it was worth all the trouble. There's always been more important things."

"Prince Elmo's got a point, though," Duke said. "Nobody ever gets a damn thing done around this place, because ever-body's got some big project in the future that's more important than anything you can do right now."

"I'm the smallest in this house. But I've taken the notion. Watch my smoke."

Duke looked scared. "Helen, he can't dig that outhouse. He's too small."

"There ain't nothing in the world my Prince Elmo can't do," Helen said. "Come here, you gorgeous sweetheart."

"I'm smarter than he is, and I'm bigger and older," Duke protested. "I'm not letting no little runt run past me like I wasn't even here. Shit, if there's a hero in the county, it's probably me."

Remembrances of Duke's heroism: Footsoles sizzling, I toddle naked along a wide, white ledge of stone. I'm outside my own body, or maybe I've loaned it away for the morning; the sun hisses like a blowtorch, or is that wind in the trees behind the ledge? I'm wobbling along beside myself, holding my hand to keep my mind from floating away like an unanchored balloon. "Them kids gonna fall into the water if you don't get up." "Get 'em yourself, Dick. How come ever time I got to? You own two good legs." "Lazy damn bitch. I ain't moving from where I am. I'm a man—I ain't no goddamn babysitter." The voice fade. "Well, I ain't moving either, and if they fall into the quarry and drown, it ain't my fault. It's yours, Mister Bigstuff, and you can just live with it the rest of your life." Feet scuffle behind me. Force slams me forward, and though I'm looking down at the water, I have also fallen in, and look up at myself, eyes pools of terror, "God damn it, Prince George fell off the ledge! Get him!" "Get him yourself!" Duke, hang on to Prince Elmo! Don't let him fall, too!" But I have disappeared from my sight.

The memory pushed me into my mother's bosom.

"What right has he got all of a sudden to act so important? If it wasn't for me," Duke said, "they'd of both drowned."

I strangled, face swallowed by one of Helen's soft tits, heaving and bucking. "You perfect little angel, you just go right on ahead and do anything you want. If you need a nice place to do your duty, go on down into the woods and dig it with my blessing."

I pulled away from Helen. "If I want a thing done," I gasped, "I'll damn well have to do it myself."

Imagine me in an ever-deepening hole, about fifty feet down the hill from our shack, in a small clearing cornered by three maples and one pin oak, wielding a burdensome spade which, when I began digging, topped me by a foot. I asked myself how much space six people—seven if Dick came back—might need for crap and decided the shaft should drop to my height anyway; its diameter would equal my arms held out from my sides; it would be round, like the single hole I dreamed into my wooden throne. But I grew during the project, and so the project grew. "Prince Elmo," Cerulia once said, "You always was full of shit."

So during the week, I absorbed grammar, and also discovered doodling. And evenings and weekends, when it wasn't raining or snowing, or the ground hadn't frozen, or I wasn't too hungry or tired, I dug in solitary pride, owing no respect to anybody or anything.

But I sometimes stopped digging to seek another pleasure: the movies, perhaps war adventures starring the heroic Rudolph Stayne, or Westerns with Lash LaRue, or cartoons. And one wintry Sunday afternoon during spring of my seventh year, in a motion-picture theater I'd (as usual) snuck into through the side door to escape the eight-cent ticket, I first fell in love—with white flesh, a heart-shaped face, blood-red lips, coal-black hair, and a pinafore which flowed to the shoe-toes. She was born a princess, and the queen bled three red drops into the snow and wished that her daughter might become beautiful, then died. Next the beautiful daughter looked down into a well full of rings caused by dripping water; the water became smooth and mirrored her image, beautiful, sad, and unfulfilled, and she sang a song that someday her prince would come; but the new queen listened to a mirror and now the dead mother's loving wish, in coming true, caused unanticipated problems. The beautiful princess was kidnapped from the golden palace of her childhood and taken deep into the forest by a huntsman who hacked the heart out of a deer; so she exchanged her palace for a shack in the woods, occupied by people who dug for gold and diamonds; before sleeping, they plumped up each other's butts for pillows. But a wicked saleswoman, who earlier had kicked a human skeleton to pieces, gave the former princess an apple which she ate, then died; the diggers stuck her in a box in the forest, and a prince trotted up on a horse and kissed her mouth. She woke up queen of the world.

That night, I slept in the glass box with Snow White. It was winter, and we kept stuffing handkerchiefs into the box with us to keep warm. "I love you, Prince Elmo," Snow White said, "and I'll be your sweet girl friend." The box changed into a gold castle, which I'd built years ago with my own hands but only now remembered. Canned food packed the kitchen shelves to the ceiling; hot, salted mashed potatoes filled one whole room—open the door, stick in your spoon, eat. I slept with Snow White in a huge white bed, under the intricate leaf design of heavy lace. We crawled inside each other for warmth, and I recalled that my real father was king and that I was prince of the world.

Walking beside Duke on my way to school through the cold, I prayed silently, "Dear Snow White, please come out of the woods just up ahead, come out from under the wooden bridge, be in the schoolyard, on the swing set, inside the school door when the bell rings, be in my classroom sitting at my desk."

Digging laboriously at my hole, I'd feel her eyebeams tickling my back, but never whirled fast enough. She'd vanished behind a tree, flown into the sun's hot ball. As the days warmed and I swam again in the Gorge, I looked for a hilly surge of bubbles to precede her rise. Swimming underwater, peering into the bottomless green murk, I sought her hovering languidly, white pinafore undulating like the fins of some fancy fish.

Then one July morning after first grade ended, as I loped with my shovel from the shack, Duke raced up our hill, shouting, "Hey, Elmo, there's a naked lady down in the Gorge!"

Grampa jittered up and down in the door behind me. Helen and Cerulia had gone on "errands."

"What's Duke say?" Grampa asked.

He repeated it for Grampa.

"Thuh-uh hell! I'm too old for them tricks," Grampa said. "Drop that shovel, Prince Elmo. She's got a much more interesting hole to dig into."

Duke started back down.

"Wait just a god-duh-damn minute there," Grampa said. "I'm a-comin' on down, too."

A gleaming island of white, black triangle thatching its center, floated in the Gorge.

"What's that?" I asked Grampa.

He squinted; tongue played between his cracked lips. "Probly ain't nothing you'd appreciate."

The island disappeared, and a head punched through the water. "Oh," I said. "For a minute, it didn't look like anything."

Duke peered at me.

"Hello, over there!" the lady called. "Hope I'm not trespassing."

"Missus, you want to swim that there quarryhole, you just go right on ahead," Grampa bellowed. "And if thuh-uh damn sheriff come along, he won't tell you no different, or he ain't a proper man."

Treading water, she stopped near the wall. "Many people swim here?"

"Why, thuh-uh boys here do, missus. We live just across thuh-uh road and up that 'ere hill. Reason I'm so palsy, I was shellshock by thuh-uh Hun during thuh-uh first war."

"Well, I didn't notice." The lady seemed about Helen's age. "Just got here yesterday, and I'm only staying about two weeks."

"How come you're not wearing any swimsuit?" I asked. "Bet you feel embarrassed." For some reason, Cerulia always wore a ratty old swimsuit in the Gorge, and Helen never swam. For seven years, I'd been living in a single room with three women, all of whom crapped outside and undressed in the same room with me. But I never snuck down into the woods after them, like Duke. And either they'd always wait till after dark to undress, or like Granma, Cerulia, and Helen never did undress completely, or I was never interested enough to notice. Anyway, looking down at that bare naked woman, I knew something was wrong.

"What's the matter with no wearing any clothes?" she smiled nervously. Long hair streamed out behind her broad, plain face, and she sounded like the kids in school reciting the pledge of allegiance. "Don't all other animals, except man, go without clothes? Nothing in nature tells man it's evil to go naked—quite the contrary. Nakedness is far more in keeping with nature's simple laws. It promotes a healthy body, it allows us to develop more healthy mental attitudes toward human relationships, including sex. The first Americans, our Indian ancestors, went naked, but now so-called civilized law forbids it."

"Well, missus, there ain't nobody in sight about to argue if you don't want to wear no clothes!" Grampa bellowed.

" 'Cept the weather," I said.

"Well, you'll have to excuse me." She pushed away from the steep wall. "We're all expected back at camp to eat."

"What camp is that?" Duke asked.

"Don't you read the papers?"

"Ain't got none," Grampa said. "Nor radio or electricity, neither."

"Well, I'll be darned, now, I really envy you." The lady trod water. "It's Fern Hill, about a mile up the road. Darned nice nudist camp. If we win this court battle, we'll be there every summer. Drop on by. But you can't wear clothes. We'll skin them off your backs."

"Just once more before I die," Grampa groaned, "just once more . . ." He licked his chops. His eyes focused sharply across the Gorge to where the lady stiff-armed herself over onto a ledge one foot out of the water. Glistening white in the sun, she squatted a moment on all fours, back to us, shaking off a spray of bright droplets like a dog.

"Lookit that one bobble up and down!" Duke whispered. "Them boxes sure make peter stiff."

Kids and grownups played volleyball.

"Handfuls of hot snatch," Duke went on.

A plump woman spiked the ball into a hairless little boy's stomach; he plunked down in the dust. The woman's heavy tits swung and joggled, the boy stood, the ball flew back into play. Men's paunches bristled with hair; one man's gut flobbed over his cock. Wearing hornrims, another man lounged in a canvas chair, fat book split open over his lap. Years of undershorts and trousers had bit the men's flesh, like a belt of scar tissue. Bottoms and hips shivered like Jell-O when the women jumped.

"Something's wrong with these people," I whispered, "but I can't put my finger on it."

"Probly eat like hogs."

Pressure built inside my pants. "Freaks," I whispered. "These women are freaks." In a carnival tent, I'd seen a slant-eyed creature floating upright in yellowish fluid, in a yard-high bottle.

"Hell, they look pretty sweet to me."

"But they all got something wrong with them. It's bit off, or maybe never even grew."

"Well, I'll be." Duke's mouth flopped open. "Women are different, Elmo. They're built in another way entirely. Jesus. hasn't Cissy ever flashed it in your face?"

"What?"

Totally exasperated, Duke slowly whispered, "Women—simply—don't—have—peters!"

"*You damn liar*!" I shouted, standing and shaking my fist down where Duke cowered. "*Snow White has one*!"

•2•

The war ended, and I heard rumors that Dick had seen battle; that his lieutenant had died in his own trench facing the enemy, a bullet through the back of his skull, and that Dick had been dishonorably discharged; that he was prowling the United States in an ever-decreasing spiral, town to town, jail to jail, despised, outcast, degenerate; and that he might and day, after traveling every road, passing through every town and city, converge on our hill and our shack.

"If Dick plants his carcass here," Helen said, "I'll shoot the bastard dead." Granma filled a third cigar box, and my hole in the ground deepened and widened. Cerulia spent entire weekends away from the hill, then came back, sometimes wearing a new dress and smelling like a dime store. And a new breadman replaced the old ("Looks just like Tyrone Power," Helen sighed), and left off bright-covered magazines, ragged collages like a child's scrapbook. Grampa began watching Helen's every move about the room. "That old man's peepers burn holes through my frame," Helen complained. "Hey, Grampa, try lighting a fire in the stove." Duke grew a foot and a half and spoke of "going to Chi and robbing a bank and living like a king." And one week when no salesman pushed open our door, Helen sobbed on the bed and let Grampa, sitting beside her, lay one massive, veined, trembling hand on her shoulder. I dreamed of crapping in private just outside the shack, and when I slept, Snow White came demurely in her white pinafore and reassured me, "Prince Elmo, I ain't built like other girls, and don't let nobody tell you different."

Then I fell in love the second time—or maybe just added onto the first.

The "new girl" stood regal and haughty in the middle of our playground one hot September morn, protected by a beagle, a squat wad of muscle writhing and rubbing like a tomcat against her calves, while the rest of us squalid bumpkins ringed her charmed circle and gaped. A plastic bow clamped her long black hair together in back. Her deep-cushioned lips parted hungrily. Her nose tilted downward, delicate, hawklike. Eyes large and black, almond-shaped, slanted like a cat's, fierce with animal juices. Her face gleamed brown from the sun. Her name was Nina. In Duke's grade, she matched his height, and hot fluids bubbled through my chest. I would drape my future over this girl's thin body.

I cartwheeled in the gravel, skinned-the-cat fifty times in a row, picked fights with larger boys, who beat my ass into the ground, but she ignored me. I threw rocks at the shut door of the four-holed girls' outhouse, squealed piggishly at the muffled shrills of outrage from inside—and she gazed scornfully into the distance, petting her lamb of a beagle, who lingered outside school each day to greet his mistress with ecstatic whines. Duke also eyed her with longing. But, demigoddess chosen by Zeus, democratic in her scorn, she ignored all humankind.

After dark, though, she shared my snug bed with Snow White in the castle of my skull.

Once she spoke to me, after I'd picked a fight for her benefit with a seventh-grader who smashed me until my nose bled into my mouth. I lay on my side in the gravel. My vision cleared—and she leaned against a teeter-totter, dog climbing her leg. "Down, Boots," she said. "Hello there, silly child."

I was too overwhelmed to speak. Her eyes terrified me. Groveling, I dropped my gaze to the soiled white wool ankle socks she wore. The writhing beagle's eyes, small, wet, shining brightly, glittered evilly; he whimpered.

Nina seemed so proud, so invulnerable, that her defeat one recess toward the end of October bewildered me. A pack of larger children huddled whispering and giggling until she left the building, whereupon they pelted her with gravel. A sobbing cry, low like a man's, ripped from her chest; instead of hiding inside, she lowered her face against the swarming wasps of gravel and raced toward the jeering mob, among whom I recognized Duke. I thought her beast would sic these enemies—yelp, snap, tear them to shreds. But for the first time the beagle was absent. Children scattered; she flailed and clawed their astonished faces. And that same day, through a window near my desk, I watched a car stop by the schoolyard. The driver kept his face averted from the school, and Nina, hands hiding her own face, climbed in. They drove off under the chill of an overcast sky.

That night an ugly scratch furrowed Duke's right cheek from eye to mouth. After a supper of canned soup, he asked, "Prince Elmo, how'd you like to play Halloween pranks tonight?"

"Thought you were going with older boys," I said. Cerulia sat near the hot stove.

"Listen, Cissy, let me tell you something." Duke scooted

over and whispered in her ear. He pointed at me. Cerulia giggled. Like Helen's, her breasts pooched out jiggling large and soft.

"Well, I sure hope it was lots of fun," Cerulia said. "But I didn't think dogs talked English. How'd you all find out?"

"Old lady decided she didn't have enough friends and invited some girls to a slumber party. Nina thought they was all asleep. They wasn't."

"You know, Duke, I feel kind of sorry," Cerulia mused. "What anybody does in private is their own business, just so nobody else gets hurt. I guess Nina must of got carried away with passion."

"Wish I'd been there," Duke said. "Wish I'd been in that beagle's place."

"It's a lot of fun, honey." Cerulia rolled her blue eyes up and around. "There's nothing in the world that feels better, or that I'd rather spend time doing. That is, with boys I like."

"You like all boys," Duke leered. " I'm taking Prince Elmo to do the honors, because he's so innocent and so much in love."

Cissy hauled me into her lap. "You're awful big for a little boy. Now, don't pull away. I know you like girls a whole lot. You just got one or two things kind of crooked. All you need is a good teacher, and you'll be the happiest little boy in the whole world."

"Her old man had the dog put to death," Duke added.

"Whew! Pretty stiff. How was the poor critter to know any better?"

"One of the girls got sick to her stomach," Duke said. "Me an' Prince Elmo's gonna go draw us a picture. We're using paraffin so it won't wash off."

"Did she do it on her back?" Cerulia asked. "Or on her hands and knees?"

"That reminds me of what kind of boys you like, Cissy," Duke leered. "Boys with long peters."

Cissy only shook her head. "Duke, someday I hope you grow tired of being nasty. Maybe I'm only fifteen years old, but it feels like I been through as much as a woman of forty. What counts is whether a fellow's of all-over good quality. A fellow of quality'd feel sorry for that poor girl and not go play pranks to hurt her feelings. And he wouldn't play games with Prince Elmo's feelings, either."

"My motto is this," Duke said, "and it applies to everything. If it's big, it's good. Tarze Roberts is big because he's rich, and that makes him good. Don't give me shit about quality. It ain't how good, it's how much. Now Elmo, let's you and me go out right now and have a big good time."

Duke and I charcoaled our faces, which made us fiercer than mere masks. Looking into Cerulia's small mirror by the dim lantern, I carved away hunks of myself, and Duke cackled, "You're a talent, kid. I'll let you draw the picture, since you got the know-how. Looks like you fell to sleep on top of a hangernade."

For warmth I stuffed my sweater with wads from Helen's movie magazines and a few rags from Granma's box. Then we took off, walking all the way to town. Under the crescent gleaming in a clear sky, the cold bit viciously. Our schoolhouse and playground glowed after a half mile, and my gloveless hands felt like they'd shatter if I clunked them on a fencepost, where barbed wire slashed the air along the roadside.

From the crest of a long hill, I sighted straight down the evenly narrowing road to where it plunged into a cluster of lights. The town cast a glowing backdrop into the sky, drowning the stars.

"Looks like it's on fire," I said.

"Serve 'em right if the whole goddamn place burnt to a crisp, those lucky sons of bitches," Duke snarled. "Town people think they're hot shit. The college crapheads are even worse. Coeds fuck anything. College boys fuck other boys."

I didn't even want to ask Duke what that meant. Nothing held together, and I must have felt, then as now, that as my days went by, I gained no wisdom; the world merely spun things farther and farther apart.

We stopped just outside the city limits to trick-or-treat. Limestone steps led up to a small lightless porch, extension of the house front, covered by a peaked roof, a house like first-graders draw. No pumpkin scowled at us from the stone wall which guarded the porch, only two eerily glowing front windows. The door between them probably opened onto a hallway which railroaded straight through the home's single story. House after house in Goldengrove repeated this meager design. I punched the doorbell, and a gaunt, frowning woman loomed behind the screen.

"Trick or treat," Duke said.

"You boys ain't from town," the woman stated.

"No, ma'am."

"You're filthy and ragged. Your mother ought to be shot."

"Yes, Miz Never." Duke held out a paper bag.

"What's your school?"

Duke told her. "And what about that pathetic bundle of rags?" she jabbed at me.

"That's Prince Elmo Hatcher. Good friend of Nina. She around?"

"No, Nina ain't around and she ain't ever going back to that school, and you just get off this property."

"Tell Nina, Prince Elmo Hatcher stopped by." We backed down the steps. "Tell her he was on his way to her daddy's store, to see if it was open, and if it ain't, he'll leave a message. Ruhf ruhf!"

She ran out onto the porch whirling a broom over her head like a headsman's ax. "You goddern boys!"

I ran. Duke stumbled backward out of the broom's reached and barked, "Ruhf ruhf, ruhf ruhf!"

We raced past the sign which said GOLDENGROVE, POP. 19,500. The sleek state road became a street, hushed and shaded by trees which clung to a few dead leaves. Scattered autos prowled the streets. We met noisy packs of ghosts, witches, ballet dancers, birds and beasts of prey. "Tramps! Tramps!" they cried.

"Fucking shiteaters!" Duke yelled back.

The children gasped; they danced like falling leaves.

Later, a police car moved silently past, red-glass dome on its roof glinting darkly in a streetlamp. "Act like you're just a ordinary human being," Duke counseled. Gliding by, cops ogled us through glass.

"Who's Miz Never?" I asked.

"Someone trying to keep a big secret."

Breath puffed out floating before me in a solid cloud; air chewed and swallowed it.

"Let's stop and see if somebody'll give us candy."

"Shit, Elmo, don't you know? Me and you's just trash. What Goldengrove people want to do is kill us. Candy or apples we get, they'll fix with poison. Sometimes they shove in razor blades, so you split open your insides."

"I'm as good as anybody in the world," I said.

"You innocent little shit-ass! Now Cissy's a *smart* piece of meat. She's gone out and got eaten since she was ten, but she knows where to let 'em bite so it don't hurt and don't show Poor old Dick, though—sheriff poked him into a meat wagon and hauled him off to a butcher shop. And your twin, he got eaten so long ago he don't even count."

"I'm scared. You don't like me much."

"Oh, I'm glad there ain't two of you any more. But I especially hate these dirty sons of bitches, fucking rich town people. I mean, we eat lardbread. We crap in the woods. But Tarze Roberts shits diamonds. He sleeps in a mansion with a lectric fence. How much disability Grampa get a month? Twenty? If it wasn't for that and stealing, we'd starve."

"I'm no damn crook," I said.

"Look, dumbass, anything we grab or steal, it's just paying back for what we never had. High time I did some ball-kicking of my own."

The courthouse, a dwarf St. Peter's, glowed from window lights which merchants left burning around the square to frighten thieves. A blind, fat limestone woman sat in a niche above the main entrance. Her bare legs narrowed to kneeless cones, and she dangled a balanced scale over her crotch. A bronze fish weathervaned above the dome. Mantled with pigeon shit, a pillbox-capped soldier, fifty feet high, bayonet fixed, charged Southerners, Mexicans, Filipinos, and Huns. Muzzle-loading cannon menaced the square's south side. To the east, an antiaircraft bayed at the moon. The town was negotiating with the U.S. government to buy a Nazi buzzbomb.

"Hardware store's over there," Duke pointed. "We'll write on the bank window catacorner from it."

"I don't understand."

Duke handed me a hunk of paraffin. "Draw what I tell you, quick and big, before any cops come by."

TOM NEVER CO., flaked the big sign. FARM EQUIP., GUNS, TOOLS.

I drew.

Duke spelled a word one letter at a time, and I printed on the reflecting glass, BOOTS.

The crude paraffin hieroglyph I'd drawn stared into my brain like the eye of truth. It was like adding apples and stones in a dream and getting answered by some new substance, heavy as stone, sweet as apple, threatening the canines as they slashed at its crusty outer flesh. Everything seemed possible—frogs piloting airplanes, four-mile centipedes with human faces, dogs with wives and a Walt Disney family of children with five--fingered hands and pawfeet at the end of shapely human legs, tailless, bearing the cocks, eyes, mouths of men, a hound's floppy ears, and large black rubber-ball noses. Nature chopped itself apart and slapped the oozing fragments together like Frankenstein in his castle lab, each creature more monstrous than the last. No fantasy was too outrageous to exist in matter.

A November first wind tore at the trees. Duke was playing hookey. Walking to school alone, I recognized among weeds and saplings a shape which stopped me dead: slim, brown, some graceful beast, timid, wild, sliced by camouflage. As I stared bug-eyed, the motionless figure changed from deer to girl, and I thought, "My dream!" She had appeared from the incredible blue sky, the treetops, the playground, the outhouse; erect and splendid, she would save me from despair. Her shoe soles scuffled gravel as she came at me. She grinned, elated, victorious. Sun beat against her eyes, already gleaming with sheer vigor. Spit trickled from the corners of her mouth. She caught my collar and swung me to the road.

Fingernails furrowed my cheeks. On me, breathing eagerly, she kneed my crotch in ragtime. She bit my jaw. Oranges and milk, her breath filled my nose. My ears flapped like wings. Straddling my groin, she ground and jolted; her left hand's nails pinioned my throat, and she settled into the rhythm of smashing my face back and forth. I relaxed. My nostrils gushed down my cheeks, over my upper lip, salty and sweet into my mouth, and I vomited. "Ukkh!" throated the girl, leaping up, scraping my gunk from her coat's abdomen.

And I croaked, "Nina . . . Never."

"Evil little shit! Now go tell!"

Fleet angel of judgment, she disappeared into the morning brightness.

A jungle of dying weeds buried our hill's steep car path. Winter birds hacked and sputtered. My nose froze. I wandered into the woods where the neck-deep privy received a few drops of my blood and soggy chunks oozing off my sweater. Then I trudged on. Across the bashed-out back window of the Dodge, a pearly web radiated from a drowsing black and yellow spider. The shack roof sagged like a swaybacked horse. One whole strip of tarpaper-brick, peeled from the siding, lay wrong-side up, puddle of rainwater soaking in. I staggered to the shack's single window, and peered inside.

As usual, Granma sat facing the wall. She'd begun stitching together the patches of her quilt, the kaleidoscope of maple leaves, or birds in flight, or in flames. I wondered if Helen and Grampa were around, if water remained in the washbasin so I could clean up and get what I needed, then just go off by myself and finish this business without having to explain. Remembering the first time I plummeted feet first from the high wall into the quarry and water rammed up my nostrils in frosty cylinders, I opened the door.

Two faces glued together motionless on the bed, sheets in uproar. A two-headed ghost sat up and glared.

"Every day it's Halloween," I muttered, making rapidly for the shelf.

After the swift burglary, I headed for my lair. Who would look for me in the hole? Nobody, unless *she* came back; I shuddered. But it'd be all over before then. She'd catch my blood in her warm lap and thin it with her tears.

A bird blasted up through the leaves. I climbed down into the hole, sat, leaned back against wet dirt, and opened my pretty prize. Fine rust had browned the steel since Dick last used it years before. "Like floating underwater," he'd once said, shaving himself. The handle was mother of pearl. I drew the blade before my face and saw NEW YORK SPECIAL in fine hand lettering on the shank. A light object landed in my left palm, a shiny white tablet, domed on the downside, flat on top. Pale, clay pink. Rubbery.

"Jesus Christ!" I yelled, casting the straight razor out of the hole. "I've sliced off the tip of my nose!"

My first inspiration was to eat it—like a cuticle, or like skin bitten from the lower lip. Large lazy droplets of blood oozed into the palm where the chunk lay. If somebody looked into the mouth of my pit just now, I would die embarrassed. Maybe a doctor could help, but I couldn't tell anybody or show anybody. I imagined raw flesh, the pink boneward scoop which disfigured my knees every summer. Looking at the piece, I saw, however, no half moons of nostril. Trying to picture the wound, I balanced the amputated morsel between thumb and forefinger and slid it into place like a hockey puck on ice.

Sun blazed over the pit lip. Starlings grakked and scuttered in nearby trees. I held my nose tenderly in place and imaged up the shrunken lid of a jack-o'-lantern, wrinkling toward a dead drop into the stomach of its head. Nose began itching and running. Better my nose slashed than my eyeball, I thought. I had lost teeth, then grown new ones. Why couldn't I just go backward five minutes? A time machine could transport me to when it hadn't happened. And for no particular reason, I decided that if my nose fused back, I would be like Captain Marvel, all-powerful. If I failed, I would drown myself in the Gorge, feed myself to the blind fish. But if I succeeded—maybe some things were final. But if you could undo time, you were a god; you could make anything happen. An evil genius at work in his lab: I vaporize him with my ray gun . . .

Ice cakes for feet. Moisture from my pit wall soaked through my sweater and shirt. I'd dozed. Sun behind me. A dangling, frozen earthworm glistened in a shovelmark halfway up the wall. Fingers and nose felt numb. I blew breath upward, palm a fireplace, nose a flaming log. Then I searched my hand: nothing. Nothing in my lap or on the ground under my butt. I gently touched my index finger to my nose. Snot had frozen in the nostrils; the tip still stuck in place. I hoisted myself from the pit and dropped my pants at the edge. The pin oak lowered one long branch down almost to the ground, and grabbing hold of this, propping my heels, I squatted over the hole and let go, my virgin privy's first crap. The enemy tumbled as I gunned them mercilessly down. Dead leaves to wipe. I couldn't dig there any more now, could I? Well, who wanted to dig himself a prison house and a grave? I was cut out for more important things. Careful not to step on the razor; I'd find it tomorrow. Pulling up my pants, I discovered that piss had splattered them.

I strode up to the shack. Helen was frying bacon on the woodstove. It hissed and popped. Grampa sat in his rocker, running an oiled rag on the end of a string through the barrel of the twenty-two. Neither looked at me. Granma stitched at her quilt. Duke eyed me and gaped. Prowling the floor aimlessly, rubbing palms up and down against her belly and thighs, Cerulia cried, "Holy cow, Prince Elmo! Who kicked your face? What's that funny pencil line round the end of your nose?"

I looked into her small mirror, hanging from the wall. Battered indeed, but also rugged as hell, and tough. My nose seemed flattened, like a boxer's. I had aged years. "Don't ask me questions, kiddo!" I shouted at Cerulia. "Ask Helen and Grampa why they were shakin' in bed together this morning!"

•3•

When I started school, I also started doodling, and my talent scurried out like a wild rat which had been hiding all along in some dark corner of its cage. During the barren moments of class—four grades in a single room, fifty unwashed, unhealthy, and hungry kids—after I'd ripped through the meager assignment, I doodled, even though I knew the act was criminal.

An inkwell sank into the top right corner of each hacked and splintery desk. It was Coke-bottle-thick glass, and removable. Each morning, we lined up at the teacher's desk; fat and haggard, she filled our wells from a gallon jug. Each of us in turn carefully suspended the tip of a funnel over our wells, and the funnel was not allowed to touch the well's lip. Sometimes the teacher poured too much, or one of us jiggled; whenever ink spilled, for whatever reason, teacher crushed a rattan—long flexible pointer wielded like an executioner's sword—across the student's knuckles. Our final act each day was to line up again before her desk and empty the inkwells' dregs through the same funnel into the same jug. At first, she punished the student she thought returned the least ink. After a while, she began punishing the one who returned the most. The change went unannounced; it simply happened. And she never seemed angry, just indifferent. But the change meant less punishment for me, since from the start I wasted most of my ink doodling.

Our writing pads were a hundred sheets thick, with cardboard backing and no front cover. Blue lines a half inch apart scored pages of dead-skin yellow. We tore assignments out before handing them in. I would doodle on the cardboard backing and work toward the front. During recess, while the teacher supervised outside, I would sneak through the building's back door, steal a fresh pad from her desk, stuff the used one into the wastebasket, and rush back to the playground feeling I'd stolen a fresh, new world.

I doodled blimps with patches stitched on their outer covers to keep in the gas, with button-eyed faces and shark mouths, swimming through a sky with puffy little clouds that searched the ground sadly for their children, raindrops that melted from their bellies and as they fell sprouted hair and eyes and parachutes for a soft landing.

As I became more skilled, a frog ate an ice-cream cone under a movie marquee, while the sky rained frowning red delicious apples.

By the time I was nine, I discovered that from sight or memory I could construct a likeness of any human face. Dick's head chased a garbage pail through the woods.

Women with enormous buttocks straddled fat ponies and waved sabers while they pursued some enemy off the page across my desk through the window into the countryside.

When I closed my eyes, my creations came alive in three

dimensions. But the instant I looked, they dove back onto the page and played dead. Nights, they swarmed from my desk to forage the countryside.

I drew Helen picking nits off Cerulia's scalp and mine, soaking our hair in coal oil, and wrapping it in rag turbans. A single louse grew so large it split the walls of our shelter with its soft, oily rotundity.

A whole woman's leg had grown overnight from the top of Grampa's head, and he struggled to fit a shoe over its foot.

In flat profile I screwed Snow White in the ass; wind lifted my uncut hair, goosebumps decorated my arm and shoulder. Her lifted pinafore limp-ragged downward from her waist and brushed the ground, to which her torso bent parallel. A word balloon spurted from her lips: "Happy to meet ya."

A gigantic hunk of excrement falling from outer space threatened a whole town. Eyes and mouths gaping in astonishment, a crowd watched the descent; its shadow darkened the houses. One of my allies, a woman with a big ass, rode it downward; in one hand she clutched reins, in the other a wasp-waisted bottle of Coke. The soft beauty of her face was an item of interest. I drew a small, black monkey riding on her shoulders. She said, "Fresh each morning to your doorstep."

I drew the Gorge inside the mouth of a fish, goggle eyes camouflaged by trees and bushes. Inside the fish was the world.

Grown ravenous, the whole world had eaten itself and disappeared, and I had to put it back. Where to start? I drew my inkwell, and my pen coming dripping out of my inkwell and drawing me drawing myself holding the pen. The inkwell bubbled out of my bellybutton. I drew myself a puzzled look.

But I had to be careful. When I went to bed, the new world might swarm out of my desk for a bite to eat.

Another problem. Animals, especially people, were put together with minimum imagination. Why not distribute head-organs more fairly about the rest of the body? Toe-eyeball, maybe, or a talking ear on the kneecap. A foot that could taste its shoe. How dumb to concentrate so many senses in the head; hack it off, a person was done for.

I changed teachers after the eighth grade. A nervous, moody fellow, this man was as gaunt as my lady was fat. We called him Old Man Stampler, but he was probably still in his twenties, nose like a blade cutting up into steel-rim glasses, long black hair working down his forehead as he moved. He exuded a hair-oil scent. And he wielded the rattan with brutal force; any section of the human body was fair game. One morning I was studying a map of France. Many lines between provinces were simply lines, like most between states and between countries. Lines on a page, the world a round drawing . . . Old Man Stampler's rattan thwocked across my shoulders. "Quit looking out the window, filth!" I had been looking at my geography book.

Once reading through a comic called *The Heap*, concerning a shotdown fighter pilot whose rotting corpse still hugged the spark of life and merged with its environment, becoming a large, powerful, haystack-shaped pile of compost, I spotted an advertisement. "Are you an artist without knowing it? Do you have a spark of talent which training can blow into flame?" Two drawings side by side on the page showed the same homogenized girl in a pageboy hairdo. One centered her neatly. The other lopped off the top of her head, but displayed a full cleavage. I preferred the second picture. In parenthesis below, however, the advertisement proclaimed that a person with "the spark of talent" would choose the first. I liked my doodles to ooze off the page, spilling out into the world. Everything I drew prowled free, and whenever I awoke in the dark, white creatures floated across my ceiling, stared off into space, followed the beams of their eyes toward some prey, and passed through wood like bullets.

Instead of centering my doodles, I balanced them. If one creature's back formed an arc to page left, a different creature's belly to the right might form the same arc—though different in position and size. I balanced angles, expressions, the blank spaces between objects, as if two or more pictures embraced on the same page.

I flung myself into playground fights for their solid contact. Larger boys held me off, trying paternally, condescendingly, to dissuade the heaving of a small juggernaut; finally, to douse my frenzy, they would pummel me to a bleeding heap. But well before my first school kicked me out, I was the largest and strongest person there, and for satisfaction would pick fights with three or four other boys at a time, or a half dozen hulks of girls. Fighting secured me, like cramming the mouth with food.

As I grew older, my drawings grew tamer. I felt less need to fabricate wild monsters of my own, since the world's foliage was fecund with them. That Halloween I had discovered that people and animals might, against my strongest desires, parallel what I drew, as if I imagined my entire life.

But finally I grow tired of filling these pads and become careless. The teacher turns too soon, or I hold up the picture too long.

He glows red and chokes on his Adam's apple, bulging against his throat like a second tongue. "You boy, boy, you, Elmo, bring that there up to the front of the room!"

"Don't think I will," I say. "You got two feet."

So he comes to me. He has to see it. The picture shows Mr. Stampler humping a lamb that looks like one of the ninth-grade girls.

"You couldn't of done this," he says.

"Sure. The company that makes the writing pads prints them up this way. You look at the picture and make up a story. Or maybe you sing a song about it."

"Shut up, I just want to know who can draw like this."

"I can."

"Liar." He leafs through, examining one page at a time. The rest of the class scarcely breathes.

Rising, I stand two or three inches taller than the teacher. For years, there have been passed notes, fighting, sloppy spit-balls, and deliberately screwed-up assignments. But this is the first time that anybody in the class has talked back.

"Call me something else, sir," I say. "Go on, Mr. Stampler, hit me with that dinky little switch." Nervous laughter from a couple of girls.

My drawings absorb him. He studies each page, swallows,

turns to another. "You'll get it soon enough, boy. You . . . will . . . get . . . it." A pause. "Everything's all jumbled up in the wrong place. Unnatural filth. Some escaped convict must of snuck in here last night and slept between the rows and left us muck for gratitude."

"I've been drawing right under your nose for years," I say. "I'm a thief, too. Whenever I finish one book, I steal another out of your desk." I walk past him to the front and rake my thumbnail across the blackboard. "Like sliding down a bannister, hey, and feeling it turn into a razor blade?"

Swiftly I chalk a picture of myself standing at the blackboard writing, "Kiss my ass." My jeans are pulled halfdown in back. I draw Stampler planting his thin lips on my butt, a lingering kiss.

While I work, nobody speaks. "I'm a liar, all right," I say, finished. "Like shit."

"You're not a liar," Stampler agrees. "You're a looney. When the full moon come out, you probly whoop around out in the cornfields and pretend you're the wolf-man. Boy, I don't know. I'd give you a few good whacks, but I don't feel like it. You're too far gone, boy. You lost all respect."

"Yeah," I shot back. "I don't respect you, or anybody else."

"But the worst thing, boy, is how you abuse yourself. If I was you, if I had your talent, you think I'd be here in this classroom? Hah! I'd be drawing pictures for movies or magazines. I'd be drawing pictures for God. I'd be making something out of myself. God give you that talent, Elmo, and you turn around and give it to the devil. That's how come you been hiding it all this time. Because you know it's nasty and evil. Tearing nature apart. This filth of yours"—he raises the pad above his head, the pages flap—"it's a vile swamp!" I catch it in flight, clutch it against my belly. "Get out of here!" he cries. "Don't never come back!"

"I thought of one person I respect," I say.

"Out! Take your filth! Get out!"

"I respect myself."

Fourteen, though I look twenty, and freshly booted out

of school, I stalk into a humid May morning. A thin white line travels all the way around the tip of my nose, like Bela Lugosi's neck after his chopped-off head was fused back on, and he prowled about seeking revenge against his executioners; just before snicking off their heads, he would drop his collar with a ghoulish grin and gloat, "I ham halmost a god!"

I'm a head taller than Duke, and whenever possible, he stays clear of me. Grampa gradually falls apart, and even Helen ignores him now. Granma's quilt, almost finished, spills out over her lap to the floor. Like a tomcat, I watch Cerulia. She's quit school and works in a department store, and every night she has dates. I want to lick and suck her soft flesh. And I'm growing tall, over six feet, a bronzed, gold-haired Apollo, on beans and cabbage, white baloney, white bread, and lard, stalking into the woods mornings, grabbing hold of the pin-oak branch which has thickened with my wrist, squatting into the cool breeze, crapping like a wild boar free in the open air.

I decide to kill the day exploring a cave I had discovered in April, just past the sorghum mill a mile from the Gorge, when, penetrating a thicket, I'd squeezed sideways between two huge moss-covered rocks in a hillside in the forest. Like falling through a crevice into a pharaoh's sarcophagus. No light then, so I'd given up. Next day I'd hooked a five-battery flashlight from Never's Hardware in town, shoved it down inside my pants head first, and held it by the ring, thumb-in-belt, playing tough. Carrying a hunk of limestone to mark my way, extending the flashlight heading in, I'd gotten cramped so tightly in the first passage I couldn't move the other arm from my side. My heart almost froze from panic. But after a hundred feet, the tunnel widened, and down I'd gone, room after room where tunnels branched off, each room larger than the last, and lower, and more wet. Water had oozed down slick limestone walls. Finally I'd dead-ended in a room so large my light had scarcely touched its ceiling. Three white pyramids of frozen mucus had risen twenty to thirty feet in the center. Delicate pearl icicles had dangled above. Beyond the pyramids, the floor had sloped sharply down to a river roaring through a low, wide arch, rushing the room's width, and frothing through a second arch, down into the earth. Returning crouched through low-roofed tunnels, I had knocked loose dreaming bats clenched half my fist's size; they had spiraled blindly peeping into the dead black. I had blazed my trail through virgin cave, and I would return.

Today, after a brief stop-off at the shack for light, I meet Cerulia coming up the hill toward me. Frock clings to flesh; she carries underpants wadded in one hand. Hair hangs in thick wet snakes onto her shoulders, down her back.

"Hello, Elmo. I been cleaning off at the Gorge."

"Out on a date all night?"

"Ain't going to work," she mumbles sadly. "Get me a little rest." Her pupils gape wide in sunlight. Breath hisses through her teeth.

"When you gonna marry, Cissy?" I stand a head above her.

"How come you care about me, honey?" She shoves me tenderly. "I'm hunting a man that ain't all shirt and no pants, with enough loot to change my life."

"How come you're not happy?"

"I should be happy. I'm a pretty girl, ain't I?"

"Sure."

"Naw, come on. You been looking at me for years without taking me in. You growed about six feet this year, honey. You'd squash my lap now. Duke thinks he's the one that's going somewhere to be somebody. But it ain't so." She falls against me and squeezes, and my shirt drinks her wet warmth. "You're the one. Like holding a piece of myself. I just had a long bad night, and I feel like kicking off."

"Aw." Forearms clumsily attack her shoulders, lips taste her wet forehead.

"Cause I just don't give a fuck no more what I do, and that's bad." Her cheeks and body make a warm meal. "Some john gets me juiced, all I can think about is how many times with how many guys. And, honey, I want it to hurt. Your big sister's a whore, ya know."

"Aw." Now I blubber her cheek. First kiss I ever gave. Tongue hair aside, nibble an ear.

"Just want love," she mumbles. "This ain't no kind of life. You better go off now to school."

"That old sonbitch Stampler kicked me out of class for drawing dirty pictures on the blackboard."

She pulls back smiling sadly. "Keep yourself fresh and sweet," she says. "Don't feed it to trash like I did. Save it up like honey for the right time. Maybe we could just move off somewheres and talk, okay? We ain't never really got to know each other before."

She tugs gently at my hand and I come along like a blind, starving dog. Can't think. All the blood's lost between my guts and knees.

Her back faces me. Dress clings to a wet body, catches in the hungry cleft of her ass. "Come on, Prince Elmo," the body seems to say, "don't be afraid. Come dig a hole right here." I'm not responsible.

She hisses, "Don't," twisting around. Lost my flashlight. A tongue drives into my mouth. Nobody's arms ever swallowed such muscle and movement. The trees, glutted themselves with leaves, drop their woven lid on a warm green box. "This ain't happening," she whispers. "It can't." I lunge in whinnying blindly for a feast. Spastic cloth sails upward, clings to the tip of a low branch, bellies an instant and sags. "No, honey, wait a minute. That's not the way. Not in there." Sun bites my drooling eyeballs. A touch, a peristaltic tug, and I can't believe how smooth, sliding into velvet pudding in a dream, a hot mouth, the curve of a tongue beating like a heart. Taste buds explode all over my body, and my eyes cook against the quick of shut lids. "Hurt yourself, honey, easy." Hands clutch my curved and sumptuous front, fused without seam, scuffling against branches and last year's leaves. Mouth fills with live meat, dripping like the Gorge, soft thighs devour my hips. "You'll be wore out." I gobble a mouthful of breast. "Rip myself wide open for you!" Rushing through the crack in the Gorge bottom, I paddle toward the morsel of sky. "Jesus, tearing me up!" I burst through the water's surface. Forest, road, abandoned stonemill, have been digested into a plush world of grass where thousands of slender naked folk mingle, a tangled, writhing potluck of human flesh sunk into the green carpet where they frolic. With amazed eyes, they eat me. White bodies blush: scattered stop lights. I fall splat on my face, mouth gaping, gorged with a living curve of shoulder joint.

Gorge

•1•

"JESUS, HONEY, don't ever tell nobody what we done."

"How come?" I was curious to find out what we *had* done.

"You and me ain't supposed to do that."

"Why not?" I punched the ground by her bare waist. How many years had I already been cheated out of this?

"We're related."

"Well, so's Helen and Dick and Grampa. Isn't this what they do? Make *sense*, Cissy!" Lying between her tits, I nuzzled one soft tilting mound and sighted the nipple at a hazy column of the sun. "Cissy, I want to see exactly where I've been."

"Naw, honey. We got to hide from each other. You know it ain't right." She struggled softly, shoving my shoulder.

"Sure felt good. That's how come you go out at night, huh? How many boys knew about it, while I just flopped up there on my pad? Jesus, what a dumb shit!" I socked the ground again. "How come I never really knew till now?"

"Holy cow," Cerulia murmured, "what a fix. Don't you know, Elmo, sheriff could pack us both off behind bars the rest of our lives?"

"Then the son of a bitch could send us to prison for spitting on the road or jaywalking. Make sense. How come people bother with anything else? Let's do it again."

"Get off, Elmo. I'll scratch your eyes. It was my fault this time, cause I'm a wrecked person."

"When'd you do it first? I'll kill him."

"Never mind. That time I couldn't help it. I was innocent like you, and too small to know anything or do anything."

"Was that time wrong?"

"Yeah," she snarled through her nose. "Million times worse than now."

"Who? Tell me, Cissy. Because I'm telling you something

and you listen hard. You ever do it with anybody else the rest of your life, and you answer to me. I swear the same. Never with anybody else. I swear it!"

"You crazy."

"Swear it, Cissy, or I'll tell. I'll go right now and tell Helen and Grampa. I'll tell Duke. I'll tell the sheriff. Swear it to me, Cissy. Because goddamn it, I love you."

"Hmmmmm, listen, honey. We'll put on clothes and go back down to the Gorge and take a swim to cool off."

"Swear it!"

"Okay, hon. I swear. Because it don't mean a goddamn thing. Satisfied now? Get on off the top of me, honey, okay? That's a good boy."

"Can I look close?"

"Later maybe. After I clean off."

"I'm not putting on clothes!"

"Somebody might be coming down the road."

"What difference does it make? Let 'em look. Anybody who makes noise'll beg for mercy while they gulp down their teeth. Oh, why didn't I ever know before?"

She stood back toward me in sunlight; her white loaves squeezed spit from my tongue.

"Wonder what"—Cerulia lifted her dress off the branch and dropped it over her head—"the rest of the world's doing now."

"Hope it's fucking."

"Wonder what's going on down in hell." When she turned, the dress covered her front; I belched in relief. "Cover your thing," she said. "I don't want to see it." She tossed my pants to where I lay on my side, and bunching them, I bandaged my crotch.

"Is it big as other boys?" I asked.

"That ain't important."

"Did I fuck right? Was there something else I should've done? Did I end up okay?"

"I hope you make me angry," she said. "I really do."

"How come we did it if it worries you so much after we're done?"

"Don't you know nothing? I mean, maybe nigger sisters do it with nigger brothers. We ain't niggers."

"But how come?"

"I don't know. Quit asking things I can't answer. You do things because you want to. You—you lose hold."

"It's okay if Grampa and Helen do it. I guess a girl can do her dog."

"Shut up."

"Cissy, I bet the more I do it, the longer my thing'll grow."

"Whyn't you just quit talking!"

Hands in prayer, I split the black surface, cold as cave water, and sank in a billowing cloud of bubbles. Terrified silver darts scattered before my splayed fingers. Balls buried themselves in my body, silence hissed. Twenty feet above, apple-green, she swam through heaven in her undulating frock. The face looking down resembled mine—older, sadder, shaped and worn like a pebble by water, currents, the atmosphere of slow, continuous change.

"You promised."

"I never did promise. But I'll do it because I owe it to you, honey. So you can see once and for all what you ain't and what you'll never be."

I trod water to my neck. Cerulia sat inches above me on the low ledge, a slick lip green with moss. She squinted over my head at the high wall we'd plunged from; her toes touched my armpits; she raised the soaked cotton above her navel.

"Aw," I sighed.

"We should of played doctor years ago. Maybe this never would of happened."

"Oh," I breathed. Her thighs began a long, slow blush.

"Is that okay?"

"No. Show me exactly where I was. Oh. What a invention!" I exclaimed. Her face softened.

"There'll be lots of other girls that look no different. But you'll never see me or touch me again."

I knew what she said was true, because it was what she wanted.

"Never take a girl," she said, "unless she wants you. Never

beg." She dropped the curtain over her knees suddenly and said, "Something's moving in the trees on the other side."

"I love you, Cissy," I sobbed. "I know I'm gonna be a man."

"Something's looking," she said. "Someone been watching us."

The formless jumble of bones held together by the ragged overcoat said, "After the Army spit me out, I just hit the road. I been everwhere. I seen it all." Dick's eyes digested in his skull's sockets. "I seen a priest come out the door of his big house beside the church and kick a starving man in the teeth, and him just asking for a bite. I seen a man in the Chicago yards grab a moving freight in a snowstorm and climb on top and snag the powerline under his chin. Lit up like a bulb. Melted flesh dripped like water off the bones, and the burnt skeleton dropped in the cinders aside the tracks. I seen a blond woman that looked like a goddess come slow down Third Avenue in her big car with a driver at the wheel, and stop and pick up the filthiest pig-down-and-out she could find and haul him and all his smell into her fancy bed for pleasure. Two summers ago, I come awake on a beach near Frisco and watch a brown girl without no suit come from way out in the water up onto the sand, sun in her face, thinking she's all alone. Sees me lying there like fishfood the tide tossed up, cries out, and off she run a half-mile curve of the beach out of sight. I couldn't of done nothing and I wouldn't of anyway. I seen a male witch in a rail camp out of Seattle drink the blood of a rabbit and his whiskers dripping, tell me and six others in turn the best route back to our homes, which we never told him what they were. Dozen bums in a boxcar strap my wrists to the crossbar on the door, me bent over looking through a opening to where the engine pushes on way up ahead where we'll be in less than a minute, and use me like a woman. Standing in this overcoat in a blizzard, whole body's been kicked half dead the night before back in some Wyoming town, face stuck into dog crap, I got my feet tied up in the Sunday paper, then this young wife with four young children in the station wagon, picks me up when I'd of died out there all alone in them hills, takes me to the next town and gives me two dollars.

All I can think about is finally coming home." He looked at me hard through decayed eyes. "Ain't a thing surprises me any more." He watched Helen, who fiddled her fingers in her lap. "Even now, when it's hot, I got chills like winter." To Granma, he said, "Wasn't you working on that before I left? Ain't you finished yet?"

"Maybe you need some medicine," Helen said. "Maybe you ought to take some pills."

"I ain't surprised nobody wants me back. I'm just a tramp like old Gabe Cord in town."

Duke had been gone all day. In spite of the years and the changes, and the distance across the quarry, Cerulia had recognized Dick and decided to stay away from the shack. Grampa watched Dick the way a dog watches a cat that's just raked his nose.

"Maybe there's some medicine you could take," Helen went on. "Of course, you ain't planning to stay."

"Worked some along the way for my feed," Dick said. "Dug postholes for a farmer's wife, and she give me poison food. Retched out my bowels in a roadside ditch."

"You can't stay," Helen said.

"That's a fact." Dick focused through Helen at a point somewhere ahead in time. "I always knowed I couldn't stay here. But I guess I will. I guess this is where I'll stay."

•2•

One Sunday in late June, another unexpected visitor appeared; and he kept coming every Sunday morning after that. He was a clean, well-dressed town boy my age who walked from Goldengrove clear to the Gorge, bringing a Daisy pump air rifle, fifty-shot magazine screwed down into the barrel. I'd long wanted a Daisy of my own, wanted it almost as badly as I wanted Cerulia, and once gawked at one in the window of Never's Hardware, wondering how to steal it. But it was just too big to shove down inside my pants like the flashlight I'd stolen to bust my cave. Engraved on its breech was a hunting scene—golden dogs, guns and men, sensual, erotic. I thought the boy's parents must be wealthy and successful; years from now perhaps Duke's children would be armed like that.

Thousands of pigeons dwelt across the Gorge in the abandoned stonemill—a corrugated iron building five stories high, an enormous bin, one floor, one ceiling, bare girders, sixty-foot-high idle saws which once sliced blocks of limestone into slabs. Outside the building, facing the water and about a hundred feet apart, two fastened-down ladders ran up to the flat roof. Beside each ladder, a sign read, NO TRESPASSING BY ORDER OF TARZE ROBERTS, OWNER. SURVIVORS WILL BE PROSECUTED." The building had been shut and locked.

The boy came to shoot pigeons. He'd found a narrow opening between wall and ground, wide enough for his body, so he could get inside the mill and shoot pigeons from below. Or he'd climb to the roof and, through the broken-out skylight, shoot the pigeons from there. Sometimes, treading water in the Gorge, I watched him on the roof. He could hit one of the fat birds in flight. Pigeons would spurt through the skylight; feathers speckled the air. But the stung pigeon would fly on. BB's don't kill pigeons, Grampa told me, unless you strike them square in the head.

The boy and I didn't speak to each other yet. I watched, hoping that only once he would forget his Daisy outside the shed when he crawled in. Or that he could climb the ladder to the top and leave his Daisy leaning unprotected against the wall. If he challenged me, I was bigger, and I would have the gun. If he called the law—but he wouldn't. He himself had been breaking the law every week. But I'd wait until he forgot the gun. I didn't want to start a fight—maybe because he walked in a kind of duck-waddle, because he had dimples or wore thick glasses, or because his pipestem arms would have bent in my grip. Maybe I liked him. At any rate, I didn't want to hurt him.

But he owed me the rifle. He was rich and I was poor. Sunday after Sunday, he'd had the use of it, and I never had. It was my right to take it away if I could.

I pushed a coal-oil lantern ahead through the tight opening

passageway of my cave. The stolen flashlight's batteries had died by the end of its first exploration; besides, I wanted more general illumination. Behind me I dragged a small cloth bag at the end of a longish drawstring. Heat filled the morning outside. All day into late afternoon the temperature would rise. Birds were on fire, wind tousled leaves, vegetation rustled in process of growth, flux, and change. But down here, the only life seemed to be myself, and tiny bats, warts on limestone. June or December, the cool scarcely varied. I followed the rock scratches I'd made during my other visit; the deeper passageways widened into rooms, nearly the same as ten thousand years before. No sounds except my heart and lungs, pressure adjustments inside my ears, pop and gurgle of my empty stomach. If the coal oil burned up or a draft put the lantern out, I'd die down here. I'd forgotten to bring extra matches.

The passageway's angle sharpened; I slid on my ass, edged down a cliff of crumbling rock, walked waist deep through a subterranean stream. The ceiling loomed so high sometimes that the lantern wouldn't light it, or so low it made me bend, stroked the back of my head; my nose touched water, and I peered up from beneath the surface and made faces. Soaked and numb, dizzy from cold, I padded along a dry passage opening onto a flower garden of translucent rock, passed one floor-to-ceiling column sectioned like a spine, thick as an old forest oak. Slippery rock intestines flopped through a large slash in the wall. The ceiling formed a sow's underbelly, pearly udders ripe for sucking. Further, the whole floor of another room heaved up a dome of shimmering rind, a giant cortex. The wick flickered, held its flame. I kept moving. A long slender frog's tongue darted down the ceiling; I waited for the tear on its tongue tip to fall. How many weeks had it been growing there? I bent, stuck out my own tongue, and drank it in, a cold, melting crystal distilled from pure darkness.

Water roared far off, breath deep from the earth's lungs. Soft, organic shapes surrounded me. A thousand eyes, crying icy tears, watched my plodding. Lips parted. A breast sloped against my shoulder. Though my signature on rock still blazed the trail, I didn't recognize this territory. One difference lay in the light. The five-battery flashlight had opened its eye straight ahead, tunnel vision. The lantern, though dim and diffused, saw spiderlike through many eyes, until finally I recognized nothing except the flow of shapes, the sullen, indivisible roar of change.

Once more I sat on globed and slippery mineral rock. My back rested on a luminous pyramid. The cloth bag lay between my legs. Twenty feet away, the floor lipped into a roaring sheet of water. Smoke curled like black rising yarn, and I twisted up the guttering wick till its flame grew, then unscrewed the reservoir cap: less than half full.

Unpuckering the bag's mouth, I emptied out a box of pastel chalk, a lock of black hair waisted by a rubber band, and horny bits of toenail grubbed off the dark floor after Cerulia groomed herself and left the house. I looked about listlessly. The borrowed rite I'd come for—part of a scrap of the only social-studies Lesson which ever grabbed my interest, part the memory of a threat Helen once made against Dick—no longer meant anything to me, but I decided to go through with it.

First I searched for a place to bury the leavings of Cerulia's body, but the floor was rock, brittle and impenetrable. So I walked to the water's edge and tossed them in. Then I searched for a smooth patch of wall where I could draw the mural which would bind Cerulia against me. Wherever we touched, a seam, like the cross-stitching on a baseball, would yoke us, biting shoulder muscle and scalp. Now try to divide us!

No level surfaces. Even the "pyramids" were globed and fluted, massive humps, nearly shapeless. But the wall contours seemed to form a breast here, there a thigh—disjecta membra, nothing I could fuse into a whole image. I tried, though, racing the coal oil, fashioning eyes without a face to enclose them, one breast, one lone red-brown pastel nipple eyeing a frenzied stripling, her crotch disembodied in the flicker of gloom, a sex maniac's butchery. I slashed thick black lines connecting the organs—a lopsided, four-sided star. And gave up, it seemed so simple-minded and futile. Bearing the lantern I returned to the water, knelt, and dipped my hands into the icy rush.

A school of tiny minnows, white and blind, clustered nibbling about my fingers.

•3•

None of Helen's steady doctoring helped Dick. Day and night, he lay in a crumpled wad on his pallet near the foot of the bed, never complaining, sitting to take a little food or a pill, leaving the shack to relieve himself in the woods, but allowing nobody to assist or follow him. "Had a accident before I left home the last time," he said. "Slept too long with a frigid woman and got frostbite on my peter." When the Welfare Woman first saw him lying there, she said, "That fellow's in bad shape. He needs a doctor."

"Naw, all I need's a great big woman underneath me here on the floor," Dick said, "to warm me up. Need to sink in between two great big titties and feel 'em flop shut over the back of my head."

"Some people sure live like pigs," the Welfare Lady said. "And they talk like pigs, right in front of their own children."

"I don't know how pigs talk," Dick replied. "I never went to college and learned. But no matter how awful you badmouth me or what horrible things you say, you big beautiful hunk of woman, I'll always love you dearly."

"Some people shouldn't be allowed to have children. There ought to be a law made."

"Ever night since I got back," Dick said, "I only dream about one thing, darling. I dream about you, about rooting and snorting around on top of your big old sweet sow's body. That's how come I returned in the first place, honey. I always knowed a fat woman would end up being the biggest love of my life."

"You ornery thing," the Welfare Woman said.

"He don't need no doctor," Helen said.

"Sure I do," Dick said. "To sew my filthy mouth shut."

Dick liked to talk. During his month back home he talked incessantly, to anybody who happened near, whether they listened or not. He even talked to Granma, to whom everybody spoke so seldom we were uncertain whether she could hear at all—half-animate fixture in the room, eternally bent over the eye surgeon's stitching of her quilt.

"God help me, Mamma, you sure give a poor, feeble vagabond of a son into the hard world," he said. "If you knowed how he'd end, would you ever of gone through all that trouble and pain? Oh, I know, working away on that cover of yours, trying to hide all the misery in the world from your old eyes. Well, don't think twice about it. He deserves everthing he's getting ten times over. Can you hear what I'm saying, Mamma? You borned a son for the cemetery. A piece of meat for the worms that live in the cold ground. Hoo boy. Now that thought started me shivering again, just when I was beginning to feel warm. Ain't that a laugh? Hunnerd degrees outside, and old Dick's cold as a winter turd. Army doctor asked questions bout what I done back home. Not a whole lot, Doc. What sort of work, Mr. Hatcher? Well, now lemme think, Doc. Swum a little, smoked a cigarette or two, made a little whiskey, raised a little hell, poked holes in some frisky late-night women, wrecked a couple cars, burnt down a house, been inside a jail or two, got married, got some kids, had bad dreams and good dreams —not a hell of a lot for as long as I been alive. Is that all you done with your life, Mr. Hatcher? Well, Doc, I could pump out as much bullshit as the next man, but it don't seem worth the trouble. I mean, what's better and what's worse? What makes a man proud and what shames him? I just sort of tried to do what I thought I liked, what give me pleasure. That's all. Now if I was Mr. Roosevelt or Mr. John D. Rockefeller Junior, hell. Why, Doc, I inherited a ton of money, is the first thing, and everybody loved me. Then I spent a ton of money and bought the most wonderful life, you wouldn't believe. Then the worms licked their chops and said, Brother, did that taste good! Pass the olives."

"Maybe you better stop blabbering long enough to swallow another pill," Helen said.

"Never did like doing what anybody else said, though," Dick continued. "Maybe it was my greatest fault. I always did want to be my own man. For instance, I never saw no advantage in stopping clear through a red light when there wasn't nobody coming the other way. But what if everbody did that, Mr. Hatcher? Hell, what if everybody did *anything*? I mean, what if everbody decided to stop on that red light? You'd have cars and people piled up clear to the moon, wouldn't you? Jesus, you'd never be able to clear the intersection. What if everbody walked on the grass? Hell, what if everbody walked on the sidewalk? People be standing on each other's shoulders twenty mile high. Pulverize the goddamn see-ment into dust. What if everbody decided he didn't have to join the Army? Well, what if everbody *joined* the Army, what kind of goddamn mess would that be? See? I truly believe I ain't the only dumbass in the world."

"Sure. Here' some water in a cup to wash it down with."

"Where's Grampa?"

"I don't know."

"Wanted to tell him about this goddamn second looey they stuck me under. Boy if he wasn't the biggest dumbass, I don't know what."

"Whyn't you just take your pill and tell Prince Elmo all about it?"

"Was your second looey the guy you shot?" I asked.

"Did I already tell that story? Helen, them pills must of done something to my memory."

"If you don't want to get well, that's your business. Just loaf on your ass the rest of your life and make everbody happy," Helen said.

"Did I tell that story to Grampa? Was he there when I told it?"

I shrugged. "Don't recall that you ever did tell it. It's just something I heard about a long time ago, while you were still gone."

"If I don't get a chance to tell Grampa, maybe you—" Helen shoved the tiny white pills into his mouth as if she were dunking a basketball. Dick eyed her a moment, propping himself on one arm. Then taking the water, he washed the pills down. "Jesus it's bitter!" he said. "Whew! Right to the head." He shuddered. "Pumps me up like a tar."

"Vitamins," Helen said. Duke told me that she had been seeing a young druggist in town. "Builds the nerves."

"Don't want to take too many of them things," Dick said. "Might get well. If I was a well man, I don't have the slightest idea what I'd do."

"We're working up to it, honey," Helen said.

"Where's Duke at? He might enjoy this story, too."

"How the hell am I supposed to keep track of everbody?" Helen shouted, and stalked outside.

"That second looey was a bastard from the word go," Dick said. "Can you hear me, Granny? Pick the wax out of them old ears. Oh, boy, was he a bastard. He took one look at me and that was it. Boy, if I'd of kissed his ass ten thousand times per day it wouldn't of done no good. Private Hatcher, he must of thought, now there's a man too good for this imperfect earth. I'll just have to grease his way up to heaven. Ooooo, wait a minute. That medicine sure jacks up the boy in me. Whew! That stuff is fierce. Helen sure could throw a hot one ever now and then when the mood hit her. Where was I? I've had some fine times, Prince Elmo. Remember that night, how far out in the Gorge I fired my stream? One time I cracked a woman's kidneys. Rolled her eyeballs back out of sight. I'm a stump of my former self. Just enough so it couldn't keep me out of the Army, but scarce enough to piss standing up. It screws your sense of values. Where was I? Boy, listen—I hope you ain't jacking off. Fuck sheep and ducks and knotholes in trees, if you have to, but don't jack off, it rots the brain. There was a time when all that seemed worth doing was getting laid. Whatever you do, don't wear tight undershorts; give your thing breathing room, space to grow long. Let it hang down your left pants leg always for correction, our family tends to curve right. How come Grampa's been such a funny old bugger since I come back? Naw, don't tell me, I know. It don't make a bit of difference. Poor old Grampa, I hope it soothes his last days. Just so he don't feel too much guilt is all. That's the worst feeling. Whatever you do, don't feel guilty or you'll feel awful. Tell Cissy I'm sorry. I done some rotten things in my life, but the way a man runs his life is his own damn business. And if you already done something, it can't be not done. Like my second looey, with the eye in back of his head. Now what I wanted to know was, how come the whole platoon always had to run across the open places right straight to where they was shooting at us?"

Dick lay on his back, placed his palms behind his head,

and reminisced at the ceiling. "Just to let my mind wander over that territory again gives me the creeps. I seen a buddy hit by one of them kraut M.G.'s fall in two pieces. Dick, old boy, I said to myself at the time, you should of volunteered for tanks. Hell, no, we couldn't sneak around behind them, there wasn't no time. And then you bet your boots there wasn't no time left at all for seven, eight guys. Rooty-toot-toot. When you stick your bayonet into a man's stomach, the muscles clamp tight; sometimes the only way to get it back out again is blast off a round, really messes you up. You pound a dead guy's tag in up under his chin so it won't get lost. It's for the family. But we protected the country from them goddamn foreigners. I'm one-hunerd-percent American, and proud of it. Wrap me in the stars-an-stripes and drop me out to sea. It's been a pretty good life all told, but I can't quite figure out what the point was. It's amazing how a man wants to keep on living no matter what drops off him in the process. Women have a rough time of it, Elmo. If I had it to live all over again, I'd of been nicer to the women in my life. Ya know, when you just give up entirely, and there ain't no future any more, it's a damned good feeling. Relaxing. You're a nicer person. You get back a sense of humor. But that goddamn second looey. Oh, Mamma, Mamma, he killed seventeen American boys in one week, and the colonel give him a medal. No fuss bout sneaking up. Take those sons of bitches head on. Eeeeeyow! It was good to kill him!" He smiled.

I waited for him to go on, but he lay still and kept smiling the same way, eyes gleaming through the crinkled flesh of glee.

"He only come back anyway to spite me, damn him," Helen said. Under the spread-out handkerchief, Dick's face still smiled. His palms still cradled his head. Nightbugs ah-chahed outside.

"Now we got to figure out where to put him," she said.

Cerulia sat off in a corner, rubbing her thighs. "How bout a undertaker, Mamma?"

"Thuh-uh boy must of gone peaceful," Grampa sighed.

"I don't begrudge Dick a happy death," replied Helen, "but that don't solve our problems. Undertakers cost a mint. Anyhow, I don't want no stranger messing with Dick. There's enough of us here, we ought to figure out some way to handle this ourselves."

"There's a potter's field to the south of Goldengrove cemetery," Duke suggested, staring dead at Helen. "I think the county handles the whole thing. Welfare Woman'd know."

Helen looked at her dirty palms, in her lap. "I got my pride," she said. "I ain't gonna have my own husband laid to earth like a pauper."

"We could bury him in the hole Elmo dug." Duke plucked an earlobe. "That goes way down, and it ought to be filled up anyway. Go out into the woods at night, you're liable to stumble in."

"Huh uh," I said.

Cerulia agreed.

"How come?" Duke asked.

"Because I've been using it to do my duty," I said. "And so've you. And I don't like the idea of burying my own father in a shithole."

"They ain't too hot on home burials no more," Grampa said. "Used to be, somebody died, you buried him on your property."

"Dick'd like it in a cemetery," Duke said. "That was one of his big schemes. The Garden of Roses. Jesus H. Christ."

"We don't need no trouble with thuh-uh sheriff," Grampa said. "I own this here land in my own name, legally registered in thuh-uh courthouse. But if thuh-uh law gets after me, some rich sonbitch might take into his head to grab it away for a song. I don't know, Helen."

"How come nobody's crying?" I asked. "I thought families cried when one of their own died."

"There ain't no rules about mourning," Helen said. "If you feel like crying, you cry, that's all. Some of us have more control over our feelings. It's more dignified."

"Sure, Mamma. I'm crying deep down in my heart," Cerulia said.

"Helen, let's just go ahead and bury him in Prince Elmo's shithole," Duke insisted. "I mean, I thought we already—"

"What's that?" Helen interrupted, eyes widening.

Duke palmed over a grin.

"What's the big joke?" Cerulia asked. "What's wrong with Helen?"

"Shut up, Duke!" Helen snapped. "Uh . . ." She appeared to think, rolling frightened eyes.

"Shee-it!" Duke spat. "Plans is plans."

"Wish we could find something else to talk about," I said. "Maybe there aren't any rules, but I watched Dick go and—" Suddenly I knew what had really happened to my father.

"Plenty of blabbing all right," Helen was saying, "and not much action. We can't just let Dick rot here on the floor. Hell, the poor man ain't even got a shroud. Three big men in this room, and all they do is talk."

"Okay, I guess I know what to do," I said, checking the size of Dick's long scrawny body. "We're not going to undertakers because Helen doesn't want to. Right?" I scowled into Helen's eyes. "So we got to put him away ourselves, but that's against the law. Right?" I looked at Duke, who covered his mouth and turned away. "And the shithole's out because I say so. And we could dig another hole, but that's not going to be necessary. All I need is for Duke to help me with the food wagon. How bout it, Duke? You owe the old man a favor."

"I don't owe nobody," Duke said. "What's on your mind?"

"The solution to everbody's problem," I replied. "Now, besides us, who knows Dick ever came back?"

"Old Two-by-four," Cerulia murmured.

"I'll just tell her Dick took a notion to hit the road again," Helen said. "She won't know the difference."

"Sure," I said. "Everybody's dumb except the Hatchers. You coming along to help, Duke?"

"I want to know what you got in mind."

"To hell with that!" I yelled. "Don't you worry about a thing. I'm just going to hide the evidence, like a good son and brother."

"Keep your voice down out of respect for the dead," Helen scolded.

"Old Dick never had enough respect for anybody," Grampa mumbled. "But he wasn't such uh-uh bad sort." A vein of quartz gleamed among the furrows in Grampa's cheek.

"You ain't taking him out on the road in no wagon," Helen said.

"Naw, Helen, don't worry," I told her. "I'm sneaky for my age. You'd be proud."

"Well . . ." She pondered her cracked and jagged fingernails fingernails.

"If he'd of been born with money in thuh-uh bank," Grampa said, "he'd of had as good uh-uh life as any man alive. It's thuh-uh goddamn rich that run thuh-uh world. By God, dead before his time!"

Granma rose from her rocker where all along she'd been stitching, and knelt beside Dick's corpse. Her quilt hung from her hands, a waterfall of flame and autumn leaves. Only half the backing was properly stitched down. The rest she must have tacked hastily during the past two or three hours. The quilt crumpled in a fiery heap beside her. She whisked the handkerchief off Dick's face and closed the eyes that focused on the ceiling. Closing the mouth, she softened his grin to a gentle, amused smile. She spread her quilt the full length of the body, tucked it loosely beneath the head, the torso, and the legs. Returning to her rocker, she hid her face in her hands.

I carried the lantern lighting our way and pulled the load through the woods. Branches and brambles slashed me. I didn't bother holding limbs for Duke; I just let them whip back.

"Yow! There's somebody behind you that's alive, damn it!"

"Maybe you better crawl under the quilt," I said. "Hug up next to Dick. Draw a little warmth inside your body."

"Look, uh, Elmo, I wouldn't go around shooting off my mouth, okay?"

"I wouldn't screw my own brother." I catapulted another branch into his face.

When we reached the thicket, I said, "This is going to take some maneuvering."

"I never did mind honest work," Duke said. "But we can't just throw him in the bushes."

Holding the lantern in my right hand, I lifted Dick's feet with my left. Duke hoisted his shoulders. We'd tied the quilt in three places with rope—around the neck, waist, and feet, from which a yard's length dangled for hauling.

"Granma sure wasted a pile of work," Duke observed.

We struggled through the thicket to the moss-covered rocks.

"We'll have to twist him sideways a little," I said. "Think he'll float?"

"Hey?"

"I'll go first and drag Dick. For the first hundred feet, crawl along after me, on your belly like a snake."

"My sweet Jesus, lookit that hole in the ground!"

Dick wedged to a halt almost at once. Grunting and twisting, Duke worked him loose. I flicked a bat which spiraled down the black tunnel. "That's a bat!" Duke cried.

"Cute little devils," I said, and began waking every one I saw. "Feel great flapping inside your mouth." The dead heels trembled.

"Don't try and frighten me," Duke said. "Hey, we can't slide down there, can we? Fuck. Guess I already wrecked this good pair of pants."

Dick kept wanting to sink. Duke complained, "Boy, this shit go much deeper? I ain't tall as you are." He slipped and gurgled, "Jesus, Elmo, this your idea of a joke? What if it decides to rain out there? Ain't a foot between water and ceiling. God-damn, that bottom's slippery! Hope there ain't no gullies. Already got my face turned up like a lily pad to breathe."

But later, moving through one gem-encrusted room after another, Duke exclaimed, "Gorgeous! This here's just fan-tas-tic! Boy, if we could find another route into this joint, we could sell tickets. We could have weddings and funerals in here, and banquets. If it wasn't so cold and damp, we could make a underground hotel. Any of this rock worth money? I read once where they found a thousand-year-old mummy in a cave, perfectly perserved. Hey, wait a minute, what's that?"

"Where?"

"Over there."

"Column," I said, "where a stalactite and a stalagmite got together after a few million years."

"Naw, dumbass, I mean where I'm pointing with my nose."

A long section of ceramic pipe ran through the room's ceiling on down through the floor. I hadn't noticed it until now.

"Hell, buddy, I know what that is," Duke said. "It's well pipe. This virgin was already popped before you ever got inside. Wonder if there's anything else you're ignorant of."

"I know all I need to."

"Mister, go ahead and talk in riddles if it makes you feel good. It's just that I don't feel safe in a closed-up space with a walking, talking asshole who's carrying a lantern. Don't you know fartgas explodes? If there's one thing that makes everybody in this world sick, it's some goddamn holier-than-thou self-righteous little prig."

We reached the last room. "Hell's bells!" Duke crowed. "It's like the inside of a castle. Jesus, put your little boy down here with a endless supply of food and beautiful girls and let him live forever! What's those funny squiggles on the walls? It looks like the walls of an outhouse. Hey, Elmo, somebody's been down here drawing dirty pictures."

"I don't see a thing."

"You fool! Look up there. Here, let's lay down this bundle. Right there on the wall. See? Don't you recognize that thing? You still think women carry peters tween their legs? Elmo—tell me, boy. Did you draw that? Huh? The light ain't very good in here, but you must be blushing from your horny heels to the top of your dirty little mind. You drew that, Elmo. I know you did, you ornery fart!"

I grabbed the bundle's foot, hauled the soaked, mud-smeared quilt-shroud down toward the water.

"It's okay, boy," Duke snorted. "I won't tell a soul, I promise. Come all the way down into the guts of this place to put dirty pictures on the wall, after God spent a million years digging it for you. Just for that! Haw haw haw! Hey, wait up. I'll give you a hand there. Dick hardly weighs ten pounds any more. Water for a grave and filth to mark it. Look at that river move! Whew! Okay, now—one, two, three, *heave!* Down, down, down! Never come out, 'cept maybe as cold broth into a farmer's tin drinking cup. Oh, I can tell, that river flows right straight down into the earth's guts."

Dick sank deeply into the fluid of my mind.

"Jesus, I don't believe it," said Duke, "the dumbass is crying."

•4•

Duke was sixteen, but he looked twenty-five. Like me, he seemed to age fast. One afternoon a week or so after Dick died, I came across Duke sitting against the Dodge's rusting hulk, a stack of slick and colorful magazines in his lap. "Hey, gimme one."

I thumbed its pictures. Morning-glory dresses to the shinbone. Pastel bathrooms. A handsome youth named Robert Lowell. Green chlorophyll-scented sheets, a woman in green pajamas. City woman, thin arm on bony hip. Air evac from Korea. Mrs. Leopold Stokowski, "strange beauty . . . slanting eyes." A bride gazes past her veil at floating knives, forks, and spoons. The cool hostess. Albert Einstein in his study at Princeton. Three country debs. Ladies of the Bedchamber to her Majesty. The Coronation of H.M. Queen Elizabeth II: above the froth and flow of white cloth, washed-out skin. Not a shadow of a doubt with Kotex. Jockette, stolen from men, made pretty and practical for you. Men on their way up. The woman who dresses for a man. Sparkling gold, invisible beauty strap, are you the woman for a great and lasting love? Whistler's mother. Famous artist shows how bosom in motion requires a bra with stretch. Sea nymphs.

And for an instant, the magazine reminded me of another treachery by Duke, a memory fragment back before I was even five, when for some reason he got pissed off at Granma and took his revenge on her old album of copperplates. These pictured strong people—men with heavy jaws, and big hands thrusting from the tight sleeves of their awkward Sunday clothes; women young, middle-aged, and old, not one of them fat, their bodies hard under the harsh, stiff dresses they wore; men in Civil War uniforms, proudly holding their brand-new Springfield caps and ball rifles—all relatives whose names even Granma did not know, since not one single name appeared under any picture in the entire album; no family name on the front, only, in large, bold, regular handwriting, which Granma read out to me once, pointing with her finger, a directive by the dead, *"Remember us!"*

But one hot, bright, summer morning simmering with humidity, Duke handed me the album and insisted that if I dropped it in the Gorge, the pictures would come to life. Those people would rise en masse, flesh and blood, full size, from the water, whispering their names. So I staggered eagerly down the hill under the album's weight, to the limestone edge, and pitched those people in, and watched the clear green water suck them down, till they shrank to a speck, then disappeared in the quarry's icy memory.

No one rose from the dead. No names breathed in my ear. I remember that Granma cried softly when Duke tattled what I had done. But after her eyes grew dry, she seemed to forget the album forever.

Now Duke was watching me closely as I stared at the magazines. "Hooked 'em from a drugstore," he said. "Say, Elmo, how much you know about Cissy and me? About what's been cooking all these years?"

I shook my head. Drawing pictures for movies or magazines, I thought, remembering Old Man Stampler.

"How you think we eat regular? Where do we get the cash? Ever wonder?"

"You and me steal. Welfare Lady brings food sometimes. There's Grampa's disability. Cissy's been working ever since she dropped out of school."

"All together it's not enough. You eat like a hog. By yourself, you'd polish off most of that. And what about clothes? I mean, even we need shoes. There's not much, but it's been enough to survive on."

"Never thought about it."

Then where do you think we're heading? You just gonna run out your days sitting on your ass on top of this hill waiting to die like poor old Dick? You think me and Cissy's gonna do that? Maybe you better start living for tomorrow."

"Living for tomorrow," I repeated.

"Yeah, what I'm doing right now, why I'm reading that mag. In three months, I'm seventeen. This war keeps up, I'll get drafted. Can you see Duke Hatcher kicked around in a Army uniform, getting his butt shot off by slant-eyed chinks way out across the ocean where nothing meets nowhere? Time to move on, buddy." He paused. "Now Cissy's up near twenty. Handsome girl. Scrub her up, fix her hair, wrap that nice soft body in some high-style clothes—she beats them there bony models all to hell. Cissy's sitting on a million bucks."

I shook my head. "Cerulia's not leaving."

"Dumbass! Elmo, I saw you at the airport rink a week back. Hell, buddy, you just simply got to know. What world you been occupying there inside your damn head?"

"Naw. Cerulia's staying here with me."

"Buddy, I been that girl's manager for years, and you ain't got a thing to say. Cissy's been selling tail since the cradle. Dick and Helen knew all about it and pretended not to. Grampa knew, hell yes. Only you and Granma didn't know, two people who never counted anyway. That girl's taken 'em like a pro and shaken herself off like a cat, like she's never been touched. But here's the ticket. She's satisfied the richest man in the county, who's had the fanciest gals in the world. Had her in his mansion. Told her one night in the sack he'd take her over anybody else in the world. Sometimes a sinkhole family like ours breeds a prize. But too many people been eating out of your sister's body too long, and now it's time to say goodbye."

"Naw, please."

"What's the matter, Elmo? You ain't hot for your own sister? Everbody's got to draw the line somewheres."

"Don't want her to leave."

"Wouldn't she look slick in something like that? Tightened some round the tits and ass? I got visions of smart management, up in Indy or Chi, or maybe New York City. We saved a tidy hoard to get us there and keep us eating awhile until we make it. There's lots of woods round here for burying a little bag of oilcloth full of green paper."

"She could model clothes," I said. "She's more beautiful than any lady in here."

"Naw. I thought about that, but the fags that design clothes want skeletons. Cissy looks too much like a woman."

"She could be a movie star."

"Yah, pow! Even a movie actress starts out whore, fucking

producers for her part. Cissy already is one beautiful whore—Ho! Wait a minute, boy. Let go, there! Just get your goddamn paws off."

"Have you—" I gasped, "have you ever—"

"Ever what? Huh? Hey, I'm a businessman, not a goddamn degenerate!"

A red devil's-eye winked through the trees that evening. Veined with red, the Gorge glowed metallic blue. By August, road and stone dust would dull the leaves, ripen them toward death. Now they gleamed mint-green. Some ancestor had tramped up this hill years ago, braved whatever Shawnee still remained in the area, and decided, To hell with planting crops, to hell with working, with going any further or climbing any higher—to hell with being a success, this is where I stay.

I clutched a pencil, and the writing pad which Stampler had thrown into my hands when he ordered me out of school. I wanted to show my pictures, my only hope and bribe, to Cerulia, and so waited for her where we had strangled on the hot broth of our flesh.

She came, sweating, cloth sticking to her thighs. Her face was soft, mouth full and soft, but I traced the skull in her cheeks. Seeing me, she shook her head slowly side to side.

"Only want to show you something," I said.

"That's nice, honey."

"Duke says you're leaving. Going away to a city and not coming back."

"Sweetheart, I'm such a sleepy girl." She pushed her arm against me.

"I'm going to tell," I blurted out. "Duke and Helen and everbody else what we did."

"No." She shook her head again. "Duke'd think it was only a dirty joke."

"You promised you'd never do it with anybody else and you lied."

She just shook her head.

"I saw you out at the skating rink," I sobbed. "How many boys was it?"

A few nights before, I'd pursued Cerulia to her destination.

Several times I had tried and failed; tracking her as she walked along the roadside. I had sneaked through trees and brush, plunging for cover when I heard a car behind, or an aurora glowed in front. Hiding, giving a brief head start, I marathoned after until taillights closed to a single red star and disappeared. But on that particular night, she'd screwed up by mentioning the skating rink, next to the county's asphalt airfield, where, among weeds and crunchy grasshoppers, behind the cyclone fence, I sometimes watched local doctors and executives from the town's RCA plant pilot their Cessnas in and out, and imagined a fieldful of Japs strafed into gold-tooth-salted pulp; or, reversing sides, I ak-akked a thousand hours' labor into flying junk. I'd stare into the sun, then at the runway. The rink had been stuffed into a gutted hangar. Inside, they rented shoe skates with wooden wheels, Duke told me. You shoved your foot way down inside and laced them tight.

I had stood beyond the parked cars, listening to the organ, watching windows change red to green to purple. An open window exhaled cigarette smoke, and I smelled popcorn, hot dogs. Shadows scuffled in parked cars. Preceded by her honor guard of boys, Cerulia had emerged from a side door. Long black hair swung like the tail of a horse. She laughed, easy and loose in the tense huddle. I crouched near the fence. Holding his mouth, one boy tumbled suddenly to the ground. A shout. He turned on his side. One of the group kicked his ass, and he scrambled off. Cerulia shook her head despondently.

I strode among the boys, lifted her light and soft into my dive-bomber, and we took off. Circling back, I pressed the button on the stick and strafed my enemies.

All four doors of the Ford had slammed at once. They couldn't even wait to form a line. An airplane droned overhead, blinking its small red light. My imagination cruised to the red-hot fleshpocket inside the car. A bare arm jutted through the window, panties fluttered in its fist—beachhead.

I spilled into my palm. And saw Duke slouching in the doorway of the rink . . .

Now, closing her eyes, Cerulia whispered, "Shouldn't of followed. Wasn't none of your business."

"Duke says you take money."

"And I do it," she sighed, "for no money. You didn't give me no money." She pointed at the pad. "Is that what you wanted to show?"

"I bet you never saw anybody who could draw like that," I boasted. "Maybe I'm the only person in the world who can." I displayed my fantasies in the fading light. "Look." I drew on a blank sheet. "You don't even have to stay still."

She shook her head slowly. "Well, forevermore." When she smiled her cheeks dimpled like mine. "Ain't that pretty."

"You're beautiful," I said. "I can't even begin to get it down."

"You always was the smartest one, but I never knowed you could draw. How come you never told us?"

"Would it have been different?"

"I'd of liked to know. You could of done pictures for the family, on the wall. It would of been so nice." Delicately, with her little finger, she lifted back into place a strand of hair that crossed her forehead.

"Look—I've been fighting and stealing, getting into trouble here and there. But what's important enough to kick me out of school maybe forever? This. I'm better than Duke. You don't have to leave."

"We ain't got definite plans yet," Cerulia said. "But you know, I really have made my choice. When I go, I go."

"Then you'll spend the rest of your life thinking of yourself like you told me. A worthless whore."

"I ain't gonna slap you, if that's why you pull back."

"Wait till I make something out of myself. I'll take care of you the rest of your life."

"Taking me for a backpack, that wouldn't be no fair to you. It's my life, honey. You ain't my boss, neither is Duke. When I get where I'm going, I'll only have myself to blame. Now, I got a very important date tonight. I know you want to help, and I know you love me"—she tugged the writing pad from my hands—"and I won't let you help. But maybe I can help you. I'm taking this to somebody I know. He's smart. He hangs pictures all over his walls. He lives in a paradise on earth like where me and Duke are trying to climb, and—I don't know—maybe you're someone he'll want to toss out the line to, and reel in."

•5•

I sat on a tree stump, while Cerulia barbered my hair neatly, lubricated it with hair oil, and savagely parted it above the left ear. She also presented me with my first pair of dress shoes: smoothly gleaming mirrors of black leather, pointed at the toe. A man in the shoe department of her store, she said, had swiped them for her.

"Elmo, cleaned up you are the prettiest boy." Her large, sad eyes searched my face for dirt. "Just relax and watch where you put your feet, and hold the tray level, and don't act smart with anybody. You'll get by fine." Resting one hand on my naked shoulder, hot in the afternoon sun, she tongued a rag and poked around in the whorls of my ears.

Duke said, "Be careful as hell, old buddy. It's a more delicate operation than picking cans off a grocery shelf. Best bet is to criss-cross the bags under your shirt, and let the shirt sort of balloon out above your belt. First good chance, slip down to the fence and sling the loot over where I showed you. Hoo ha! You come back in the wee hours tomorrow morning, Elmo, and we dig up the rest of our treasure, then down to the bus stop with our goods, two—I mean three—one-way tickets, and by God we're home free, old buddy." Two squirrels spat and chattered among the branches. Duke armed me like a knight. Lifting the two puckered cotton bags, one of which had carried pastels into my cave, he noosed their drawstrings over my head. I wriggled my arms through; a bag hung near my waist on either side. Then he dangled the small hacksaw like a holy medal against the sweat-beaded flesh of my chest. Cold steel tingled. "Through the kitchen," he said, "up three flights, make a sharp right and clear to the end of the hall. You won't believe your eyes."

Cerulia said, "It'll be like cutting butter. He's interested in you. That's why he give you this job. Still, you got to be careful when you do it."

"Yeah, wait till after midnight when they're drunk and rolling in the grass."

"Tarze don't ever get drunk," Cerulia said. "He's in complete control."

"Aw, you done harder jobs, old buddy," Duke said. "Don't you know that? This is just a leetle tiny caper compared to what you helped with. Tomorrow you'll be far gone, with me and Cissy in a coach and four."

"I just want to stay with Cissy."

Cerulia stood tiptoe, reached behind my head, pulled my mouth against hers. "Sweetheart," she murmured. "Baby bear."

It was early evening when a sheriff's deputy, standing beside a telephone box, checked my name on a list and admitted me through the gate. "I know about your family," he said. "Mr. Roberts is getting him some pretty low-class help these days."

"Sure," I said, "nowdays they let anybody be a lawman."

"How old are you, boy? We got strict age laws about who handles liquor."

"Twenty-one."

He peered up into my face. "You're big enough. But you look awful young in the eyes."

The wide asphalt curved a half mile up the slope where Tarze Roberts' mansion loomed against the red sunset like a fairytale palace. I stepped into the grass, barbered and moist. "Hey, you goddamn idiot, keep off!" the deputy shouted.

Chlorine's sharp tang polluted the air. Reaching the top, I saw a crescent-shaped pool whose water seemed perfect blue, and beneath the surface, long and lithe, creature from a dream, a naked woman frog-kicked. The low diving board, jacketed in hemp, still vibrated from her last dive. But when she surfaced, treading water, I saw the flesh-colored swimsuit blending with her skin. She smiled, white-toothed, licked her lips; her long gold hair floated about her shoulders.

"Hi, I'm Barbie." She waved me over. I just nodded and gaped. "One of the football players?"

I shook my head.

"What's your name?"

"Prince Elmo."

Jump in here with me, Prince." She breast-stroked to poolside; tits bulged against cloth.

"No suit," I mumbled.

"Well, aren't you the silent type." Against her chin, a finger width of hair floated; she stirred it aside. "Our hair color's the same. Maybe we're related. Whew! I need the swim. Started boozing around noon. Much rather smoke. Gin puts me out like a light. I'm in movies. What's your line?"

"Gee!" I cried out. "A movie star?"

"Well, yeah. Prince, how old are you?"

Old enough to know the score," I announced.

"I mean, you seem so innocent. It's kind of attractive, but, well—"

"I'm an artist."

"How thr-rilling!" she exclaimed. "I love artistic men. Can I pose for you?"

"Yeah, I mean, you know."

She looked up coyly, flickering lashes over her blue eyes. "I'll pose nude."

"Hey, you out there, will ya get over here please?" A fat man in mushroom hat, long blood-stained white coat, gestured violently beneath a flying buttress.

All about me in the warm bright air, invisible doors opened. The man yanked my wrist. His face was sculpted like a bacon jowl, seamed and suety. "What're you, asshole, making like one of the guests?"

"Touch me once more, mister, you'll need an adding machine to count the bruises."

The man's face softened, amused. "Kid, maybe you just didn't know you ain't supposed to talk to the real people."

"She talked to me."

"It's got to do with class. You got to know your place."

"She wanted me to come swim with her."

"Buddy, your place around here ain't no swimming hole." He shook his head. "Boss had that girl flowed out here for the party, two thousand miles, bought and paid for. He finds ass growing all over the place. He shakes the bushes in those grubby hills south of town where even poor folk like you and me wouldn't stoop to scrounge. And nigger wenches and half-breeds? Let me tell you!"

As we entered the kitchen, I noticed a fifty-pound drum of lard, viscous spikes and loops growing from its mouth like stalagmites. Several fly-studded strips of tape dangled from the kitchen ceiling. Further on, wired in hairnets, a dozen nondescript ladies, strung side by side along a fifty-foot butcher-block table jutting out from one wall, sliced and spread and stuffed and stirred and pounded into shape a gargantuan chaos of food.

Juice spurted out the corner of my mouth, trickled cold and slender down my chin. I wiped it.

The man pointed to another butcher block, ten feet on a side, where three mute sides of beef lay. "Got to work up the meat. Whyn't you wash up—can's around to the left of the range—and when you get back, help that lady on the end spread gunk onto crackers." The mound of gray paste, into which she jabbed a small silver knife, dwarfed her.

I tweaked the kitchen-bathroom's fixtures—handles, faucets, spouts. Stainless steel. The low, wide bowl swallowed soundlessly—rich man's crapper. Then I washed my hands and started out. A tall lean stranger talked with the cook. I paused at the door. Except for a close-cropped crescent of gray above his ears and around the back of his head and neck, he was bald, and though his neck and hands were deeply tanned, his dome shone translucent pink. He wore a two-button jacket of dust-blue fabric, which at his slightest movement reshaped against his flesh. His trousers were mother-of-pearl gray, cuffless, narrow, unpleated, and he wore a gray ascot. In repose his face lacked seam or line. When he frowned, however, muscles contorted the face into angles—like a feather pillow packed with rock. And when he smiled, the whole face drew up into a contour map of creases, jolly and benign—but twenty years older than before. The cook pointed me out to this man, who motioned me over.

"I'm Roberts." He reached out.

The cook shrugged and ambled to the chopping block.

Roberts' palm felt dry and soft. "You really should learn a firm handshake," he said, smiling, crinkling instantly into a well-razored Santa of seventy. "But that's not your fault. How's your father?"

"He's away from home."

"Really? I must have the wrong information. Understand he was pretty ill."

"Sure. But that's over now." He still clung to my hand; I pulled away.

"Thought you'd look younger," he said.

"I thought you were nearly dead from old age."

"Ha! See? There's been some talk back and forth, hasn't there? Loosen up, son." A lady stared dolefully at her employer, then returned to stuffing some small animal. "Hell, let's take a guided tour around a rich man's house."

The hacksaw stung my chest. "I'm supposed to be working."

His pupils were refrigerated blue surrounded by clear white. "You'll get paid," he said.

"Give me something to eat."

He signaled the cook. "Fix a sandwich for Prince Elmo." The cook scowled, so Roberts added, "Prince Elmo isn't like the rest of your help. He's my apprentice—right, kid?"

The cook handed me a sandwich on a plate, and water in a diamond-faceted glass.

"We pump our water out of the ground," Roberts said. "No chlorine to louse up the taste. We put chlorine in the pool, though, because of our filthy bodies."

I washed down a mouthful of bread and meat with a swallow of icy, pure water. "Look, I don't know about this water," I said. "But I got a nicer-smelling place to swim than that girl out there."

"My niece? We'll introduce you."

"We already met. I would've walked on by, but she called out. It was her fault."

"You sound like a guy who beats them off with a stick."

"Mister, I don't know, but I think you're making fun of me, and I don't like it."

He patted my shoulder, a fatherly gesture. "Prince Elmo, you're a charming boy. But you ought to practice indirectness. Feelings dive off your tongue naked as a jay." And taking my elbow, he pulled me into a stairwell.

"Listen, mister, are you a queer?"

He just regarded me with doleful tolerance. "I don't have any morals. But I wear a few manners around the house. They keep things from falling apart."

I felt limits melting away. Morals, manners—any distinction between these words meant nothing to me. It was the way he spoke, the material gesture of sound, of where I had been in my life and where I stood now. Nothing, it seemed, could be accurately predicted, except strangeness, surprise, difference. I could hardly separate my hands and feet from the world, from smoke fading in the air, mote-filled shaft of sun, walls, strange white creatures flowing about me.

Gray and functional, the stairwell rose clear to the roof. But the rest of the house bombarded me with incredible complication, like an architectural Proteus. Narrow, elbow-cramping hallways and circular staircases alternated with vast golden rooms where the Sun King might have flopped, planting horns in the foreheads of his nobles. A dark-paneled, claustrophobic den like the inside of a nut opened into a state-house rotunda with columns and dome, gleaming floor-medallion of bronze, pastel furniture. An audible rush of water in the distance fought the Fourth of July heat. Of one large, bare, marble-floored room, Roberts said, "Shipped this back piecemeal from a Venetian palace." Bending, I snapped a fingernail against the "marble," and the brittle click betrayed it. "Plastic," Roberts noted. "Canal water wrecked the original. A lot of the decoration here's plastic. It's cheap, and it lasts. Even looks more the way the real thing *ought* to look."

In one narrow wooden room whose Gothic slits opened west, Roberts poured himself booze over ice in a small globed glass. Bars of light scored an oil painting—colors soft and hazy, as if a foot of water drowned the scene—of a child whose eyes expressed stark candid innocence, and reflected the daylight of some past world. "Painting of his son by Renoir," Roberts explained. "I've bought lots of art treasures. Great investments. I've dicked around a little with paint, but that's not my real talent. Artists project some imagined world onto canvas. I project what I imagine onto the real world. A shallow person'd call me a frustrated artist. But I say every artist's a frustrated

Tarze Roberts. Ha!" He saw me watching the underwater child's eyes. "You know, living my kind of life, I keep stumbling across the past. Some young man or woman drops by the office and insists on an appointment. Curtain raiser's usually, 'You've never seen me before, but my mother told me you were my real father.' Mostly they're dirt-poor, and I don't know whether they're telling the truth. It's pretty ticklish if the adventuress is some sexy gal. Shouldn't bang her, she might be my own daughter, and it might be traumatic for her. I look carefully for some track of myself—looks, mannerisms, even turns of mind. Then if the whole enterprise seems an obvious hoax or a complete bore, well—one young thing said that if I didn't help her out, she'd marry some damn grease monkey. 'My dear,' I told her, 'it's no concern of mine. I don't care if you fuck dogs.' "

Keep things from falling apart? I wondered.

"Then again, I've arranged good jobs, sent young men and women through college, medical school. If I could find a particularly promising young bastard, I might take him on as an apprentice. For instance, I can picture my ingenuity grafted onto the energy of some black buck; of course, I'd have to teach him impeccable manners. But when I want to be, I'm blunt. I've earned the right to control my world."

"How'd you get so rich?"

"Boxes," he said without hesitation. "Bottles, sacks, cans. It came out of an almost religious feeling. I was even poorer than you probably, and like everyone I wanted to be rich. So one hungry morning, in this county right here—you know I'm a local boy, don't you?—after eating a breakfast of garbage—No, I'm not exaggerating. Membranes from inside eggshells, for the record. Huddled up against a tree, sick from hunger, I asked myself, 'How do I get rich? What's the best way?' And the answer came, so simple, like a natural force: containers. Whatever's made must come or go in a bottle, sack, wrapping paper, a can, a box. The common denominator, the heart of the world. Even containers are packaged in containers. This, inside that, inside this. The more I thought, the more universal it seemed. The human body's a container, and comes out wrapped in a sack and goes out in a box. The whole earth is a container, the solar system, et cetera. Two questions remained: Which compartment of this vast system should I plunge into, and Where would I get the cash?"

He financed himself at first, he told me, by stealing from a grocery where he managed to get a job as carry-out boy. "Two to three hundred, a lot of money then. Statute of limitations ran out eons ago. Besides, it wasn't enough by one millionth to pay me back what I'd lacked since birth." He looked much older than his age, he explained, and was "smart as hell." Traveling to New York City, he'd started as stockboy in a company which made containers for shipping food. At twenty-five, he owned the company. "Course, since then I've diversified like crazy. Right now, for instance, I'm making a killing on chinchillas."

Though for some reason he kept trying to put me at ease, I checked to make sure the paneled door remained open. Something hidden went on in this room from which sunlight had faded. I remembered two stray mutts, lean and ragged, down at the Gorge on the bare stone, luxuriously and with great ceremony sniffing assholes.

He was saying, "Once I thought I'd filled my life going after wealth and pleasure. Now I see I've been searching instead for value, the meaning of life. And I've failed. Look, this vast empire, and no heir. What a piece of shit!"

"Mister, I want to know," I said, looking him squarely in the eyes, "what the hell you've been doing to my sister!"

"Aristotle in debt," he smiled, "stands at the mercy of a shop clerk."

"That's Greek to me," I retorted.

But he bent his forehead against the paneled wall and roared.

Independence Day rockets, courtesy of the American Legion, explode kaleidoscopically. On the sloping lawn, several tipsy men choose sides for football. Jacketless in shirt and tie and razor-creased trousers, Roberts captains one team. Dressed in a starched white jacket and bearing highballs on a silver tray, I move among lovely ladies on the sidelines.

One lady tells another, "He was wearing a white suit like

that the first time I saw him. He walked into the room where we all were—like Phaeton in his chariot! He went to the piano, it was a vision. And my God, I thought, what an utterly gorgeous man!" She wears a green gown cut low on her breasts, full, soft like her arms, shoulders, all her body. Her face is heart-shaped, wide, lovely. Torches and bursting rockets show green eyes, a sprinkling of freckles, red flowing hair. She must be thirty-five. "Bob!" she calls into the group of men. "Please don't play in your jacket."

A tall fellow approaches, removes a white summer suit coat, smiles, teeth white and perfect. His blond hair's parted a half inch left of center. Dimples carve his cheeks. He hands her the coat. "Honey, it's a friendly game of touch," voice high and pleasant, eyes the most amazing blue. "Nobody gets mussed or hurt." The fat tie he wears is hand-painted, black palm on an island of green.

"That's what you think," she murmurs, taking the coat, tenderly draping it across the arm holding her highball. "I've seen what happens in these games."

He walks back, duckfooted, to captain the other team. "I should have done a better job on his shirt," the green-eyed woman says. "And look at the poor man's pants. You'd think after so many years I'd be able to do something about them. Bagging at the knees. It's my fault."

"Oh, Anne, why do your own ironing? Sheer perversity!"

"No, thanks, I've had way too much," the green-eyed woman tells me. "Well, wait. Which ones are scotch?" I point with my nose. "Oh, why do they bring children to alcoholic parties?" she asks. "To see grown-ups all soused and acting like kids? I'm glad my own aren't here." She takes a glass. "Too young," she murmurs. "Bob!" she cries. "Can women play? I'd love to be on your side! I'll hike it!"

"Not through that mass of crinolines, you won't!"

"Then let me block. Oh, what am I going to do with all this *energy*?"

"Save it," he calls, youthful and doomed, running downfield to kick off. "The blessed balm, the hero's reward!"

"You told me fibs." Barbie Wilson, sucking a crude cigarette. "How can I ever explain to Mamma I offered myself to a hired hand? You *should* blush." She stuffed a delicate seashell crust, heaped with gray paste, into her mouth. Her gown dipped to the dead end of two hard little teats. The breasts of the red-haired woman bulged full and soft, breasts to nurse babies. But Barbie's looked like tough mouthfuls. "Unfaithful to my class in life." She lowered her face, rolled her eyes up staring into mine, hot juices bubbling, relaxed cheeks and mouth—cold submission—and pressed her fingertips against my chest. "I'm free, white, and make my own rules— What in heaven's name is *that*?"

Glasses in my tray teetered. Booze sloshed out. "Holy medal," I blurted.

"Feels like some kind of hard *tool*!"

She giggled, and her off switch suddenly shorted out. She covered her face and bent down, giggling. A lady pursed her lips. Barbie Wilson still giggled as I made my escape.

"Wasn't that girl on Arthur Godfrey?" somebody asked.

The football game had sucked attention away from the fireworks display. Women squealed and shrieked with each hike. Men rolled grinning all over the grass.

"Touchdown!" Roberts yelled.

"Wait a minute," protested the man with the hand-painted tie. "I thought the goal line was over here." He prodded a spot some five feet beyond where Roberts, carrying the ball with graceful swoops and dodges, had been tagged.

"Nonsense!" Roberts said. "I set the goal here, even with the end of that table. Touchdown! Touchdown!"

The other waved his hands in the air and shrugged. "If you say so."

Roberts kicked off, straight to the man in the hand-painted tie, who began his runback with the astonishing speed of a natural sprinter, not merely dodging but brilliantly outrunning all competition. Every motion of his body, every surging leap, announced in gesture's mute language: This person is extraordinary, he is gifted, a child of the gods. Yet whenever he came to rest, breathing hard, he stood awkwardly with turned-out feet; his shoulders stooped, as if from defeat and despair.

Now it looked like a clear runback, the full length of the "field," before a gallery of admiring ladies.

"Out of bounds!" Roberts cried. "Ball's down here! Come back!"

Far ahead of all pursuers and blockers, the runner awkwardly slowed bent-kneed to a walk a few feet from his goal, and slogged back. No boundary markers broke the lawn. With good-natured puzzlement, the runner asked, "Heavens, man, are you lining up with the stars?"

Roberts seized the ball. "I had the top of that tall tree in mind." He pointed to the limit of his property, a half mile away, where a pin oak's silhouette loomed against the glow of Goldengrove. "But you were way out of bounds. *Miles* out of bounds!"

"Just in case the problem arises in the future, where's the west boundary?"

"Why, my television tower." Roberts pointed up at the blinking red light four miles off.

"I was thinking of the north star," said the man in the hand-painted tie.

"Bob, oh, Bob!" the red-haired woman called. "Maybe you'd better take a breather."

"Nonsense. I'm in great shape."

"He's doing fine!" Roberts cried. "Great runner! We need him out here in the field."

Both sides huddled. On the next play, "Bob," quarterbacking, retreated with the ball to pass. But Roberts and an extremely heavy man broke through the blockers. Together, they crashed into Bob. Impact dislodged the ball, and Roberts leaped across the pile-up and recovered the fumble. The fat man huffed to his feet, but Bob still lay gasping on his back, tie flung across his face. The red-haired woman knelt beside him.

"I'm all right, Anne," he panted. "Listen"—he got to his knees—"I thought this game was supposed to be touch."

"Pickwick, I'm terribly sorry, really I am." Roberts helped the runner to his feet. "We built up so much momentum, we simply couldn't stop in time."

"Oh, that's all right. Forget it."

"Grass stains all over your pants!" the red-haired woman cried.

"Game's almost over anyway," Roberts said. "Let him finish it out. I'll handle the cleaning bill."

On the next play, Roberts made a run around end. Pickwick seemed not to have fully caught his breath, for he scarcely moved.

"Touchdown!" Roberts cried. "Twelve points! We win!"

"Who said the game ended with twelve points?" a woman near me asked.

"I didn't hear anybody," replied another.

I decided to offer the loser first chance at what booze was left in my tray. Sweatless and unwrinkled, whirling the football above his head, Roberts strode to where Bob Pickwick and his wife scrutinized the green stains on Bob's clothing. Roberts held out his hand, which Pickwick took a very brief shake.

"Fan-tastic game!" Roberts said.

"Like a banana with bones. I'll help you patent it," replied Pickwick, hitting the winner with a blazing smile. "No, thanks," he told me. "Rather have water." He took his wife's hand, turning his back on Roberts and myself.

She whispered, "I wanted to come out there and—"

"Now, now," he murmured, and glancing over his shoulder at Roberts, waving his free hand as if a night insect had buzzed too close, said, "Enjoying the party. Many thanks."

In touching unity, the couple moved gracefully off.

Anger hardened Roberts' face. "Goddamn spoiled little rich boy," he growled.

Waiting for a chance to make my move, I walked among guests and played waiter, picking up fragments of talk.

"I know why you married me, baby, you married me for my tight little nigger ass, hey?"

". . . sent a letter saying I felt this really deep love. He wrote back about this great disproportion of affection, and we shouldn't even see each other again. Yeah, I mean I think about him a lot . . ."

"I did *not* throw myself at him. But if you keep this up, mister, I just damn well might!"

Two jacketless, shirtless, grinning men one-for-the-moneyed a gowned and bejeweled lady of uncertain age howling into the pool. "Oh, you beeeeeests!"

Roberts and Barbie Wilson in tête-à-tête near the pool. Both waved at me, across the mermaid in the water.

"I stick this salt lick up on my mantle, looks so much like a sculpture in marble. Anybody asks who's the artist, I tell them, Le Boeuf."

"At the Elks, after a movie they shave the screen."

Dragging deeply on a cigarette, Barbie Wilson kept about twenty feet from me.

"There isn't any Midwest. There's only this breeding ground, this great big bedroom sandwiched in between the coasts."

"One day in the shower, notices this swelling in his scrotum. They operate at the hospital that same day, then send him home to die."

"I just wish you wouldn't keep acting so friendly. I mean, you keep following him around like a sick dog."

"Boy, I know, but when things start falling apart, they never get better. Me and her, we were killing each other over the phone bill."

"I walked through the door and first thing stepped on their kid's pet newt. Then they got this big sheep dog that jumped me on the couch and wouldn't stop till they beat him off with a newspaper. Whole evening was like that."

"Suddenly I feel free, like nothing matters!"

Pickwick was shaking Roberts' hand. Then Roberts tried to kiss the red-haired woman's cheek, but she jerked away. Hand in hand, the Pickwicks disappeared into the black tree line and the night.

A man pulled a woman's gown strap from her naked shoulder. "Beautiful tits, have a look."

"*Stop* it!"

"Captain shot out of the whorehouse window with his forty-five, and the little yellow bastards down the bottom of the hill really scurried. Then we got this little Jap bellhop to do it with one of the girls and she keeps telling us, Oh, G.I., he so tiny, he so *small*."

Several men and women in various stages of undress churned the swimming pool to a boil.

"Got clap on tour from a fourteen-year-old chick. Doctor

says he can't fuck his wife for three days after the shot, so he tells her he's nervous, can't sleep, ya know? Spends three nights pacing around the living room pretending he's too nervous to lie down in bed. And, I mean, he's been gone three weeks and the wife's hot to fuck, and he says, 'Jesus, I'm too nervous, I just can't figure out why.' "

"Look, *you* were gone forty minutes and *he* was gone forty minutes. I mean forty whole minutes. Now, what the hell is going on?"

"He's working in the library with this girl who's getting married next day, and he tells her, 'Look, your husband's gonna be out tonight on a bachelor party, one last big old fling, so why don't you drop by my apartment and open up, yourself?' And this guy's three-quarters queer, but sure enough she knocks, and brother, does she waddle down the aisle all reamed out."

"This guy, it turns out, was having an affair with his pet chimp, and his wife says, 'Either that chimp goes or I go.' "

Men and women raced down the lawn shedding clothes in ragged, flapping shadows, as if silent gunners blasted their bodies apart—businessmen, professors, doctors, lawyers, and accountants, respectable and unrespectable housewives, golf widows, country clubbers, elementary-school teachers, graduate-school wives, grandmothers, down the hill into the trees.

"Back to nature, folks!" Glass held high, wearing his grandfatherly smile, Roberts watched nymphs and satyrs blocking all thoughts of daylight. The fireworks died unnoticed.

A furious wife dragged her husband down the drive. "Come on, you drunk degenerate!"

"Wheeee! I feel so goooood!"

One empty glass rolled back and forth across my tray when I set it down.

"Where's my wife? Hey, have you seen my wife?"

A bloated slob in boxer shorts dead-manned face down in the pool.

I stealthily faded into the blackness surrounding the mansion, and shoved my toe against a man's pants. Feeling for the wallet, I slipped out the bills and pocketed them against my groin. A woman's silver lamé purse next to a bush: eagerly zipping it open and reaching inside, I clenched some wrapped cardboard tubes, then dodged the hand grabbing at my ankle.

"Jesus, whatever your name is," a woman whined somewhere, "I could keep doing this forever."

I moved briskly toward the noise, found another pair of pants draped over a bush, and stuffed another wad of bills into my pocket.

In the stairwell's gray light, I recalled Cerulia's directions, climbed, padded down a movie-set hallway. "I'se the captain of the comfort station," I hummed, "at the Honeymoon Hotel." All felt familiar, even noises crowding from some rooms—elephants making love, grunting like Dick and Helen.

I opened, whispered, "Room service," then snapped on the light. Mirrors on the ceiling. Red-velvet wallpaper. Marble cathedral gargoyles sticking out from the corners. A football-field bed, great, smooth gleaming expanse of woven gold counterpane. Sinking ankle-deep in a lavender bear rug, I suddenly began believing my preposterous errand.

An oceanic painting loomed above the bed. Nobody had styled hair that way for years. Several layers of varnish, split, veined, and fissured with an infinitude of tiny cracks, formed a unity which counterpointed the main design, total merging. If my teacher had found the cartoon for *that* in my writing pad, I'd be serving time. Which were men, which women? Mouths opened and closed, bared teeth snarled, muscles knotted, straining upon matted tufts of hair. But there was peace, too—the cool sweep of some citizen's flank in repose, the gaze of one centered pair of eyes regarding all existence with chill, grim calm.

Then I saw flaws about this sumptuous room. The mirror, which covered the whole ceiling, had cracked like a leafless tree. Its silvering had blackened in spots. Wallpaper peeled near the ceiling; touching, I found it wasn't velvet, just crimson chintz. The gargoyles—obscene, lecherous death's-heads biting into well-fleshed thighs, gryphons dangling pearly genitals like intestine—were plaster-of-paris castings, sifting fine dust to the rug.

My grail lay through the door opposite the picture. I turned on the light, dropped my pants, and sat. A leopard-skin bath mat lay spread out across the floor. The lavatory knob, the spout and handles on the bathtub, the shower spray, drain, the little red delicious apple pull-knob on the medicine cabinet—all solid gold.

I reached for toilet paper—and saw my drawing book lying shut on the tank. So Cerulia *had* given it to him. But weren't pages missing? No time to make sure.

It wasn't cutting butter, but the work flowed. Kneeling, I bagged the toilet handle. As an afterthought, I removed the wad of bills from my pocket and bagged them, too, then sawed at the lavatory's "hot" handle, fancy little nugget.

"Better hurry, doll. At the stroke of midnight it turns back into shit."

Smoking, she lounged in the door. The room behind her was dark. "Backbone of America's out there on the lawn fucking. I just wandered in to water the potty. Mind? Wait, doll! Run out, and I'll sic every cop in the country on your botsy-wotsy. Whasat line round the tip of your nose? Maybe you're dangerous, huh? Cut my little throat? Here goes a good siss . . . dum dee dee." Silver sheath hiked above her waist, she sat on the john and smiled fuzzily, lace cradle taut between her ankles. "Mamma caught me in a trunk doing it with the neighbor kid when I was eight. Bet you feel like I did then. Like a little dingdong on the wing," she sang, "at the p'liceman's ball. Saw picture once, p'liceman's ball, bare girl standing on a pedestal hiding her pussy from a hundred flying peckers. Wow, I'm stoned."

I sighed.

"Yeah, I mean, it's good to hear you're alive. What's your name? Prince Elmo? What fuck kind of name's that, honey? Whew! Feel like somebody's giving my brain a good juicy lick with his tongue. Almost said fuck on Godfrey one morning. Kiddo, the whole world's hung up on toothpaste and deodorant soap. All the sloppy housewives, fresh out of the tub, spreading sweet and dewy for an army of hairy, overweight clunks. Down in Reno, the dude ranch cowboys had their tubes cut. But by god they wanted you fresh from an aromatic douche. Everybody's got culture up the ass. Except you, Prince Elmo." She kicked her panties onto the animal rug, stood, shook herself like a wet dog. "Want to, don't you?" She kicked off a pair of transparent plastic slippers, performed some Indian footwork on the fur. "Boom boom boom boom! How's it from behind? You low-class bum! Flush the potty! Okay, now—give me everything, the cash you hooked out of billfolds and purses, you sneaky little thief. In the Folies Bergère in Gay Paree, they bring clunks up out of the audience and tell them, feed these bare-tit broads up here on stage some sweet shit. So tell me, low-class citizen—you!—tell me how much you want me. Don't swallow your tongue!"

"So bad . . ."

"Great. You've got the gift."

"So bad . . . I can taste it."

"Smooth beast. Want a lock off your scalp." She pulled me down and chewed a forelock loose with the hacksaw. "Spun gold." The severed lock sifted to the floor. "Only time I ever touched hair this fine was on a twittering, limp-wristed fag." She held out the smoke between her fingers. Take this, lover. You're no good to me knotted up."

"I, uh, never smoked."

"Swallow the smoke. No! In your *lungs,* fool! Hold it. Yes. Till you feel like exploding. That's the way. Watch this magical rabbit leave the hat, mild-mannered Clark Kent enters the phone booth and emerges"—an upward flash of mercury, a streak, whack! against the ceiling, snaking down the wall —"Ssssuperman!" A cloud of freckles on the long lean back, on her breasts. Red porcelain lips soften smiling.

"No more work, bright baby. We're going sswimming," the creature hissed. "Right now. Slush, the room fills with invisible waves of water, churning currents."

"Falsies!" she cried, ripping at my bags of loot, "sagging tits of an old woman, off with them this instant! Mmmmmmy beast, my god, my natural blond!" She flipped two switches on the wall. Eerie redness bathed the room.

"I feel so gooooood!" I cried.

The golden cloud kneeling before me murmured, 'Mmmmmm, and I'm a wegetarian."

Shuddering, grabbing our hair in one hand, then an ear,

some bright creature forced us slowly down—dry lips grazing belly—sinking until a spasm jarred over us, tugging our mouths into a salt-lick churn between our thighs

•6•

Naked and by myself, I awoke on the roof of the mansion, no memory of how I'd come there, body scratched and bruised, stars whirling above my eyes. I lay beside a massive chimney of brick on a gently sloping shelf, leopard skin shielding me from humped, hard tiles. The roof began its abrupt mansard drop at my heels. If I'd moved . . . It seemed as if I'd slept with open eyes, watching the galaxy's low pivot about the pole star, while a breeze cooled the juices of debauchery to a crust.

Silver needles pricked my brain: bird cries. My tongue plopped in my mouth like salt pork. Congealed light oozed lard-colored into the blackness. Where were my clothes? What had I done before blacking out? In what rooms, with what people? Muscles felt torn. My coach had turned back to a pumpkin.

A silver carpet, ocean of dew, lay across the land. Tiles all slippery—steady. I'd make an excellent target for some bloodthirsty guard. Shadows moved in the pool's twilight. Five minutes there, dissolving the crust from my body, would make the water saltbroth.

Protruding as if from a capped cellar, a door loomed upon the roof. I wore the leopard skin like a cape and stumbled down the gray stairs.

I needed a plunge in the Gorge.

Four naked citizens lay heaped and tangled on the cold floor outside the kitchen, one woman, three men. The men wore watches, the woman her wedding and engagement rings. A barbershop quartet of snores and heavy breathing. I could smell them as I moved on.

"What uh kind of animal is that?" asked a man in the pool.

"Pooh Bear," a woman answered.

A fringe of woodland surrounded the property, hair around

a monk's tonsure. Through the trees loomed a chain-mail fence, and I began scaling it, when a pool of white flesh beneath a tree murmured, "Hi. Know where to find my duds?" Delicately she fanned her crotch with a maple leaf.

Galvanizing jolt: I lay heaped by the roadside and smelled my own singed flesh and the nymph called, "Y'okay?"

I jogged along the roadside. The light grayed. A car, headlights burning, horn blaring, swerved wide, throwing gravel.

I floated numb and free through the green atmosphere of the Gorge and sensed nothing beyond the deep translucence verging into black. Finally I climbed to the stone shelf. A spotted rug undulated on the water.

Folded in quarters the penciled note had been stuck between the Ford's rotted wiper and windshield. "Old buddy, couple things ocerd to me outside the fense with all kinds of nakid hijinks gon on. 1. you got caught. 2. you are one greedy basted. Not wanting to risk the 1st, we are on are way. Maybe one day are paths will cross. Meanwhil if your no doublecrosser, lotsaluck from the Real World." And below, in another hand: "Sory."

Couldn't sleep.

I kept indoors, seldom left my pallet, breathed the hot, close air, and dreamed of Cerulia's smooth thighs.

The Welfare Woman huffed in. "Where's everybody?"

"Here," Helen said.

"What's the matter with that child?"

"Don't ask me. He already learned to talk."

"Prince Elmo, don't just lie there and twitch. Does this household need a doctor?"

"Ain't nothing wrong in here," Grampa said, "that killing wouldn't cure."

"Now what sort of talk is that? What's the matter with you people? This place smells like a stinkbomb. No wonder that boy looks sick. It's summer out. Clean air and sunshine. Dick somewhere in the woods?"

"Dick got tired of family life," Helen said. "Hopped a freight."

"How long ago?" Her little bright eyes glanced here and there. "Last time I saw Dick, he couldn't push a wheelbarrow."

"Dick does what he likes," Helen grumbled. "How come you got to pry, lady?"

"I see some things he didn't take," the fat woman said. "Isn't that Dick's razor over there?"

"Left it for Prince Elmo," Helen said.

"Thuh-un boy's gone," Grampa said, "and that's all there is to it."

"What about her?" She indicated Granma. "She know anything?"

"Completely bats," Helen said. "Fire a gun behind her head, she wouldn't blink. Don't eat enough for a goldfish. Pining away for that piss-ant Dick. Lady, it's lucky you was too fat to ever marry. Bearing kids ain't for shit."

"Like some hill apes I could mention. Hopped a freight, eh? I bet if some deputies start digging up this hill, they'll find out different."

"Take your food and scram, lady. We'll get by."

"Where's Duke? Where's Cerulia? Somebody tell me that."

"You got the hots for Duke, too?" Helen asked. "Hell, I knowed all about you and Dick, but Duke's just a little boy. He'd get lost in the folds."

As hours slogged on, I daydreamed about the razor. My body floated across the room, lifted the blade, and hacked flesh off my arm to stimulate a nerve; I fell through the wound and slept. Maybe the shack would burn down on top of me. At night I heard harsh rustling, a thud. Helen cried out, "Take your filthy paws off! Granma's more man than you!"

Helen grew careless during the day. I opened my eyes and saw her naked on the bed. Grampa was somewhere in the afternoon sun. "Whoopsy, you awake?" She faked cover with her hands. Then she gave up all pretense and sat on the bed's edge facing me, and asked, "Know anything about women? It's about time. Maybe get you off your ass." She stood, displaying herself. "Feast your eyes on a real woman, Elmo. Sometimes not eating too good keeps a lady slim." She looked like Cerulia, more pouchy, and brown-nippled where Cerulia was pink. "Still in my thirties. Deserved better than life give me. I'm a handsome woman. Well, ain't I?"

"Sure."

"You ain't ever supposed to see me, I guess. What the hell's the difference, if we don't touch? See? It's held up good, in spite of everthing. Those marks on my belly, from popping four kids. At first they was awful red, but now they don't hardly show. Unless somebody points them out. It ain't every woman my age after four kids that looks so good. Know where you come out of? Who'd believe a tiny little hole like that could grow so huge all of a sudden, then shrink back tight?"

I nodded. "It's a sight."

"You're about the age to start going after girls. But there won't be many in your life that look this good. You're awful big for your age. Maybe you'd get jealous if I went out for dates with other men. One boy I heard of beat his mother up for going on dates with a young druggist in town. You wouldn't do that."

"No."

"Duke's the type to beat his mom. Where's that shift at? I just laid down for a nap and lost it. Put it on before Grampa gets back. He's got crazy ideas. What kind of woman he think I am, anyway? My titties you lookin at? Bigger'n most women's by half. All made for a purpose. Well . . ." Her shift hung from the bedpost, in full view. "You figure where a man sticks his thing, don't you?"

I nodded.

"All right. You're plenty old enough to know. A boy should learn from his pa. I guess it's okay—so you don't have to find it all out from scratch."

One night, Grampa said, "What's thuh-uh use? I got uh-uh burning fuse, and I might just as well explode. But I ain't got thuh-uh guts. Wish thuh-uh goddamn Hun'd shot me right atween the eyes thirty years ago, so I wouldn't spend thuh-uh rest of my life shakin' like a dog after a rainstorm. This here land, boy, after I'm gone it's yours. There's the deed in the courthouse. It ain't worth much, but it's a place to live. Ain't everbody owns his own piece of earth. Dick never did, and now he never will. Thuh-uh poor boy ain't even buried in the ground." His whole body trembled, and his voice rattled like tumbling rock. "I'm guilty, boy. I deserve to die, if man ever did. And when I die, I'm going straight to hell. That's why I ain't got thuh-uh guts. Cause I'm scared to death of hell."

One morning as if sleepwalking I got down to the Gorge and lay in wait for the boy with glasses and dimples, duckfooted walk, the Daisy fifty-shot pump air rifle. He appeared, dressed for Sunday school, whistling, cradling the gun in his arm's crook—as if I'd drawn him through a circuit in my brain.

He waved across the Gorge. My hand waved back. "Hey there!" he called. "Whadjaknow?"" Then he cocked his gun. "Watch!" He fired. Gently the stonemill rained feathers. A fat pigeon launched itself over the high roof.

"Shoot with me!"

I walked around the edge of the quarry and joined him.

"You look sick," he observed. "Hope it isn't catching."

"Not sleeping."

"Insomnia? At your age? You're big, but I can tell you're not much older than me. I have this instinct for judging age. Dad tells me when I grow up, I'll lose it, especially with women. Take a crack at that one perched up there."

I missed.

"You jerked the trigger. Let your breath halfway out, hold it, and squeeze. Watch. Heck of a strong spring. Up to a hundred feet this thing shoots straight as a twenty-two." A pigeon flapped some feathers loose. "What's your dad do?"

"Feeds fish with his dead self."

"Wow, I mean, sorry. My dad teaches college, but he's really not getting anywhere. He keeps trying different things. Now he's trying to write a book. Go to school near here?"

"Teacher kicked me out for drawing dirty pictures."

"This guy at my school came in with eight-page bibles. You know, Smilin' Jack and Mae West and Popeye, and Blondie and Dagwood. Too dirty for me. If Dad found out I looked at those things, wow. You ever get punished?"

I thought a minute. "Dick'd get drunk sometimes and smash me on top of my head with his knuckles. Still got the knots. That's a ways back."

"The eight-page bible guy got sent to reform school last spring. Stealing from lockers. I go to school in town."

"We're poor folk."

"That's too bad. My grandpa's filthy rich." He looked embarrassed. "Know anybody in reform school?"

"My dad was in the pen," I said.

"Mine never even got a parking ticket. He doesn't drink. He never even swears. I mean, he's something. Got any cigarettes?"

"Nope."

"Girls admire a guy who smokes because he knows his way around. You ever been on top of a girl?"

"Maybe."

"Boy, I don't think I ever would. The poor kids in my high school do it. No offense. They say your dick grows twice as long. I started swearing last year. Shit, fuck, piss. Only when I'm alone. Dad'd wash out my mouth. And Hazel tells on me. One evening I locked myself in my room and wrote five pages of dirty words. Felt great—till I tried to figure out where to hide it. Finally I locked the bathroom door and tore the paper into tiny pieces and pushed them through the used-razor-blades slot in the medicine cabinet. If they ever tear down the house, I'm dead."

"Here, let me take a shot."

"Sure. Here's the way inside the building. Tight squeeze. It's against the law. Two-hundred-dollar fine. If Dad ever found out, wow!"

"I'll stay out here."

"Hand me the gun?"

"Fuck off."

"Hey, I thought we were friends."

I walked away. A scrambling, scraping force slapped the small of my back. "You damn crook! Give me back my gun!"

I landed face down. The Daisy slid across rock. A figure blurred past me, swooping down. "Double crosser! You asked for it."

"Look, you got me all wrong," I said.

"The hell! Back where you came from!"

"Don't point that thing at me."

"Self-defense. Go away, damn you!"

"You've been breaking the law a long time," I said. "What's that gun cost?"

"Seven ninety-five."

"Maybe I'd take seven ninety-five from you. But you owe this place two hundred bucks for every time you broke in. Hypocrite."

"You're bigger than I am, and I'm going to shoot."

I picked up a rock. "Go ahead, chickenshit. I'm gonna bust your ass, and if you call the cops, I'll tell them all about you."

A flaming dot seared my thigh.

"Jesus Christ," the boy murmured. "You all right?"

I raised the rock.

"Come on, now. Don't force me."

I laughed, and he shot me on the kneecap. I dropped the rock and grabbed myself. "Yow! I *felt* that!"

"You asked for it," he announced. Eyes gleamed behind the thick glass rind, vindictive and gleeful, like a man who's just dug his way out of prison. I scrambled running around the Gorge toward our hill. Flames pricked my ass.

Lying around had sapped my legs. I dodged behind a car. He shot me through the busted windows, and I ripped clear around the shack—and there stood Grampa, shaggy and shaking, singleshot twenty-two like a bar across his loins.

"What thuh-uh hell is going on?"

"Uh oh!" The boy halted suddenly behind me.

"Son of a bitch, you shooting my grandson?"

Pupils expanding behind the glittering glass, the boy muttered, "No, I mean, it's a mistake." He dropped his gun and ran.

"Come on, Grampa, let's get him!" I raced in hot pursuit. The old man's labored breathing rasped close behind.

The boy waved his arms, stumbled, caught his Sunday shirt on a branch, tore loose, raced with death's bootsoles slapping earth at his back. I ran wide through the woods to cut him off. A charging bull, head down, Grampa swung the rifle like a scythe.

The boy scrambled into the open across the bare rock skirting the Gorge. When he reached the stonemill, I leaped from the trees and blocked his path. He looked back: the massive, terrifying old man rushed across limestone the same dead gray as his skin, his eyes. The boy clumsily scaled the wood ladder up the corrugated wall of the mill. I heard the rapid, clear intake of his breath.

Grampa stopped fifty or sixty feet from the building. "That's far enough!" he roared.

The boy leaned into the ladder like a crushed spider.

"You sons of bitches rich boys think you can come all the way out here and treat us like shit!" Rage purified the tremor from his voice, thundering like the Day of Wrath. "You break the law, like you're a-doin' now. You torment our children, and stalk over the earth like you owned it lock, stock, and barrel. Silver spoons and gold plate and meat on the table all your lives, and never a goddamn worry. And if the coppers haul you in for being goddamn worthless punks, Daddy comes down to the station, pays the cumshaw, and bails ya out." In tones of afterthought: "I'm a-gonna kill ya, boy."

Who looked down at me, and with matter-of-fact incomprehension said, "You can't kill *me*."

"Take a deep breath, boy, cause here it comes." Grampa steadied the rifle at his shoulder.

"No, not this morning," the boy said.

A pair of glasses ticked into the scrub grass at my feet.

Grampa became rigid as stone and spat a puff of vapor from the gun muzzle. Bulletwhack against flesh. A pigeon hustled against the blue sky. Grampa's shoulders collapsed forward as if he'd shot himself. The boy's legs bent like rubber. He slipped one rung at a time slowly down the ladder, catching his fingers in each rung to break the fall and slid against me, looking into my face. Grampa shuffled out of focus.

"Sorry," I murmured.

Tears from the blue nearsighted eyes. Gently, I laid the boy on the ground, stumbled back a few feet, then began running toward town and a phone.

•7•

Monday evening, Helen dropped the newspaper into my hands and said, "For Christ's sake, don't let Granma see this. There may still be a little bit of brain left between her ears."

Yellowed by lanternlight my picture stared up puzzled and annoyed, snapped the previous day in the sheriff's office by a pouchy, middle-aged fellow who said, "Look up, kid," and blinded me. To save the life of another innocent boy, said the story, I had taken action which caused the arrest of my own grandfather, would-be slayer, a deranged, shellshocked, impoverished veteran of World War I. The boy lay in a hospital bed, condition fair. The sheriff guarded Grampa under lock and key.

Beside my picture on the front page was another, the smiling boy I had helped shoot."Honor Student," said the caption underneath his picture, "Gunned Down in Cold Blood by Lunatic."

The full story hinted around about somebody named Prince Elmo Hatcher, who'd been raised in a low-class, criminal environment, but who somehow still embosomed a spark of natural humanity. Remanded for the time being to the care of his mother—something about Miss so-and-so of the Department of Welfare recommending such and such. On page two, a picture shot through steel bars showed Grampa, "Elmo Hatcher," face in hands, sitting on a narrow bunk held up by chains.

After we'd watched attendants load the wounded boy into an ambulance, red light silently whirling, the same sheriff who years earlier had delivered me naked and shivering from an April cornfield, and two deputies, had prodded me toward the shack. Shaking, leaning against the rusted-out hulk of the Ford, Grampa had been waiting for us.

Revolver cocked and aimed, the sheriff twanged, "Mighty easy thur, podner. Better grab some sky."

"Prince Elmo's innocent," Grampa said, wrists extended for handcuffs. "Take me to thuh-uh hoosegow."

"Sure thing, old-timer. Boys, careful now. Cuff the old

galoot's hands behind his back. Then search the shack for the firearm."

One returned with the twenty-two and the Daisy. "Nobody inside," he announced, "except a old lady in a rocking chair."

"Don't let Granma know nothing's wrong," Grampa pleaded.

"Old-timer, if that boy dies," the sheriff glowered, "I'll spring the trap under your feet myself."

A deputy said, "Roy, cut that out. This ain't the Old West."

I rode between Grampa and a dozing deputy in the back seat of the sheriff's car. The second deputy drove. Sheriff sat up front, revolver in lap. Leaning over, Grampa whispered against my ear, "Listen, son, it's all okay, but there is one thing I wish you'd sneak me, without tellin' nobody . . ."

Helen said, "I'll sure miss old Grampa around the place. Wonder if the govermint's gonna keep up his pension for Granma to eat off of."

Late Monday night, while Helen and Granma slept, I wrapped a cheese sandwich and some cookies—sticking what Grampa wanted into the sandwich—inside the newspaper Helen had brought. Tuesday morning, I carried it into town.

"Hatcher," the sheriff said, unlocking the cell, "your grandson's here with a little home cookin."

The steel bars clanged shut behind me, and footsteps faded.

"Hi, Grampa."

"Hi, boy." Sitting on the bunk, he took the package.

Grampa gave me one last long hard look in the eyes, then bent to unwrap his food. "Don't worry about a thing, Prince Elmo," he said. "I always loved you more than a son and still do. Want you to understand, that ain't changed a bit. You done what you had to do. And you done thuh-uh right thing. But you got to help me one last time."

Moving swift as an athlete, he stood, razor open and forearmed a powerful hammerlock about my neck.

"Hey, Roy!" he cried. "Sheriff!"

"What in the hell!" As Grampa let me go, the sheriff pumped six bullets into him. "Guess the old bastard was tryin' to get even."

The VFW arranged Grampa's burial. I didn't know until I read it in the paper that Grampa's been awarded the Distinguished Service Cross for killing all those Germans the day he lost control of his body. He never talked about the medal. At the VFW's request, Helen and I combed the shack looking for it, so it could be pinned to his chest when they buried him. I found a flat, rectangular case, nickel-plated and tarnished hidden beneath the woodbox. Embedded in velvet, the medal had been lying untouched for years. The prosecuting attorney told the paper, "We didn't know he was a hero. It changes the whole disposition of the case. You know how a war sometimes knocks the nuts and bolts loose inside a man's head." Besides, the boy Grampa had shot, one William Pickwick, was off the danger list.

We couldn't reach Duke or Cerulia. "Maybe they'll read about it in the newspaper somewhere," Helen sniffled. The closer to the burial, the more sob-ridden Helen became. "Poor old geezer. Who'd of thought he was so far gone? He should of had more children and grandchildren to gladden up his final years. Just thinking about it breaks my heart. Poor lonely old thing. I hope them French whores is waiting for Grampa up in heaven."

Whether or not Granma ever knew what happened or where Grampa was, remained uncertain. "I think I'll ask one of them VFW guys if they run a home for war widows," Helen said. "I mean, pretty soon Granma may just start wettin' the bed."

One day the sheriff dropped in twice at the shack. Both times he poked around, in corners, even inside the stove.

"By the way, Helen," he asked, "Where's Dick at?"

"Well, Roy, ever thought of looking under the mattress?"

"You wouldn't of seen nobody suspicious—"

"Sure. There's this feebly escapes from Muscatatuck asylum every night, with his magic beanie that flies him through the air. He's albino with pink eyes that glow in the dark."

"Is that a fact?"

"I seen him driving down the street once in your car."

At the foot of the Goldengrove cemetery—a hilly area, several acres rimmed by a high stone wall—lay a weed-filled patch with tiny stone markers lined in rows. Potter's field. No names on the markers, just numbers. They sowed the first crop a full six feet deep. When they'd planted the whole field shoulder to shoulder, they started all over again, digging the next layer of graves a foot more shallow—or until the shovel hit wood. Now they were on the third layer.

Grampa was laid to rest here amid a gaggle of strangers, gathered because of local publicity. The air drooled humidity. No preacher attended—nobody in the family went to church—and the VFW planned no ceremony, though one blue-uniformed old codger in a blue, peaked cap drove us to the cemetery, then teetered back and forth under his ribbons' poundage. A youth knelt over the deal crate to drive in nails.

"Hold, on, there!" Helen sobbed, "Let's have one last look to make sure it's Grampa." Off came the top, and there he lay, wearing the clothes he'd been shot in—unpowdered, undisguised, unembalmed, unwashed, crusted with dried blood, peaceful. I had closed his eyes in the cell. His medal lay against the bullet-ripped shirt. I was supporting Granma, and when the lid came off, she shuddered.

Helen shouted at the crowd, "You goddamn dirty sons of bitches!"

The VFW codger drove us home. Helen and I rode in the back seat with Granma, still shuddering, between us. Helen sobbed, "Elmo, who brought Dick's razor to Grampa? He was the only father you knew."

My face dropped into my palms, and, astonished, I found myself crying bitterly.

•8•

"It's like a dream," Helen said, "like it all sort of floated past, you know? Help me here, honey. Set Granma back in the chair. What the hell's left to do? Now there's really only you and me to handle things, Prince Elmo. Jesus, I don't know. Help me here, loosen this damn button. I never done a thing in my life I really wanted, because all I ever wanted to do was close the door behind me without saying goodbye, and hear the new world say, 'Helen, it's no shame, believe me, it's no shame.' Whatever happened in my life, I'm not the one responsible. There was always some asshole calling the shots. Maybe me and you both can start everything all over somewhere. There's got to be a little money in this place. You know, ride a bus out to the Golden Gate? Warm there, never snows the whole year long. There's a street with all kinds of fancy eating places. You can just stand on the curb and watch the movie stars sashay by, all those handsome fellas in sunglasses. Whoever wanted more than that? Come on, honey, help me here. This air's so hot and thick you could slice it. Honey, hold Helen tight, it'll make you feel better. Easy. We're gonna miss old Grampa, ain't we? And Duke and Cerulia, and even old Dick. Never thought I'd miss that sonbitch. Don't you mourn too much for him, though; he ain't even . . . I don't know. I done some pretty sloppy things in my life, but I never had no other choice . . . It's okay, honey. If it makes you feel better, go right on ahead . . . Oh Jesus, honey, we better lie down, hadn't we—"

The door slammed back against the wall, and the Welfare Woman shouted, "Hussy! Jezebel! What have you done to that child? Roy! Make them stop that filth!"

"Well, I'll be mothered and fathered," came the voice, amused, surprised, and pleased.

"Hey, don't you know, you simply got to stop!" the woman screamed. *"Stop them!"*

"Now, maybe this ain't none of our business."

"White trash! *Stop that filth*!"

"You simply got to give them a little time," Roy explained. "It's might near impossible to stop a speeding car on a dime."

I was hoisted violently. My head bonked the floor. The room scattered in all directions. The Welfare Woman's massive crimson bulk loomed waving and roaring above the bed. "Slut! You've done everything in the book to your menfolk. And now you've dropped into the last cesspool of vice!"

Calmly from the bed, Helen asked, "Have you all got a search warrant?"

"Have we—? Did you hear that, Roy? You low-life brazen Belle Starr, have we ever! We kept it a secret, what we found yesterday floating face down in the Gorge, so skinny and fishbit there was scarce enough of it to bloat up! Kept it a secret till we did tests and knew for sure, so you wouldn't try and make a run! The coroner found enough strychnine in that poor dead man to kill a army. All the license in Babylon wasn't enough by itself, you had to murder your man. And then on top of everything else, you had to go and do *this*! And right behind the back of the poor, innocent boy's grandmother!"

"Podner," Roy said, smiling down at me, "we're a-takin' your mommy to jail for murder. And I give you my word, ain't nobody sayin' a thing about what we just witnessed, not if you live straight from here on out. We're a-gonna outfit you with a new home and a new family. The parents of that boy your grandaddy wounded have offered out of sheer generosity to take you in. It's a chance afforded to very few in this world. Atirely different life."

A different life.

Hazel

•1•

ONE BLAZING noon, the Welfare Woman delivered me to the Pickwick house, which stood fifteen feet above street level. A girdle of rock held its small yard from tumbling onto the sidewalk. Through a heavy pelt of ivy, dull green and luxuriant in late summer, only a few bricks gloomed. I noticed outlines of a trellis, like the skeleton of some lost explorer, flesh gobbled by man-eating creepers.

I had been caged two days in the Salvation Army, outfitted with clean clothes, assiduously scrubbed and barbered—and indoctrinated by the fattest woman in the Indiana Department of Welfare. "This is a good family that's taking you in, better people probably than you ever run across. Which doesn't mean they don't have problems of their own. You should act like the most grateful human being in the world. We can scrape filth off your body, but nobody can get it out of your head. There's children in that household, one of them a girl. They don't need somebody to spread slime over the whole operation. With what I know—but you deserve at least one chance. I only hope I'm doing the right thing."

"Where'd they take Granma?"

"Downstate. That poor old lady's going to be treated like a human being for once in her life."

"Are you going to fry Helen?"

"Up to judge and jury. If it was up to me, wild crocodiles'd be chawing her carcass right now."

"When can I see her?"

"Boy, there's only one hope left for you in this life, and that's to forget your whole past. Pray these fine people'll want to change your name and make you one of their own. You done things that'd send a older person to hell a million times over. Listen to me, Prince Elmo. Have you got a conscience?"

"Huh?"

"Do you feel any guilt about all you've been involved in?"

I stared down at my clean nails. "I feel bad about Granma. Never got to say goodbye."

Just then a red-haired woman opened the door.

"Missus, here he is," the Welfare Woman announced, "with all he owns in the world on his back."

"Won't you both please come in?" She seemed imprisoned by nervousness.

A typewriter machine-gunned upstairs.

"Now, this boy's been raised in the original trash heap of the universe, and I can't promise that he has one lawful impulse inside him."

Mrs. Pickwick frowned and shook her head.

"Maybe there's some natural human good buried in there still, maybe there isn't," Fatty continued. "If he was a product in a store marked down to half price—"

"I don't think you ought to hurt his feelings," Mrs. Pickwick interrupted.

"You're a good-hearted woman. But watch him like a hawk. Plenty of places to salt away a bad boy." She left.

"Lady, I promise I won't bite."

"Ha ha . . . well . . . you seem much older—"

"You grow up fast in a trash heap."

Ivy shagged around the windowpanes. The living room floated in watery, twilight cool. A quiltwork wallpaper pattern flowered through the coat of gray-white paint, and somebody had sketched the beginning of an abstract mural above the fireplace; timid, spidery strokes, unconnected forms floating in a void. In one corner of the room slept a baby grand.

"How's your son?" I asked.

"Billy?" She peered up at me wide-eyed. "Upstairs convalescing. What a terrible experience all that must have been for you! We've seen you before, but where on earth was it?"

"Last July Fourth. I was a servant at that rich guy's."

"Of course! Let me show you something," leading me to the mantle.

"My drawing pad!"

"Yes, Roberts gave it to us, and it made up our minds to help you."

"You mean you saw the pictures in this, and you still wanted me in your house? Lady, you must be nuts."

Her cheeks reddened. "We tore out a couple for Hazel's sake."

"It's only doodling."

"If I could draw like that!" She shook her head vigorously. The typewriter kept thundering. "Hazel and I started this mural, but you can see how untalented we are."

"Good thing you left that party early," I said. "You're a nice person, and you'd have been mighty embarrassed about what happened later on. Those fancy people went wild."

"*Really*?"

"You never saw so many people naked in your life. Sure makes you stop and think."

"Oh shoot!" She slapped her sides.

"I mean, in the bushes, and down in the woods, and in the bedrooms, and in a big pile just outside the kitchen door."

"*Shoot*!"

"Anyhow, I'm glad your boy isn't dead."

"God, I envy people who're free!" she suddenly cried. "Cutting loose just once in your life! Where's Bob? Where *is* that man? *Bob*?" The relentless typewriter kept mowing down the world.

Instead of Mr. Pickwick, an incredibly gawkly female emerged, all knees, elbows, and endless shanks, bared uncharitably by shorts and halter—a stork with girl's head, some poor glorious creature whose pituitary short-circuited in the womb ("Weighed thirteen pounds at birth," she later told me. "Poor Mother!"), flooding veins and marrow. An elastic stretch bandage wrapped her left knee tightly, holding the joint together. And yet—this whooping crane devoured her world through the most gorgeous eyes, almond-shaped, green. Her rich black hair, against fashion, flowed in curls and eddies to her shoulders, siphoning excess life-force from that chrysalis of bone.

I'd felt ashamed few times in my life. But now here I was incestuous, glandular, ignorant, depraved, fatherless, a pigsty child—and here was this superb flamingo of energy.

"Hazel. Thank God!" Mrs. Pickwick cried.

The green eyes narrowed. I was being thoroughly seen.

Reaching out, basketball center making the tip, she gripped my hand. "Hi. With you on top of everything else, our happy home threatens to turn upside down."

"Hazel!"

"Just kidding." Hazel dropped my hand. "My brother gets shot all the time, and every day we take somebody like you in as a family member."

"Honestly!"

"I've wanted a sister for eleven years. You're good-looking, but you'll make a lousy sister."

"Hazel's embarrassed," Mrs. Pickwick said. "This is her way of bluffing through."

Hazel rolled her eyes toward the sound of typing. "Hasn't Dad finished his chapter yet?" Wrinkling her nose, she stage-whispered, "He's upstairs writing a dirty book. It's his latest get-rich-on-my-own scheme."

"Young lady, you've said just about enough for the time being."

"Mom, if I can't be beautiful, can't I practice being bright and witty? Maybe Prince would like to jaw a little with Billy, you know, my brother, the one you helped—"

"Stop!"

"Look," Hazel said, "Emily Post hasn't written a whole lot about situations like this, so we'll just have to muddle through."

Wringing her hands, Mrs. Pickwick murmured, "I wish Bob would hurry."

"We're a busy family. Dad's got his novel, Billy's got a bullet in the back, I've got rotboxes in the basement, everything from dead birds to a whole dead sheep, which is going to take several weeks, by the way, Mom." She smiled at me. "I string skeletons together for the university. For mad money. Thought I'd get to work on Billy."

"Go outside," Mrs. Pickwick ordered. "Your father will handle you later."

"Aw, c'mon, Mom. I'd like to sound this guy out. He's becoming a brother under sinister conditions."

"She's just showing off," I bluffed. "She'd have a hard time hurting my feelings."

"Because you don't have any?"

Mrs. Pickwick threw up her hands. "Honestly! Even Hazel's father's no match for her, and she's not thirteen yet. Come upstairs and meet Billy—again."

The typewriter drummed and frothed in mechanical fury through the closed door opposite Billy's room.

"Hey, whaddayaknow?" From the bed, Billy held out his hand.

"Hey there."

"No hard feelings?" He appeared to be apologizing.

"Billy's a natural Christian," Hazel observed.

"Aw, go back to your corpses!"

"I'm going to call your father," Mrs. Pickwick said.

"Better not," Billy cautioned. "He gets pissed when he's interrupted. He screwed up his Ph.D. thesis on Ralph Waldo Emerson because we were all too noisy, and he couldn't concentrate."

"Will you please not swear?" Mrs. Pickwick cried, high and nervous.

"Trying to loosen Mom up," Hazel said. "But here she is, tight as a drum."

"I'm okay, Mrs. Pickwick. You don't have to worry. I really appreciate this"—meaning, I suppose, that I appreciated being taken into a family whose son I'd almost murdered—"and I don't want to cause you any trouble. Otherwise I'd leave right now."

"Con man," Hazel muttered.

"Oh, bug off," said Billy.

"Make me."

Throwing up her hands again, Mrs. Pickwick left the room. Billy pointed, "That's your bed."

"If you don't mind," Hazel said. "I'll stick around awhile and make sure he hasn't come back just to finish a bad job."

"Lousy way to welcome a guy into his new home. Ignore Hazel, old buddy. Nobody can keep her under control. Please, sis, knock it off."

"Well . . ." She thought it over. "All right. But you'll have to prove yourself to me, Prince Elmo."

"That works two ways," I bluffed again.

"But your name sounds like a cornfield king."

"Listen, uh, Prince," Billy said, "I'm sorry about what I did to you."

"Did to *him*?"

"What's that?" I asked.

"Shot you in the ass."

"I didn't know you did that," Hazel said.

"Don't tell the folks. I got carried away."

"With a BB gun is all," I explained.

"But you might have put out his *eyes*!" Hazel wailed.

"Naw, he was too good a shot for that," I said. Healing from a back wound, Billy was reaching for my forgiveness; it was too much. "I won't tell anybody. And don't ever think about it again, okay?"

"Now promise me something, Prince Elmo," Hazel said.

"Sure."

"Well, look. Things just aren't going smoothly here. What's happened to Billy isn't the cause. But I wonder if anybody was really surprised when pow! there stood the cops with bad news. It just seemed like part of the general progression. Then Mom had the bright idea of pulling you into the family—I mean, don't take it personally, but . . ."

I was looking about the small room: cluttered secretary, tall glassed-in bookcase filled with books; typewriter and piles of type-splattered paper; telephone extension; on the walls, clipped-out newspaper photos (of Hemingway, Faulkner, Steinbeck, Cummings, Ted Williams, and Roy Campanella, I later learned); tacked-up Harvard, Yale, and State University pennants; a small plastic forty-five record player and its stack of large-holed records; the ragged overstuffed chair; and two large open windows, one on either side where the walls cornered; the bed on which Hazel and I sat; my bed, crammed into the narrow room which could gracefully hold only Billy's. Wallpaper sank away in vistas of beige Corinthian columns.

". . . Dad's under a lot of strain. Don't get him more bothered than he already is."

I visualized the impressive man in white who, with such

grace, had played the losing football game at Roberts' party. Surely such people owned the world.

Downstairs, knuckles rapped imperiously. The typewriter's steady drumming slowed to a halt. We heard Mrs. Pickwick open the door. "Oh, it's you."

A male voice grouched, "It's me, lady. Think the whole thing'd just go away? We done a job. Now when are ya gonna pay up?"

"That's the roofer," Hazel whispered. "He came around last week."

"I'd kill the son of a bitch," Billy hissed. "If I were well."

"I don't know what to tell you," Mrs. Pickwick said.

"I mean, my kids got to eat, too, lady, or don't you people ever think about that? My wife'd like to live in this part of town, you bet your ass."

"Watch your language. Children live in this house."

"Yeah, there's children in my house, too, and I can't afford to put no clothes on their backs unless the people that hire me pay up. I can't pay for no more roofing material. I can't even pay the help. You owe me three hundred bucks," the man's voice rose angrily, "and you tell me not to cuss!"

In the next room, a chair raked the floor; the door opened timidly, the footsteps padded down the stairs.

"Hiya, buddy. Heard ya typing when I come up the walk. Thought you was gonna hide up there all afternoon."

"There's no point behaving like a fool," the voice flat and angry. "We pay our bills. We'll pay yours when we can. But don't come around here abusing my wife, on my property."

"Three hundred bucks worth of this property is mine, mister, in case you forgot. Deadbeats—in my time I heard a hundred. Don't use them words to my wife, get off my property, they say. Well, I say *bullshit*! A bad debt's like stealing money out of a man's pocket. I say a deadbeat oughta be shoved into the clink like any other damn thief."

"Call the police, Bob."

"Yah, call the cops. That beats hiding behind a woman's dress. What's the good wasting breath on a buncha damn edjicated idiots?" The door slammed.

"It's all right, Bob."

"I'll clean that bastard's low-class ass," Billy whispered.

Hazel's shoulder blades rose and settled like wings. "Wish we didn't owe so much money."

"It beats me why your parents needed another mouth to feed."

"Because they're nice people," Hazel replied.

". . . up there with the children," I heard.

Mr. Pickwick emerged from the stairwell, cheeks and mouth limp beneath the dead stare of guilt. Suddenly he lit the same blazing smile which had demolished Tarze Roberts. "Hey there," moving swiftly, extending his hand, "so busy I didn't know. Don't stand. Settled?"

"Uh . . ."

"We're busy knocking him into shape." Hazel embraced her father, who was taller by only about two inches.

"Where's your suitcase?" Mr. Pickwick asked me.

"Don't have one—but there's lots of clothes over at the Army." I had no right bringing these people extra trouble.

"Well, back to work. See you at supper. We have a surprise, by the way. Show him, Hazel. Not much, but a start." He bolted into his room and closed the door. Within seconds, the typewriter was off and booming.

A brown rectangular box of corrugated cardboard, three inches deep, lay on the dining-room table. "Who's Sargent?" I asked. Inside lay neat and gleaming tubes, their labels poetry: viridian, burnt umber, alizarin crimson, cobalt blue, zinc yellow, yellow ochre, and a big fat tube of titanium white. "Oil paints! Hey!"

But as I began my doze that night in my first bed, as muted headlights brushed the walls, and Billy breathed regularly a few feet off, raised voices pinioned me.

"You agreed, " Mrs. Pickwick was arguing. "You said it was worth a try."

"Because of the pressure. Roberts and the Welfare people and you—"

"By all means don't forget me."

"—ganging up at once."

"Like the salesman who sold you the Kaiser when we couldn't afford it, right? We didn't really need that roof, did we? But you didn't want to hurt the man's feelings. After all, he wanted so badly to put a roof on the house."

"We're talking about that juvenile delinquent upstairs." Mr. Pickwick said.

"Yes, let's talk about him," said Mrs. Pickwick. "This time it's not a roof we can't afford. Or a car. It's a human being. Maybe if you stopped thinking about yourself once in a while."

"Oh, come on, for pete's sake!"

"You're afraid of saying no to some damn stranger who's out to pick your pocket, but when was the last time you agreed to take your own family anywhere? Even a picnic, or swimming? I'm always the one who has to suggest it, just to get out of the house."

"And you always choose the worst times, when I'm busy, trying to make something out of my life. Or when I'm down in the dumps," Mr. Pickwick said.

"You're always down in the dumps. If I had to wait till you actually felt like doing something, I'd be dead from old age."

"It might surprise you to know that some people find me charming."

"Oh, I believe that," she said. "I really do. People have *told* me how charming you are. I've actually *seen* you be charming—to strangers, or your parents. But around your own wife and children, you don't even exist. It's taken me years to get this clear in my head, but if I'm going to live any kind of life, I'm just going to have to make it for myself."

"What does that have to do with—?" I felt the thrust of his index finger.

"I don't know what it had to do with anything," Mrs. Pickwick sulked.

"I'll just bet you don't."

"What's that supposed to mean?"

"Nothing." He paused. "I just don't see why with all our other problems you—"

"We!" she interrupted. "I *knew* you would try to dump it

all off on me. I sat there and watched Roberts literally bowl you over, like that football game when you told me you *despised* the man, remember? And there he sits with the Welfare people and says"—her voice assumed a mock pomposity—"'Now this isn't one of your ordinary boys from the sticks, Mr. Pickwick. I think he has incredible potential, and I'd take him in myself, but he needs a family, a home to bring out the best in him, and it's utterly impossible for me to give him that.' And you just nod and smile. You were afraid to say no, because then those people you could care less about might stop thinking, 'What an utterly charming man!'"

"If you knew it was a pile of baloney, why didn't you say so?"

"Because," she answered in a flat tone, "I just happened to agree with them."

"Well, after all, the State is going to foot his expenses." A momentary cheer came into Mr. Pickwick's voice.

"Sure they are," his wife responded. "Don't you have any idea what it costs to raise a boy into a man?"

"He already is a man. Or didn't you notice."

"Oh, I noticed, all right," she airily replied.

It was a challenge, but he declined, saying, "The lady from Welfare mentioned if things didn't work out, we wouldn't have to keep him on. It's only a foster home arrangement. Maybe we can just keep him for a decent length of time, then send him on his way. I mean, I really think my boat may finally come in with this novel if I can finish it without distractions."

"Why not blame the boy because you never finished your Emerson thesis and can't get promoted or even a decent raise? What about that horse farm you tried to start? Or those mortuaries you invested in—weren't they supposed to hook up with some big national motel chain? All that money down the sewer."

"Borrowed from my parents."

"And now, my God! I saw how your eyes lit up after the Welfare people left our house and Roberts went into that little song and dance about chinchillas. Ten thousand dollars on a one-thousand-dollar investment! Almost like he was offering you a bribe to take in"—this time it was *her* index finger I felt—"except that you'd pay good money to Roberts for those disgusting rodents, with absolutely no guarantee! What is the matter with you?"

"I haven't bought a single chinchilla yet, so far as I know. But thanks to you I got manipulated into bedding and boarding one Prince Elmo Hatcher."

"We've already been through that, but okay. He *is* talented. Why else would a man like Roberts be so concerned about him? He's had an absolutely miserable existence! Just once in our lives can't we do something we know is right? I mean, it's an awful old chestnut, but what's wrong with really doing good?"

"I'd rather do good for some poor beautiful deprived girl," Mr. Pickwick muttered. "What about Hazel? What about . . . you?"

"Well. At least you've said it." Her voice was suddenly weary. "I hope it sounds as insane to you as it sounds to me. I know Hazel pretty well, and she can take care of herself, believe me." Then, after some moments of silence, Mrs. Pickwick added, "Of course now you'll have to borrow from your parents. It's the only way I see we can get by until you finish your novel."

"Back to money."

"I even told the breadman and the milkman to stop delivering, because we couldn't pay. Your parents are so rich, maybe it's high time you borrowed regular sums every month till you finally begin making it on your own. Oh, they'll grumble some, but then they'll come around. They always do. So it's not as if we were *really* poor."

"For you, it all comes down to money."

"No, it comes down to life," she said matter-of-factly. "Nothing is happening in my life. Except bills we can't pay. Look at you. Maybe you'll get your success; who knows, maybe all sorts of strangers will start praising you to the skies. So where does that leave me? I sit around this house listening to that typewriter and I feel right on the edge of blowing up. Sometimes I think I'd do anything, just to make something different happen."

"Guess I don't satisfy you."

"I guess not," she said.

"What's the matter with me?" he moaned, giving in utterly. "If anybody should have made it by now, it's me. I know that's probably just my rotten ego sounding off, but lord! Look at my record. Everywhere I graduated, valedictorian! Where did I slip up? Sometimes I dream you're with other men, just can't get the image out of my head . . . I'll borrow. I kept thinking I could make it on my own this time, but you're right."

"And later you'll use it against me. And that stranger upstairs."

"No, he'll just have to stay for now. It's like I'm somnambulating, doing things in my dreams that seem right and natural, then waking up, wondering what the heck's going on. I guess he did save Billy's life. What *is* wrong with doing somebody a good turn now and then? I'm under a strain. He doesn't deserve this. Neither do you."

"It's all right," she acquiesced. "Most of it probably is my fault."

"I used to have so much energy!" he wailed "Remember? High as a kite, the whole world came together, I felt like a god. Now I can't even pull myself out of bed. I don't understand myself, but maybe something does need to happen. Why did you ever marry me?"

And I heard Mrs. Pickwick murmur, "You're my poor gorgeous man."

"Elmo? You awake?" came a whisper from the next bed.

I stayed quiet. Nobody should have to feel any worse because of me than they already did. Logically, I should have cut out at once, that night if possible, for my sake as well as theirs. Or just "taken them" awhile, played the tame animal till I caught my breath. Instead, lying there the first night in bed, I found myself wanting to please them, as Mr. Pickwick seemed determined to please everyone except his wife and children. Two people had thrashed around trying to understand why they'd acted— and now here I am trying to understand not only why I stayed, but why I wanted to make these people love me; though even then, like a pet who sniffs danger in a room, I must have sensed in their gesture more neurosis than generosity. Maybe I wanted a family, any family, and false order still seemed preferable to no order at all. I was a stray who doesn't care what motives have opened a house; he stays for the meal, the mat on the floor. But that isn't quite it. If nurture had determined my mind (and it did not determine my body), I should have been a psychopath. Yet as children from the fattest, most loving homes turn out monsters, maybe—

I'd show these Pickwicks. I'd actually make things easier: eat tidbits, help around the house. Incredible! they'd exclaim. What a guy! Remember all those problems riding us? Why, it's as if his very presence made them dissolve into thin air!

Lulled by these reveries, I slept . . . and toward morning dreamed I was looking down from the ledge at a white shape floating just beneath the surface of the Gorge. All was washed in the noon sun's brilliance. Rising, the shape revealed itself as some bird, vulture or falcon. It slowly pumped great albino wings, cascading water as it hovered above me, then, with the gentlest pressure, sank claws and beak into my right forearm. My left hand clutched its feathers, trying to loosen the creature; whereupon it dug in still more firmly. Sinking fingernails through feathers, I tore at the meaty breast. But the bird matched my violence: the more I hurt it, the more it maimed me. Horrified, I battled more powerfully, but the bird returned force for force, bruising muscle and bone, tearing flesh until pain awakened me into gray, hazy light, and I found my right forearm pinioned in my own left hand, blood oozing where fingernails dug into the flesh.

•2•

One blazing afternoon toward the end of August, at Helen's request, Mrs. Pickwick drove me to jail so I could visit. We parked the Kaiser right next to the new Police Emergency Unit in front of the limestone courthouse, with its fat blind Justice, its charging soldier, and a black Nazi buzzbomb on a limestone block the size of a beer truck. TOM NEVER CO., said a weather-beaten sign. The jail occupied two floors over Kresge's, opposite the courthouse.

"I'd love to meet your mother," Mrs. Pickwick said.

In his office outside the cellblock, the sheriff searched me carefully. "We don't none of us know for certain how your grampa got hold of Dick's razor," he said. "Wouldn't have no idea yourself, would you, Elmo?"

"Leave that child alone," Mrs. Pickwick commanded.

"If this here's a child, ma'am, I'm a motion-picture star. You intend going through that door yourself?"

"I do."

"Wait here a minute. I'll check and make sure Helen's decent."

"Poor woman," Mrs. Pickwick sighed after the sheriff left. "She must be miserable in this place, without any privacy."

The sheriff returned. "She'll be ready in a minute," he announced. "Wanted to run a comb through her hair."

"Don't you have a female attendant in this place?" Mrs. Pickwick asked. "I think it's terrible, your just charging in on that poor woman."

"Shoot, old Helen don't give a damn," he laughed.

Helen occupied the same cell in which the sheriff had killed Grampa. Seeing us, she called through the bars, "Hey there, Prince Elmo. Long time no see. Howdy, lady. You Prince Elmo's new mamma?"

"I'm Anne Pickwick. But I certainly wouldn't try to replace Prince Elmo's real mother."

"Well now, you're a sweet pretty thing," Helen said, "and darn considerate, and I'm sure glad my child here's in your hands."

"Thank you," Mrs. Pickwick murmured.

"Roy, are you gonna let these people inside for a visit, or am I just supposed to sit here looking out this cage like a monkey in the zoo?"

Roy unlocked the cell, let Mrs. Pickwick and me inside, locked the door, and left.

"Hell, that Roy's a good egg," Helen said. She looked cleaner than I ever recalled. Her gray denim dress was starched, pressed, neatly belted. "Food's right agreeable around here. Old girl's beginning to fill out." She patted her tummy's slight bulge. A portable radio and a pile of magazines filled the shelf of the cell's one window, steel mesh inside louvered glass slats which the prisoner could crank open and shut. A breeze came through. The plank bed hung on its chains. No mattress, only an army blanket on top of wood. The toilet lacked seat and dropcover. A roll of toilet paper squatted on the concrete floor. Above the bed, ragged dents marred the concrete blocks where the sheriff's bullets had passed clear through Grampa. Turned low, the radio wailed a tinny hillbilly cry.

"Honey, this has got to be the nicest jail this side of heaven. I never had it so easy."

"What are they going to do with you, Helen?" I asked.

Peering into my eyes, she naughtily bared white teeth in a grin. "We'll talk about that later maybe, in private, after we visit a little with your new mom."

"If you'd rather discuss something alone with your son, I'd be happy to leave."

"No, honey, I want you to stay right here. Come sit beside me on the bed. Prince Elmo there, big healthy clunk, he can sit or stand as he pleases. Wish I had a nice soft place like you're probably used to at home."

"They haven't even given you a mattress! It's a disgrace."

"Honey, when you been through as much hardship as me, it don't matter a bit. I just flop down here, eat my three squares a day, enjoy the radio, read me a *Movie Romance,* and relax. Poor old Dick. Buying my comfort with his dead body."

"Good heavens!" Mrs. Pickwick exclaimed. "You shouldn't talk like that. Don't you have a lawyer?"

"Sure, and he don't cost me one red cent. Pleading me guilty."

"But you're entitled to trial."

"Sure. But the D.A. said if I was to be tried, it'd be for murder one, and if they found me guilty, some old judge might decide I ought to fry. This ain't the best possible world for a woman, ya know. It's men that hold the whip, even if most of them ain't worth a fart."

"Well, I think it's simply terrible that they don't have a woman here to look after the lady prisoners. Why, they ought to have a completely separate wing. Or at least"—she blinked at the stark toilet—"grant you some privacy."

"Shoot, honey, before I come to jail, I always done that

in the woods anyway. We never had no outhouse. Prince Elmo here started to dig one once, but he got sidetracked. Naw, that don't matter a bit."

"Oh."

"And like I said, Roy's a good egg. Anyhow, I plead guilty to manslaughter. And then there's—extenuating circumstances? Dick never was worth a damn, running round with other women and stuff. Plus a thing or two which we got up our sleeves as softeners." She flashed me another grin. "Get me off with maybe five years at the outside. But thanks for thinking of me. Us girls got to stick together."

"That's the truth."

"What's Prince Elmo's new daddy like? I bet he's really loaded."

"His parents are," Mrs. Pickwick said. "He just teaches at the university."

"Hey now. Think maybe I got through grade five."

"He doesn't make much. He never finished his doctor's degree."

"Well, almost a doctor. I bet you're really proud married to a man like that. I never had reason to be proud of Dick. My husband, you know, the one they say I poisoned."

"I know."

"Is your husband a living doll?"

"What? Oh. I think he's very handsome."

"I bet he is, with a babe like you for his wife."

"Well, thank you."

"If Prince Elmo starts getting fresh, just let me know, and I'll take care of him."

"What?"

"I say, if he starts getting in the way, let me straighten him out."

"Oh."

"Prince Elmo, sounds like you got a great new daddy."

"It's not as if Bob were his real father," Mrs. Pickwick said.

"That don't mean much. He thinks Dick's his real father."

"What's that supposed to mean?" I asked.

"La de dah," Helen singsonged.

"Now that you brought it up, who is he?" I asked.

"How the hell should I know?" Helen snapped. "Honey," she said to Mrs. Pickwick,"when you've cut loose as much as me and with as good a reason, you can't always know what caused what. Dick was gone so much on me running around, and as you can probably tell from the way I look now, I was a handsome girl, though Jesus knows how hard times have aged me—"

"No, you're still very attractive," Mrs. Pickwick said.

"Thank you. Anyhow, I'm not sure I know, and it don't make any damn difference. Roy? C'mere! Honey, I want to say a few words in private to Prince Elmo. Roy! Get your skinny buckaroo butt in here!"

"Settle down," Roy said, coming to unlock the bars.

"My head's swimming," Mrs. Pickwick said.

"She do something, ma'am?"

"No, it's all right."

"So long, honey. And you listen here. Don't take no crap off of men. You listening? They ain't worth it."

"Happy to have met you, Mrs. Hatcher."

"Pleasure's all on my side, honey. You go out and wait, Prince Elmo'll be out in a minute. Go on, Roy, get out of here."

Roy relocked the bars. Chuckling, swinging the keys against his thigh, he left.

"Listen, Helen—" I began.

"Now don't crowd me, fella. I want to hear from your own mouth how things're going for you."

"Aw, you know."

"How's Granma?"

"In a home downstate. Welfare Woman says she's fine. Haven't been to see her yet."

"You don't seem to care a whole lot 'bout your own blood."

"I miss Granma. I miss you too. I mean that, Helen. And I miss Cerulia. Heard anything from her?"

"Ain't heard nothing from nobody. It kinda pisses me off. But you always was my favorite. You understand, don't you?" That grin again. "Prince Elmo, just thought I'd drop something on you so you could think about it from time to time. You ain't no kid. I oughta know. But if your old man's who I think, he's got one shitload more dough than this Pickwick you're living with."

"Who you talking about?"

"For me to know and you to find out. It don't make a bit of difference anyway. Won't get you a damn thing. And besides, that ain't what I wanted to say. Which is, I'm pregnant again."

"What?"

"Ain't made you much smarter living with a professor. I'm having another baby, dumbass."

"Jesus Christ, Helen."

"That oughta ream out some old judge, huh? They ain't about to send a woman with child to the stake, are they? Hey, baby boy—how come you're lookin' at me thataway?"

I just blinked my eyes.

"Whatsa matter? It's a scream, that's what I say. Listen, this family you're living in, nice clean upright bunch? Sure hope you don't wander in like some French disease and screw 'em up."

"You mean—"I could hardly say it—"you and me—?"

"Ain't that the limit?"

I just shook my head, forcibly holding my eyes from the swelling traced by the starched cloth over her belly.

"Don't dare tell that pretty sweet little lady about it. She'd flip right out of her skull."

I nodded.

"That's the limit, all right. I told my lawyer it's Dick's. Also that fatass woman and old Roy. Not that it makes a damn bit of difference to him. Roy's one good old egg. You're pulling a mighty long face there, son."

"Gotta go."

"Well. Just wanted to leave you a little food for thought."

"Sure."

"You might be in some sort of shape to help old Helen by the time she comes out of the clink."

"Righto. You said it."

"Maybe them Pickwicks got more dough than that little lady let on."

"Don't think so, Helen."

Roy wandered back, digging a finger into the side of his nose, sniggering. "How's this here reunion coming?"

"Hi there, you old buckaroo."

He unlocked the cell and motioned me out. "Time's up till next time, podner."

"Don't take no wooden nickels," Helen said. Metal clanked. I kept on walking.

"Honey, keep your nose clean now, y'hear?"

Kaiser idling, waiting for a red light to change green, Mrs. Pickwick said, "Don't think you have to apologize for your mother. I admire her. She's got spunk. Locked into that tiny cell, nothing to look forward to except a long jail sentence, she almost seems free. Isn't that ridiculous? Something that would just destroy somebody like me—well, it doesn't concern her at all." The light changed, and Mrs. Pickwick warmed to her subject. "The more I think about it, the more I really envy her. Lord, what some people wouldn't give for her inner sense of freedom. Not that anyone would want to be in jail. But her spirit! You deserve to be proud of your mother, Prince Elmo, and it's not the least bit condescending when I say that sometimes I wish I could break loose from some of the old hidebound patterns that make me feel so *cramped,* and take off into a clear blue sky!"

•3•

In September, just before school started, Mr. Pickwick's parents, who lived one hundred miles to the north, paid their first visit since my arrival. Grandpa Pickwick, a heavy-set energetic little fellow with enormous hands and feet, was a retired oilman and also an amateur student of American history. Born in Indiana and trained as a lawyer, he had been circuit court judge in New Mexico until certain mysterious dealings with Indians who were about to be tried in his court left him the owner of oil-rich lands. Well before middle age, he was a millionaire. Grandma Pickwick, whose eyes were a gorgeous luminous blue, was an active Christian Science practitioner. Both wore Phi Beta Kappa keys.

"Well, young man," Grandpa Pickwick asked when we were introduced, "what do you plan to be when you grow up?"

"Don't know."

"How could the poor child possibly be expected to know?" Grandma Pickwick said.

Mrs. Pickwick pointed above the fireplace, at the swirling, clashing colors of my turpentine-wash sketch, beginnings of the mural I was painting. "That's his work," she offered nervously.

It stunk.

"You don't want to be an artist," Grandpa Pickwick said. "You couldn't support your family. You'd end up starving in a garret."

"Money should never be the most important consideration, Dad," Grandma Pickwick admonished. "You know that."

"Hmmph. That's true enough. Audubon was an artist. But then he spent most of his life starving. Wouldn't have eaten if he hadn't been a criminal on the side." Turning to Mr. Pickwick, he asked, "When's vacation over, sonny?"

"Two weeks."

"Bob has been working extremely hard all summer long," Mrs. Pickwick said. "I've never known a man who worked harder."

"Of course he has, Anne," Grandma Pickwick said. "Dad and I know that."

Grandpa Pickwick stood before the cold fireplace and scrutinized my work. "Reminds me of redskin art," he said. "Scarcely changed at all over the past two thousand years. Visited some reservations five years ago. Remember, Mother? Those primitive fellows are still knocking it out, same old stuff. Thank your lucky stars for progress. If the redskins owned this country, we'd all be squatting around a dusty campsite eating raw bear meat."

"Better that," Grandma Pickwick said, "than all this constant grubbing after a dollar."

"True enough," agreed Grandpa Pickwick. "I liked some

of those fellows. You know, Elmo, I've got Shawnee blood flowing in my veins. So has Bob there, and Billy and Hazel. Rugged fellows, those redskins. A drop or two improves the stock."

"Dad's proud of his Indian blood," Grandma Pickwick said. "Shows up in Hazel, even though Bob has my coloring."

"But the pure line's going to run out before long, mark my words. The pedigreed redskin can't keep up with the modern world. Place firewater in a redskin's hands and he's out of control. When I was judge, I'd sentence twenty or thirty redskins a day for drunken behavior. Indian's a child. Never grew up. Most of the Shawnee that stuck around here mixed its blood with the niggers."

"What are you writing about, Bob?" Grandma Pickwick asked.

"Rather not talk about it, Mother," Mr. Pickwick replied. "You know the saying. If I talk about it, I won't write it."

"A lot of nonsense," said Grandpa Pickwick. "Talking clears things up. If you're ashamed to talk about it, you'll be ashamed to have anybody read it when you're finished. Anne, tell us what sonny's book's all about."

"I haven't seen it."

"Won't even show it to your own wife, eh?" Grandpa Pickwick grumped.

"I have faith in Bob," said Mrs. Pickwick. "I respect his feelings, and I think he should feel free to do this his own way."

"Nobody questions that, Anne," Grandma Pickwick said. "I only wondered what he was writing about. Why get so defensive?"

"Too many dirty books around these days," Grandpa Pickwick said. "If I were in charge, I'd bring the country back to what it was when I was judge. We tarred and feathered purveyors of filth. Of course, you wouldn't write a dirty book, son. You were raised better than that."

"But they make the money, all right," Grandma Pickwick said. "You have to grant them that, don't you, Dad?"

"I'm not sure this is a fit subject to be discussed around children," Mrs. Pickwick said.

"Oh, nonsense, Anne!" Grandma snapped back. "You get upset easily these days, don't you."

"Sorry, Mother Pickwick."

"My father was such a wonderful man, you know." Grandma Pickwick gazed upward. "A poet and a genius. Only man in my whole life I ever completely admired"—as she looked from Hazel to Billy, her eyes flicked an instant over me—"until your father grew to be a man. Robert reminds me so much of your great-grandfather Wilson, it's uncanny, like the transmigration of souls. My father realized the true values of the spirit. Material objects, things of the flesh, money, didn't mean a thing. He knew that the real world was one great spirit, and it inspired everything he wrote. He could never write filth."

Grandpa Pickwick grumbled, "What about that poem describing the young widow woman in her bath—"

"You wouldn't understand!" Grandma Pickwick cried.

"Sonny, this book you're writing, is it going to be a money-maker?"

"I'd have to know first if it were ever going to see print," Mr. Pickwick replied. He sat on the piano bench and knitted his long, slender fingers, and kept his eyes on his feet, as if trying to read his shoe toes.

"Thought you'd have some publisher beating down your door," Grandpa Pickwick said, "throwing in Fort Knox just for starters. Let's hope this fares better than some of your other projects."

Mr. Pickwick said quietly, "Folks, I feel as if two or three teams of horses are tugging pieces of me in all different directions."

"Pshaw, Dad!" Grandma Pickwick exclaimed. "This obsession with materialism in front of the children. What will they think?"

Hazel, who had been unusually subdued, now said, "It's okay, Grandma. We know when to take adults with a grain of salt."

"Why, I don't like that sort of talk at all," her grandmother said. "Anne, do you allow that sort of backtalk in your home?"

"She was just trying to reassure you," Mrs. Pickwick said.

"Well, I don't know what to think. This is very trying. Maybe we should shift to some other subject of conversation. Prince Elmo Hatcher." She looked where I sat beside Hazel and Billy on the couch. Grandpa kept pacing the carpet in a huff. "That is one of the strangest names, now, isn't it?"

"Yes, ma'am," I said.

"Your parents must have been monarchists at heart."

"You'd have to ask them."

"His father's—" Hazel began.

"Your grandmother," Mrs. Pickwick interrupted, "knows all about Prince Elmo."

"But I've never had a chance to chat with him in person. I must say, Anne, you've done a wonderful job making him presentable."

"For heaven's sake, Mother," Grandpa stormed, "you've never seen the lad before. You haven't the slightest idea what he looked like when he first entered that door. He may have been a veritable peacock!"

Grandma ignored this onslaught. "Have you and Billy become fast friends?"

"I like Billy a lot," I said. "I like the whole family. They're fine people."

"The finest people in the world," she confirmed.

"Monarchists!" Grandpa gruffed. "My God!"

For a while nobody spoke.

Suddenly an energetic stir arose from the piano bench. "Just a moment, folks, listen," Mr. Pickwick said, waving his hand nervously. "I can say one or two things. I'm writing about—you'll approve of this, I know, Dad—the Meaning of America."

"First-rate subject, sonny."

"And the American Dream."

"I like that," his mother said. "Because the whole material world is a dream. Mrs. Eddy taught us that."

"I'm writing about the American character," Mr. Pickwick went on, "the sort of rugged individualism we associate with the early capitalists in this country and the whole free-enterprise system as we know it."

"Excellent!" Grandpa Pickwick approved. "That'll knock 'em dead."

"But of course I wouldn't want to slight the poet and dreamer—know what I mean, Mother?—the fresh and visionary child hiding beneath the firm features of every true American. The essential American innocence, and the desire of our Founding Fathers to recover on this continent the Garden of Eden itself."

"A lovely idea!" his mother sighed.

"Of course, in order to give the work shape, I'm having recourse to the classics, the old Greek and Roman myths, the Bible, and, of course, Dad, the lessons and patterns which derive from the study of Man's History through the Ages."

"By golly, sonny! You've really hit it this time!"

"Ultimately, I suppose, I'm trying to discover the secret of the universe, as embodied in the secret meaning of America. I'm taking a crack at nothing less than the Great American Novel!"

"It's beautiful, a beautiful idea!" Grandma Pickwick exclaimed.

And Grandpa cried out, "It'll bring down the house! You'll succeed big, sonny, the way Mother and I have always expected. Top of the charts, I can see it now. A million dollars and a crack at the Silver Screen!"

Mr. Pickwick fell silent, features eaten hollow by their very expression of relief. "Dad," he whispered, "do you think a small chinchilla ranch might be a good side investment?"

As the old man's mouth gaped in wonder, Hazel said, "Folks, let's peek in on some of the skeletons I'm stringing together."

•4•

Hazel kept her room locked. She locked it when she went inside, she locked it when she left. She seldom allowed her mother to clean the place. "Mom, you might put something back in the wront place. I've got everything exactly where I want it."

According to Mrs. Pickwick, Hazel still slept with the scraggly, bald teddy bear which had been her first playmate.

A ragged brownish scrap of wool, last remaining relic of her baby blanket, hung like a pennant nailed to the wall above her pillow. Even the lace curtains, which Hazel herself laundered every two or three years, were hanging there when the squawling oversized package of female brawn was first bundled home from the hospital. "It's my room," Hazel insisted, "and what I do with it is my own darn business."

So while Mr. Pickwick's typing in the master bedroom slowed to an occasional peck and finally petered out altogether, and he began negotiating with Tarze Roberts to buy a half dozen pairs of chinchillas, and Mrs. Pickwick grew more and more disgruntled, and Billy and I in our joint cubicle bull-sessioned to an incessant background of rhythm and blues emanating from the fat black spindle of the forty-five, Hazel would lock herself into her room and, I supposed, string together the boiled cleaned bleached bones of crows, chickens, rabbits, possums, cats, and other animals found along the roadside or in the family cookpot.

Helen had long since been incarcerated in the Women's Prison, Indianapolis. I never visited. The prosecutor had accepted her belly's plea, but the judge crushed her with a fourteen-to twenty-five-year sentence. "God help a poor abandoned woman," she sighed, leaving the courtroom. And one day in late April, a nameless baby girl, perfectly formed and healthy, was taken from the prison hospital to one of the orphanages about the state. "You have a baby sister," said the warden's brief note to me.

Two months after Granma died in the State Home, I got information of her death in a package containing her belongings: a crochet hook, various-sized needles for quilting, a handful of brightly colored scraps. Cerulia and Duke, so far as I could tell, had been swallowed alive by the land. I had lost my family.

One afternoon, Billy and I returned from high school with Bo Diddley's new record, *I'm a Man.* But when we raced upstairs to put it on, we found the record player missing—and heard a falsetto whine throbbing through the locked door of Hazel's bedroom.

Billy pounded the door. "Hazel, give me back my record player!"

"Go away!"

"You're a *thief,* Hazel!"

"And you're a selfish—I don't know what. You've had a record player for years. Now it's my turn. Go away!"

"You're bigger than I am, Prince Elmo. Break the door down."

"What's that you're playing, Hazel?" I asked.

"You don't really care. Nobody cares. Go ahead, you lunk!" she cried. "Break down the door."

"Aw, come on."

"I just want to be alone!" she wailed.

"I know who it is," Billy said. "She's listening to Johnny Ray."

". . . feel-ing ver-reee sa-ud insi-ighed!" caterwauled the tinny sound.

"I love him! Go away!"

"Aw hell, let's just let her borrow the thing," I suggested.

"Whose side are you on?" Billy asked.

"We can hear Bo Diddley later."

"No wuh-uhn cared if he li-uhved or die-ihed . . ."

"Johnny Ray!" Billy spat. "Christ Jesus in heaven!"

On those rare occasions when I was afforded a glimpse inside Hazel's room, I saw new patches of color sprouting from her walls: Robert Taylor, Alan Ladd, Rudolph Stayne, Randolph Scott, and, of course, Johnny Ray, hearing-aid cord twining down the side of his face, earpiece plugged in like a badge of humanity. There was also a picture, clipped probably from one of Mrs. Pickwick's *Bazaar*s or *Vogue*s, of a lean, blue-eyed young man in bathing trunks, torso oiled by the pool from which he'd just hoisted himself. He smiled; dimples dented his cheeks; his teeth were even and white.

Once I awoke to little mewings and whimperings from Hazel's room, the rustle of body-tousled sheets. "Oh, please, pleeeese. Ohhhh."

One howling winter night, a large stained object, gauze and cotton, discarded dressing for a wound, whispered against my bare toes in the john when I got ready for bed. Had Billy been hurt? Then I recognized dressing and wound for what they were. After all her years of being a woman, Mrs. Pickwick wouldn't make this mistake. To protect Hazel, I swaddled it in tissue and hid it in the wastebasket.

Soon after this discovery, Billy took me into his confidence. One drawer in the secretary remained locked, and Billy owned the key—his treasure drawer.

"Want to see something?" He opened the drawer, dug to its bottom, and pulled out a fading snapshot. "Don't tell a soul."

It showed Mrs. Pickwick, perhaps ten years younger, facing camera, standing in a shallow stream which covered her ankles. Her arms and face were raised skyward, and she was naked. Another naked woman, photographed from behind, abased herself at Mrs. Pickwick's feet. "Remember us," I thought, and the harsh dresses of Granma's album suddenly fell away, exposing the lean bodies of a hundred dead ladies in my mind.

"Who's she?"

"One of Mom's college friends. She married some rich guy."

"Who took it?"

"Don't know. Found it one day rummaging through Mom's dresser. Don't think I'd dare ask, do you?"

"Your mom is one handsome woman."

"Yeah," Billy sighed.

And borrowing undisclosed thousands from his disgruntled parents, Mr. Pickwick filled the basement with rows of wire cages stacked to the ceiling.

"Think I've found the royal road," he said. "They're gorgeous. Go down sometime and just blow against their fur!"

Mrs. Pickwick appeared to gag on a mouthful of dinner.

"Think of it!" Mr. Pickwick went on, "A chinchilla coat big enough to cover Hazel! Look how she's filling out. She's almost a woman!"

"You're making fun of me," Hazel protested. More and more often, her bright eyes looked like those of a kicked pet.

"Mark my words, Hazel, you're going to be a knockout," her father insisted.

"Bob, stop it. You're hurting her feelings."

"Nonsense. There's nothing wrong with old Hazel a few

years won't fix. Then you'll thank God you have those long legs, to keep you a few strides ahead of all the boys."

"That'll be the day," Billy said. "She's already in love with Prince Elmo."

"All of you just go to *hell!*" Hazel cried, shoving her chair over backward and flying from the table like a big gawky bird.

As the still air resisted her blouse, I saw two little mounds, sweat glands outdistancing the rest. And in the next months, I noticed bras in the bathroom clothes hamper, draped over doorknobs, at the foot of the stairs in fluffy piles spotted black by tiny hooks and eyes. And terrified to find her glands pouring poison into her veins, as after a rainstorm giant mushrooms explode overnight from flat barbered lawns, Hazel walked about the house, shoulders hunched, wide eyes pained, burdened with an enormous reversed knapsack bound to her mercilessly by shrinking straps. I'd hear Mrs. Pickwick murmur condolence; then suddenly mother and daughter would pile into the Kaiser, for a custom fitting in a department store on the square. Flat bra boxes lay empty except for splayed tissue-paper tongues.

Hazel sobbed, "They hurt me, mother. They're *killing* me!"

"You'll be okay, honey. You'll see."

"What's it all for, Mother? I can't stand it!"

Summer after my sixteenth birthday, Billy and I and glorious Hazel were horsing about the house. It was squirtgun season and Hazel had loaned us money for the most advanced dime-store weaponry, black drummed tommyguns which propelled a jet twice the living room's length. "Promise not to squirt me," she'd said, handing us bills and silver.

When we returned from town with the artillery, all promises were off. The only targets worth a stream bobbled from the chest of Billy's six-foot little sister. "Bet if we moisten her blouse enough," Billy said, "the nipples'll show."

Hazel stretched out on the living-room couch, procrustean bed simultaneously propping her head and feet. She was reading a college text, *Modern Biology,* for Hazel's brain had kept pace with her breasts.

"Hi, Hazel." Billy scored bull's-eye on her left boob. I drilled the right.

"Ooooooh!"

"Lookit. Her bra shows through!" Billy cried. "Keep pumping."

"How could you?" She was looking at me.

"Attaboy!"

Hazel beaned Billy with her book, jerked away his squirtgun, and blasted streams into my face, while I stumbled and plopped on the rug. She dashed through the dining room and kitchen, where Mrs. Pickwick was trying to fix dinner, and out through the back door, Billy and I pursuing.

A concrete ramp in the back yard led down to the ancient pair of basement doors, which swung inward. The door bottoms were wood, with panes of glass above. The basement had been designed to double as garage, but it opened too tightly for the Kaiser, which remained around front, at the curb. Hazel's rotboxes and workbench filled the area with the rich scent of loam.

"Will you kids settle down?" Mrs. Pickwick pleaded.

Hazel scooted down the ramp into the basement and held the doors shut.

"Try and push through," Billy said.

I shoved. Hazel grinned through my reflection.

"Keep trying, Elmo. I'll go through the house."

As I turned to watch him, Hazel parted the doors a crack and squirted my cheek. "Ha ha." She clapped them shut again and threw the inside latch.

I shoved with both hands. My right arm crashed through a glass pane. And I heard a chaos of small animals whirring about their cages.

"Hey, that'll cost you a dime." Hazel squirted through the jagged hole.

The forearm stung slightly. "Must have scratched myself."

"Tough tittie." Hazel squirted me again.

Pulling myself gingerly from the door, I turned my arm over. Two huge open mouths gaped—lips of skin and fat, yawning muscle, unslashed sheath around the bone. A red dot rhythmically spat blood into my face.

"Hey, Hazel, look."

Billy ran up behind squirting Hazel's bottom. "Elmo's hurt," Hazel cried. "Stop that, you damn idiot!" She pushed rapidly through the doors. Crimson geysered diagonally the width of her sopping blouse.

"Yukgh!" Billy turned green all at once. "Make a tourniquet."

"Here, just let me—" Hazel pressed her fingers beneath my armpit, and the fount stopped. *"Mom, Elmo's injured!"*

Mrs. Pickwick appeared in the yard. "My God, what'll we do?"

"Billy, go call Dr. Demetz. You got to drive us, Mom. Let's get going." Her fingers slipped, and a jet arced against the blue sky.

Leaning against the bricks which lined the side of the ramp, Billy vomited in front of his feet.

"Get a move on," Hazel commanded.

We made it to the Kaiser, Hazel and I in the back seat, Mrs. Pickwick driving. Blood dribbled and oozed onto our clothes and legs, onto the seat between us. "Hurry, Mom. He's losing blood."

"I'm going the speed limit."

Hazel's fingers slipped. Blood splattered the back window.

"Press your fingers where I am," Hazel told me. "Quick." She ripped off her blouse, twisted it into a rope, and knotted it wetly around my bicep. Thin white stretchlines triangulated down the bulging roots of her breasts toward the cloth-covered nipples.

Mrs. Pickwick glanced into the rear-view mirror, then craned suddenly around with a look of horror. "Hazel, put your clothes back on this instant!"

"Sorry, he's bleeding to death. Watch out, Mom. Red light."

Mrs. Pickwick looked front and jammed the brakes.

"Cars coming?"

"No, Hazel, there aren't," Mrs. Pickwick snapped.

"Run the light."

"I can't. It's red."

I said, "For Christ's sake, Mrs. Pickwick, go through the goddamn light."

"Stop that swearing! It'll turn green in a minute."

"It's green now," Hazel snorted. "Move!" We moved. "Should've called the Police Emergency Unit," she muttered.

"You can't go into the doctor's looking like that," Mrs. Pickwick said.

"Watch your driving, Mother."

"The waiting room's liable to be full of strangers."

"Turn right," Hazel said.

As Mrs. Pickwick turned, a man stepped from the curb, and she braked.

"Mother!"

"He has the right of way," Mrs. Pickwick whimpered.

"Stop being such a goddamn imbecile!" Hazel shouted. The pedestrian whirled midstream and gaped. "Hit your horn!"

But the pedestrian scrambled across.

Mrs. Pickwick sighed when Hazel supported me out of the car, across the sunlit sidewalk where walkers stopped and gawked, into the waiting room where an old palsied man looked awestruck over a trembling *Life.* The nurse ushered us at once into a room containing a long table with an aluminum top, the reek of ether, and a kind-faced woman of middle age, the family doctor.

"Well, who's been playing with knives?" she asked, helping me onto the table where I lay on my back. The ceiling swirled. "How much blood's he lost?"

"Ton," Hazel replied.

"Feet up, that's it. Color's okay." The doctor smiled across my carcass. "Quick thinking, Hazel." Already she was tending the wound, salting it with white powder. "Wait a min. Your mother needs something. Watch him a moment, Hazel."

Hazel smiled down between her jutting shadows. "Hey, how's it going?"

A towel fell over my eyes. Mrs. Pickwick said, "For heaven's sake, cover up with that."

"Sure. But I'll probably need two of them, huh, Prince Elmo?"

I could see again. Hazel had draped the towel over her shoulders like a fighter, each end brushing a breast. The doctor passed around paper cups half-filled with bright red fluid, then propped me so I could drink. "Wish I could have some," she said. "You won't believe how good this'll make you feel, Anne."

It oozed over my tongue, thick, sweet, cherry-flavored.

"Wow, delicious!" Hazel exclaimed.

"What's in this?" asked Mrs. Pickwick.

"Just drink."

The doctor dripped clear fluid through a needle into the beautiful Grand Canyon of my forearm. Hazel and Mrs. Pickwick had gathered their chairs up close, noses practically inside my wounds.

"That's really fascinating," Mrs. Pickwick said. "I've never seen the inside of an arm before, have you, Hazel?"

"Not a live one," Hazel replied. "Lots of dead ones on the fourth floor of the med school, pickled in formaldehyde."

"Look at all those different colors," Mrs. Pickwick marveled. "What's that little red hole?"

"Artery," Dr. Demetz said. "Severed. If your daughter hadn't acted, he'd be dead as a doornail."

"Hazel, you're a hero!" Mrs. Pickwick exclaimed. "I mean a heroine."

"Thanks. Wow, how many stitches you think that'll take?"

"We'll find out," the doctor said. "Got to clean out the gashes. But first—better get your heads back—arm needs a little blood." She unknotted the blouse, and gore spurted a yard.

"I could hear that," Mrs. Pickwick said. "It hissed sort of."

"Now let's sew that pipe together," the doctor said.

"Wonder what it tastes like."

"Honestly, Mother!"

"Well, you don't think I'm about to lick it!" Mrs. Pickwick giggled.

"If you think this is something," Dr. Demetz said, "You ought to drop by the emergency ward some Friday night. By four in the morning, there aren't very many organs of the human body that haven't been staring up into my face."

"Is it true what they say about Negro men?" Mrs. Pickwick asked.

"Now, Anne," cautioned the doctor, looking significantly at Hazel. "Try to put how you feel now into perspective. That dope doesn't last forever."

Fifty stitches and a tetanus shot later, we left the office. Hazel wore a starched white patient's gown the doctor provided. "Who's driving?" Dr. Demetz asked. "Anne? How do you feel?"

"Grrrreat!" Mrs. Pickwick cried, crimson with pleasure.

"Maybe you should stay awhile. I'll tell my nurse to call Bob and have him take a taxi over."

"Don't you dare. I want him in a good mood."

Hazel supported me tenderly. The sedative seemed to have sunk into her large body without a trace.

"I think that boy bled less than if he'd donated to the Red Cross," said the doctor.

Mrs. Pickwick danced a little jig around to the driver's side.

Hazel and I sat in front because of the back seat's caked and fly-speckled gore. Mrs. Pickwick sailed through the first red light without touching her brakes or checking traffic.

"You just ran a red light," I observed.

"So what?" replied Mrs. Pickwick.

"You're also going sixty miles per hour in town."

"Wheeeeee!" Mrs. Pickwick cried. "I feel wonderful."

We squawked to a halt before the house. Mr. Pickwick was waiting on the steps, an empty cardboard banana box hanging from one hand. Blood seeped through the heavy gauze pack taped over my wounds.

"How bad?" Mrs. Pickwick asked.

"Fan-tastic!" Mrs. Pickwick sighed. She clung to her husband's arm, smiling seductively into his face.

"I phoned the nurse while Jane was working on Elmo. Hazel's our girl of the hour."

"Mrs. Pickwick was a great ambulance driver, though," I said.

Still clinging to her husband's arm, Mrs. Pickwick was hopping tiptoe up the steps, beaming, planting little moist kisses on his cheek.

"Hey. Take it easy."

Billy lurked shamefaced inside the door. "Sorry I was such a sissy."

"Prince Elmo's so brave," Hazel murmured, looking admiringly into my eyes.

"Mmmmmmmmmmm!" Mrs. Pickwick threw her arms around her husband's neck and kissed him on the mouth. The banana box fell upside down, jarring straw wisps onto the rug. She pulled him toward the staircase.

"Uh, I think maybe you'd better stretch Prince Elmo out on the couch," Mr. Pickwick said. "Anne, for heaven's sake." She had tugged him halfway up the stairs. "Or maybe he'd rather use the reclining chair in the back yard. Why don't you do that?" he asked me. "Sunlight and fresh air might be just the thing."

"Move, you gorgeous man."

"Go on out of here, you kids," Mr. Pickwick urged. "Your mother needs to lie down and rest."

That evening, Mr. Pickwick was meeting with other chinchilla "ranchers" from the area and told Billy to come along. "Somebody from the family ought to be there, to admire what an animal expert I am."

"I'm nursing Prince Elmo," Hazel said.

Mrs. Pickwick slept like a log upstairs.

After they left, Hazel said, "Bet you'd like to see my room."

"I have, from the hall."

"Nice room isn't it?" She nudged me inside and shut the door. "That's a horse's skull on my dresser. We came across him in a ditch, on one of those county roads outside town. Mom and Dad blew their tops when I told them what I was going to do. Anything for science."

"Hazel, I was thinking, maybe I just ought to go lie down in my bed."

"Meet Mr. Wobbles." The bald teddy bear buttoneyed me from Hazel's pillow.

"Hi, Mr. Wobbles."

Hazel still wore the starched badge of heroism above a pair of floppy shorts; I wore pajamas. She paced silently, looking at the bare wood floor.

"I feel like I'm the patient with this gown on," she said. "Maybe I cut myself, too. Maybe I'm bleeding to death."

"You're a good girl, Hazel. You're okay."

I knew I should leave. But I stayed seated on her bed. "When you say I'm 'okay,' what do you mean?"

I just looked at her.

"Well?"

"You're the best person I know." I meant it.

"Ohhhh." She dropped beside me on the bed, wide green

eyes level with my eyes, and bumped my face hard with her lips. "I'm so happy you're here," she whispered, kissing my face and ears under the agonized grimace of Johnny Ray, stroking the back of my neck with her long, slender hands. "I love you, Prince Elmo. So much I can't stand it."

Twisting off the bed and facing me in a half crouch, she lifted the short gown with its single tie in back and pressed my face into her bra. Her knee bumped my right arm, and I let out an involuntary "Ow!"

"Sorry." She dropped to the floor and began kissing my fingers, which protruded through the gauze gauntlet. Grabbing the pillow from under Mr. Wobbles' head, I smothered my engorged adolescent groin. "Want you to make love to me," she murmured, "if it'll make you feel better."

"No," I whispered, pressing down hard against the pillow to keep from moving. "It's like an operation. You'll bleed all over."

"We'll say it was your arm." She embraced my calves. "Mother lets me clean up my own room."

"It'll hurt."

"I'm a big girl. Anyway, it's only supposed to hurt a minute."

"Your mother'll hear."

"She's conked out. I'll lock my door. What happens doesn't matter, don't you understand?"

I understood.

She threw herself back on the bed, bouncing Mr. Wobbles to the floor, and with the sigh of total surrender pressed my quaking left hand against her wound.

"You'll get pregnant." I leaned above her.

"More than anything in the world," she moaned, "I want to have your baby."

Whereupon I fainted—waking in my own bed, feet elevated on a stack of pillows. Hazel sat beside me. She bathed my forehead with a cold washrag.

"Hi, there." She bit her lip. "You fainted. Been out cold about fifteen minutes. I've been thinking. You're such a good, kind, understanding person, Prince Elmo. And I'm nothing but a rotten whore."

But I just smiled weakly and lay there like a limp carrot, noticing that my wounds itched. Soon I flopped off to sleep.

A few days later, while I convalesced upstairs, Billy handed me a present. "Summer's a lousy time to be ill. This might ease the pain." It was a slick, fat magazine called *Scamp.* A nude woman, color-photographed head to bellybutton, smiled from the cover. Tinselly pasties sparkled over her nipples.

"That's nothing," Billy said. "Wait till you see inside. Middle page folds out."

I found the place.

"What's the matter?"

"Where'd this thing come from?" I asked.

"Drugstore."

"I mean who puts it out?"

"Some incredibly rich guy named Waldo Whitman in New York. Used to publish a clean magazine, but now he's switched to filth. Isn't she fantastic?"

"Yeah." I thumbed through the front advertising and read the masthead. His name—you know whose—was listed there, "Associate Editor in Charge of Long-range Planning." Then I turned back to the centerfold and took a good look at Cynthia Love, full length on her tummy, naked as a jay, the same coppery hue all over. She'd slimmed in the flank and butt since the last time I'd seen her this way more than three years before. Her tits bulged larger, more firmly developed, unreal. Trimmed and smoothed, exercised, she'd been trained like a thoroughbred mare. The eyes had changed, too—all innocence fucked out, blue whore's eyes looking softly into mine.

"She's got to be the most beautiful woman in the world," Billy sighed.

"Yeah. I know her, Billy."

"What?"

My heart missed beats.

"She's my sister."

Chinchilla

•1•

MOUTH GAPING, Billy looked from me to the foldout, and said, "I don't believe it—Jesus, I wish Hazel looked like that."

"It'd drive you nuts."

"Boy, having a piece of ass like that around your own house all the time—oh, my poor, stiff, aching dong!" His glasses rode down his nose; he jammed them impulsively between his eyes.

"But your own sister, Billy."

"I'd close my eyes. I'd pretend—she was *your* sister!" he cried in triumph. "And you could pretend that she"—he jabbed his finger into the page's fold—"was *mine?*" He danced around the room, clasping hands above his head like a fighter. "I'm sending off for Charles Atlas lessons. I'm getting contact lenses. I'm going to change my name to something hairy and masculine, like one of those fag movie stars. Up on the marquee right now, in letters ten feet high. BUCK PICKWICK! Don't you think Cynthia Love would fall at the feet of a guy named Buck? By the way, that's not your last name. Did she get married?"

"Being married wouldn't make much difference to Cerulia. Cynthia Love must be her stage name, for whatever she's doing these days."

"Let's call a family reunion!"

"No."

"Write her a letter. Send a telegram. Tell her about this stud friend of yours named Buck."

"Billy, listen—"

"Buck," he said.

"You're crazy."

"Shit!" He pointed at his portable typewriter, a battered old reject of his father's, and behind it the reams of type-filled paper—poems, stories, fragments of novels, sex fantasies, daydreams. "I'm going to sit down at that typewriter for three days and knock out the Great American Novel. My father's balls'll drop head first into his socks. And your beautiful babe of a sister'll melt into my massive, muscular arms." He flexed his skinny biceps and suddenly collapsed backward onto his bed and groaned, "Man, I sure would love to get laid right about now. Hope you don't mind when I say I'd like to fuck your sister."

"Naw, Buck. I don't care."

"That's a true friend. Listen, I've heard the way to get girls hot is tickle their palms."

"I've heard the story."

"It drives them up the wall. And if you touch a girl just above the knee it's even better, or bite her earlobes, or tickle her neck with your tongue. And if you ever get your hand up a girl's skirt, they say it's clear sailing into the tunnel of love. Wish I knew. Elmo, haven't you ever wished we were homosexuals? Make everthing so much easier. You know how horny guys are compared with girls. Hell, we'd be laying each other all the time. Cool and relaxed." He shook his head. "Next best thing would be to have a sister who looked like that. I'd be the biggest damn incestuous pervert in the world. Like that hillbilly brother in the joke. 'Gee, sis,' he says, 'you're even better than Mom.' And she replies, 'Yep, that's what Pa says.' Hee hee. Don't get pissed, I'm only half serious about screwing your sister. Anyway, to make you feel better, I'd marry her first."

"She's older than us," I said, "seven years. And she's no virgin."

"How do you know? Anyway, I want a girl to show me the way, somebody who knows all the positions. Of course"—he scooted up onto his pillow, and cradled the back of his crew-cut scalp in his hands—"you got to let them know you respect them first."

He lay silently awhile, dreaming ceilingward through his thick lenses, while Cerulia and I gave each other the eye.

Billy sighed. "I've also heard that women really turn on to an intelligent man. Just start reeling wisdom out of the old brain, and all a woman's blood rushes to her crotch, a big swooshing tidal wave into the tissues. A woman's like a pinball machine, full of burning little erogenous red-light zones. The words of a brilliant fellow make her tilt!"

"Tilt means you lose," I said.

"Never played pinball either," he admitted. "Christ, I wish I'd had a life like yours, without all these fucking restraints. Bet you got laid before you were ten years old."

"I used to think women had peters."

"Hell, I used to think they didn't have anything at all, just a little hole in the thigh where Mom said babies came out." He gestured his thumb toward Cerulia. "Bet that girl doesn't have a peter."

"May have grown one by now. Maybe that's why she's lying on her stomach, to hide it."

"Elmo, are you going to get in touch with her?"

"No."

"Understand, I wouldn't screw your sister if it wasn't all right with you. We're too good friends for that."

"Thanks, Buck."

"You wouldn't screw my sister either, would you?"

"That would be kind of rotten."

"Well—I mean, that would be almost as bad as if you screwed my mother, wouldn't it?"

"I wouldn't do that either."

"Not that she'd let you or anything. But Mom's really a gorgeous woman for her age. You have to admit that."

"She's beautiful."

"But you'd never mess with her. Not even if she went crazy, you know, and thought you were somebody else, and threw herself at you naked? Would you do it then?"

"Oh, come on, Billy."

"Naw, listen, I'm serious. Would you screw my mother if she said she was going to kill herself if you didn't? And there she was, completely naked, holding a razor against her wrist and saying, 'Do it, or I'll cut'?"

"That's a phony question. It'll never happen."

"I sure hope not," Billy mused. Silence. "After all, you're not blood relatives. She's old enough to be your real mother, but that doesn't necessarily mean anything. Look at animals."

"Will you knock it off, Billy?"

"I wouldn't be saying things like this if I weren't bothered and confused. Probably it's just my age. I worry about all kinds of crazy things, and if you're going to be my friend, you'll simply have to try and understand. I mean, take my father. I think he likes you better than me."

"That really is crazy."

"Maybe. But that's the way I feel. Even if feelings aren't based on truth, they're true. The point is, I like you a whole lot, Elmo. You're my best friend. But sometimes I feel you've sprung in here like some healthy jungle thing to eat me out of my world. I mean, I'm sure glad that you don't want to be a writer."

"I wouldn't like it, either, " I agreed, "if some guy suddenly came barging into my life." Who could blame him? Who would want to compete with a shark, a tiger, a cannibal king or prince? I admired his candor. Maybe I loved him.

"Old buddy," he said, "give me another gander at that gorgeous hunk of flesh."

With my good hand, I tossed it the intervening yard to his bed, and listened to its rustling leaves. He tore the picture out and thumbtacked it to the wall above his bed.

"Buck Pickwick," I heard him murmuring. "That's a good strong name. Hey, listen, I have a great idea, Elmo."

"No, absolutely not."

"Let's phone her." Cerulia's bronzed sun cast its glow over the room. "I'm tired of whipping my meat to specters. I crave the touch of another's flesh."

"Who knows where she lives?"

"The magazine." Billy grabbed the extension phone between our beds, dialed 0, and leafed frantically through the front matter of *Scamp*. "Operator? Prince Elmo Hatcher here"—he grinned wickedly—"I want to place a person-to-person collect call to my older sister, Miss Cerulia Hatcher in New York City. What's that? Yes, Prince, as in Ranier. I know it's a strange name, but it was the gods' fault."

"Okay, Billy Buck, you win," I said. "But people who fall in love with photographs are full of shit."

"No, you spell her name, see, as in cun—I mean peaches and cream—"

"I'll pick up on it downstairs."

I surprised Mr. and Mrs. Pickwick necking on the couch.

"Hey, let's watch it," I said.

At the kitchen table, Hazel was wolfing through a stack of peanutbutter-and-jelly sandwiches, her usual evening snack to gain weight. "Hi, Prinsh Elmo."

Receiver to my ear, I heard a click, followed by giggling and a girl's lilt, "Scamp Magazee-een."

"We are trying to locate a Miss Cerulia Hatcher," the operator said. "The party calling is a Prince Elmo Hatcher, relative of Miss Hatcher's." Electronic pops and buzzes, breathing, muffled voices.

"Operator," the receptionist said, "I have a number you might try." She reeled it off. "Stop that, you *beast!* . . . Interference on this end," the *Scamp* receptionist shrilled. "Happens when we work late."

"I am trying the number now," the operator told us.

A rich voice answered, "Waldo Whitman residence."

"Wow!" Billy exclaimed.

"I have a long-distance collect call for Miss Cerulia Hatcher."

Long silence. "Who is calling?" the man asked.

"Lady's brother."

Now a second man spoke. "Operator. I'll accept charges. Duke, boy. Waldo. Where you calling from? Thought you were still across town burning a little midnight oil for the company."

"This isn't Duke," I said.

"Oh, sure thing, buddy." The voice deadened. "Half-assed crank."

"I'd like to speak with my sister."

"Sister, my ass," Waldo Whitman snarled. "By the way, the bitch changed her name to Whitman."

"You mean she's married to *you*?" Billy cried.

"*Two* tomcats yowling in the backyard! Who's the other creep?" Waldo Whitman asked.

Static and commotion.

"I'll tear that bastard apart," Billy mumbled. "Rip his eyes out."

"Wait, here she is, boys," Waldo Whitman announced. "Miss Crotch!"

Through a mouthful of sandwich, Hazel observed, "Sounds like a live-wire exchange."

"I don't know what's going on," a high-pitched desperate voice near the receiver, "you filthy bastard."

"Haw haw . . . " A door slammed.

"Prince Elmo," I said. "How's things, Cissy?"

"Long time no see," she murmured. "You *must* be him."

"Yep."

"Oh, honey, I married the nastiest bastard on earth. He ain't—isn't worth dogfart."

"We'll kick his teeth in," Billy growled.

"Who's that?"

Briefly I explained where I was living. Mrs. Pickwick appeared in the kitchen doorway and asked, "Who's he talking with?"

"Part of his real family," Hazel replied. "I guess his sister."

"How'd you find where I was?"

"Saw your picture in the magazine. Billy—"

"Buck!"

"—fell in love with it. So we called."

"Didn't you want to call me for yourself?" The question was plaintive.

Distant sounds of furniture banged around. Waldo Whitman shouted, "Get the fuck off! You're running my phone bill sky-high!"

"You tight-assed rich fairy!" Cerulia muffled the receiver.

"That's how the upper classes carry on," I told Billy.

"He thinks you're a lover," Cerulia softly explained. "But I locked the bastard out. He can't disturb us."

"If you had to run off and leave me, Cissy, I'm glad it was for a—"

"Can it, Elmo. All day I eat crap inside my cage."

Billy said, "Cerulia, I'll help you any way I can. I'd even die."

"You sound like an awfully nice boy. What do you do?"

"I'm a writer. Novels, poems, short stories, everything. I'll write you a letter, if you promise not to show that creep."

". . . like that very much, Buck," Cerulia murmured across a thousand miles of wire.

"He's only a kid, Cissy. Lay off!"

"Don't pay attention to Prince Elmo. I'm more man than your husband."

"I'll just bet you are, Buck," Cerulia said.

"Ooooowow!" Billy sighed.

"How's old Duke?" I asked.

"Fifty miles ahead of the game. The new mag was his idea. He runs it. Waldo just pumps in the juice when Duke says to. Everybody calls him a . . . uh . . ."

"Prodigy," I said.

"You always was smart as a whip. Why can't it be you with me now?"

"How'd you get there, Cissy?"

"Be surprised," she said resignedly, "all the places this little motor carries you." In the bastion of some richly furnished room, her face must have nodded sadly toward her fork of flesh. Muffled thunder, a pounded door. "Have to hang up now, Prince Elmo. Give me your address. We'll keep in touch."

Billy spewed the information.

Upstairs, I asked my glassy-eyed foster brother what he knew about Waldo Whitman.

"Son of a bitch inherited five thousand department stores across the country. Can't do anything except spend money or lose it. But he's always marrying gorgeous chicks. Your sister must make it a half dozen. If he managed his own stores they'd have failed years ago. Instead, he hatches all these projects. Resort hotels, airlines, art museums, you name it—kiss of death, they all fold. Once the jackass negotiated with Egypt, Saudi Arabia, Ethiopia, Yemen, and the Sudan to buy the Red Sea and turn it into a private resort."

"I'm beginning to admire the guy."

"Chiefs of state found conversation difficult with a person whose head was wedged up inside his ass," Billy said.

"Wonder if Whitman knows Tarze Roberts."

"All those rich assholes are thick as thieves. Would you like to borrow my private airplane for a little side trip to Iceland? Borrow my privates, my tongue, my wife?"

"What about your rich grandfather?"

"I'm going to lead a revolution. Down with rich cocksuckers.

We'll lop off their beans in the town square and piss on them." For a while, he dreamed silently into his pinup, then went on, "Man, my life's becoming clear. I've just got to bust out of this goddamn narrow middle-class zoo. Break a few stinking rules rich men make up to keep themselves rich. That's the only way to win when all the decks are marked, and all the high cards already dealt out. I'm going to have that girl, Elmo. Any way I can."

"You're too nice a guy, Billy."

"Buck."

•2•

I want to catch up with the animals that filled the Pickwick basement. Their coats were light gray and softer than goosedown; a darker stripe covered their spine to the tail's tip. Our slightest breath could part the fur, baring the gray hide. Adult chinchillas grew to the size of squirrels or medium-large rats.

They remained wild in their cages, and hostile. When one of us filled their feedbox with pellets—processed from fruits, seeds, herbs, and moss—they scurried with amazing rapidity around the wire. Agile as giant spiders, they whirled three hundred sixty degrees up the side, across the top, until we finally slammed the gate shut. These rodents, royal chinchillas, were native to the foothills of Chile and Peru. Inca gourmets once prized their meat.

Each pair occupied a separate cage as more or less permanent mates. Interbreeding damaged the stock, and the Breeders' Association required that careful pedigrees be kept. But occasionally things went haywire. Three afternoons a week, Mr. Pickwick, Billy and I descended together into the basement to clean cages. "Valedictorian of my college class!" Mr. Pickwick chortled. "Now look at me!" Cages would stand open while we scooped out soggy, reeking newspaper and straw and stuffed it into cardboard banana boxes to haul outside and burn in the backyard incinerator. We thrust arms amidst the whirling chaos of small animals, and over the months received painful bites from incisors like those of a small beaver.

Once, as if by diabolic plan, six animals suddenly whirred through the door, then rebounding off our bodies scurried lightly into the basement. They whizzed over the ceiling as if it were floor, snicked our fingers when we lunged and jumped. After a couple of hours, we finally captured them in nervous, bleeding hands. And hastily caged together two males, two females, and a female with a male not her former mate. The paired males became lovers—though at first we thought they were male and female breeding. The paired females squeaked and spat at each other, then settled to glowering from separate corners of the cage—a temporary lovers' quarrel, we said. We did not discover the error until the female chewed her interloping male almost to death, a thousand-dollar pelt half ground into raw meat. We tried, nevertheless, to save him for breeding stock, and during several weeks caged with his true mate, he seemed to recover, even thrive. Then for no reason we knew, he fell dead.

To make sure each rodent stayed where it belonged, Mr. Pickwick bought a pliers-like device which punched serial numbers into the delicate ear; this caused no problem, since ears were amputated from pelts before they were stitched into wraps.

But we had further difficulties. The mated pairs sometimes ate their newborn young. There was no predicting when they might crave such a meal. Once a male killed his mate; by the time we found out, he had already eaten her top half.

Mrs. Pickwick refused to help feed or clean up, and soon refused even to enter the basement. "They're repulsive! I can't stand to *look* at them!"

But I could. And sometimes, alone, at night when I couldn't sleep, I'd walk down, snap on the light, wake them, and peacefully brood upon the silent spinning chaos of fur.

It was here one midnight while the Pickwicks slept that I noticed, sticking through the newsprint inside one cage, a crumpled wad of typing paper. I fished it out and straightened it. Stained with urine and dung, it appeared to be two ripped-apart, unrelated fragments of Mr. Pickwick's manuscript. I read:

. . . knelt and rested my forehead against the pew in front. From the center of her rose-window above the altar, the Virgin smiled sadly down upon me. My brain throbbed . . .

I tore loose the brassiere and pushed my face between her huge, firm breasts. With wild, animal impulse, she grabbed a fistful of my hair and bored a hard, hungry thumb of nipple against my tongue. "Loverman!" she cried. "Ram me with your big, hot cock!"

After more than a year passed, and the rodents had multipled and, along with them, problems, Mr. Pickwick complained while we cleaned cages, "I don't understand these beasts. I can't control them."

•3•

A bleak, harsh winter passed—then in early spring, on the State University campus, while the season's last snow drizzled from branches and melted into the softening ground, I saw my playground girl grown up. Each day after my high school classes, I hiked across campus on my way home to the Pickwicks'. Gingerbreaded with limestone abutements and narrow Gothic casements, even the largest buildings blended into woods and pasture, the pastoral landscaping of some nineteenth-century genius. Several bucolic wooden bridges crossed a winding stream, at most three feet wide after the thaw.

Leaning on the rail, looking sadly down at her distorted reflection, she stood center-stage on one of these bridges. A well-clipped miniature male poodle, whiter than the bridge itself, sat beside her. She wore a coat of black sealskin, thick and heavy like her own long gleaming hair. I recognized her first by the thin, delicate hawk's blade of nose, its downward tilt, straight, flaring nostrils. When she looked up, filaments of white surrounded her black pupils.

Screwing up my courage, I strode the hollow-sounding ramp. "Hello, Nina."

"You know me?"

"We went to school together."

Up went her guard. "You weren't in Boston."

"Not Boston."

"Oh." She looked over the rail into the flow. "I don't remember my young girlhood."

"All I remember," I fumbled out, "is you."

"Complete and utter stranger, why don't you leave?"

"I had a crush on you back in the third or fourth grade. You were older. I've never been able to forget."

"Tell me your name."

"Uh—Pickwick. Prince Pickwick."

"You're smooth. 'Secret crush, never been able to forget.' One serious flaw you'd better correct, though. 'The only thing I remember is you'—that makes you sound dumb." She stared me down. "Can't you think up a comeback?"

I couldn't, so I asked, "You in the university?"

"Let's operate on that level, it's simpler. I'm waiting for somebody—maybe you'll help me kill time. I am in the university. That is, when I feel the urge, I take a class or two. Next."

"Why don't you ask me what I do?"

"What?"

"Make cast-iron jockstraps," I said, "to protect myself against bitches."

"One point for a foul shot." She smiled grimly. Her gloved hand clutched the railing, and she rocked back and forth. "Find somebody who looks depressed, then move in for the kill. So you're not stupid, you're smart and nasty like me."

"What's the problem, Nina?"

"Where would you like to start? The disposition I inherited in the womb? My last speeding ticket? Daddy warned me, never talk with strangers."

"Your last name."

"So you do remember me from grade school. And I thought you were just the average muscle-bound liar and seducer. Never know what you'll hit when you walk the dog. If you weren't handsome and your teeth weren't in good shape, I'd kick you in the groin and call the cops."

"What's your dog's name?"

" 'Dog.' Here, Dog." The poodle tensed, pricked up his ears, and raked his knobbed tail across the boards.

"Like animals?"

"Sure, Prince. Especially horses. The feel of twelve hundred pounds of muscle between my legs. How's that?"

"That's all right."

"You're beginning to bore me stiff."

"Love to ask you for a date."

"That's better."

"Drinks downtown?" I looked old enough to buy booze. But I was broke, and bluffing for time.

"Are you rich?"

"No."

"Too bad. Get rich. Then proposition me. And I'm not talking about a few drinks." The pelts molded her body, sleek and lean, heating my juices. The muscle gives way there, I thought, and there, and it's unbelievably soft. "Of course, you could be famous."

"I'm not."

"Strike two. But maybe you will be someday, and I'll be around awhile. What are you, when you're not molding those jockstraps?"

"Artist."

"That doesn't score brownie points. I've known a few talented neurotics. Not college kids taking art courses, the real thing, in New York, Paris. I'm an advanced little girl." She pursed cushioned lips, and kissed me off—as a tall young man, wearing a camel's-hair coat, strode up the bridge from the other side. Like Nina, he was lean, black-eyed, brown-skinned, as if both had spent the winter searing themselves at Cannes. His nose angled patrician to the tip, which dropped suddenly as if broken off. But the effect made him more handsome.

"Hello, darling!" Nina cried, bright and shrill.

"Who's he?" the man asked.

"Why, an old childhood chum of mine. Prince, I'd like you to meet my husband, Ivan Rhodes."

We shook hands. I remember the sad triumph in her face. Everyone who read the local paper knew that in addition to being the only son of the richest trucker in the state, Ivan Rhodes had once been the university football team's starring quarterback, and God knows what all else in the way of golden success. Looking into his spoiled face, I could tell that at any opportunity he was unfaithful.

"Let's go, Nina."

"But don't you want to chat awhile with my friend? Or are you all—what's a polite word for it—*talked* out?"

"We're late."

"*You* are. Poor dear. She kept you so long. You must be simply exhausted."

"Let's go." He seized her elbow. Turning cold eyes on me, he said, "Buzz off. You've served your function."

Nina threw me a wink, let it linger so her husband could see, then puffed a soft kiss.

I ran straight to Billy's typewriter and hacked out a letter to Duke, in his powerful capacity as Associate Editor in Charge of Long-range Planning of *Scamp.* I also executed several erotic sketches, watercolors, pastels, and ink, just to the right of what the Postmaster General might confiscate for his private collection. I told Duke this should give him some idea of my talents, and that if he would publish my work, I would adjust my skills in any direction he wanted. Craving success, I relied on the thick, reek of blood for help.

•4•

One evening at the end of May, shortly after Billy and I graduated from high school, Mr. Pickwick announced that the Chinchilla Breeders' Association, of which Tarze Roberts was president, would stage a convention around July 1, in New York City. "We'll *all* make the trip!" he exclaimed. "Anne, it'll be a second honeymoon!"

"I don't see why you're so excited," said Mrs. Pickwick. "It just sounds like another big expense we can't afford."

"You don't understand. This is the moment of truth. All

the big buyers will be there, and we get to auction off our pelts!" He licked his lips, blinked at the dining-room ceiling, then dreamily murmured, "We could clear fifty thousand dollars."

"Pelts?" Billy asked

"That's what the man said," replied Hazel.

"How many of the hideous little beasts does that mean you'll have to murder?" Mrs. Pickwick asked.

"Mother!" Hazel cried. "Honestly!"

"Why can't we just sell live pairs to other breeders," Billy inquired, "the way Tarze Roberts sold us ours?"

"I looked into that months ago," Mr. Pickwick said. "The whole market seems to have been filled. Maybe prospective buyers are waiting to see how the rest of us make out, before they plunge in themselves. Anyway, I don't know how to go about selling them live. You need the right contacts."

After dinner, Mr. Pickwick took Billy and me aside, beneath my fireplace mural of violent movement and livid colors. "I didn't want to discuss this while we were eating."

"Don't tell me," Billy shuddered. "I don't want to hear."

"How're we going to do it?" I asked. "Feed them rat poison? Gas them in the car trunk?"

Mr. Pickwick shook his head. "The Breeders' Association Manual says that if they die slowly, their follicles relax, and pretty soon all the fur starts shedding. You have to kill them fast, so the follicles contract." A long silence followed, during which I didn't look anybody in the face.

Finally I said, "Okay, tell us how."

"That's what I wanted to discuss. There are two possible ways." Mr. Pickwick lifted a thick paperback from the mantel and began leafing through. "Here." A line drawing showed two strong hands. One clutched the balled-up animal, the other, hair sprouting from its back, drove a hypodermic needle into the animal's heart. "Strychnine," Mr. Pickwick explained.

"Jesus Christ in hell!" Billy snorted.

"Look, son, let's not have that kind of language in this house," said Mr. Pickwick.

"The other method couldn't be that bad," I said.

Mr. Pickwick turned the page. This drawing showed the animal strapped to a small plank. One wire had been clamped to the animal's head, another to its tail. A hand swiveled the toggle switch shut. "You just need ordinary household current," said Mr. Pickwick.

Another long guilty silence.

"It's really terrible, I know," he whispered. "Hideous and disgusting."

"How did we ever get into this?" Billy asked.

"I must have had my eyes only halfway open, son. But we're in it all the way. We can't back out."

"The hell we can't. This makes me goddamn *furious!*" Billy cried and stomped up the staircase to our room.

"I don't really blame him, sir," I said. "Maybe we'd better hire a professional to do it."

"Too expensive. I'm already in over my ears." Mr. Pickwick covered his eyes with one palm. "You'll stick with me, won't you, Elmo?" He was pleading. "I can't do it by myself. Won't you please help me out?"

When we snapped on the light, their bodies whispered in my brain. We pulled translucent latex gloves over our hands to prevent electric shock; at once, my fingers began sweating.

"Let's start with an old one," Mr. Pickwick said, "one with a little less value. See if we can't get the hang of it."

The creature whimpered sharply on the plank.

"Golly, I feel terrible." Mr. Pickwick turned the switch. "Wait a minute. Do I smell burn?"

I took the warm body, bunched up like a lobster boiled alive.

"We didn't singe any of her coat, did we?"

I examined the thing carefully. "Looks okay."

Mr. Pickwick walked to another corner of the basement and faced the wall, while I worked the short, razor-sharp skinning knife. "Hope I know what I'm doing," I said. "I'm not really sure."

"Nonsense. You're doing just fine."

"Skinning a thousand-dollar squirrel," I muttered. "Feel better if it was for food." My gloves were filling with liquid. "Finished," I told him.

"Get the carcass out of sight," Mr. Pickwick said. "I'm coming back now."

But after he electrocuted our fourth, Mr. Pickwick stayed and watched me skin it. "Like Byron when he saw those Italian highwaymen guillotined," he said. "After the first, the others didn't have as much effect. Mainly he felt thirsty."

Though the pelts showed no damage, the smell of burn lingered. "Maybe we'd better go to the needle," he said.

"No, thanks."

"What's the difference? It's horrible either way. Maybe I can manage alone."

"No, I'll help." I owed it to him.

The clear strychnine came in rubber-capped vials, a doctor's shot medicine. I clutched the chinchilla like a cat, by its scruff, and stretched the tail to hold it still. When its muscles balled together in a climax of agony and I wanted to yell, I sensed that motion in the cages had grown to frenzy. Then I realized that all this time we'd been slaughtering in full view of the cages, and that these animals were crazed by fear.

"Better stop doing it where they can see."

"I know," Mr. Pickwick said. For some reason, he was sterilizing the needle. Our hands still swam in rubber, as if we feared contamination of some sort. "But this is the only place the light's good enough. I know it's indecent, Elmo. But what can we do?"

Enjoy ourselves a little less, I thought.

When it was over, four frenzied couples remained behind, to breed a new batch. I cleaned the knife and put it in the kitchen's utility drawer. Then we lugged a covered garbage pail through the basement doors, up the concrete, into the black night. It took one of us gripping each handle to heft the pail: small fetal shapes, pale and slick, filled it to the brim.

We set the pail behind the garage, next to the alley, and I began crying. Our hands clutched each other's. When we reached the kitchen door, I saw by its yellow light that he was crying, too.

Nearly a month later, amid packing, and phone calls to rail stations and airlines and travel agents, I slunk up into Billy's room and placed a long-distance collect call to Duke, who'd never answered my letter.

"Hey, kiddo," Duke said over the giggling, squealing, and lowing of human heifers. "What I miss most about that section of the country's the healthy stench of nature. What's the deal?"

"I'm coming to New York."

"Whoopsy. Let's haul out the old schedule. By the way, Pennsy Turnpike's banned hitchhikers."

"Not riding my thumb." I told him when I'd get there. "What about my pictures, Duke?"

"To use a phrase, ha ha, they came. Think I got them somewhere in my desk. We run on a pretty tight budget around here."

"I'll work for nothing," I said. "I just want people to know who I am."

"Want to snow the chicks, huh?" A mild commotion, the receiver clattered about, Duke grunted, "Easy, kiddo. On the phone. At least let me tap a kidney first . . . Elmo? Look, I've got an awful tight schedule. No time for palaver. What say you give us a buzz when you hit town?"

"Hurry up," a woman's voice.

"Look, kid. Hanging up now. Got to work over a layout." The line died.

None of us had ever flown, so Mr. Pickwick booked us on an airplane. "Never been so excited in my life," he said. "It's like being reborn."

Hazel and her mother charged new wardrobes at the best department store downtown. Hazel called me to the door of her room to model a sleek summer frock, flowery cloth clinging to her tits. "Um, slobber," I said.

I caught Billy on his knees at the foot of his bed, mooning piously before his naked icon. "Elmo, join me in adoration of this daughter of the gods. O Lady, rain thy bountiful goodness upon thy servant, suction him into the thermal sanctuary of thy . . ."

At breakfast on departure day, Mrs. Pickwick said, "I hope everybody isn't expecting too much."

It's a tidal wave of good fortune," Mr. Pickwick said, "crashing upon the beaches of our lives! By the way, I left a key with the Richardses next door. They'll feed what's left in the basement while we're gone."

Gazing into my egg yolk's crystal ball, I too dreamed of fame, riches, a woman's hungry praise.

Except for one black cowhide suitcase, weighing about thirty pounds, which Mr. Pickwick kept beside his bed, the Kaiser had been packed the night before. But when Mr. Pickwick tried to start it, the battery failed. We lost a half hour waiting for a service-station jeep. "Don't let the engine die," the rescuer cautioned. "That battery's got two dead cells."

"All I want to know," Mr. Pickwick asked, "is will it get us to the airport?"

"Sure, like I said, just don't kill it."

Mr. Pickwick crawled behind the wheel. "When we come back, I'll hire a chauffeured Rolls to meet the airplane. I'll—" The Police Emergency Unit, a bakery truck with a whirling red light on top, roared around the corner and past us, siren shrieking.

"—hire a flight of angels," Hazel said. "Come on, Father. We'll miss the plane."

After a fifty-minute drive to the airport, plus ten minutes creeping through the half-mile-square parking lot terrified that Mr. Pickwick would kill the engine and murder the trip, we huddled in the rear of the plane and looked out on its four roaring, belching piston-driven pods.

"We're going to crash!" Billy shouted as we shuddered into position on the runway. "Jesus Christ, here we go!"

I glanced across the aisle. Hazel had propped her feet against the floor, clenched fists in her lap. Her eyelids were puckered shut. Mrs. Pickwick glanced nervously from Hazel to her husband, who gaped happily through the porthole. The expensive black suitcase rested above him, in the rack for hand-luggage.

"Tingles your balls like a Ferris wheel," Billy sighed next to me.

I saw the quiltwork farmland of Ohio and then Columbus, like crabgrass clawing some suburban lawn. Then a turnpike knifed through the choppy green water of tree-foamed mountains. While we ate Swiss steak steamed to mush, a tongue of New York state flowed below our glass-bottomed boat. At last, fore and aft decks jutting skyward, our destination oozed its golden canopy.

"Beautiful!" Mr. Pickwick cried into the engine's throat. "Augustine's golden paradise!"

"Smog," Hazel corrected.

Loping behind the Pickwicks down the rolled-over staircase, I saw a Piper Cub warming its engine nearby, man and woman in the cockpit. The man stepped onto the wing, slipped, stumbled, cartwheeled into his propeller. The airplane bucked like a shotgun. Its engine belched deeply, then built to a smooth roar. The woman grabbed her hair and lifted herself toward the cockpit ceiling.

As we entered the terminal, a siren shrieked. Mr. Pickwick casually asked, "Wonder what that's all about?" I kept my mouth shut.

Buses to the city throbbed outside the terminal. But we piled ourselves and luggage into a taxi whose driver got lost in a tremendous amount of early-evening traffic jamming the labyrinthine route he'd chosen to the Hotel Taft.

Hazel and I got headaches. Billy complained he was "carsick or something." But Mr. Pickwick's excitement grew. "Look at that building! Look at that derelict lying right there in that doorway! Poor fellow doesn't have anyplace else to stay. Wait, isn't that the Chrysler Building? Didn't we pass that ten minutes ago? Boy, that city air's something else."

Our driver honked at pedestrians, at other vehicles, at fellow taxi drivers. In his terrific rush to reach our destination, he raced through intersections as the light changed red. The meter ticked away nickels, dimes, quarters, dollars, a total of $8.70 when we jerked up before the Taft. With difficulty, since the black suitcase filled his lap, Mr. Pickwick tore a ten from his billfold. "Keep the change. When in Rome," he told his frowning wife.

We crawled out on the curb and stood in a hot chaos: engine roar, broken ranks of people, subway vibrations, cold burn of neon reflected from a million glass panes, stench coating the tongue. I saw nothing alive except bared pale faces and hands.

Then I recalled the Piper Cub. In the granite and tile lobby, before the elevators, I reeled and almost fell.

"Easy there." Mr. Pickwick supported my arm with his free hand. The other clutched his cowhide suitcase.

Billy and I occupied a room together, Hazel one by herself, Mr. and Mrs. Pickwick a third. When we regrouped in the adults' room, Mr. Pickwick announced, "I'm going to check in with convention headquarters."

"For heaven's sake, Bob. Can't we at least have dinner first?"

He hefted his suitcase with its precious load. "I want to register this baby and stash it away in the auctioneer's safe. Won't rest easy until I do."

The fruits of our slaughter weighed so little and occupied such small space.

Mrs. Pickwick said, "Oh, go ahead, if you think you have to. Leave the rest of us in peace."

"Sorry, I just can't rest until—it's the first important thing I ever finished."

"Yes, go on, get those nasty pelts out of here!" Mrs. Pickwick cried. "I need aspirin. My head's splitting. Come back when you feel like it."

Mussed from the trip, he shuffled to the door. "Hey, kids," he smiled wanly, "you'll all feel better after a good feed." His eyes appealed to Mrs. Pickwick, but she stared at the gray carpet. Hugging his treasure, he closed the door gently behind him.

Hazel said, "Mother, that was absolutely unnecessary."

"Leave me alone."

"Let's go eat," said Billy.

"Let's all eat," I joined in.

After gorging myself in the hotel dining room—kidney-stuffed double lamb chops, baked potato with sour cream, blue cheese globs dressing the salad, Dutch apple pie with two scoops of ice cream, four cups of coffee—I felt great. "Let's look around this place tonight."

"Not without Bob," Mrs. Pickwick cautioned. "You'd get lost."

"I'll make chalk arrows on the sidewalks to show us the way back," I said. "I'll drop bread crumbs behind us, like Hansel and Gretel."

"I feel terrible about poor Bob." Mrs. Pickwick forked blueberry torte to her lips. "He tries so hard."

"Poor Daddy," Hazel said. "I love him."

Billy said, "What're we waiting for, man? Let's go!"

Hazel announced she was coming, too, and Billy said like hell, and Mrs. Pickwick said don't swear, that Hazel had no business out after dark, weren't some good movies on television? And Hazel said she was bigger than Billy, and besides Elmo knew the ropes, and Mrs. Pickwick said everything was beyond her control, like a herd of wild buffalo.

As soon as we hit the street, Billy went wild. "Yow-wee, man, this is *New York City!*" He whirled and cavorted. A passerby smiled. Hunched over in a flowing black tent which dragged on the concrete, in a pointed dunce cap like a sorcerer's, a little old lady with nutcracker chin and nose paused in his wake and tornadoed a forefinger against her temple.

"What was in that coffee?" Neon glowed on Hazel's face, pleasure burned inside.

The buildings heaved with breath. "Hey!" I cried. "This place is *alive!*"

We walked arm in arm, Hazel caught in the middle. "Fine lady and gentleman," Billy spieled, "this unguided tour is sponsored by the Curb-your-dog Weenie Company, accept no substitutes. On our left, you will observe a plate-glass window with strangers inside eating and drinking. The smiling face in the glass is Miss Pickwick's. The bum at the counter hunched over coffee and crumpled tabloid, that's me. The fifty-story building on our right is toppling in our direction, watch your step. And there is Prince Elmo Hatcher, proud possessor of the roundest mouth in history, advertising blow jobs for camels."

"Bil-ly!"

"Buck Pickwick, lady, if you please, peripatetic stud, the damsel's friend. News of the hour follows: Simulated hydrogen bomb attack destroys sixty-one cities, kills an estimated five million persons"—moving lights girdled the building—"Wall Street executive passes through prop of private aircraft at LaGuardia, remains donated by widow to Nedicks, maker of the burger with the full quarter pound ground meat inside—"

"Did it say that?" Hazel squealed.

"Change, please, for the cripple." Billy paused. A blind man with no legs sat in a hod carrier on roller skates. "The beast eateth its offspring!" Billy gestured about the teeming streets. He pitched a dime into the man's tin cup.

"You hurt his feelings," Hazel scolded.

"Deaf and dumb!" cried Billy, "on a placard about his neck."

A beast swooped from a theater marquee advertising *La Strada.* The black thing whirled silently before our faces, spun upward through the bright haze into darkness. "Bat," I said.

"My God, a mystic experience!" Billy gasped. "Was that a soul flying past?"

"Your tongue," said Hazel, "flapping from your mouth."

A tiny middle-aged man eyed Hazel, ankles to flowing hair. He winked and deeply bowed. Hazel blushed. Beautiful. So was Billy.

We plunged down steps into a subway, haggled our tokens from an exasperated black, raced for the turnstile as a distant train screeched. But the four-leaf clover caught as Hazel attempted to pass. One massive wooden arm jutted up her dress, between her long legs, exposing a soft, white thigh.

"Help, Mr. Policeman!" she piped. "I'm being raped by a turnstile."

Bill and I hoisted her over. We reached the platform as a train pulled out. Billy waved frantically at the last car, where a young girl peered at him through the glass. "Ah, did you see that look? Face like an open white flower in the soot!" He clasped his bony chest and reeled. "Gone! The one true love of my life! Elmo, listen. When do we ring your sister?"

"We could double-date," Hazel suggested.

"I have a whole sonnet sequence knotted up inside my head, waiting to be thrust into her heart."

An express thundered and shrieked. We tumbled through its gaping jaws, nestled swaying in its belly, which disgorged us at Wall Street: buttes and cliffs, lonely deserted pavements.

"Graveyard," I said. "The end of the world."

"Most gorgeous thing I've ever seen in my life," Hazel sighed.

"The last few winking lights," observed Billy, "bosses grinding away their passion on top of moaning secretaries, cushioned by the plush carpets of executive suites."

"Maybe Daddy's up there someplace," Hazel said.

"Oh, to be rich, famous, and in New York!" exclaimed Billy.

"Kiss me, Prince Elmo!" Hazel cried. "On the steps of the Stock Exchange!"

"We'll turn our blushing cheeks aside," Billy chuckled, "for the intercourse of giants."

Arms flew around me, soft mouth mashed mine, her breast cushioned my heart's bump and grind.

"Stock just rose six points," I whispered against her ear.

A half hour later, we sailed without mishap through another turnstile, and stood inside an enormous building. "We're doing everything tonight," Hazel said. "Won't be anything left for tomorrow."

A reeking cloud of muscatel parted momentarily to reveal a husky T-shirted youth loping toward us. "Gu mafa da," he said. He wore a sailor's cap.

"Hey, there, pleased I'm sure," Billy replied.

"Muh fa dum." The young man scowled angrily at Billy's feet.

"Let's scram," Hazel whispered.

"Guff!" The young man powerfully gripped my arm. His bicep, elaborately tattooed in blue with a woman whose legs fused into a serpent's tail, swelled gigantically. The woman's breasts bulged. *"Gavoom!"* Pitching me aside, he vaulted the turnstile and disappeared the way we'd come.

"We're the only sane people here," Billy said.

We leaned against the bow, as the ferry eased vastly into the harbor wash.

"That tang," Billy said. "Ocean! Amazing!"

"This isn't a boat, it's a city!" Hazel cried. "The continent's starting to move."

"There she is!" I pointed toward a numbus of spotlights.

"Can't go up inside her arm any more," Hazel said. "It's cracked."

"Imagine making love to that big woman!" Billy cried. "You'd have to lead with a lantern."

"Imagine making love to any woman," I said.

"I am," he sighed.

"You boys have dirty minds," Hazel scolded, leaning against

the railing while sea breeze wallpapered the dress against her belly and thighs.

"Let's make love to Hazel, Elmo, while her head's turned."

"Yes!" Was it my voice?

Later, in Washington Square, Billy whispered, "Wow, *bohemians!*" We wandered into a smelly maze of side streets, and heard brushed cymbal, piano, vibes, saxophone, jazz labyrinths. Several streets converged in a piazza. Weird couples shouted, gave one another the finger. Leaning against a lamp-post, two women felt each other's breasts. "Wow, lesbians! God, Hazel, for the first time tonight I'm glad you came along. So everybody won't think me and Elmo are a couple of twittering, limp-wristed faggots."

We saw a small theater decorated with life-sized photographs of women. An elderly couple slunk from a limousine and oozed through the glass door.

"Strip joint," Billy said.

"Those aren't women,"said Hazel.

"You're kidding!" Billy protested.

"I can feel it. Because *I'm* a woman."

I saw a creature with blue eyes, heart-shaped face, body naked except for bra and G-string. My own reflection in the glass stared out.

"What's wrong?" Hazel asked me.

We walked arm in arm up Fifth Avenue by Central Park, woods to our left, glacé palaces looming against the dark cool glow of 3 A.M. A taxi braked, hissed on. The boat pond reflected night-blackened foliage, tops of buildings.

Billy said, "That's her address. Up there she's sleeping in that monster's arms!" He dashed across the bald street.

Hazel said, "The last sane person in New York just went berserk."

Billy flattened his front against the building, a gigantic dirty angel food cake. He spreadeagled writhing in agony, clutching limestone. "Goddess!" he moaned. "My queen!"

"We'll all be arrested." Hazel crossed to her brother.

But I looked though shaggy blackness into the vanity glass of pond. Cerulia's palace. I lost control, imagined her up there in the arms of her rich monster, thought of the time I took her, and the night she left when I betrayed her. And bracing my gut against the low wall, I spilled double lamb chop and kidney, blue cheese, and Dutch apple pie into the woods.

•5•

At breakfast next morning, I learned Mr. Pickwick had come in reeling at 4:30 A.M. and fallen asleep fully dressed. When steaming plates of scrambled eggs lay before us, he finally staggered into the dining room, suit crumpled. Haggard, with a fine blond beard and black crescents cushioning his eyes, he glanced about bewildered. The room was nearly empty, but Mrs. Pickwick had to wave before he saw us and shambled over.

"Second honeymoon," Mrs. Pickwick grumped. "We'd better have this out right now."

" First I got lost," he said. "This homosexual on the subway platform—"

"The children!"

"—gave me wrong directions, and I ended up somewhere in Queens. But I groped my way back. Had to jump off the train two stops early, because I was just about to vomit. Walked the couple miles to headquarters—that cleared my head."

"Poor Daddy," Hazel said.

"Yes," he agreed, "that may be the word. Man in charge of numbering and grading lots for auction looked through our pelts."

"My God!" Mrs. Pickwick cried. "What's the matter?"

"I really don't understand. We were following instructions to the letter, weren't we, Elmo?"

"You mean after investing all that money," Mrs. Pickwick began in a tone of wonderment, "you loused up everything just because you were too cheap to hire a professional—"

Billy, Hazel and I stared at our cold, congealing mounds of scrambled eggs.

"Look, I don't know *anything* yet! He just commented, it seemed like a do-it-yourself job, but that it might not make any difference. He didn't say anything definite. I won't know for sure until tonight, at the auction."

"Probably just some joker pretending he's a big man," Billy said.

"Then I saw Tarze Roberts in the lobby. He shook my hand and slapped me on the back, and I told him I was afraid of losing my investment. He said he felt a certain responsibility, since he'd sold me the things in the first place. Maybe if I lost, and it wasn't really my fault, he'd consider bailing me out. He thought it might be fun to bail a little rich boy out of trouble."

"Little rich boy?" Mrs. Pickwick inquired. "Did he say that?"

"His own words. Then he said that too many chinchilla coats seemed to be shedding fur, and it might not matter if I'd done the skinning with a meat-ax. By the way, Roberts asked, How's Prince Elmo? Fine, I said. Take good care of that boy, the man told me. He's a real prize."

"Maybe we should breed *him*," said Mrs. Pickwick.

"What's that supposed to mean?"

"Oh, nothing at all," she sighed. "Continue."

"Then I went into a bar. First time in my life. And I got drunk."

"What on, Daddy?" Hazel asked.

"Think I ordered scotch and tonic. Whatever it was tasted awful. I got the impression people in the bar were laughing at me. After a couple drinks, I realized that my youth was gone."

"*Our* youth," Mrs. Pickwick sighed.

"That I'd wasted our youth chasing swamp fires. I should have played tennis with Billy, taken trips with my wife, paid more attention to Hazel. I have varicose veins from sitting too much. My eyes are going bad, I'm losing my hair. I thought I'd never find the hotel again."

Mrs. Pickwick reached across the table and held his hand. "You poor child." Closing her eyes, she shook her head. "Scotch and tonic?"

Right after breakfast, I called Cerulia. "Those rich women," Billy said, "are never home. After the naked friend of Mom's in the photo got rich, Mom never could reach her. She was always meeting somebody for lunch."

But I tried anyway, while Billy waited tensely.

Cerulia's sleepy voice: "Whozat?"

"Prince Elmo. I'm in New York City."

We decided to eat lunch at the Museum of Modern Art. "It's kinda nice and rural," Cerulia drawled. "I'd have you all up to the place, except my prick husband might barge in, the bastard. Even though I ain't—haven't seen him for two weeks."

"Getting divorced?"

"Naw. He just flies around the world getting laid, while I compare recipes with the butler. Your friend Buck—pretty neat guy?"

Next I reached Duke at his office. "Four this afternoon," he said. "Ain't it nice to have a family in the big city, huh, to cushion the blow? Me and Cissy had one pair of underpants between us when we come, haw haw."

Billy brushed his hair for a quarter of an hour. "Wish I had enough dough for contact lenses."

"You'd be a knockout."

"At least these hornrims make me look smart as I really am. And older. Hello there, Buck, you rugged devil. Let's polish up those strong, even, white teeth."

Hazel insisted, against Billy's objections, on coming along. "I want to meet Prince Elmo's flesh and blood."

"Thought you already did, last night at the Stock Exchange," Billy quipped.

As we lingered outside the cafeteria, Billy yanked a virgin pack of Luckies from his suitcoat, ripped off the top, stuck one into his mouth, and lit up. "Heh heh," he cackled.

Hazel exclaimed, "Child, oh, child!" Then she looked between us in amazement. "I simply don't believe it! The girl over Billy's bed!"

The Lucky plummeted from Billy's mouth, smoking ember smearing ash down his front.

And up flounced Cerulia wearing a little-girl white pinafore dress, pink bow cinched above the waist. Another pink bow gathered her rich hair. Wispy ringlets of innocence circled down her forehead. "Oh, Elmo!" she squealed, embracing me wildly about the neck. "How good you look. Oh, how many years has it been?"

"You look younger," I murmured. "Like a little sister."

Bill trembled another fag between his lips, soaking it at once like a T-shirt armpit. Hazel slowly shook her head.

"And you're a man," Cerulia said. "Strong and fine." Dancing back, she cried vivaciously to Billy and Hazel, "Isn't my brother a gorgeous creature?"

Hazel extended her big hand. "I've been his sister the last few years."

"Yes?" Cerulia's eyes narrowed. "Who is this?"

"Buck Pickwick," Billy croaked. "Uh, hi." Releasing Hazel, Cerulia tenderly took his hand and smiled. "I loved your letters. They seemed so sensitive."

"Uh." Blood invaded his cheeks.

"I didn't know you wrote her," I said.

"The dearest things," said Cerulia. "What I could understand, anyway." She still clung to Billy's paw.

And Billy's whole carriage began changing. Swagger came into his torso though he stood still. The cigarette fit. His shoulder angle, his head's cocky twist, seemed tough, manly. With a smooth easy sweep, a gesture he must have practiced hours in secret before a mirror, he palmed the book of matches to his lip and thumbed himself a light.

"Hey there," said Cerulia.

"Hey there, yourself," Billy replied.

Hazel looked on wide-eyed. Her lips silently formed, "I'll be goddamned."

We lunched outside in the courtyard, near the jutting virile black column of Rodin's *Balzac*. An overcast caged the noon sun. Facing Hazel across the table, Cerulia kept reaching out to touch my hand or Billy's when she spoke. Her knee, like a tall soft cat, kept rubbing mine.

Billy said, "Old Balzac, my hero! Locked himself in a little closet sixteen hours a day, drank coffee like a fiend, and wrote. Art, that was the main thing in his life."

"He looks so energetic." Cerulia's fingertips brushed the back of Billy's hand. "He reminds me, well, of a bull."

"Moo for her, Billy," Hazel said.

"He carried on a rich and varied love life by mail," replied Billy in his new worldly basso. "Now Rodin—his models became his mistresses. To sculpt the human body, he needed to touch flesh."

"Even Balzac's?" Hazel asked.

"Aw c'mon, Rodin wasn't any fag."

"Wish you'd speak normally," Hazel said.

"That's my little sister for you."

"She looks enormous," Cerulia said. "By the way, honey, are you Billy or Buck?"

"Buck."

"Ever sculpted anybody, Prince Elmo?" Cerulia flashed a little-girl smile, brushed my hand, pressed my knee.

"Just an amateur painter."

"Your new sister here looks like a little old live-in model."

"You bet," Hazel said. "I never have been able to keep my clothes on around Prince Elmo."

"By the way, honey, what did you say your name was?"

"Mona Lisa," Hazel replied.

"Well, I've posed for a few artists in my time," Cerulia looked coyly down. Billy swallowed convulsively, and the planes in his face shifted.

Hazel said, "We own one especially artistic pose."

"Don't you like me, honey?"

"Not particularly."

"Well, honesty makes up for a lot of failings."

"Why don't you just beat it, Hazel," Billy said.

"Thanks, I'll do what I please."

"That picture," Cerulia said, "I'd never do it again. I was poor. Getting it done wasn't bad, though. Photographer was a lovely man."

"Oh," moaned Billy.

I realized my napkin was shredded in my lap. "What the hell's going on, Cissy?" I asked. "I mean, you used to wear dresses that looked like feedsacks and say ain't and—I don't know. Now you dress like an angel and talk like a cocktail party."

"Everything changes, honey."

"And you're married to some damn plutocrat."

"There was a rich man then, too," she said, as napkin fragments sifted between my knees to the cobblestones. "And I still slip and say ain't. But you take me back to old times, Prince Elmo. They wasn't all bad."

Her eyes, her touch closed a circuit of corruption and I wanted to throw over the world, and run with her down imaginary roads, with only the clothes we had on now, and escape backward to our source.

"We always was mighty close," Cerulia said, "me and Prince Elmo. Are you and Hazel close, Buck?"

Billy gave me a puzzled look. "She's just my sharp-tongued sister," he said.

"Has Prince Elmo ever said anything about what his life used to be like?"

"He doesn't enjoy talking about it," Hazel snapped.

"There was good things," Cerulia said. "Sometimes they come back, when the bad just seems to melt away. Ever swim in the Gorge now, Elmo? That was the purest water in the world. We ate crap and froze our butts off during winter. But life seems awful free back then, when I think about it now, cooped up breathing smelly air in these dumb buildings."

"I never go back," I said.

"Sort of let your new life take your whole self over, huh, Prince Elmo? Just let the old things go hang."

"Yeah." I felt a great swelling beyond my control. "Like you and Duke. The way you both took off without giving me a thought, and never a letter, never a glance behind. I haven't forgotten that, Cissy."

"Duke made me."

"He never did. You wanted to."

"That ain't fair."

"Sure. And you never came back for Grampa's funeral, or wrote Helen in her trouble. And never called for *me!*"

"Lay off her, buster," Billy commanded. "Brother or no brother, I see a guy right here who never visits his mom, never visited his grandmother before she died, never gave a damn about calling his own sister till I forced him."

"You big baby!"

"Calm down," Cerulia said. "That guard's looking at us."

"Probably giving you the eye," Hazel said. "Don't all men?"

"Honey, you wouldn't know if they flashed it six feet five inches high."

"Great family reunion," I said.

"For you and Hazel," said Billy sullenly. "Thick as thieves. She insults your real sister, and you egg her on."

"Look, twirp—" I rose.

"Sure, go ahead. You got me a bullet in the back, friend. It's like having a goddamn rattlesnake in my room."

Leaning toward Cerulia, propping splayed fingers on the table, I hissed, "You little whore. You look so innocent and fresh, and every opening in your body oozes slime."

In a bright little voice, holding back tears, Cerulia replied, "They gave you a good home, but you just went rotten."

"I want to kill you," hearing my words before I knew I spoke.

"Sweet Jesus," Billy whispered.

Cerulia was crying. Even the fear in her wet eyes seemed delectable.

I pulled myself up straight. "I'm leaving, friends. Bye bye, Cissy. Buck, old boy. So long, Hazel."

I walked back inside the building.

Hazel breathless at my elbow. "Elmo, come back." We headed toward the angry, gleaming lobby. "*Please* don't let her have Billy."

I stopped then.

"Even if she is your sister, you know what she is. Please, help me stop her."

I shook my head stupidly. "She wouldn't."

But already we were running. Afternoon blazed like a phoenix now, and the table stood empty.

"Oh, *no!*" Hazel cried.

"What's the fuss?" I spat. "It's his piece of ass."

Hazel clenched her fists. "Oooh, I hate this city! All at once I decide I don't like your sister. So I keep jabbing like a catty little bitch and drive Billy right into her damn bedroom."

"He's a virgin, too," I said.

"God, it's like incest."

We meandered to the second floor, talking to keep our minds off other things.

"Back at the Gorge, people did pretty much what they felt like. If you wanted something, you stole it. If you wanted to screw, you screwed."

"But you came out all right—like somebody who went through so much he became a saint. You didn't take advantage of me."

"Some saint," I snorted. "Must have been born with natural morality in my bones—like the way I can doodle. Where that came from's another mystery."

"And where it's going?"

"In a couple hours, I'll sell it to my brother. It's a natural quirk, like being able to lick your own nose."

Then we looked at a real picture. "He couldn't draw," I said.

"Isn't it supposed to look like a child's work?"

"He wasn't trying to paint like a child, any more than a child tries to paint like a child. That's my opinion."

"What's she dreaming about?" Hazel asked.

"She's not. Rousseau's dreaming up that nice world in the picture. For instance, the lion's vegetarian. He'll admire the woman because she's beautiful. She's vegetarian, too. No butchers or police. Everybody's naked. People and animals go around touching each other. They even feel like screwing the ground."

"Oh, honestly! Anyway, you've got it backward. It's a world where *nothing* touches. The lion just doesn't care enough about the woman to eat her. The woman's naked because she can't afford clothes. She's sleeping in the woods, because she's kicked out of the house. And she's asleep—as far as she's concerned, the outside world isn't there. Maybe she's dead."

"Well. It doesn't make any difference. I had a feeling once, in a cave, that I'd like to paint, because I thought it did make a difference. Everything kept changing and coming together at the same time."

"Were you hungry?" Hazel asked. "Sometimes low blood sugar can cause a mystic experience."

"Then maybe that's my ticket—starvation. Cerulia and Duke

dreamed of wealth; now they've got it. And Billy—wild with sex. Today he gets the girl over his bed. And your father—peeling dollars off the backs of animals."

"Then there's Mother," Hazel went on, "like a capped Coke that's been heated. Pop her top and she'll blow all over the place. That's her dream: exploding."

"What about Hazel?"

"Oh, she doesn't want much. Just a big rotbox for the world, so she can wire it back together. I'm kind of depressed. I don't excite you much, Elmo. You're a sweet old fellow, but I get the message."

"No more fights."

"I wish I was the most incredibly sexy girl anywhere. But I'm big and gawky and skinny. If I were somebody else, we wouldn't be spouting all this crap right now."

"Come on."

"A minute ago, I said you didn't take advantage of me. Hell, who wants to be impaled on a kneecap? I'm sick of being bright, it's a pain in the ass. Why did *my* pituitary have to go haywire? I'm so miserable!" she wailed. "I'm going to jump off the Brooklyn Bridge."

She stalked away. I looked about, thankful nobody else had heard, not even a guard.

•6•

A penthouse complex on Fifth Avenue, near the Village, housed *Scamp*. I walked the whole distance, and while pavement scarred my feet, a gorgeous phalanx of women blistered my eyeballs. There seemed to be plenty of models, lean and tight-skinned, with regular plastic features. How could bodies breathe through that plaster makeup? I kept trying to snatch a smile and failed.

Next to Duke's building, a restaurant spewed onto the sidewalk. People sat at little round tables, under beach umbrellas. They sipped drinks, picked at food, and watched people who walked past. I watched a few of them watch me. At the curb, an elegant lady's poodle shit into the gutter.

The guard looked me over, took my name, telephoned. "Okay, mister. Elevator to forty."

Creamy pastels inside the elevator, and unnatural, rich blues and reds. The operator fingered a small square plaque. Without seeming to depress at all, it lit, doors slipped together, the elevator whirred.

"Penthouse," he muttered. Open Sesame.

Girls, the quintessence of those in the street, leaned against blue-and-gold corridor walls, bent over drinking fountains, lounged in swivel chairs, undulated through red swinging doors. All wore the same uniform, an ermine bikini. Fragrance, soprano murmur, squeals of hysteria. The receptionist's plastic desk was more transparent than glass. Red letters on its front: LOOK, DON'T TOUCH!

Smiling, luxuriously crossing her legs for my eyes, she sighed a little "Yes?"

"Hatcher."

"Wait here." Rising, she undulated down the corridor, past a pair that Indian-wrestled foot to foot, giggled, twitched buttocks, jiggled bosoms. Reaching the last red door, the receptionist knocked, then looked inside and motioned me along. An Indian wrestler tumbled across my path. "Hey, you, come relax me!" I stepped over.

Duke lounged behind an enormous desk. He looked dry and small, and though in his early twenties, he seemed at least forty. He was talking on one of four desk telephones. "Yeah, old buddy. We'll cream the bitch." Motioning me into a straight-backed chair, he cradled the receiver. "Hey, it's Prince Elmo."

"Hey, Duke."

He lifted another receiver. "Baby, bring in the hooch." Cradled it. "Room service. Nobody round here wants for nothing."

I couldn't restrain myself. "Wow! Man, Grampa would've loved it here. This is paradise!"

"Tickles the old tastebuds, don't it?"

A doll with fur on her ass and tits wheeled her tray through the door. Bottles and glasses jingled. "Hafta do something about the air conditioning," Duke remarked. "The chicks sweat. Turning into a locker room. Go for a dip, baby."

"Yessir." She left.

"Show you the pool sometime. I swim with the chicks, when I'm not working my ass off."

"Nothing to drink, thanks."

"Eighteen-year-old scotch. Burn the stuff for energy. So. Guess we ought to hug and kiss or something, huh?" A phone clanged. "The Duke . . . Sure, Freddyboy, we'll send a check out—when you layout bastards turn in something that doesn't make me vomit." He flattened the receiver. "If we ain't gonna smooch, let's shake paws." We shook across the vast cherrywood expanse of desk. "First time you ever saw me in a suit, huh? Dig this tie. Oriental silk. Fifty bucks. Got maybe fifteen like it."

"Great view." I pointed over his shoulder through the picture window.

"That's the Hudson. Bet you'd rather see the view in the hall, hey? Takes a few months outside the boonies before you develop taste, you know what I mean? It even took me a while. But now it's hard to remember how life was."

"Where'd all this come from?"

A smile tightened flesh over his powerful chin, and he tapped his temple. "Out of the old skull. I probably got the highest natural I.Q. in the city, and more energy than all its goddamned power plants. Understand your new father's a prof."

I nodded.

"I got ten profs wiping my ass, figuratively speaking. And thanks partly to you, we didn't have two hundred bucks when we started out, not knowing which way off the train, nothing. Prince Elmo, how come you fucked up that night?"

"Smoking dope. I finally woke up on the roof."

"Well, everything worked out. And that guy, the one you didn't rob"—Duke thumped his desktop—"he's sunk plenty in this little venture."

"That character has his finger in every pie."

"Sure. He's no silver-spoon-in-the-mouth dumbass like

Whitman." Duke looked around conspiratorially. "Hope the idiot doesn't have this place bugged. This magazine's the first thing he's done right since getting born rich. Christ, a poor boy like me just naturally hates some bastard who's had it all from the start. Cissy and I played with him like pussy swallowing mousie. At first, I hired out for common labor. Garbage collector, fried hamburgs, developed ass calluses on a highchair in one of those Forty-second Street smut joints making sure customers didn't bust seals on the trash or jag off in the store. Then I hired out as stockboy on this mag before I made it into *Scamp.* So I spot this imbecile Whitman and begin edging in, suggesting, and get made supervisor. In addition to being a total jagoff, Whitman has this weakness for marrying and divorcing chicks, so then I play my queen. Receptionist job opens, so I get Cissy all dolled up—you know how innocent she makes herself look—"

"Don't need to hear the rest. When Jerk divorces her, what happens to you?"

Duke tapped his temple again. "All thought through."

"I'm impressed. But right now I'm mainly interested in making a deal."

"You're a talented kid, Prince Elmo. Problem is, do you have the right sort of talents for us?"

"I'll dance to any tune."

"I got artists beating down the door, guys who graduated art school. But I tell them, go scrape your pen across a bathroom wall. We're building fantastic circulation, Prince Elmo. I give you a break, you make it fast. What I'm thinking about is a foldout that's drawn instead of photographed. You can improve on a real woman only so far—makeup, stuff injected into the boobs, caps on the teeth. It's still a real woman, and a guy might think, Hey, I'm getting something like this back home in my creaking sweaty bed, why buy a mag and jag off? See the problem?

"Now what I got in mind is pictures of chicks so unbelievably fantastic you won't find them anywhere—and yet they ain't from outer space. Perfect, only they ain't real women. Get it?" He lifted two phones at once. "Of course, this ain't just a cockbook we're marketing— Hi, the Duke. Kid brother's here. Bring the coloring book. Now!—Rachel baby?" into the other phone. "Carry it all up to my office." He banged them both down. "We're trend-setters. All the latest gadgets and styles in our ads, things people don't even know they want yet. We're into politics, the best causes. Took a stand to integrate schools. One of these days, I'm even putting a nigger into the centerfold. You'd be surprised, the number of women reading us to find out what men want."

"But mostly men buy the magazine to masturbate."

"Nothing wrong with that," Duke said. "We ran a article by some schmuck Ph.D., who called it the greatest indoor sport of all time. Relieves tension. No emotional involvement. Unless people fall in love with their own paws, heh heh. You know what Charles Goren says, you don't need a good fuck if you got a good hand."

A knock, the door swung open, a little man in tight checked pants came in. He deposited a large drawing pad on the desk, pastels, charcoal, watercolors in tubes, and left. "So long, Mary," Duke called after him. "Mary's a fag," he explained. "We're running an editorial next month, supporting the homosexual movement in America. Those guys have the most beautiful imaginations. You can learn a lot about style from a fag."

A person in the standard ermine bikini waltzed in without knocking. The rest surpassed anything I'd seen. Long and incredibly curly blond hair swooshed back, as though a strong wind blasted her face. She was a taller, more powerful Barbie Wilson—a sleeked-down, full-breasted Jean Harlow. Muscles gently rippled beneath her soft flesh.

"Rachel's the best in the joint," Duke explained.

"Who's Mr. America?"

"Kid brother, Prince Elmo. Stand up in the lady's presence, boy."

"All biceps and gonads," Rachel commented. "Why don't we take off our clothes?"

"Rachel's a college grad. Also, she's a kike."

"My father was a moyle," Rachel said, flouncing about the room. "Rabbi Smegma, better known as the Prepuce Kid. Sold head cheese on the side."

"Wait a minute," I said, "run that by again."

"I'll spread it on toast if you like."

"Settle down, Rachel. This is just another job assignment."

"I'm the magazine's Girl Everything. Right now, it's staging a theatrical event to impress the kid brother."

"You're a dick specialist," Duke said. "Whenever you start talking my ears fill up."

"Probably with filth," Rachel said. She stretched, raising her breasts, flattening her lean torso, reeking sweetly of perfumed flesh. "Do I peel off?" she yawned.

"We never photograph that hairy thing," Duke said. "It's ugly."

"The real reason's because we're all female impersonators," Rachel leered. "Those poor straight johns hacking off."

"If you're not a woman," I said, "I'm leaving."

"First nude model?" Duke asked.

"Yes." I worked fast, charcoaling her movements as she reached behind her back. "Always work from imagination, or memory."

"Mammary?" Rachel dropped her top pelt to the carpet. "I'm especially proud of the nipples. Pink and small. Not shot full of brown like a giraffe's nose."

"Too abstract," Duke commented over my shoulder. "Don't like it."

"Give him a chance. Elmo, darling—is that your name?—looky here."

I gasped.

"I trim it," she teased. "So fresh and neat."

"Oh, settle down!" Duke yelled.

"But doll, you said make his eyeballs pop."

I dropped the charcoal.

"I'm bored just standing here. Why doesn't somebody feel me up?"

"You know the policy around here. Let the kid work. He has one hell of a knack. But you can tell she's got pores, lets off human odors. Just what I want to avoid."

"Duke sublimates everything into work," Rachel taunted.

"Wait and see," Duke threatened. "My biggest problem is, I fuck too well."

"Now. Look," I said.

"The crotch is really criminal," Duke insisted. "You simply got to hide it, Prince Elmo."

I slashed a two-edged crusader's sword diagonally across her.

"What a amazon!" Duke exclaimed. "All muscle and gold hair, ready to trim your nuts."

Rachel stirred warm air behind me. "I'm always proud to take part in cultural events."

"Want to show Mary," Duke said. "Back in seconds."

A breast nudged my nape.

"Feel my ass," she murmured. "Fine, go ahead, do that, too. But we can't do it here. And there's a guy in my apartment. It isn't fair, all these locked-up desires. Anybody you can work them off on?"

Duke barged in. "You two stop that!" Rachel sauntered to the doorjamb and lounged. "We hype up your creative energy around here!" Duke cried. "What you do with it later is your own fucking business. But don't make a mess here." Then, "Mary likes ya, kid."

"She'd *love* him," Rachel purred.

"We're giving you this contract. You either sell to us or through us. Sole buyer, sole agent. Only contract we offer, take it or leave it."

"How does it feel to screw your own brother?" Rachel asked.

As if palming from his sleeve, Duke produced the paper. It sifted to my throbbing lap, and in an erotic delirium, I signed.

"You'd never of gotten this fantastic break if you wasn't my blood brother."

Rachel tiptoed, gathering her white pelts off the rug. "Before I package the American dream," she announced, "I'll give it a warm-Coke douche."

I staggered onto the dusk street. Traffic crammed together unmoving. Red lights trapped cars bumper to bumper, constipating intersections. Horns screamed like the maimed.

A trapped Plymouth, windows shut tight, crowded the curb. Behind its wheel, a man strained his mouth wide open and pounded the shoulder of a well-dressed lady huddling against the far door.

The light said "Walk"; I crossed into an intersection. A black woman gunned her Buick at me. Children, overflowing the back seat, howled. I barely dodged the crazed charge and slammed against a mailbox.

The logjam gradually broke. Sore and weak, I mounted a crowded uptown bus and dipped my ass toward its one empty seat—when I saw a little old cane-carrying man and started to offer the seat to him. In he darted, snarling like a mongoose crushing a cobra's skull, and elbowed me violently out of his way. As I teetered in the aisle for balance, he rammed my belly with his cane. An old lady glared furiously. "You might have given it to him without a fight!" she snapped.

I clung to an upright metal pole as the bus stopped again, and a cripple climbed slowly aboard.

"You can't come on this bus!" the driver shouted.

"Fuck you!" the cripple shouted back. "I'm getting on this bus!"

The driver screamed, "You can't bring those crutches on this bus, you bastard! Get off of here!"

A lady seated behind the driver shouted, "Can'tcha see you're holding up the bus? Get the hell off!"

"Give it gas!" a man thundered. The driver pushed his handle, the doors started shut. But the cripple jammed his crutch between them. *"Let me on this bus!"* he shrieked.

A man near me muttered, "I'm going to smash that son of a bitch. I'm going to slit his guts."

The driver killed his engine, stood, and faced his passengers. "Breakdown!" he shouted, "Everybody clear the bus!"

Grumbling and snarling, we shuffled for the exits. A lady bopped the cripple with her purse. "Dirty inconsiderate bastard!" she shouted.

The cripple fell on his back against the curb between two cars. Somebody had thrown one of his crutches inside the bus. The lady kicked the other under a parked car. "Help me, I can't get up," the cripple said. I felt like wringing the bastard's neck.

Sweating from the thick soupy air, I felt a bumper nudge my leg. An old lady's Chevrolet had stopped too slowly for the red light, and I whirled and began hewing her hood with my fists. Then I bashed my shoe sole against her grill. Moving around, I kicked the driver's door hard. "Watch where you're going, you old bitch!" The light changed. But I landed a good violent one on the trunk before she scooted off.

I stormed into the Taft. Finally an elevator yawned. Midway across the lobby, somebody was running. "Hold the doors!" he cried. I pressed the "close" button and through the narrowing crack saw him shuffle to a halt.

Billy grimly contemplated gray shapes on the television.

"Thought you'd still be dipping your wick," I said.

He kept watching the fuzzy screen.

"Couldn't you get it up?"

Silence.

"Did she blow you and make you vomit, or what?"

"Lay off."

"Hey, Billy, how was that good old first piece?"

"Look, man, I'm sorry. Okay?"

"I know, you went off in your pants and spent the day apologizing. While my reeking whore of a sister entertained you, telling about this or that stud with the V-8-engine-powered ass and the really big cock, who reamed her smooth."

Rising, he heaved a glass. I ducked, and it broke against the wall.

"You bet I fucked her!"

"Liar," I shot back.

He fell moaning on the bed, face buried in the pillow. "Oh, Jesus! I'm sick with guilt! Oh, man, I'm sorry. Help me out of this!"

"Even I fucked her, Billy." I had clubbed him before I knew the weapon was in my hand.

"What?" Picking his glasses from the mattress, thrusting them on, he wide-eyed me.

"Fucked—Cerulia."

"I don't understand." He sat bewildered on the hotel-room bed. Then he charged me red and roaring, flailing his thin arms. I planted my palm against his forehead, but he slipped under. His fist hooked my jaw. "Yahhhhhh!" Billy lay writhing on the floor, and I spat on him.

He wore suit trousers, shoes, and a T-shirt. Coat, white

shirt and tie lay crumpled on the floor. His glasses peeked from under the bed. He crawled on his stomach, reached up, opened the door, pulled himself through, and staggered blindly down the hallway.

At 6 A.M., just after Mr. Pickwick staggered in again dead drunk, police phoned Mrs. Pickwick. Around three that morning two cops had parked their patrol car before an all-night diner on Lexington. While they drank coffee and waited at the counter for hamburgers, one of them watched through the plate glass as Billy tugged open the patrol car's back door and pissed onto the seat.

•7•

At first Billy refused to leave his cell or talk to anybody he knew. "Says his whole life is finished," explained the desk sergeant, a bald man with thick, hairy forearms and a raw whisker-shadow where scraps of toilet paper still soaked blood. "Maybe his old man can talk him out. Where is he?"

"His father," Mrs. Pickwick icily announced, "is incapacitated."

"Can't let you ladies back there. Maybe his brother here—"

"I wouldn't be any help," I said.

"Does he have enough blankets to keep warm?" Hazel asked.

"Girlie, all he has is a smoothed plank, scooped out a little where his behind lays. Too many new guys use blankets to hang themselves. We even took away his belt."

Mrs. Pickwick, Hazel, the desk sergeant, and I remained alone in the room—until Tarze Roberts walked in.

"Are you a lawyer?" the sergeant asked.

"No, but *my* lawyer's on the way over right now." He dropped a name.

"Oh," sighed the sergeant, staring down at his blotter. "Anyway, it was a pretty disrespectful thing to do."

Roberts left the sergeant staring at his blotter. "We'll have him out in ten minutes," he assured Mrs. Pickwick. "There won't be a spot on his record, I promise."

"It's all happening too fast," she said. "I didn't come along last night. Bob wouldn't have let me if I wanted to. Did he lose it all?"

"He had a lot of company," Roberts consoled her, smiling, bald pate gleaming, blue summer suit tailored and pressed. "Including me. First bad investment I ever made. You can't imagine how embarrassed I feel. Couple years ago, everything pointed toward a real killing. Otherwise, of course, I'd never have recommended—" Suddenly he beamed and reached for my hand. "Prince Elmo! It was so good of you to phone me this morning. It's been so long!"

Gritting my teeth, I shook with him.

In breezed a fat man with a thick, wiry shock of gray hair. He carried an attaché case. "Back in a sec," Roberts said.

"Wait." I handed him a pair of glasses. "Get them to Billy."

"Everything is so incredibly awful," Hazel said. "I don't want to live through the day."

Mrs. Pickwick tightened her lips. "Maybe it's not so bad. Maybe we needed something like this all along."

"Mother!"

"I don't mean your poor brother. But now maybe your father will come to his senses. And maybe your grandparents will come to theirs. Because I'll tell you one thing"—she looked Hazel, then me, in the eyes—"I've come to mine."

The lawyer and the sergeant left the room, and Roberts returned to where we stood. "They're going in right now to unlock him. Jack will talk to the night-court judge. You have to sign something. And that'll be that."

"His father should have been here to handle this," said Mrs. Pickwick. "I can't thank you enough."

"Nonsense. It was the least I could do."

"Right," I said. "The least."

"Now, here's a pleasant surprise. I'm inviting you and your husband, and even your children, to a party I'm throwing this evening for a few close friends. In my brownstone. I only use it to entertain when I'm in the city." He gave a Village address. "You need to unwind."

"I'd love that," Mrs. Pickwick said. "Ever since we came,

I've been cooped up in that awful hotel room, watching television and worrying about those disgusting chinchillas."

"You're a beautiful woman. You deserve better."

"Yes," Mrs. Pickwick agreed.

During the taxi ride from the jail, Billy refused to speak—until Mrs. Pickwick mentioned the party. "Fuck it," he said. "I did all my unwinding last night."

Mrs. Pickwick did not correct his language.

Back at the hotel, I hung around the lobby alone, moving aimlessly among sand-filled ashtrays.

"Elmo, listen." Hazel. "What's happening? Billy won't tell me."

"Who gives a damn?"

"You were such good friends. We all were."

"Hazel, will you beat it?"

"All right. I just want to tell you something, in case you think you're some kind of innocent in all this mess. I don't know how, but you're partly responsible."

"Like everybody else," I said.

"Isn't that Roberts a disgusting hypocrite? Elmo, I'm not sure I like you any more." She walked away.

Later, pausing to unlock my room, I heard voices through the door across the hall. "We're going to that party, mister. If you don't, I'm going anyway, alone! I intend to get *some* pleasure out of all this miserable business."

"Look at me. How can you talk about pleasure?"

"You threw me the key, mister. *You!* Now I'm going to unlock my cage."

The hell with it, I thought. Maybe Billy was in my room. I couldn't face anybody right now. So I walked the city until it bored me, then, on Forty-second Street, saw an old Bogart movie twice. Bogart escaped from Devil's Island to fight Germans and at the film's climax machine-gunned several Hun off the wing of their plane, which he'd shot into the ocean. He was angry because they'd strafed his ship and killed some faggy-looking kid. At the end, Bogie gave a patriotic speech looking dead-on into the camera. The *Marseillaise* boomed in the background.

Roberts' brownstone was in fact two connected brownstones with the separating wall knocked out. Mounting the steps I noticed, across the street in Washington Square Park, a bearded muscular Nature Boy, bare-chested, in leotards, doing handstands and pushups. He was standing on his head just as the artificial lights went on.

A guard inside the door checked my name against a list, and said, "Down the hall, mister, past the staircase, and get your shot."

"Shot?"

"Doc's set himself up in the can. Ain't you ever been to one of these blasts?"

A perpetual 4 A.M. gloomed inside. I touched the crimson wallpaper: chintz. Farther in, the bathroom door opened on a blaze of fluorescent light. A goateed little fat man sat on the toilet's pink pouf cover, and a bottle of Merthiolate stood beside a box of cotton balls on the tank. On a stand next to the lavatory gleamed a tray holding rows of plastic-encased needles. He fingered the large hypodermic in his palm.

"What's this all about?"

"Skin." He fitted a needle to the syringe and filled it halfway from one serum bottle. From a second bottle he filled it full, then squirted the ceiling.

"Hospital or party?"

"This," he lifted a bottle, "makes you healthy. And this," lifting another, "makes you high. Vitamins, amphetamine."

"You're really a doctor."

"If anybody at Yale told me I'd be doing this, I'd have said he was wacko. I get paid more shooting dope into rich asses in one night than most G.P.'s make in a year."

"Nobody sticks needles in my ass."

He pointed to a rubber stamp and pad. "Nobody gets upstairs till he's processed. I stamp your hand with fluorescent ink, you hold it under ultraviolet light. No needle, no stamp; no stamp, no party. Man, you will really fly."

"Oh, what the hell."

A freezing touch, a pop like icepick through inner tube, searing pain.

"How was Cal last night?" asked a woman behind me.

"Very sweet," another answered.

"Give that about a minute," the doctor told me. "Ladies, you'll just have to hoist your skirts again. But I'm a doctor. It won't affect me."

"Oh, shoot," one pouted.

The doctor stamped my wrist.

"Should we spread our legs?"

I brushed past into the crimson hallway and headed upstairs. On the third or fourth step, cupped hands hefted my ass to the top. I turned. Nobody. On my wrist a number briefly glowed 7/4/58. "Okay, you're in."

A crowd milled about the enormous room in slow motion. I'd never seen people in less rush—odd, since many whirled about in a manner suggesting violent, chaotic motion, arms above head, fast-dancing to a band which played rock music at what seemed to me a bafflingly slow tempo. I felt impatient. Distances seemed incredibly great. I gave the wainscoting a hard kick, and pain took eons traveling from toes to skull. Something slapped my face. My hand.

"Enjoying your new life?"

Turning from the wall, I noticed a slender, bald man, pale carp floating motionless in its tank. "Which one?"

"The stable new home you've been living in the last three or four years." Bubbles rose from his mouth. "Don't you recognize me?"

After staring an hour, I asked, "Why isn't anything touching the floor?"

"Beg your pardon?"

"Downstairs. I lost the key to my engine."

"You're in quite a state. You were like this when Barbie caught you sawing fixtures from my john."

"Couldn't turn the hot on," I said. "It kept speaking French." Seeing his puzzlement, I tried a further explanation: "All these colored lights ooze onto your guests. They might sue."

"Oh." He smiled. "You can't predict how it'll affect different people. How's the artwork?"

"One of these days I'll dig through to China," I answered. "Right now, nothing mixes. I keep trying to eat that cake. It's hard to see the difference between men and women, you know?

Like screwing your own mother. I'm trying to figure out, does that bring things together, or pull them apart?"

"Deep problem," he said. "Wait a while before your booster, okay?"

"How'd you get out of prison?"

"I'm not Billy," he said. "Or do you think I'm Helen?"

"Don't know."

"Remember the cuckoo? How it lays eggs in other birds' nests?"

"Always did wonder how you survived," I mused. "You like to go slumming."

"At every chance," he laughed, aging instantly. "And I wish you success in your career, whatever it may be. Now I must corrupt a few choice guests. We'll see each other soon, I hope."

I found myself facing a blond, athletic young man. We both talked at once, so I pointed, meaning, "You talk." But our fingers met; rather, I touched the thick glass separating us. We shrugged. We moved on.

A familiar gentleman slumped on a sofa.

"You're depressed." I sat beside him.

"Stupid enough to get shot with that stuff," he said. "Look, that goddamn Prospero of chaos fiddling around over there! I'm in a roaring funk, but I'm damned glad Billy and Hazel didn't come."

"Who?"

He gazed through smog-filled twilight into my eyes. "You shouldn't have come here," he said. "As your guardian, you know, I'm responsible."

"In a manner of speaking," I replied, "it turns out that I'm your father." People grew roots down into the floor. "No wonder they can't move fast," I observed.

"Moving so fast they'll all have coronaries. Elmo, man—get hold of yourself. Whoooooh!" Green wind rushed from his lungs. "This is the good life. Freedom. Look how happy. Careful what you want—you'll get it."

"I've got two heads," I commented, "and enough fetal parts to make me think you're going to have twins."

"America the beautiful." He indicated the slow-motion forms. "Frenetic, whirling frenzy."

"Used cars," I added. "Bones."

"Have you seen Anne?" He frantically gripped my arm. "Have you seen my wife?"

I'd stepped into some sort of bedroom. "Pardon me. Looking for the river."

"Come to the right place." Lean and pretty. Her head touched my shoulder. Freckles clouded the bridge of her nose, her hair was brown, half her bosom spilled up over her gown's low cut. "But it's occupied."

Her tongue swelled to a cylinder, tip squirming against the roof of my mouth. Then I rammed a tongue into an ear. "Wild man." We grappled. "Lift me up."

Bare shoulders against the wall, silver-gray cloth mushroomed above her waist. Chin against collarbone, brown churning sea of crotch. Palms under soft thighs. "Christ." Bone grinding bone, creamy velvet thrashing against the wall, breath all tobacco. "Harder." Bones jellied inside the soft pelt sagging over my shoulders.

She lay limply against the wall, open fork wet like her mouth. "Now me." I faced a red triangle, white full thighs. Red hair, soft bed of tongue, knelt at my feet. Inside a rocking horse, soft rockers in my hands, two hard, dry pebbles rake my chest. On my back, submerged in a salt sea, "He's a workhorse." Hot whirlpool sucks me in. Mattress groans like a man holding a power line. "They still going to it?"

Lurching free, I peer upon a locker room of flesh, at naked women draped exhausted against floor and walls. A whole male platoon casts off clothes—as an old bald man charges through. He shoves me savagely aside. Puffs of gray hair shag each shoulder blade. Liver spots mottle his bony back. Snarling like a panther, he piles on top of the woman on the bed, broom-handle frame pressing into her plump softness. Sweating, giggling, she greets him and everybody else, and squeals. "My energyyyyy!" Red hair spills like blood from her head.

•8•

We sailed back across the sunny continent—the green sea of farmland, the vague cities—in a flagship of death. Nobody spoke. Nothing of me lay "out there" except the scattered, digested, and absorbed fragments of a forgotten child. Though once, for a minute or so, I was distracted by a faint halo about the propellers.

We struggled our bags the whole blazing distance across the lot to where we'd parked the Kaiser. Mr. Pickwick turned his key in the ignition, but nothing happened. "Fuck this goddamned thing," he snarled. Beside him in the fiery front seat, Mrs. Pickwick pressed her temple against the rolled-up window and sobbed gently into her hands.

It took an hour for a garage truck to bring the new battery. After Mr. Pickwick cursed other drivers for fifty tedious miles, we came to Goldengrove and the ivy-covered brick house. Its front door stood wide.

"Goddamn neighbor forgot to lock the place," Mr. Pickwick said.

Entering, I noticed a penciled scrawl, like a backward F, on the doorframe.

"Anything missing?" Billy asked.

"Bastard should have burnt down the house," Mr. Pickwick snarled.

"What's this?" Bending, Mrs. Pickwick lifted a delicate object from the living-room rug, a kind of sculpture from two hair-thin wires twisted together at the center, dovetailing, a double V. "Vacuum must have missed it last time I cleaned."

"Animals seem alive and well," Hazel called from the basement.

"Fuck the animals!" Mr. Pickwick shouted back.

In the dining room, a piece of red yarn hung delicately draped over a chair arm. "Call the cops," Mr. Pickwick said.

"But nothing's missing," his wife protested. First she tried phoning the neighbors, but nobody answered. "We must all be getting paranoid," she said and phoned the police.

"Getting what?" Mr. Pickwick asked when she hung up. "Laid?"

Two policemen arrived to inspect the house. "You must be imagining things," one said, "if that's all you noticed.

Billy called loudly from upstairs, "Officers!"

I followed their blue butts.

In our room, Billy gestured toward his pinup of Cerulia. "You could get arrested for drawing filth onto a picture already that filthy," one policeman commented.

"I'm innocent!" Billy argued.

"But there's no evidence of a break-in."

"Let's take one more look at that door," said his partner.

Downstairs a cop shut the front door, thumb latch frozen in lock position, then pushed from outside, and the door snapped open. "Oh. Latch doesn't hold. Check your lingerie drawer."

Mrs. Pickwick rushed upstairs.

"There's this underwear nut," an officer explained. "Been operating in Goldengrove three years now. Sometimes passes up hundreds of bucks lying on a dresser, and steals bras and panties."

Hazel nodded in dumb stupor.

"Better check your drawer, too, young lady."

Hazel trudged upstairs, just as Mrs. Pickwick came back down. "I can't tell," she said.

Hazel wasn't sure either. "I never did keep count."

"If he picked my wife," Mr. Pickwick observed, "he picked the right woman."

"I don't know anything about that," an officer commented. "He seems to be a gentle enough guy. Been surprised a couple times and always runs away. Just some poor lonely nut who wants people to know he exists. By the way, kid, burn that picture or we'll haul you in for possession of filth."

They left. Billy crumpled the picture into a wastebasket.

After dinner, which nobody ate, Mrs. Pickwick discovered a small red dot in the crotch of a pair of panties. She phoned the police, who reassured her this was a distinguishing trademark of the pervert. "He probably imagines it's him being worn next to your body," the desk sergeant explained.

Mr. Pickwick spent the night alone downstairs on the couch. Next morning, Mrs. Pickwick awoke with threads tickling her face. The bedspread had a sewn-in quiltwork, and it seemed the pervert had cut backing stitches near the spread's edge, pulled loose the top threads, and dangled them over.

Later, Mrs. Pickwick noticed that two dresses, left hanging

in the closet while she was in New York, sported a whitish crust, like dried gruel, on the bosom.

Mrs. Pickwick cried most of the time now.

Billy was getting ready to settle at Harvard that fall. Though a senior in high school, Hazel would attend a program for gifted students at the State University in Goldengrove, where I had gotten a partial scholarship to study art. I knew that I'd outstayed my welcome, that I was waiting for the end.

In mid-August, a copy of *Scamp* came by mail. Duke had published my idealization of Rachel. He also dictated a letter: "This may be your dream break for Success, depending on how the readers take to your style. If an uncultured slob like myself can offer you advice for the future, it is this: stay away from real women, that is models (ha ha) when you work. Nobody's going to care if you know the names of muscles under the skin, or anything beyond lips, tits, and ass, just so what finally comes out does the job. Ha ha. We will pay any reasonable expenses, such as paint. I hope the enclosed helps boost you on your way. By the by, it looks like my boss is going to divorce our sister. Seems Cissy's been a little indiscreet about the men in her life, not to mention the life in her men. Ha ha. Yours truly may come out of all this, believe it or not, in better condition than ever before, and you may have even further reason to rejoice that I am, Your brother, Duke." The envelope contained Duke's check for three hundred bucks.

When I showed Billy my first "success," he nodded indifferently. "Congratulations. Boy or girl?"

Mrs. Pickwick seldom spoke to me. We passed without looking. When she learned I'd been paid for my work, she motioned me into the kitchen. "You'll have to go," she said. "You know that."

"I understand."

"What do you understand?" Sharp, angry.

"Nothing."

"You'd just better believe it, mister!"

She sobbed bitterly behind me. Invisible locusts of chaos buzzed everywhere.

In the basement, where only eight chinchillas now skittered and whirled, Hazel busied herself stringing together the skeleton of a lobo wolf, gift of the university's biology department. "Understand you're going to be famous, Prince Elmo."

I showed her the picture.

"My, my." Coldly. "Friend?"

"Imaginary."

Carefully wiring the gray-and-ivory jaw into place. "It's heartening to know that one member of this family, at least, is living up to his best potential. When you're famous, you'll probably forget all about us plain folk."

"Wish I could help—with things."

"You can't."

Billy cried us both awake once out of his nightmare.

"Hey, man." Shaking him. "Easy."

"Who? Oh . . ."

"What was it, man?"

"Intruder." Billy's face glowed yellow from the streetlamp. "Coming up the stairs to slaughter us. Rifle melted in my hands."

Grandpa and Grandma Pickwick paid an unexpected visit.

Mr. Pickwick greeted his mother from the couch. "How's the First Church of Christ Science doing these days? Raking in the old loot?"

Grandma Pickwick nodded coldly. "Hello, Robert."

Grandpa Pickwick, who paused several moments before walking through the door, which Mrs. Pickwick held open, finally stepped inside.

"Hello there, you old Phi Bete!" Mr. Pickwick called. "Hanged any redskins lately?"

Grandpa Pickwick grunted and began pacing the whole downstairs, scowl crinkling his broad, red face.

"Looks like Dad *ate* the redskin," Mr. Pickwick observed. "Indian meat's a major cause of indigestion."

"You seem to be in pretty high spirits, Robert," Grandma Pickwick said.

"I'm right on the verge of breaking into a goddamn song," said Mr. Pickwick.

Grandma Pickwick's luminous eyes widened. "Robert!"

Granpa Pickwick suddenly stormed out of the kitchen and marched upstairs. "First door at the head of the stairs, Dad," called his son. "Jiggle the handle after you're through."

In a low voice, almost a whisper, Grandma Pickwick told him, "Robert, you'd better handle Dad with kid gloves. He's terribly disappointed in you."

"Oh? And why is that, Mother Pickwick?" Mrs. Pickwick asked coldly.

"Don't be a simpleton, Anne!" her mother-in-law answered.

"Wait wait wait wait!" Mr. Pickwick fired in staccato. "Does this concern something in the real world, Mother? Eh?" Upstairs, the toilet flushed; the handle jiggled. "Isn't the whole thing inside *your* head? Didn't you make it all up? Hell, it's all *your* fault!"

"You must be making fun of Mrs. Eddy," his mother said. "You never did understand the subtlety of *Science and Health.*"

"Tell Mrs. Eddy to squat on it," Mr. Pickwick said. "Tell her I said she should. Use my name."

"There are children present," Grandma Pickwick scolded. "You must be terribly unwell."

"Why don't you send over a practitioner?" asked Mrs. Pickwick.

"If I thought your suggestion were at all serious, Anne, I would."

"But, Mother, she *is* serious! And please, make him muscular, six feet tall, and extremely well hung."

Grandpa came stomping down the stairs.

"Please," Grandma Pickwick whispered.

"Laryngitis, Dad? Can't you speak?"

The old man grunted disgust.

"I've tried to please you all my life. Spank me. Get it over."

"Has everything fallen apart completely?" Grandma Pickwick asked.

Grandpa Pickwick broke silence. "You failed, sonny. You took my money and made another rotten, lousy investment and lost it all. You've stepped across the line. Nothing I can do, no punishment, will help any longer. You're a lost soul."

"I feel the flames right now," Mr. Pickwick cried, "burning my ass. I'm sitting on hot coals. Don't worry, Dad. I'm being punished."

"Nonsense," said his mother. "Dad, you simply place too great an emphasis on material greed. It's obvious that Robert should put his nose to the grindstone and finish his thesis.

At least that's exercising the spirit, and maybe he'd get a raise so he wouldn't keep having to borrow money."

"I'd like you to tell me, Mother," Grandpa Pickwick snorted, "just what's been putting food into that spiritual stomach of yours all these years. And what about the twenty-five-dollar fee you doggoned practitioners get for one single house call?"

"Folks, it's a fascinating dilemma!" Mr. Pickwick cried. "I spend my nights thrashing about, polishing both prongs with my lower anatomy. By the way, Dad, can that toilet glug down a whole Shawnee?"

"My own father passed through a very dark period in his life," Grandma Pickwick reminisced, "and managed to survive it."

"That old coprophage, God bless him!" Mr. Pickwick's eyes gleamed.

I saw that the old people were baffled and hurt, and that suddenly even Grandpa Pickwick was worried. He said, "Listen, sonny, is the strain too much?"

"Ouch!" Mr. Pickwick clutched his abdomen. "Would someone pull that beak out of my liver?"

Hazel hugged him against her bosom. "He's in trouble. Please, Daddy."

"Hazel's taken over my role around the house," Mrs. Pickwick said.

"If I ever get to sleep at night, Dad," Mr. Pickwick went on, "I have the American dream and wake up soaked with seed."

His voice magnetized people in the room around him. Grandma Pickwick now sat on the couch and held his hand. Embarrassed and pitying, Billy approached. Grandpa, features softened and anxious, looked down, shook his head side to side, and murmured, "Sonny, sonny." Even Mrs. Pickwick, crouching before her husband, reached out and almost touched his leg. My head ached and my stomach knotted painfully.

Looking up at me, Mrs. Pickwick commanded, "Leave. Only his real family should see this."

For a while I looked at apartments, lying about my age to landladies, until I wandered upon a gray '49 Ford, keys dangling from the ignition. Stealing it, I blasted dust on country roads in the waning afternoon. Leaves had matured to a dull, flat green. When the sun stuck swollen and orange just above the trees and the bone-dry air breathed chill, I braked at my hill's base. Like a hungry mongrel, I sniffed the clear water of the Gorge.

While I fought up through thickets of weeds, mosquitoes attacked and I smashed blackish smears against my palm. On the shelf against the Dodge's back window lay a dusty, crumbling bird's nest. Hinges rotted loose, the shack door had caved in. A few scraps of tarpaper-brick stuck to the boarding, like filthy dressings on wounds. Inside smelled of earth. Night bugs began clearing their billion throats.

The mattress of Helen's bed had rotted into the floor, which had rotted into the ground. A thick brown crust mantled the stove; nearby, a constellation of prophylactics clustered like slugs smashed during a mass invasion.

In the forest of coughing insects, I squinted over the caved-in ruin of my privy to the darkness where once I'd shaved off the tip of my nose and daydreamed of unlimited powers.

Sitting on the limestone ledge, I dangled my feet toward the water. Moon and stars: the stonemill turned gold like a phosphorus skeleton. I undressed and plunged twenty feet into ice water. Minnows nibbled my toes. I battled my body until it numbed.

At the Goldengrove sign, I abandoned my stolen Ford, walked a mile to the brick house I would soon leave, and eased myself noiselessly through the front door.

Voices from the kitchen, words whispered and furious.

"Just tell me how many?"

"Hypocrite," she hissed back. "Those scenes I peeked at in that awful novel. You couldn't have made them up. It was that little slut in college."

"Way before we were even married."

"There was another girl, too. After we started dating, you ditched me for her. When you had enough, you snapped your fingers, and I came crawling back."

"I know that in my deepest misery, I sat in a room of strangers while you—"

"What lies do you know?"

"I saw what you looked like after it was over," he hissed. "Mussed, unzipped. And I smelled you. I'll never forget the smell."

"I can tell you something about smells. About the way *you* smell. Among other things, you're stinking drunk, yes? If you were more of a man—"

"Now it comes out."

"You *want* me to be a whore. Asking me to tell you all about it. 'Give me the juicy details, give me a thrill!' "

"Load my ears with filth."

"On that huge investment, what was the highest offer you got for all those pelts—three hundred bucks? And you took it? How long do you think any woman can like you, a man without force, a loser?"

"Roberts has force. Yes indeed he has! And what about your stepson? Was *he* in that room? But you've probably fucked him all along. That's why you wanted him here, so when you were miserable because you didn't have the imagination to give your life meaning, you two could run off somewhere together and screw."

"You're a sick man."

"I know that I'm married to a crawling, degraded woman. Was it a whole roomful of men? Hey?"

"I lost count. However many would make you happy."

"Now I know you want me to die," he said. "The knife's in your hand. I'm your guilt, so when I'm dead, you'll be free."

"When you're dead!" she scoffed. "You'll be wallowing in self-pity when you're eighty, crying in your daughter's lap. You're doing your best to ruin her, too. And what a weak Milquetoasty example you're setting your own son!"

"You've won," he said suddenly and quietly.

"Aw, did the bad woman hurt the poor little baby?"

"You can stop now."

"Me stop? Who started this?"

"The children might hear."

"Now he's worrying about the children. Well, little man, it's too late now. They're already ruined, thanks to you."

"I need help."

"You've been sucking my blood for twenty years," she said.

"No more tit, baby. Find your own help. You put on a great show for your parents today, whined so much you got yourself *two* mothers! Dear sweet Hazel! Listen, we're just wasting time. Am I calling the lawyer tomorrow, or are you? No, don't answer. You couldn't take action if your life depended on it. I'll call. Now, I want you and everything that stinks of you out of this house by noon tomorrow or I'll throw a restraining order in your face. Clear? Don't give me that hurt, speechless act. Okay—nod. I'm going to bed. Clean yourself out of my life."

Footsteps. I huddled under the piano. A ghostly nightgown flowed upstairs. Cramped, uncomfortable, I waited for Mr. Pickwick to make some move. Kitchen sounds, drawers opening, closing. Maybe the man was fixing himself a snack. I got ready to sneak out through the front when the basement door opened and shut, and there sounded a faint metallic click.

After noisily opening and shutting the front door, I breezed across the dark living room, into the kitchen. Several high-pitched clangs from the basement were followed by tense, sustained moaning. "Uuuuuuh!" I twisted the doorknob and pushed: locked. "Uuuuuuh!"

Rushing out the back door into the yard, down the concrete ramp, I shoved the wood bottoms of the basement doors: locked from inside. So I yanked off a shoe, smashed glass, dropped the shoe behind me, reached in and threw the latch.

The basement was black. I hopped so I wouldn't cut the shoeless foot. Stumbling against Hazel's workbench, I heard a bony rattle. Something scurried beneath my foot, and I whirled to see a rodent disappear up over the ramp's lip. Deeper in the smelly basement, a thin, small voice asked, "Who's there? Is that Anne?"

"Prince Elmo," I answered.

"Leave me alone," he whined. "Let them eat the rest of me."

"What the hell?" I began waving my hand above my head to find the light string.

"Don't turn on the light. Get out of here."

Too late. The yellowish glow oozed among the wires. Several cage doors had been flung open. Mr stockinged foot hit the cement when I saw Mr. Pickwick on his back, arms stretched at right angles from his body. Near him lay the fat, squat skinning knife. Chinchillas swiftly scurried here and there. I knelt and began searching his body for wounds. "My wrists," he murmured. "I slashed them." Tiny slice marks feathered both wrists, but no cut gouged in deep enough to draw blood. His booze-breath filled my nostrils. "Let me die in peace," begged Mr. Pickwick.

Somebody pounded the door upstairs. "What the heck's going on?" Billy shouted.

"Your father tried to kill himself!" I shouted back.

A shadow. Nightgowned Hazel stood above us, blood flecking her bare feet. "Daddy! Oh, Daddy!"

"Just got back from apartment hunting," I lied, "and here's Mr. Pickwick. He'll be all right, though."

She sat on the cold floor and cradled his head in her lap. "Oh, poor Daddy, poor Daddy," she moaned. The half dozen or so remaining chinchillas crouched in corners, scurried up walls. They were quite uninterested in devouring human flesh.

"I don't want to live," insisted Mr. Pickwick.

"What's going on here?" Mrs. Pickwick coldly asked. She had crossed the glass safely in slippers.

"Daddy tried to kill himself!" wailed her daughter.

"No! Let me see!" She knelt and examined his wrists. "Where's he hurt?" she asked.

"Right *there!*" Hazel shouted. "Where you're looking!"

Mr. Pickwick began to cry.

"Oh," said Mrs. Pickwick.

Then Billy joined us. "Police Emergency Unit's on its way," he announced, working a glass sliver from his heel.

"The what?" Mrs. Pickwick twisted frantically toward him. "Oh, God, no! Go back! Tell them not to come!"

But feet scuffled, crunching glass. Two blue-uniformed men, faces red from exertion, rushed in hauling between them a stretcher with wheels. Badges gleamed. Their free hands waved flashlights. It was too late to call them off.

Eating

•1•

Suicide was illegal; the police who came to save Mr. Pickwick's life stayed to arrest him. Mrs. Pickwick furiously phoned her husband's parents, who phoned a prominent lawyer in town, who, that same night, arranged to have all charges dropped on condition that Mr. Pickwick be placed in a private mental institution. But the Goldengrove newspaper already had its story fresh off the police blotter: "Millionaire's Son Slashes Wrists."

The next morning, Mrs. Pickwick told me, "I don't want to see you any more. If you ever hit bottom, contact me through the lawyer. But leave us all alone." At once, I arranged by phone to rent an apartment which I'd examined the previous day.

While I stormed about the room packing my few belongings, it was Billy's misfortune to wander in, dazed, miserable, lamb entering a wolf's lair. "Don't know what Mom has against you," he said, "but it's not fair to send you away. You and I were awfully good friends. I just want you to know"—he held out his hand—"I don't keep grudges."

I glared him down. "Thought you'd be kicking up your heels now that the competition's gone."

"Man, don't."

"Maybe Harvard'll help you grow up, so you can join the men in the locker room."

Hazel lingered in her bedroom door. "So long, skinny," I said.

"Elmowwww!" she wailed. "Don't be a fool."

"Fuck everybody." I slammed the front door and charged down the limestone steps without looking back.

A mile from the Pickwicks', across town, my apartment occupied the third floor of a hundred-year-old house: turn-around kitchenette, one large low-ceilinged room, a screened-off alcove for the double bed. The john I shared with other tenants. The place was "furnished"—two overstuffed chairs with springs punching through, caved-in couch, Navajo rug whose foot-worn chevrons vanished in the center. But three large windows opened onto plush foliage. An oak jutted from the postage-stamp front yard; its roots shouldered up the sidewalk. A hard maple topered beside the house. Morning sun flowing between branches and leaves veined my dingy lair with gold.

I lived here against university housing regulations, which allowed only married students, graduate students, or students twenty-five and over to reside off campus. During registration in the cavernous field house, I showed authorities a forged birth certificate which made me twenty-seven. I looked it.

I guess I had reasons for attending college. So many young clean-bodied women, for example, a Mississippi of responsive flesh, flowed the university's asphalt paths. They bent over library books, over drinking fountains. In winter their breasts pooched against cashmere. Spring saw them lounging in grass, legs up, skirts falling back, soft thighs drinking air and sun. And they liked my looks, even though I didn't: blond lion's mane a little too long, six three, two hundred pounds, long-legged, narrow-hipped, I could collect bodies when I wanted to.

The equipment available free to an art student on scholarship was almost limitless. My teachers, for the most part, ate me up; they may have envied me. When I told them, "Leave me alone and let me work; if you were a real artist you wouldn't be teaching," and other juvenile nonsense, they responded, in effect, "Give him all the freedom he needs." And when they found my creamy nudes in *Scamp,* my teachers said, "You're whoring away your talent, Prince Elmo," and imagined rescuing me from some goldfish-tailed siren mating in the murk with giant squids goggling fishbowl eyes, waving man-thick tentacles, clacking horny beaks.

And I wanted Nina. This was the only place I knew to wait—though her family had moved, she and Ivan had graduated, and the alumni association could disgorge no record where they were.

I began paying monstrous attention to my meals. Working

afternoons in a splintery prefab World War II structure that housed the art department, I imagined the dinner I'd prepare: spaghetti, or pizza, or sausages sizzling in garlicky pepper broth. Steak was too healthy. I lusted after coarse, complicated dishes which demanded hours of preparation to shock my system, burn tongue and palate, bloat me with indigestion, punish me with nightmares. I'd simmer a pound of hot Italian sausages, gently rotate them in their own bubbling juice, where they tumesced and split. Then I'd dump them sliced into a deep pot with pear tomatoes, tomato sauce, and garlic cloves grubbed from the dirty waist-high refrigerator; I minced a half dozen each of onions and green peppers and nursed the brew, adding oregano, garlic, parsley, tomato paste for thickness, until finally it digested itself. Then I'd boil salted, buttered water in another deep pot for number 8 spaghetti. All the while I drank gin, beer, or cheap wine to aggravate hunger and fire a euphoria which killed time: indifferent to classes, to snow collecting against my windows as afternoon burned out, to evening air blending with fumes of cooking.

I never shared one of these meals with another person.

I also grew overwhelmingly concerned with money. When I first began living alone, I was flush with my brother's check —which I blew making a down payment on a '49 Ford, maroon V-8, ninety-horsepower, two-door convertible. Dick couldn't have done better. I also hooked gasoline like Dick, with a three-foot siphon of garden hose I sliced from a homeowner's lawn one black 3 A.M. after brawling and screwing.

A good month would bring maybe two hundred bucks —depending on whether Duke thought *Scamp* might be able to use my work. Some months I got nothing. *Scamp* kept several of my pictures in reserve; if they used one, they paid. I knew Duke was shafting me, that I should scrounge an art teacher's year's salary for a single dirty page.

I would pinch like a miser, dream of sudden hoards, agonize about my overdrawn account, spend evenings in the dark to save on the electric bill and stare down at the yellow street, that urinous light flung by Goldengrove's ancient lamps. The scholarship paid only tuition, so in the bookstore I ferreted textbooks into the lining of a baggy overcoat I wore for stealing. I even mooched off women, living a week in the apartment of a one-eyed divorcee because she fed me. As soon as Duke sent money, I left.

When I had money, I spent it maniacally. After one day, half or three quarters would have washed away and the rent would still be owing. I seldom knew what I'd bought or where I'd spent. Once I wasted twenty bucks on caviar which proved to be rotten, and I didn't even try to get my money back.

And I consumed women, without all that much pleasure, at Don Juan's pace. I'd lust after a girl—breasts, thighs, ass, swell of lips, dazed odor which fumed from her meat—and her power to arouse me would make me furious. Soon I began fearing that I unknowingly had syphilis, that microscopic corkscrews had stolen inside without raising carbuncles on my prick. My body was their universe; they ate kidneys, liver, and heart, and swarmed dividing and redividing through my spinal fluid. I imagined that syphilis had attacked while Helen still lugged me in her bag of flesh, that my fetal head bumped the stiff cocks of strangers, that my father had plunged in spouting me from his coated dong filthy and fish-smelling from some reeking woman. Spirochetes splashed in the swamp of my brain. They rotted my dreams.

Often I hit the stoneworkers' taverns on the levee where the railroad split town, and there I'd pick up a bar girl, usually a country queen divorced from some no-good bastard serving six months on the farm for nonsupport. "Girl's got to pick up a few bucks to feed herself and the kids." My phony I.D. lied about my age, though bartenders stopped even asking after my face had been punched crooked: sometimes a jealous husband or boy friend would kick my ass off.

I remember the worst time. Soft in the cheeks, still pretty, Rena Ann was heading down the dead-end road of her thirties. Bright red hair, bangs down her forehead, the rest a tumbling pageboy onto her shoulders. A black quarter inch grew next to the scalp. Dishbroth had puckered her hands.

"Where's the good old husband?" I asked.

"Michigan City. Shot a buddy in the face."

Hillbilly band behind the bar—steel guitar, drums, piano, guitar-strumming stonecutter singing through his nose—knocked out "Satisfied Mind" like a mechanical toy.

"He couldn't satisfy a woman with a dose of vitamins in his jeans. Bastard couldn't even shoot straight."

"Seems to me," I said, "the men in this country have one hell of a time satisfying their women. Never yet come across a happy wife."

"That's cause you're hansum. One look at you—what's your name?"

"Prince Elmo."

"Hey now." She pointed to her empty glass.

"Tell me what *I* get."

"Your manners ain't exactly sterling silver."

"Think it over, Rena Ann, while I go tap a kidney."

"Maybe you was thinking of charging me?"

One dirty john without lid or seat. Pissing, I read the bank of slim machines lining the wall. "Retardo"—picture of a man, diagonal blush lines down his face and naked shoulders—"don't be embarrassed with your girl," "Knights"—picture of a horse—"the Big Man's Buddy, the TICKLER (sold for prevention of disease only), surprise her *tonight*, MAKE YOUR FANTASIES COME TRUE! Twelve genuine art pix to the pack, let *her* choose the position tonight, PIONEER, reduce her to a TREMBLING BUNDLE OF NERVES, with the new miracle invention SUPERCOCK"—Clark Kent in the phone booth ripping off his business suit—"pat. pending, the FANTASIZER, patented blow valve, easy to clean."

From the john door, I saw a man join her at the bar. His hands hacked near her face, but I couldn't hear him over the band's ricky-tick. When I reached them, she announced, "This here's my husband, Fred."

Younger, he'd probably been handsome; dimples thumbed into his tallowy baby face, and his eyes were almost intelligent. "Sure do hope you ain't going to cause trouble," he said.

"What is this shit?" I asked.

"I didn't know he was in town, honest." Looking at my chin. "We're separated."

I asked him, "Why don't you mind your own goddamned business?"

"Easy, Elmo," cautioned the bartender passing by. "This here's a friend of mine."

"Lying whore!" Her husband snaked out of her wrist, and she hustled behind me.

"Make him leave me alone. My lawyer says what I do's my business."

"Hell with your lawyer! You an' me both know how you pay that edjicated sonbitch his fee. Mister, this here don't concern you."

"I don't like seeing a woman pushed around," I bullshitted.

"Take a good look at him, you bastard," she taunted. "This here's the sort of man I like. You never did know how to treat a woman."

"So haul ass," I said. "Plenty of women out prowling. One might be able to stand you."

Ice from my own glass struck my eye. "Jesus Christ," the bartender said. The band tickety-tocked. I recalled the philosophy exam I was supposed to suffer through next morning.

We snarled into the December night. My back slapped a slushpuddle, Fred piled on. We struggled in the tavern's blinking neon. I strangled him. Light snow lilted down. His face purpled, eyes bulged. The woman tugged my shirt collar. "Don't kill. Ain't worth that."

So I let go and stood. Fred rested in the slush, while his smashed lips sucked breath.

"Hurt?" she asked me.

"Maybe a black eye tomorrow."

"Mister, I'll cut your balls off," Fred gasped.

"You and who else," taunted his wife.

Snow hissed quietly through the feeble light. The railroad's black spine lay stiff down the middle of the street. Beyond jutted ragged hotels for traveling men and bums.

"You gonna catch cold, mister," she told me. "Come warm up over to my house."

"What about Fred?"

"Got him a room somewheres."

He lay in the slush, snow melting on his hot face. At the rear of the windowless gray one-story building of concrete blocks, the tavern, we got into my car, and she gave directions to her bedroom.

A 3-D Technicolor head of Jesus hung nailed to the door. "Who watches the kids?" I asked.

"Ain't got no babysitting dough." Clothes peeled, and I remembered that my coat still dangled from a hook in the tavern. "They look after theirselves. Better snap off that light."

"How come?"

She clutched her bosom's sag. "They was fine till my fourth brat sucked all the bounce out."

I pushed her back onto the bed, which groaned and lurched.

"Careful! Look, mister, it just ain't necessary to be so rough!" After a time, she said, "Honey, you're one of them position hounds. Wish you'd of turned off the light."

A gentle knocking at the door. Her squirming died. "Shhhh, quit a minute!"

The small high voice whimpered, "Mommy?"

"Jodi, you get on back to bed right now!"

"Mommy?"

"Get the hell on back to bed or I'll knock your block off!"

Light feet padded away.

"Give some head," I told her.

"Now, listen, mister, that's something I ain't about to do with nobody."

"I'm not asking." Gripping her wrist, I twisted her arm.

"You win." Then she was stumbling out of bed, tripping to her knees over a wad of clothes, rising, staggering into the hall, where she gagged and threw up. I flopped back on the mattress and slept—until a barrage of nudges and pokes awoke me in the dark. Rena Ann leaned over hissing, "Hey now. Come on, mister, I want another go-round."

"Lemme 'lone."

"I knowed you was too pretty to be all man." She juggled me like a bag of marbles. "That's how come you made me do that, like them fag movie actors. You should of picked my husband. Go on, you got from here to the moon to prove you're any kind of man!"

Bruised, scratched, and defeated, I staggered into 7 A.M. cold, damp clothes glued to my flesh like ice. Roofs sagging, windows sealed against winter with bellied and split plastic sheeting, tarpaper shacks lined the slushmud road. Fat-lipped slashes smiled from my tires. The trunk yawned: my spare, too, was slashed. And the convertible top.

"Hey there, old buddy." Wrapped warmly, earmuffs clapped against the freeze, Fred shuffled around the corner of Rena Ann's shack. Snuggled into heavy coats, three large men, including the bartender, followed. Heavy boots clasped their ankles. The bartender juggled a crowbar hand to hand, and Fred held out two ripped hunks of cloth. "Here's your coat, old buddy."

Turning to run, I slammed against my car. Then I gripped my crotch and felt the shit kicked out of me. Above the drumbeat of boots, a woman called, "Killim, Fred!"

"Lay off him now," Fred was saying. "I ain't traveling back to no state farm for this bastard."

Children were off to school when I stumbled into my street. Joy rose at the sight of me. "Tramp!" they cried. "Crazy!" Handfuls of garbage pelted my retreating shape.

Later, as I shaved in the second-floor can, a long gash peeled across my cheek.

•2•

"Haven't seen you in over a year," Hazel said. "Who'd guess we're living in the same town?"

Midnight in early spring. My bruises had yellowed in their process of dying away; the scar on my cheek was a faded pink. Emerging from the Princess Theater with the crowd that flowed under a darkened marquee as I was passing by, she clung to some boy's arm—and called my name. While we talked, her date, a head shorter than Hazel, lurked in the shadows and eyed me suspiciously.

"How's Billy?"

"Oh, knocking his professors dead. Don't you two ever write?"

"No."

"Too bad. I'll get after him."

"I'm living at—"

"I know." She looked down.

"You could visit."

"You'd have to tell me when, wouldn't you? I hear stories about this good-looking guy overextending his adolescence."

"You're the only person I feel guilty around."

"Then I'm not very polite. Not for good friends renewing an old acquaintance."

"You're not skinny any more."

"Ah, I know." She made flapping motions with her arms. "We worry about the dumbest things."

"Still stringing skeletons together?"

"Passed beyond that. I'm almost a biologist now. How's your work?"

"I'm sculpting the human figure in clay—then I cast in plastic. New technique. It takes a hell of a lot of time."

"You and the human figure," Hazel sighed. "Maybe you're the biologist, and me with my bones—was I the original sculptress?"

Now I wanted desperately to talk. "My teachers say the human figure is absolutely out. It's all abstraction now. But that bores me, splashing colors around. So I tell them, let me do my own work or kick me out."

"You say that to their *faces*?" Eyes blazed in mock surprise. "My my. Listen, Elmo, I've got to run."

"How're your parents getting along?"

"Oh." She bit her lower lip. "Divorced. While Dad was in the hospital. He's living with his parents now. They're supporting all of us. Mom, too. She's not well, hangs around the house. We sold all the cages and the two or three chinchillas that didn't escape to a pet store for fifty bucks. So you see," brightly, "it wasn't a total loss. By the way, have you ever found that childhood sweetheart you once told me about?"

I shook my head and left.

But then I did find Nina again—Nina Rhodes. The September after I turned twenty-one, I found her in the social waste of Goldengrove's Sunday paper. Facing the movie ads, the smartest modern hemline above the knee, Nina posed at the railing of an ocean liner cruising mid-Pacific. The caption announced that she'd already settled with her husband in Goldengrove, where, as vice president of his father's trucking company, he would soon begin managing its operations in the southern Midwest. There she posed, Ivan's advertisement—my gorgeous Nina, whom I determined to pursue and steal, in order to give meaning, purpose, and happiness to my time.

•3•

My creations began with a coffin-sized steel tubful of clay, moist under its polyethylene shroud. I sculpted naked women of the mind, who armored their flesh in chic originals; perfume fogged out of their panties when my women shimmied them down, then kicked them floating like tissue wrap through the Danish modern boudoirs of my brain. Their breasts felt so firm and fine—fat globs of clay, splat!—beneath my deft palmings and tweakings. And my visions whispered, "You'll have to forgive me, never done this before, it'll take a while to loosen up." I'd tell them, "Stay tight, baby. Clothes are your natural state, act like it." They were my sphinxes, impenetrable and sleek, objects of worship, and I loved to sit them down and cross their legs, hangman's noose of thigh, the one part I'd let relax, drooping in the clay, while shoulders, propped by elbow-locked arms, jutted, and breasts clenched, and eyes slitted in an ecstasy of embarrassment, and stomach muscles went tight, widening the slender torso.

Sculpting a model hindered my work. I'd be overwhelmed by odors, pores, the way muscles disheveled skin I wanted smooth. I didn't know the names of muscles or bones, or where organs turnpiked over each other, and I didn't want to know. That was Hazel's business. All I knew was ass, face, lips, nose, tits, thighs, the trimmed and perfumed triangle of a woman totally civilized. "Shouldn't be here," one protests. "My lover will be furious if he sees this. He'll beat me up, sleep with my best friend for revenge. And oh, my husband!" And I whisper back, working madly, "Yes, you *should* be worried." "Am I supposed to be part of any special scene?" she asks. "A nude party? Sitting on top of some man?" "You're whispering into my ear, that's all. You're telling me, baby. The meaning of the universe." "Fantastic," she murmurs. "But so does a gob of spit," I explain. "It's a matter of taste. Your shape just interests me more."

I was trying to crawl inside a new technique which few had tried, and in which nobody had yet done significant work. First, I inserted shims, overlapping squares of copper sheet in the clay. From a container the size of a frozen-orange-juice shaker, attached by hose to a tank of compressed air, I then sprayed a plaster swathe about my hallucination, hiding her like the coma-trapped survivor of some flaming auto wreck. After the cast dried, I gouged out the moist gobbets of my darling, and, at the copper seams, dismembered her death mask. Wearing a filter mask with two cotton-stuffed cylinders projecting from either cheek, I coated the mold with a compound of car wax and carbon tet, whose fumes destroy the liver in seconds. The new technique consisted of brushing on thin layers of epoxy resin, whose fumes can irreversibly destroy the entire human organic system—a process so dangerous some schools have outlawed it.

She comes from the mold in jigsaw chunks, which I weld together with acrylic glues. Then she shimmers again before me, smooth as pearl, capable (if reinforced with fiberglass) of resisting the Victorian hammers of prudes. Then I oil-paint nipples, fingernails, hairline of skull, of crotch; and I fill the eyes with sight.

Then came the evening I rubbed the phone and summoned, for the first time since the chaos in New York, my genei.

"Ah, Prince Elmo."

"I'm lucky you're in town."

"Not at all, Prince Elmo. I'm the lucky one."

"I'll come to the point. I'd like another favor."

"And I like an honest man," said the miniaturized voice from the mansion.

"Look, you've already stuck your hands in my life when I never wanted you to," I said. "I've got a few ideas why, but I never asked and—"

"What do you want?" Roberts interrupted.

"Another man's wife."

Electronic chuckling. "I *love* that, Prince Elmo. Are you well cared for?"

"I'm caring for myself."

"Terrible, that Pickwick business, wasn't it?"

"You rode that one all the way home," I said.

"Obviously," he chuckled, "we are two moral upright gentlemen, the very souls of—honor? Well, now. You're a senior in art school. Right?"

"Haven't checked recently."

"Fierce sense of independence, but not afraid to ask help in powerful quarters. Tell me about this woman."

I gave him a few superficial details, then added, "Her husband's a cheat."

"Terrible," he sighed. "How his wife must suffer. Let's have him bumped off."

"What?"

"Murdered. I could arranged it—let's see, riches, social class . . . say, eight thou? Too steep?"

"Let's consider something less drastic," I said.

"Yes?"

"Throw a party at your mansion. Invite Nina and me."

"I'd have to invite her husband."

"That's okay."

"You're a wonder, Prince Elmo."

"Meaning?"

"Let's just say I have an interest in you. But if I'm doing you a favor, I want something back. Maybe one of your sculptures. How many are done?"

"Four."

"At the apartment?"

"One. Three in the art building. You're probably too busy to come over and see them yourself."

"But I'm *never* too busy for you, Prince Elmo," he cried. "In my opinion, you're an excellent long-range investment."

"If I survive."

"Yes, please do that. Extend yourself into that woman"—dirty old man's snigger—"and leave plenty of blond little Prince Elmos to carry on after you're dead. Speaking of which—I won't come over in person. As a matter of fact, I'm being called out of town. But I'll dispatch a very clever young man in my place. My private secretary. He'll look your pieces over, and help us do our dirty work."

"Without violating the laws of man and nature."

Roberts jovially shot back, "I don't know about you, boy—I'm at war. Stay in control, don't get caught. Above all, as you put it, survive."

"Is this choirboy of yours a complete bastard?"

"Certainly! Like me." Controlled ebullience at the other end. "Like you!"

•4•

The night Roberts' emissary tapped on my door, I lay buried to the hilt in a blond coed of eighteen. "Man, this is a creepy time for visitors," she moaned.

"Mr. Elmo Hatcher, please, it would be to your distinct advantage to answer your door before too very long. My name is Krishna Singh, and I am doubling for Mr. Roberts in a matter of great urgency."

"We'll finish sawing this log later."

"Ohh!" Her tongue fluttered against my ear. "It feels creepy to stop in the middle." She shrouded herself with a sheet whose shadows molded her shape. I crawled into a bathrobe and opened the door.

"No doubt terrible of me to interrupt your rest in this manner," said Krishna Singh, "but I must carry out my job." He entered and looked about, and since he loomed so tall, spotted my coed over the divider. "It would seem as if you are leading a rather disorderly existence, Mr. Hatcher. I understand, for example, that your off-campus apartment is entirely against university regulations. But please let us shake hands now." Krishna Singh, chameleon-slender and exceedingly good-looking, smoldered through black coals of eyes. "I would return another day, if the matter were not so urgent."

"Why didn't you warn me by phone?"

"You will observe that your telephone, Mr. Hatcher, has been removed from its cradle."

"Because I didn't want to be disturbed."

"I am overwhelmingly sorry, lovely lady." Krishna Singh bowed gracefully above her and straightened like a knife. "I was given no other choice."

"Cree-py!" she smiled. "Where did you manage to get that creepy tan?"

"I am"—he smiled a moment at my Navajo rug—"from the isle of Trinidad. Except perhaps for a slight gathering of pigment over the summer, my body at birth was already shrouded in this creepy tan."

"Are you a Negro?" she asked.

"My blood stream may be enriched by the seed of African kings." He scowled; the smooth cheeks knotted suddenly below the high, flat cheekbones. "But in the main, my blood line is reputed to have been pure Inca. My ancestors wore the first coats fashioned from the pelts of the Peruvian Royal Chinchilla, whose meat formed their chief aristocratic delicacy. Most likely, however, there are few blond personages in my lineage"—again he bowed, coals smoldering, and this time flashed at her his tiny, white teeth—"and certainly none so entirely attractive, as you, hiding your charming mermaid's shape beneath the sheet."

"Cr-eeepy!"

Creepy indeed. But then Roberts had raised chinchillas. So perhaps the coincidence was not so totally strange.

To me, he explained, "My family is the richest in Trinidad. I am here being trained by one of your leading capitalists, in order that I may better manage my hereditary properties." He seemed to enjoy saying this so much that his stomach muscles visibly clamped a silent laugh.

"Where'd you learn that phony English?" I asked.

"At the feet of the best tutor in Trinidad," he answered, gleaming all over. "I am every inch"—he bowed toward my coed, who at that moment lost hold of what little cloth concealed her sloping right breast—"an aristocrat." His eyeballs almost popped their sockets.

She covered again—to the nipple line. "Isn't it creepy?" Swelling and contracting, her boobs pointed now at me. *"He's* a prince. Did you know?"

"Yes, that is one of those dramatic ironies with which real life is shot full, beautiful girl." His hand made a suave gesture, and hers darted reflexively an inch toward it. And I knew that here was a man who could seduce any woman in the world. Sucking air through the nose, he held it against his tight, trim vest, buttoned down to the waist. Suit, shirt, and skin, it seemed, had never suffered a wrinkle, or a hardship. "The atmosphere of this room," he sighed, "is impregnated with the ocean-mackerel perfume of persons making love, which makes the accomplishment of my work most difficult. A man of the world like yourself"—turning toward me, bowing slightly—"will most certainly understand."

"As a man of the world yourself," I said, "you know how much I wish you'd get to the point and beat it."

"Hey now, brother!" His eyes blinked. "A man who blows his temper always loses to the man who holds himself in control."

"Mickey Mouse," I said. "The sorcerer's apprentice."

"You know why I have come. Good." He took a deep breath. "I have seen the three sculptures which reside in the building where you practice your craft, and it hurts me to tell you that good as they are, they will not suffice, singularly, or even as a group." Now he motioned toward the resinous sphinx, all blacks and whites, hawk-poised tensely in the center of my living room. "However, this very one, on that injun rug—hey?—will suffice for the favor my employer is planning to bestow upon you. My nerve endings are quite sensitive to excellence in works of art, and this is *the* best product of your craft. You will undoubtedly concur."

"Take the other three. I'm keeping this one."

"I can well understand. Not only is she the best, she is also the one most resembling, shall we say"—gleaming once more upon my coed—"your own true love? But she will be payment. You must choose between a plastic artifact of your own manufacture, and the flesh and blood siren you love."

"He talks so poetic!" the coed exclaimed.

"Of course, such casual affairs of the heart are of concern

to nobody," said Krishna Singh. "And although I am liable to become close friends with your Nina and her husband, your secrets are safe inside my breast. As an aristocrat, I could never betray you, even if such were my desire." That killed him; he seemed about to explode from repressed laughter.

"Liable to become what?"

"My dear fellow, I must get to know them both. It should work entirely to your advantage. I might add that the gathering you requested is being arranged, invitations are presently at the engravers—it is to be a party in your honor, my friend, in honor of a rising young artist whose reputation is rapidly being established, in honor especially of my employer's recent acquisition of this very work of art." He suavely gestured at my sphinx. "All the best people from far and near are being invited, including, of course, the dear Rhodeses."

"What ominous good fortune."

"You have a way with words. Of course, you will consent to the arrangement. This could prove the definitive launching not only of an *affaire de coeur,* but also of the reputation of a rising young star in the firmament of art."

"Creepy!"

"You see, Prince Elmo Hatcher, my employer may be prepared at some future time to negotiate with your broker and, himself, draw up a contract for the purchase of all your work, present and to come, a type of security known to very few young apprentices to their craft, such as yourself."

"And *your*self." I hated him. I also felt a strange kinship.

"And myself. Shall I call you Prince? You, my new friend, must call me Kris." He pronounced it "crease." "For that is my name among friends."

"Kris. I hate giving her up. But all right, let's make the deal now." We clasped hands like duelers crossing daggers. "We can carry her down ourselves," I said. "She's not heavy."

His long-fingered hands, nails long and lovingly pampered, shaped a gesture of horror. "I never take part in manual labor. Workmen will arrive tomorrow morning with a truck." He grinned. "And now, my new friend, I can take my leave. Yes, such an added pleasantness that you also were here, my beautiful young lady in your charming attire." He glowed and smiled; she squirmed, she sighed. Bowing himself gracefully through the door, Krishna Singh was gone.

"What a beautiful man!" she sighed, clutching her sheathed bosom.

I dropped my robe, lunged for her on the bed.

"What are you doing?" she squealed.

"Finishing dinner."

"Don't be *creepy!*" Naked flesh slithered from the bed to the room's center, pulled on clothing under my sphinx's guard, and charged from the apartment. I clutched the warm, empty sheet.

•5•

The swimming pool was dry. An inch-wide crevice curved the full length of its crescent floor where the cement had buckled. I'd parked at the gate, seen my name (first on a dwarf list) checked off by the guard, and in foggy darkness trudged once more up the asphalt drive. Some loose roofing tiles cluttered the shrubbery. Only two side windows of the mansion were lit. I stumbled against the front steps, and my knees hit the slippery stone.

Winking, smiling, fluttering his graceful hands. Krishna Singh admitted me. The house smelled of dust. "Doesn't anybody clean this place?" I asked.

"Oh my, you artists!" he chortled into the gloomy air. "We have seated your ravishing Leda in the vast living room to the north. Her tender yoni forms the centerpiece of our little soirée."

"Where's Roberts?"

"I am the chief here," said Krishna Singh. "Tarze Roberts seldom utilizes his mansion, except to entertain for business purposes. This evening, unfortunately, he is winging by private jet to a small Far Eastern country where he holds vast interests in oil, rubber, and tin, and where a war has broken out in which your country has become involved."

"I didn't know we were fighting a war."

"Few people know indeed. I believe that your President himself was only recently informed of this fact by his leading generals, who were informed by some soldiers in the field. My employer is a concerned property holder within the boundaries of this warring country, and he considered it in his best interest to speak with the local government there, to make certain that whatever happens, his property falls into no jeopardy."

"Somebody dump a bomb on one of his oilwells?"

"As a matter of fact, one story tells of an airplane crashing in the middle of a rubber plantation, destroying several trees. And also several workers. And a pilot or two. Ah ha ha, most unfortunate."

"I was joking."

"You must be wary of that, Prince Elmo, for in the Far East, as elsewhere, the ridiculous is commonplace, and one's most farfetched thoughts often find real-life equivalents."

The "vast living room to the north" turned out to be "the Venetian Ballroom." Its plastic floor had weathered poorly. Split and cracked now, the imitation marble begged for a mop. At least one decorative gargoyle had flapped off, leaving a gaping hole. A dozen or so guests wandered through the vastness, lost.

"Don't know a single person," I told Krishna Singh.

"Oh, you will, you will! Kind people!" he called. "Behold our talented young guest of honor, creator of this charming work of art."

An old lady nodded my way. A man intoned, "Speech." "It's not yet a lively party," Krishna Singh remarked. "Let me get you a drink." He indicated a large bowl on a card table, shrouded by an enormous napkin, one of those disposable tablecloths. "We are drinking wine punch to save the cost of bartending. By the way, I hope your emotional attachment to that charming young lady whom I met the other night in your apartment was not too great. As one man of the world to another, I must inform you that I have, how shall I put it, alienated her affections?"

"Is that a fact?"

"Yes, sadly enough it is true. She sought me out, fairly

beseeched me to dally with her, and I would have been untrue to my cosmopolitan nature and my concern for a woman's tender feelings had I refused her." He winked. "And then I knew your real affections were directed elsewhere. You are surely incapable of holding a grudge." He handed me a cup of gingerbread glass, and proceeded to empty half the ladle down my wrist and sleeve. "Pardon, my slave quotient is underdeveloped, and I thought I heard the ringing of door chimes. Mix, please, with the other guests." He danced off.

I sidled to where a stocky fellow, fifty-five or sixty, stood smoking like a fiend before my sculpture. "Thing fireproof?" he asked.

"No."

"Dandy." He tapped loose the cigarette ash between her crossed thighs. "If you ask me, this young lady is obscene. Wife's hiding in the shadows because of it. If this guy Roberts wasn't so goddamned rich, we'd have left half an hour ago. No offense."

"Nope."

"Where the hell is Roberts? He's why I came. And who's that skinny nigger who answered the door?"

"His assistant, Krishna Singh."

"Tyrone Power this, Errol Flynn that. Nigger parents are like children naming cats and dogs."

"He's from Trinidad."

"He's not even an American nigger? Strange, I thought I had a nose forum."

Just then Nina Rhodes spilled into the room on the arm of Krishna Singh. A morose Ivan trailed behind.

"Artist boy, I've got to snag the old wife and leave." The gentleman crushed my hand. "It's pretty clear Roberts isn't going to show up. Hey, you absolutely sure that guy"—he pointed rudely—"isn't just some local nigger?"

"My dear friends," said Krishna Singh, "what good fortune coming together in new combinations of friendship, the primary gift of the gods. My Nina, my Ivan, my Prince Elmo!"

She was still brown, skin coarser than before, as if sunburn had fathered her tan. Gauze cascaded from her shoulders to her ankles, clinching in directly beneath her breasts. She generated electric leanness, her gauze wrap like dressing on a wound, as if she'd suffered some accident and her weight had drained, leaving her famished—except for the grand, soft, sloping bosom.

"We've met before," she said. "So now you're a celebrity. Congratulations."

"I told my friends about your association with a certain magazine," Singh explained.

My hand swallowed hers. "I've seen your work," she said. "You must know a great deal about women." Eyes burning in a charcoal room. "I didn't remember your last name as Hatcher—you told me something else. In school you were much smaller than me, weren't you?"

Her nails, long, narrow, pointed like my sculpture's, gently raked the back of my hand.

"Is it all right if I shake his hand?" her husband asked. "He's supposed to be my new friend too."

"Hey there. The pleasure's all mine." Releasing his wife, I gave Ivan Rhodes my most sincere warm human glance as I gripped his hand.

"You remember Prince Elmo, don't you, darling?" Nina cried. "On that bridge a few years back? You had one of your little attacks of graciousness."

"All right, so we're all old friends," Ivan said. "My old new friend, Prince Elmo. My new old friend, Krishna Singh. All gathered here in this gloomy dustbin." He lifted his handsome face and sniffed. "Smells like the rest of the house has been closed up for years. Right now, good friends old and new, I'm searching this bizarre room for a drink."

"Three cups of wine punch right away!" Krishna Singh scuttled off.

"Wine punch, echh!" Ivan Rhodes protested. Slicked back, flawless gleaming ebony, his hair appeared to tauten his uncreased forehead. Nina's hair was yanked brutally back in a bun, forcing her face against the skull.

"Ivan loves to drink," Nina sang out. "Tell our friend Prince what you drank for breakfast."

"Oh, God!" he groaned.

"He just hates his life," she went on. "He's so rich and so miserable, aren't you, darling?"

"We have a bad marriage, I guess," Ivan sulked into the floor.

"He never wanted to come this evening," she explained. "He doesn't enjoy much of anything any more. Except belting me now and then."

Ivan Rhodes looked away, shaking his head, thrashing his hands stiffly against his sides, muttering, "Oh, God, oh, God."

"Darling, you should have let me come alone. Now that you've brought me, why not go away? Prince Elmo here would be more than happy to drive me home later. Wouldn't you, Prince Elmo?"

"Don't start in on him, too," Ivan said.

"I adore male solidarity," Nina said. "What absolutely touching concern! Go away, you beast. These men won't need any protection."

Krishna Singh bubbled up with the cups. "Tch, trouble in the Rhodes ménage," he sighed. "Such lovely people, such a beautiful couple."

"Shut up, Kris," Ivan commanded.

"Tell him to go home, Kris. Tell him how my body still aches."

Ivan said, "I can assure you, Nina, that throughout this entire evening, no matter how miserable and boring it becomes, no matter how much I detest the people I meet and no matter how you assault me, I will—"

"—stick to me like a leech," she finished. Suddenly she gripped my arm. "You must work for a living. Darling, have *you* ever worked?" she asked Ivan.

"Dear Ivan, come along with me. I will show you about this fascinating house," said Krishna Singh.

"Get lost."

"Can't you see, Kris? This is a very jealous man. He actually thinks I might soil his honor." She hugged herself tightly, as if her insides might suddenly fly through the flesh.

"Look, maybe you'd both better just go home," I suggested.

Still cuddling my arm, Nina went on, "Don't you remember that dinner at our house, Kris, when he actually suspected *us*?"

"The two of you took off together for an hour and left me alone to entertain his date. What was I supposed to think?"

"But, darling, aren't you the fussy little hypocrite? How long ago was it, all that astonishment and sweat—"

"All our dirty laundry in front of strangers? Why?"

"Because of what you did to me tonight, you bastard!"

It became clear that he would never leave us alone together all evening. So I left the room, tore a stub from my checkbook, scribbled on it, returned, and the next time Ivan looked away, trapped my phone number in her palm.

"Got to leave," I told them. "You know how it is. Work, work, work, all the time."

Her smile flamed. "But Ivan doesn't know. Tell him!"

Ivan shook my hand farewell. "Sorry," he said, looking beaten. "None of this is your fault. You just got caught in something."

"Men, I hate you all. Goodbye, golden boy." And she furtively stuffed the wad between her breasts.

I stalked my car through the chill fog. Long before, I had replaced the slashed-up '49 Ford with a newer model, a '58 yellow and white convertible, sharp knife-blade chrome design slashing back from the front fenders, across the doors—gorgeous gas-eater with new whitewall tires and a powerful engine. I twisted the key, heard the engine clear its throat. Beams cut through the white soup. But when I started off, a lean form suddenly jumped before me, flung up its arms, tumbled onto the road. I jammed brakes, set the emergency, jumped out, and in the headlights discovered a black dead limb which just then had broken loose and fallen across my path. For a moment, I had thought it was Nina. I kicked it to the roadside, then drove off.

•6•

While I still slept the next morning, she called and asked, "What do you want?"

"Dunno," I mumbled into the receiver. "Thought maybe I'd sculpt you."

"Is that what you really want? Go on, say it."

I told her. "I want very badly to fuck you."

"All right now. You don't have a wife, or children, or some live-in slut?"

"No."

"Good. Let's make it"—silence, breathing into my ear—"three o'clock, so I can get home for dinner. I hope you don't mind bruises. I love to do it in the light."

"Yes."

"I fuck like an animal," she said. "You'll love me."

Late by five minutes, she came through my door without knocking, white rabbit coat hanging in her hand. "Put away my fur." I hung it in the closet and turned, waiting for a sign. "We've already wasted time," she said. "Left the car two blocks away, in case my husband takes a crazy route home from work. I'm supposed to be shopping for a winter coat. Well?"

I reached for her body, tight and hard, kissed her, stroked her waist. "Don't waste time with that," she ordered. "It doesn't do a thing. Let's undress. No. Take off your own clothes. Ceremony gives me a pain in the ass."

Her bra hooks caught. "Damn! There." Those large breasts leeched all nourishment from her—lean meat, muscle, long legs, elegant and bruised; a fat veined bruise deepened the curve of her delicate waist. "Where'd you get those ugly scars?" she whispered as we tumbled on the mattress. She pulled me against her, dry and tight, and it was like touching bait and feeling the trap spring shut. Her muscles knotted chaotically as she chewed my shoulder. Then she softened, greased velvet, eyes white slits, water drooling from one corner of her mouth. "I go crazy," she moaned. Muscular and squirming, she swallowed me. Fingernails, teeth, uprooting twist of hips. Time flowed down the drain.

Later, back against me, she whimpered, "I don't have any self-respect. I hate myself." Her tight hairdo had exploded out of its pins.

"That isn't true. You're a fantastic woman, all woman."

"You're saying that because I let you fuck me."

"I've loved you for years."

"What time is it?" she asked.

I looked at my watch on the floor, in the gloom of a gray autumn twilight. "Five."

"I have to be someplace. Oh, damn!" She struck my chest. "Why do I have to leave? Listen to me, Prince Elmo. You're the only man except for my husband. This is my first affair. Do you believe that?"

"Yes."

"I feel so guilty."

"Your husband treats you like a beast," I told her.

"Anymore I can't even stand to smell him."

"Do you have children?"

"No. Are we going to do this again?"

"We don't have any other choice. We have to."

"I know. You're going to have to be friends with my husband so he won't suspect."

"I'll do anything."

She drew back, looked at my body. "I was pretty rough. Look where I bit—ohh! you're bleeding."

"Worth it."

"I have a confession to make," she suddenly announced. "I told you I don't have children, but I do. A little boy three years old. He's with the maid."

"That's all right."

"I never want to lie to you. My husband doesn't trust me, so lying's become almost a habit. I can't even control myself now, when I don't have to lie."

"Nobody could blame you."

"You're so good. I have no right to expect anything from you. But promise me you'll be faithful, even though it isn't fair."

"I promise."

"If I refuse my husband he'll begin suspecting. So I can't make the same promise."

I felt depressed. "Stay for dinner," I said. "I'll fix something good."

"Have to go." She stood; her glance scurried about.

"It's downstairs."

"Damn! What about the other tenants? My picture's been

in the paper." Beginning with the bra and working down, she jerked her clothes on. "At least let me have a mirror for my hair. I'm running out of time. What if I get a ticket?"

Froth of white fur, she escaped through my door, then stage-whispered up the dark stairwell, "This time you call me!"

•7•

Duke wrote me, "Little brother, there's a charge of good news in the family way. Yours truly has been elevated to Editor in Chief of *Scamp*—mainly because of stamina, energy, vitality, and talent, but also because of a wee favor done to the Big Boss. Prince Elmo, I am now a rich and powerful man, a winner, and of course in an even better position to do you favors and help you along in your career. Beginning (if okay with you) with a more or less regular monthly feature of your work, and a higher and more regular salary than called for in your old contract. We'll get around to renegotiating the whole thing one of these days. Meanwhile, I also understand old rich man Roberts is still a booster in your camp, and that you are into other forms of the artsy-fartsy than what I've seen. As you probably know, Roberts now owns most of the magazine, whose circulation and readership is growing faster than any other magazine in history. Be thankful for powerful friends and blood relations—and maybe if you get the chance, slip in a good word or two with the Big One for Your Brother Duke."

One evening soon after I got this, my phone rang, and a woman said, "Hey there, Prince Elmo. Remember me?"

"Cissy!"

"Yeah, honey. Can I haul my butt over for a while?"

"Where are you, Cissy?"

"Greyhound."

"I'll come pick you up."

"Don't bother, honey. There's just enough left in the old purse for taxi fare."

"Jesus, Cissy, what happened?"

"Honey, when I get there, I'll tell you all about it. You got a little bit a whiskey on hand for a tired girl?"

When I let her in, she said, "I gained some weight." Her cheeks pooched softly fat.

"Look fine."

She rested her small suitcase, I gave her a triple shot, and she flopped into a lumpy chair. "Divorced," she announced. "We been separated years, and finally the divorce come through."

"Oh."

"But it ain't just that. I got royally screwed in the bargain. You men," she shook her head wearily, "are real live bastards. Old Waldo, the judge, both lawyers—but the real kicker was our mutual sonbitch brother Duke. If it wasn't for him, I might of got a real nice settlement to live off of. But Duke, he couldn't tell a lie, you know? Me and my lawyer come into court expecting a pretty easy go, and suddenly, without any warning, there's this surprise witness. 'Really tears me up to have to say this,' Duke says, 'but I ain't got no choice. My own blood sister is a shameless whore and adultress.' And then he comes up with date and time of day when I'm supposed to be screwing all these guys that I never seen before in my life, that crawl up on the witness stand and say, yes, I done it to her this way, and yes, she told me do it to her that way, and yes, she never could get enough of it. I think even my lawyer was bribed, he acted like such a dumbass. Thanks." She finished gulping the bourbon, and I got her another. "Of course, I ain't no lily-white innocent, you know that, don't you, honey." Looking shyly up from the chair.

"Yeah."

"Maybe Duke found out about you and me. I probly deserve anything I get, I been such a piece of trash. Sure do hope there ain't any hell."

"You're too sophisticated to believe that."

"Fuck sophisticated. Look where saying 'isn't' stead of 'ain't' got me. From now on in I'll just say 'ain't' thank you."

"Got any plans?"

"Naw. Elmo—can I stay here to catch my breath? All them

windows must look good in the sunlight, and I'm just about dry of money. Maybe loan me a few bucks?"

"Sure."

The phone rang. "Why haven't you called me today?" Nina asked.

"I was about to. You almost heard the busy."

"Good friend, honey?" Cerulia drawled.

Nina cried out, "Who's with you?"

The ceiling crushed slowly down. "Nobody."

"Thank you kindly," Cerulia said.

"You promised you'd be faithful," Nina moaned.

"It's only my sister."

"I'm coming over there!" The phone died.

"You better leave, Cissy."

"Aw, c'mon, honey. I only just got here. Ain't even got a place to spend the night. Who in hell's that, to make you shove me out? Ain't I your sister?"

"She won't believe us. Anyway, I'll look guilty. Won't be able to help it. Maybe—I don't know—maybe she'll drag out the truth."

"You really do rub a girl's face in it, Elmo. So who's she, somebody else's wife?"

"Yes."

"She still living with him?"

"Yes."

"I'll bet she tells you they never screw, not since the two of you got started rubbing bellies."

"She isn't any liar."

"I bet. She probably tells her husband everything, too. Doggone! Okay, I'll leave."

"I'll write you a check. How much?"

"Bus fare to Chicago. Five bucks? Maybe something for hotel. But, hey, who's gonna cash it?"

Whispering footsteps, violent pounding, the door heaved and labored. "Unlocked!" I yelled.

Nina charged in, sweating, eyes brilliantly manic. "I didn't think you'd be so eager," she panted.

"My sister. Honest."

"Look me in the eyes."

I couldn't.

"Liar!" she shrilled, stalking to where Cerulia sat, still in her creased and dowdy wrap. "I thought he had more taste. You look like a tramp off the street."

"I'm his sister, lady," Cerulia said. "Who are you?"

Nina whirled toward me. "Get her out of here before I kill her!"

Cerulia rose wearily. I examined the toes of my shoes.

"Lady, you'll probably take this all wrong, but can you cough up ten bucks cash? I need bus fare and a place to sleep."

"Whore!" Nina snarled. "Don't I have enough humiliations without this?" She dug furiously into her black, small purse, came up with a wad, and stuffed it into my sister's hand. "There! Is that enough for services rendered?"

Cerulia shook her head at me. "Elmo," she said, shoving the money into her pocket, "you must be paying off all your sins at once."

"See you, Cissy."

Hefting her cardboard suitcase, she walked through the door. "See you in hell," she said. I listened while her footsteps died.

"Elmo? Was she really your sister?"

"Yes."

"Are you lying again? To make me feel terrible?"

"She just got divorced. No alimony."

"Oh, Elmo." She gripped my arm, rubbed her forehead into my shoulder. "If that's true, I'm an awful person. I gave her all my money," she added. "Must have been fifty dollars, and she only asked for ten. Will she be all right, do you think? Don't make me feel this way!" she cried. "I can't stand it! When I'm not with you—I don't know, I imagine that you're unfaithful to me, don't you see? The whole world's just crumbling, and there isn't anything I can do, and I feel so helpless! Please forgive me."

"Nothing to forgive," I said.

"I called you a liar. I made you throw out your own sister. Elmo, listen to me. I want to be your woman so much. Nobody else's. Yes. Shut the door . . . Take off your clothes, oh God, I can't wait . . . Oh do that, too . . . Let me. I owe you this to make it up. We belong to each other. We have to, when we can do this, and this, oh God, and *this*!"

•8•

I became "friend" to the Rhodes family.

"Come to dinner," Nina told me over the phone. "You have to become closer to Ivan, you know, or he'll suspect. By the way, I'm also inviting Kris. It's strange how the two of you got into our lives around the same time. Listen, have to rush." Click.

December snow plummeted fat and wet the night of the dinner. Slush greased my Ford beneath a wrought-iron arch like a cemetery gate, into the development where Nina lived among expensive low ranches and split-levels, stacked new and rich among tailored hills. The developer had bulldozed a whole forest, and now wires crutched the wrist-thick saplings grafted into the raw lawns. Rich and warm, houses slept under an electric blanket. Christmas bulbs burned red, blue, and yellow in the shrubbery.

The Rhodes house was a long, low redwood box, its several picture windows sealed by glowing curtains. Nina herself opened for me. The white dress stopped midway down her thighs. A square bib of open neckline bared her to an inch above her nipples.

"Wish I could be all naked for you tonight," she whispered, eyes raised toward mine.

Stepping into the foyer, I heard a distant whine. Then a groin-high form raced past and crashed into a small table which supported a vase of flowers. The vase toppled and shattered, spreading a puddle of water, roses, and carnations.

"My God!" cried Ivan from another room. "Charlie again?"

"What's he doing out of bed?" Nina murmured.

The shape whirled against my legs, knocking me against the storm door, then headed into the room from which Ivan had called. Shouts followed, the breaking of glass.

"Hurry, Nina! He's creating havoc!"

Nina and I entered the large living room together. Arms and legs splayed out, Ivan Rhodes sat embraced by an easy chair. Krishna Singh rubbed his napkin over a big wet stain on his fly. Two highball glasses lay overturned on the rug, alongside a maraschino cherry and a section of orange.

There came a horrendous crash from the next room.

"Do something," Ivan pleaded.

"Yes, I'd better," Nina agreed. 'I'm the only person in the world Charlie listens to. Come along, Elmo, and help."

In the dining room, amidst the ruins of an elegant table setting, stood a small, towheaded boy, lovely, wearing pajamas and a bland smile. He held the tablecloth like a white flag.

"Bedtime, Charlie," Nina said.

"Hi, Mommy," he said. "This is fun." Through a picture window, I saw snow sifting across the peaceful back yard.

A fat maid, starched white, rushed into the dining room. "Something should be done about this Charlie!"

"I'll deal with him," Nina said. "You set this table back to rights. And when you finish, clean up in the living room and foyer. Come here now, Charlie. Come to Mommy."

He flowed into her arms and she lifted him. He rested his cheek against her bare neck, blinking his blue eyes at me.

Ivan appeared in the doorway. "My God. Did you do that, Charlie?"

"Somebody this child should punish," grumbled the maid, on hands and knees, cleaning up.

"Naughty boy," Nina whispered into his ear. "See how angry we all are with you?"

"Put him to bed, Nina," Ivan said.

"I'll help you," called Krishna Singh from the living room. The three of them went down the hallway to Charlie's bedroom.

"Hey there," Ivan greeted me. "You seem to get the worst of everything around us. Nina and I are friends tonight, though. At least that's something."

"Good to see you again." We shook and sat down.

Charlie tucked away, Nina and Krishna Singh reappeared, whispering to each other.

"Oh? Is that a fact?" Nina said, scowling at me. "Does anybody have a cigarette?" She grabbed a fresh pack from the coffee table and furiously lit up, sucking match flame and smoke till her breasts bulged. "Where's my drink? Ivan, haven't you given Elmo anything yet?" She fumbled her cigarette to the rug. "Damn!"

"I'll mix Prince Elmo whatever he likes," Krishna Singh volunteered. I trailed him back through the foyer into a den, floor-to-ceiling shelves snaggletoothed with a few books. Tiers of expensive booze gleamed across the sideboard.

"Kris, what the hell is going on?"

"One of those complicated situations of which you rich white folk are so fond. Scotch? I recommend this straight single malt, twenty-two years old. Roughly your own age, eh?" He dumped it over ice and handed me the glass with a flash of teeth.

"What were you telling Nina in there?" I asked him. "She looks upset about something."

He stiffened like a blade. "I am doing my job, I owe you no explanations. Except, to make this all a bit more fair, I should tell you that we are rivals in a game known as survival of the fittest, and that however much I may actually like you, we are antagonists upon the battlefield of life."

"Are *you* screwing Nina, you bastard?"

"No no no," he laughed. "Don't you have any idea at all? Listen, brother, the stakes in this game are so high that I am attempting to sabotage your life."

"Is that what they teach you guys down in Trinidad? That African king in your family, man, he must have been a cannibal."

"What's that about Trinidad?" He grinned hugely. "I'll be damned, I *did* tell you that's where I'm from, didn't I?"

Nina danced through the door. "Kris—I want to discuss a few things alone."

"Beautiful woman!" bubbled Krishna Singh. "I stand at your will."

Nina seized his elbow. As I moved forward, she said, "Not you. I found out about your little girl friend. Come on, Kris, I know a private place. Maybe we'll be back later this evening. And maybe we won't!"

"But, my dear," Kris lightly protested as she led him away.

I glugged my scotch and refilled my glass, whereupon Ivan Rhodes came in and said, "Where's Nina and Kris?"

"In private conversation."

"You like that guy?" he asked.

"Right now I hate his guts."

He stuck his own glass out, and I poured.

"You've got to say one thing," Ivan remarked, "the guy has style up the ass. Purest good manners I've ever seen." He paused, then regarded me dolefully. "Don't have many friends. Made a sorry mess out of my life. Hope you don't mind me talking like this."

"Don't worry about it," I said.

"For some reason, Nina's in a snit," he went on. "Must be something I did, though I don't know what. I just can't predict her any more. But she had that gleam she gets when she wants to embarrass me, and—well, to make it short and sweet, it looks like we'll just have to eat all by ourselves."

Nina and Krishna Singh returned around midnight. In the living room, Ivan and I slouched and watched snow fill the back yard.

"Kris took me for a little ride in his car," Nina announced brightly. "I hope you two had fun together."

"You're a lousy hostess," Ivan said.

"And you are disgustingly drunk as usual," Nina said, while Kris stood by grinning.

I stood. "Let's talk outside, buster," I told him.

As soon as we were out the door, I gripped his shoulder. "Man, I'm gelding you."

"Nonsense. I did nothing."

Raising my fist against the whirling snow, I landed suddenly on my back. My right shoulder felt wrenched. Krishna Singh towered above me. "May I assist you to your feet?" he gloated.

I staggered to the house. Turning at the doorstep, I saw him climb into a black XKE and pull away around a curve. I went inside.

"Spend the night," Nina said, pulling me into the living room where Ivan lay passed out on the couch. "We'll tell him you couldn't get your car started. He'll believe us."

"Sure he will."

"I want to make it up to you. It's all Kris's fault, he had

no business telling me about that stupid coed he caught you screwing."

"It was before you and I were lovers," I said.

"Forgive?"

"What's that?" The distant whining.

"My poodle," mouth against mine. "He's old, so we sleep him in the basement. Some nightmare's made him wake up. I know what he needs." She looked at me fiercely. "I love him." She steered me into a dark hallway. "Take off your clothes and wait for me here." Light blazed, a door shut.

Toward morning, I pried loose from her limbs and staggered, mouth full of cotton, to the bathroom for water. Fumbled the switch. Fluorescence seared my vision. Above the tub a rubber bag hung from a hook, and from the bag a rubber snake dangled, chrome clamp loose about its middle. At its head, a black, slender nozzle peppered with holes still dripped venom onto porcelain.

•9•

On the Dean's desk were a dusty martini shaker decorated with three Greek letters, the picture of a woman in profile, a half-empty bottle of shaving lotion, and a manila folder with my name typed on its tab. He reeked of sweet chemicals, and an oily gleam moistened his cheeks.

"Just finished shaving," he said. "Have a chair."

I sat, shoe toes touching an empty wastebasket.

"You—are in trouble." He gestured with a well-scrawled sheet of note paper wrapped about his middle finger. "Why did you lie about your age to the housing people? Sooner or later we always catch up."

"Took you almost four years this time."

"Can you give me some idea what your motives were?" While we talked, he folded and refolded the note paper into a tiny wad.

"Sure. Where I live's none of your business. The dorms

cost a fortune. You eat what they feed you, and even if you don't, you pay. No girls in your room. Ever seen that Roman orgy writhing up against the walls of the girls' dorms just before hours?"

"Mr. Hatcher, I'm Dean of Men. Not the assistant dean, or one of the teachers. Let's show a little respect. We have a photostat of your forged birth certificate." He tapped the folder. "That's against the law."

"So's spitting in the gutter."

"We've checked further, and it seems you've also been playing fast and loose with university art equipment."

"Do you have hard evidence of that?"

"We don't enjoy taking drastic measures against our students. You've got a rather good record here, and I understand you've been given extraordinary opportunities by some powerful people. If I decide, for instance, that you need psychiatric help—well, that's a possibility. I am not your enemy, Mr. Hatcher, and I'm trying to help you out. Do you *want* to be punished?"

"You can threaten me all you want." I smiled.

"All right, I'm through wasting time." He flicked the tiny paper wad into the wastebasket. Then, opening my folder, he ballpointed something across a form. "This means you're being expelled," he said, "permanently. What a shame. After doing rather well in all these courses, you'll never graduate." He began scribbling on another sheet. "This," he explained, "states that you've been getting scholarship money under false pretenses. That you have been, so to speak, stealing money and art equipment and must pay it all back, with interest, beginning three and a half years ago. Let's move on. This innocent little form tips off your draft board that you are now fair game for induction. It also implies that since you've been evading the draft for the past several years, your name should appear early on the induction list. In my opinion, you have a character disorder and deserve a few swift kicks in the tail."

"Speaking as Dean of Men?"

"Speaking as one angry individual who doesn't have much patience with fools. Now, that takes care of everything. Of course, you can always appeal."

"To whom?"

"To me. Appeal denied. Now get the hell out."

I rose. "This conversation's been recorded," I told him.

"What?"

"And I have witnesses listening through the door."

"Wait a minute. Come back!"

"My lawyers will have some interesting comments, all right, about your unprofessional, not to say ghoulish glee."

His mouth gaped. "Don't leave this room until we straighten things out!"

"You sorry bastard." I slammed the door back into his face and reeled in shame and fury through the empty outer office.

•10•

Roberts' voice over my telephone said, "Understand you've been booted out of college. If you like, I'll do what I can to help."

"Forget it."

"Don't worry, by the way, I've paid off your so-called debt to them."

"Thanks loads."

Giving no sign he understood, he merely continued, "Me, as you know, I never went to college. Now two universities, including this one, have me on their board of trustees, and I've been awarded five or six honorary degrees."

"Congratulations."

"Don't be bitter. Let me bull up your spirits. Some wealthy citizens are beginning to express interest in your work. Would you like to do a piece of commission? An acquaintance in New York wants you to sculpt his beloved dog."

"Have him get the thing stuffed," I said, "and ship it here. I get enough back-handed help from good old Kris. Tell that bastard I'm going to blow his brains out."

Roberts just went on, "What would you say, then, if I could arrange an exhibition, to sell your pieces for a good price?"

"You'd have to get Duke's permission."

"I have."

"I've got ten or fifteen things collecting dust at the art school."

"No. The department was junking them, so I had them trucked over to my place."

"Man, I guess I really don't follow."

"I'll take a hefty commission on anything that gets sold."

"It still can't be enough to interest a guy like you."

"What about the Army? Going to let them draft you?"

"What else can I do?"

"You can survive. I want to see if you have what it takes to get through. How is your pursuit of that woman coming along?"

"Driving me up the wall."

"What would make you happy?"

"Having Nina all for myself."

"If you really want her, take her. You have the guts. Is she afraid you'll starve together if she leaves what's-his-name? You won't. Tell her that you have a guaranteed market for your work, a patron named Tarze Roberts who won't let you starve. I expect to get my money's worth. The whole world's your dinner table. Sharpen fangs, my boy!"

•11•

Ivan Rhodes began calling up. "Elmo, man? I feel depressed and lonely. Have you seen . . .?" He'd name a movie, then glide by in his fat red Cad ("Why do I own such vulgar cars?"), and after the picture, we'd hit a bar, shamble back to my place stinking drunk, and shoot bull about his life and mine. Good friends, Ivan and I.

"You know something about women, Elmo, tell me—what am I going to do about my marriage? She used to be crazy for me! When we first started going together, she'd call me all the time, call my parents. She'd show up at my apartment, be waiting for me when I came home from dating another girl. My God! That girl tore my body loose with love, know what I mean? And she never criticized me. I mean, I'll bet if I cut a fart in bed, she'd have complimented me on my musicianship. The only thing, I got the feeling she liked to do it best when there was danger of getting caught. I'd bring Nina home, and her mother'd be watching TV in the next room, and Nina'd make me screw her standing against the living-room wall. Wonder I didn't get shingles. We get married, and suddenly I'm lucky to glimpse her naked ass. When she got pregnant, I couldn't believe it. And now she starts calling everybody she knows, especially old boy frends, long distance and talking like they lived in the next block. It's a good thing my old man's rich."

"Maybe you shouldn't be telling me these things. In fact, I wish you wouldn't."

"Sure. I shouldn't bore you with all these rotten details. Maybe I ought to see another shrink. Oh, I saw one for a while there. After I lost control and screwed a girl who threw herself on top of me with her dress up, that's hardly exaggerated—and Nina found out, and even though she hadn't been putting out for months, well— I guess a lot of things are my fault, though. That wasn't the first girl, or the last. I'm about as worthless a person as there is. Between her mom and my dad, it's a wonder we're no worse than we are. Her mom, she probably never has hugged Nina out of love. Just froths at the mouth. Her old man's like what I'm going to be probably in thirty years: furious and dried-up and quiet. His belly's one big bleeding ulcer. When Nina was in sixth or seventh grade they packed her off to private school in Boston, who the hell knows why? They couldn't afford it. Probably just to get her out of the house. I guess it's lucky Nina and I got each other. Instead of busting up the lives of two innocent people, we just finish a bad job. I finish wrecking her, she finishes wrecking me. Of course, there's poor little Charlie, however he managed to get into this world."

"Why don't you divorce her?"

"Because I love the bitch, God damn it. I really do love her."

Old fears about syphilis began poisoning my sleep, my lovemaking. I'd slump about the apartment, neglecting my work for hours—although the date for my one-man show was set for late spring, and I'd contracted to produce five more sculptures, and five paintings. Booted from all university facilities, I converted my "living room" into a studio. And fucked Nina amid chaos.

"I don't mind your filth," Nina told me. "*Your* filth is lovely. And it'll make you so rich and famous you can move into a mansion, and we'll make love in front of mirrors." But I imagined firing into her tight body a verminous syphilitic broth. I was too cowardly to face a doctor, and too greedy to tell her we had to stop. My body jammed inside hers fulminated the whole meaning of my life.

And I knew that if I could not have her wholly for myself my life would have to end. At first, I could tolerate the thought that Ivan sometimes took her and considered myself lucky for what I could grab. But now she seemed mine by right. Hadn't my childhood been total deprivation? Whatever I managed to pillage, the world, its debt a bottomless hole, already owed me.

"I'm going to take you away from him," I told her, lovemaking with murderous violence.

"Yes, take me out of this life. I'd rather die."

I gave Nina no warning when one chill March evening, I attacked.

"The family is eating," the maid announced at the door.

"Come in, Elmo. We're just sitting down," Ivan called from inside.

I stalked into the dining room. Clutching her fork in both hands, Nina glared up at me in terror.

"Greta, get another setting," Ivan said. "You'll have dinner with us, won't you, Elmo?" Filet mignon lay half finished on his plate.

"Don't want to eat," I said. "I want to talk with you, alone."

"Why sure." He rose immediately from the table. "You in trouble?"

Charlie commanded, "Bad Daddy, wash your hands! Daddy has dirty hands." A transparent plastic mat, splattered with food droppings, lay beneath his high chair.

"No," Nina whispered. "Please, no."

"Look, it's probably serious," Ivan told her. "I'll be back before my food gets cold. Don't worry. Let's go into the den,

Elmo. I'll pour you a drink." We left the dining room, crossed the living room, golden in the day's last sun. "Weather's been so nice," he said. "But man, you look like the devil."

In the den, I told him, "I'll get right to the point. Nina and I are in love. She wants to leave you. We're getting married."

"I don't hear. What?"

"Sorry, Ivan. I don't want to hurt you, but that's how it is."

"Oh." He looked down at his feet, as if ashamed to look me in the face. He seemed to shrink a foot. "Have you been having an affair?" he asked.

"Yes."

"How long?"

"I don't know. Don't want to talk about it."

"For a long time? Since fall?"

"Yes."

"Did you meet often?"

"Whenever we could," I told him. "I don't think there's any point discussing it."

"You don't." His hands trembled. He poured himself straight scotch, dribbling some outside the glass. A long streak wet his pants leg. "I don't want to either," he went on. "I wasn't a good friend, was I? Understand that I'm trying to control myself. Maybe Nina should be discussing this with us. It concerns her."

"No need. She's upset enough."

"Nina!" he called. "Get in here!" He tossed off his drink. "Want some?" he asked me.

"No, thanks."

Nina came to the doorway, where she stopped, looking nervously past Ivan and me. "Elmo's told on you," Ivan said, looking at her waist.

"Oh?"

"What are you going to do?" he asked.

"How much have you had to drink?" Nina asked. "How can you get drunk at a time like this?" She stuck a foot into the den.

"I'm trying very hard to control myself," Ivan said.

"Well, I'm glad it's finally out in the open," she announced. "All this goddamn secrecy's been tearing me to pieces."

Ivan swallowed more scotch.

"Did you two decide anything?" she went on. "Ivan and I have already lived together much too long."

"Why don't the two of you just get the hell out of here," Ivan yelled, "and leave me alone! Go off somewhere and do your goddamn filthy things! Stop rubbing my face in it."

"Hypocrite," she said. "Who was unfaithful first? Don't you say nasty things to us. Don't you dare!"

He flung the glass at short range and missed her. Scotch slopped over his suit arm. A crash in the foyer.

"Act civilized!" she cried.

He swung as if to slap her face. But I grabbed him from behind and pinned his arms in back.

"Bitch! Bastard!" he sobbed. "Leave me alone. Why didn't you just hire somebody to kill me? Look, Nina, I love you!"

"Isn't it a little late for that?" she asked.

He struggled to get loose, but I hung tight. "Why did you have to choose *him*?" he sobbed.

"All right, I'm sorry about this whole thing," she said, "which is probably more than you'd be willing to say."

"Slut!"

"Sure. Go ahead, Ivan, keep it up. How many times have you called me those filthy things?"

"Let me go, Elmo, you son of a bitch, or I'll kill you both."

"Settle down," I said. "I don't want to hurt you."

"Thanks, dear friend. You may now let go of me. I promise, I won't run amok."

I released him. He charged Nina, and grabbed her throat in his long, graceful hands. "Bitch!"

"What is going on?" shrieked the maid. "My God! Call the police! Help! Help!"

Wrenching Ivan around by his collar, I slapped his face until he let go. Then I shoved him into a chair. "I mean this," I told him. "If I ever hear that you touch her again, whatever the reason, I don't care, I'll cripple you, man."

"Leave, please leave," Nina begged him.

"What about Charlie?"

"You've given up any right to him," said his wife.

"Better go, Ivan."

"I need my clothes."

A shrill voice from the foyer.

"Maid's calling the cops," I said.

"She saw you trying to kill me. Better leave before they come, Ivan, or so help me God I am going to press charges against you for attempted murder." Nina's voice rose steadily. "Have your lawyer tell Greta where you decide to stay, and she'll see to it you get every goddamn scrap of yourself that's still lying about this house. Now out, *out*!"

"So long, good friends," Ivan called. And staggered through the front door.

Dazed and trembling, Nina watched the empty foyer. Her child screamed in the dining room; a plate clattered against wood. From her trance, she murmured, "You have to leave. I'll call you. You better get hold of a gun," adding faintly, "I love you."

At midnight, while I shook in an easy chair I'd shoved back against my door, the phone rang. Expecting Nina, I stumbled through filth and clutter to answer.

"Man," small weak voice, "Ivan."

"What do you want?"

"I'm at a hotel," he said.

"Why aren't you with your parents?"

"Too ashamed to tell them, Elmo. I blew my dignity to pieces this afternoon. Man," he sobbed, "I feel so alone."

Crying bitterly, I jammed the phone into its cradle.

•12•

Nina didn't call for a week, during which I barricaded myself in the apartment. Nothing happened. Except that somehow I performed a tremendous amount of work.

Finally, "Don't say my name. Your phone may be bugged. Meet me at the West Side Shopping Center, in the parking lot. You'll see my car. Hurry. Before they have a chance to follow."

But the battery was dead and, exhausting myself with anxiety, I finally coaxed out a service truck which jump-started me for five bucks. When I arrived, she was furious. "What were you doing? What took so long? Don't you know you're all that's left?"

A gigantic parking lot, asphalt scored with diagonal yellow lines, faced stores fused together in a solid half-mile row, like the false front of a Hollywood set.

We left my car in the lot. "Scoot down," she commanded, driving off.

"Haven't left the apartment all week," I said. "My battery was dead."

"Things've been happening fast. I'm flying down to Reno in a week."

"Has he bothered you at all?"

"His daddy's lawyer's taken over Ivan's ball game completely. Tough, nasty bastard."

"What about money? The child?"

"They're trying to cut me off without a cent." She clenched her jaw. "They've even tried to take Charlie away from me. But poor Ivan's screwed up too much and too openly during our marriage to have much of a chance. I may not get the best settlement in the world, but I'll come out pretty well. I owe you a great debt of gratitude. If it hadn't been for you, I'd never have busted up that farce of a marriage."

"You'd have found someone else."

"No. It depends whether or not the man has guts. Elmo, how much do you care about me?"

"I love you, you know that."

"Well, if we're going to keep up our relationship, I guess it's time we really leveled with one another." She turned off the highway onto a country road.

"I think I've been honest."

"I haven't," she said, stopping next to a clump of trees and killing the engine. "I told you you were the first lover since my marriage." She examined her long, pink nails. "You weren't. I was afraid to tell you, because you'd dump me. There was another man, right after we married. I was so disgusted with Ivan—I knew almost immediately that I'd made a mistake, on our wedding night—oh, God! Why am I telling you these things?"

"Did you love him?"

"Who?"

"Your—lover." The word choked me.

"Ivan was treating me so horribly."

"I understand."

"How? It was so tawdry. And he was an animal, a *brute*! Oh, I was glad when it ended!"

"Where's Charlie now?"

"With my parents," she said, "until I straighten my life out a little. Do you hate me?"

"No."

"You're sensitive. Don't let me down. Without you, I'd— Some days this week, I thought, Oh, what the hell, let's just end the whole damn thing."

"End what?" I almost asked.

•13•

Nina winged down to a dude ranch outside Reno where she'd spend the next six weeks. "I'll be miserable without you the whole time," she told me over the phone. "But no, better not see me off, somebody's tailing us. You have plenty of time to get your exhibition in shape. Become so famous and rich nobody can ever touch us."

Roberts called about my progress. "We need those last pieces," he said. "Work fast." My apartment was a battlefield of dismembered plaster casts, stacked canvases, squashed paint tubes, bent shims, and gallon jugs of poisonous resin and hardener for final casting. A blank plastic woman stood like an enormous doll, awaiting her cosmetic paint job; my best canvas yet (it recently changed hands for fifteen thou) still was only an eight-by-six-foot oil sketch blocking one wall, magnesium step ladder before it. Plaster dust, rock-hard hunks of clay, empty tin cans, hardened brushes, beer and whiskey bottles drifted about the floor.

I worked with acrylic paint, because it dried fast. As I completed each canvas and sculpture, Roberts' emissaries hustled over, photographed it, crated it on the premises ("Roberts Containers," branded in the wood), and carted it off. Day and night I worked in frenzy, interrupting only to doze on a sheetless mattress spotted with stains. All my many windows stood wide open. As I spread lethal carbon tet, then fatal plastic broth onto my molds, one large fan puffed fumes into the spring air.

"Why hold this bash in Boston?" I asked Roberts over the phone. "Why not New York?"

Because everybody opens in New York. Don't worry. My publicity people are flying the major critics in. We're renting a honeymoon suite, and hanging the walls with red velvet. In two months you'll be famous. How's your sex life?"

"I'm fucking my work."

In fact, a sublimated lather of sperm fathered the whole substance of my art: women tight, languid, erotic, languishing for cock, women who could never be mothers, creatures spawned to be eaten—breast, earlobes, tongue, cunt—into epileptic frenzy.

My big canvas, completed, showed two women against a background of crimson wallpaper decorated with oriental twists and loops of blue. Though in the same room, the women were separated by walls meeting at right angles. One wore only a sweatshirt and sat bare-assed on the floor, legs slightly apart, leaning back against the wall in an exhausted trance, staring between her legs, arms limp, inert hands palms up on a yard-wide strip of plastic tile between wall and carpet. Chrome-yellow flowers flared from the carpet's crimson. Shadow darkened her wall, and a rectangle divided by steel grids, hot-air vent, opened by her left arm. The other wall glowed eerily, and in front of it, facing out, a woman with huge soft swinging udders and brown brainless eyes rested on hands and knees—ass against the wallpaper—atop a four-legged wooden table, drawer hanging open, and in the drawer a matchbook and eraser. The picture's light flowed from a man's crumpled white dress shirt filling the lower right corner of the canvas. Roberts had this painting reproduced on the poster advertising my show.

Postcards from Nina trickled in. "Dying for you at night. You know who." "Lover, I do miss you. They detonated an H-bomb underground last night, and my mattress quaked. I thought of you and almost died." "Lots to discuss with other women getting divorced. Keep thinking you should become a cowboy, you'd take easily to this free life."

Then nothing for two weeks, until, knowing she thought my phone was bugged, I tried reaching her from a public booth. The dude ranch telephone rang several times. Finally a rough male voice told the operator, "That one ain't to be disturbed under any circumstances. Just tell the party she's having a fine time."

On sheer whim, I wrote Billy Pickwick c/o the Harvard English Department, saying I'd soon be in his territory. "Do you remember me, can you forgive, could we get together?"

His reply came air mail special delivery. "I'd love to see you, Elmo. How many years now, four? So we've wasted years of friendship because we were proud or immature or some foul and perfidious horseshit. Hope you can forgive *me.* On my part, man, I mean it, there's nothing to forgive. By the way, I already knew you'd be here and would have broken through the guards to see you. Posters all over the Yard—yes! Guys stealing them to whack off. You horny bastard.

"I graduate this joint in a week. Hard to believe. It's been such a great identity coordinate. What's left of my family's coming to see me walk the plank. Surprises, surprises. Let me know where and when you arrive, I'll meet you. Your brother by adoption, Buck. P.S. That's how I've been known around hyar these four years. Sometimes I long to be called Billy. But ya makes yer choice."

14

When the limousine pulled up outside the hotel where my exhibition would take place, several strangers were waiting in the sunlight. I admired a striking couple—tall, slender man, deeply tanned, wearing a flawlessly tailored blue summer suit; and a stupendously beautiful woman, tanned, tall, full-breasted, high hemline flaunting the most exquisite legs. "It's him!" she cried as I climbed out. "Look, it's Elmo!"

Smiling, the man shook my hand. "You don't recognize me."

"My Jesus, Billy. Where are your glasses?"

"Contacts. Had them three years. Meet my girl." But she flew against me, clumsily pecking my cheek.

"Hazel, you look—"I choked.

"Beautiful, go on and say it," Billy grinned "All my buddies are going out of their minds wondering who's that scrumptious chick I'm shacked up with."

"Billy's women are jealous, too," Hazel said.

"Billy's women?"

He blushed through his tan. Waving a hand casually above his head, he said, "Plenty of fine women in this world. Even for a guy like me. Oh man, it's good to see you!"

"Yes!" Hazel agreed. "And you don't look much older. You just—well, look distinguished. Oh, you're going to be a success, I feel it in my bones!"

"That brings back memories."

"I swore off stringing skeletons years ago. Decided sympathetic tremors passed between those scaffolds and me, and if I didn't stop, I'd never fill out."

"I tell my friends dying to grind their marbles," Billy said, "not to let that gorgeous frame fool them. She's mainly a genius."

"I'm wildly brilliant," Hazel laughed.

"A year younger than me, and she graduated from college last year."

"Where'd you get your tans?"

"Hazel got hers at La Jolla, where she's a biologist and a mystic. She melts on sunlit beaches in her bikini and communes with the All-One."

"Handsome, capable Fella," Hazel said. "But He's fussy about his martinis. So. Here we are, grown up. In a couple of days, Billy completes his rite of passage. And what about Prince Elmo?"

"University kicked me out months ago," I said. "They wouldn't let me have my own apartment till I was twenty-five, so I lied about my age."

"Man, I've had my own apartment, all legal and approved, since sophomore years," Billy said. "And am I happy!"

"Beautiful place. One of Billy's women made curtains for him. Another hung wallpaper. Didn't a little Thai girl give you that temple rubbing?"

"Yeah. She gave me another present I wasn't so happy about."

"And the ex-wife of that French ex-diplomat, wasn't she the one who did your bedroom in red? Billy just spring-vacationed with her in the Virgin Islands."

"I may be stupid," said Billy, "but I'm wildly successful with women." He flexed a pipestem arm. "They love me for my body. And because I write poetry about death and destruction and first love lost and rhyme tomb with womb. And hold advanced political opinions. My first project after graduation will be to resist the draft and spend the next few years in prison, trying to master *Finnegans Wake*. Or, failing that, spend a few years at Fort Bragg learning to be a damn good pool player."

"When the Dean of Men booted me out of school, he told me I'd get drafted."

"To cast death masks of the enemy?" Hazel asked.

"There isn't even a war going on," I told her.

"When you hold advanced political opinions, you learn we're always off somewhere fighting a war," Billy observed. "But don't lose hope. Maybe they'll send you to Bermuda. We're probably fighting a war there, too."

The three of us ascended to my bridal suite. All the furniture had been removed, red carpeting laid down, red velvet the same rich color hung floor to ceiling in all four rooms. A glass wall gaped from the largest room, one huge floor-to-ceiling, wall-to-wall picture window affording a fine view of a gasoline company sign, vast neon flower opening and closing constantly.

"And this is where the honeymooners rip off their first night," Billy explained, "so the whole tribe knows the marriage is being consummated."

"Displaying the bloody sheet in the window," I said.

"Only a king and queen on their wedding night could afford this joint," Hazel said.

Workmen grunted and strained. Wooded shards from the packing crates marred the plush rug—loose nails, seltzer, thick cottony swaddle to protect my dead ladies from being buffeted.

A motorcycle girl stood spread-legged in her crate, the front of which had been crowbarred off. Hands on lean hips, wearing only an unzipped leather jacket, she parted her small-toothed red mouth in scorn. Billy said, "You've done it, man! Our Lady of the Motorcycle-seat Sniffers. That is powerful!"

"Anything anywhere a woman might appreciate?" Hazel asked.

"God in heaven!" Billy halted in front of my huge canvas of the two girls sunned by the crumpled shirt. "I'll buy it right now. Look at those jugs! The thighs on that girl in the sweatshirt! Whose shirt is that, Elmo? Yours? That one girl really looks limp. Did you just finish socking the meat to her?"

"Just like being back home," I sighed.

"Show me a naked woman," cried Billy, "and this thin veneer of Eastern sophistication cracks and crumbles!"

"You're talented, Prince Elmo," Hazel said, "no doubt about that. I just wish you had a higher opinion of women."

"Don't you understand?" Billy gesticulated. "Those aren't women. Those are exercises in pure form! Right, Elmo?"

"Impure form," I corrected.

Hazel and Billy both said, "Touché."

My suite lay one floor below the exhibition. After I left off my suitcase, we spent the rest of the afternoon arm in arm, Hazel center in a pair of pumps ("I may be beautiful, but I'm still too tall."), stalking Boston, heading diagonally off Beacon down Mountfort past a row of brownstones decimated for what Billy called "the sphincter of the state highway system." And, as the sky lowered into deep blue, we meandered along the Boston bank of the Charles. An undershirted man eased past in his punt. Birds swirled. People sat along the opposite sward as we crossed a bridge to the other side.

"Lo! The Square!" Billy announced. Ice-cream shops and congested traffic, the subway island whose newsstand glowered behind stacks of the *National Enquirer* ("I CUT OUT HER HEART

AND STOMPED ON IT"), subterranean vibrations, then Harvard Yard, somber and gorgeous, peaceful, students in a grubby circle around a girl, standing, black hair flowing long. "When will they ever learn," she sang. "The local culture mill," Billy said. "Ecce! your poster nailed to an oak! Right above that twittering flit." Beneath mine, an ancient poster, fading and peeling, advertised a Rudolph Stayne Film Festival: Stayne in a cowboy hat, like a campaign sign for sheriff.

The Yard lay all in shadow, somber, peaceful. Gushes of steam punctuated a distant air hammer's rat-a-tat-tat. "Working twenty-four hours a day to tear up a section of street," Billy explained. "We'll pass by on the way to my apartment. One of Cambridge's gorgeous scenic attractions if you enjoy the taste of dust."

The sun had died, but the sky stayed blue, and darkness roamed a half hour off. We strolled down Mass. Ave. Disgorging fumes, cars oozed bumper to bumper, and I said, "I've never felt so good."

"Billy's still in the process of getting over a minor shock," Hazel commented above the crescendo of air hammers.

"Yes, couple weeks back in Chicago, a friend of mine was involved in an unfortunate mishap because he supported advanced political opinions. A night guard discovered him at 2 A.M., in his carrel in the stacks of the University of Chicago library. Some fellow human beings had given him a brain concussion and hacked off his right hand."

"Do you hold advanced political opinions?" Hazel asked me.

"I don't hold any political opinions," I told her. "I make dirty paintings and sculptures."

"And I," said Hazel, "look through microscopes at slices of dead tissue."

"And I," Billy said, "lounge about my well-decorated apartment and listen to Mozart on my very advanced KLH stereo, and occasionally sip hundred-year-old brandy, and support advanced political opinions. It's all unbelievably civilized."

"What are advanced political opinions?" I asked. Two turns off Mass. Ave. brought us to Humboldt Street, also peaceful and somber, leaf-heavy branches crossing the sky, automobiles crammed in both gutters, a double row of nineteenth-century houses divided now into student apartments.

"We are against war," Billy said, "against bigotry, slums, and racial segregation, against the pollution of our air and water, against big government and big business, which destroys our freedom and all quality in our lives, plus any number of other excellent items to be against. We are *for* peace and especially we are for the *pleasures* of peace, such as sipping brandy, listening to Mozart, writing poetry that rhymes womb with tomb—"

"—getting an irrelevant education," Hazel chimed in, "making love to many women—"

"And many men," Billy added. "For the women only, of course."

"Sculpting dirty sculptures and painting dirty pictures," said I.

"—going to good movies and bad movies, making good conversation," Billy said, "and knowing the secure feeling that all your debts have been settled, especially those to the doctor—"

"—and the mortician," Hazel said. "And I might also add, the pleasure of sitting on a golden beach near La Jolla, communing with the All-One while the Fussy Fellow sips his iced martini."

"Your friend still alive?" I asked.

"He died," answered Billy, "about a week ago. Without coming to. Prince Elmo, I strongly advise against holding advanced political opinions. The human race is utterly hopeless, and only romantic fools are trying to save the world."

"All Billy really desires, modest fellow, is the return of Paradise on Earth."

"Oh, speaking personally, I've been enjoying Paradise on Earth for the past three years. But it occurred to me some months ago that such enjoyments were selfish, and that for a few minutes each month I should at least turn my KLH speakers outward through my windows and offer an occasional passerby—"

"Female," Hazel whispered.

"—a taste of my fine brandy. Women deserve at least the barest glimpse of Eden."

"How are your parents?" I asked.

"Poor mother," said Billy, shaking his head. "She died last year—cancer of the adrenals."

"Oh, poor Dad!" Hazel cried. "His parents couldn't stand to have him around, so they sent him off to an institution—it was awful!"

"They gave him electric shock treatments and had all sorts of fun with him," Billy explained. "Now we don't even hear from our grandparents, except when they sign a check."

That evening Hazel prepared us a stuffed veal roast, all subtly veined with crystallized ginger, and carrots sliced lengthwise braised in a sauce of butter and brown sugar, and sautéed green beans retaining their crunch. Before dinner, we lounged in Billy's gossamer-curtained living room and listened to Mozart on Billy's KLH and sipped freezing martinis prepared by Hazel. During dinner we swilled a Cabernet Sauvignon: "Compromise, for Hazel's sake, to right-wing California," grumbled Billy. We ate a thick, custardy chocolate meringue pie. And with our rich Colombian coffee, we sipped thimbles of Billy's Napoleon brandy from its ring-shaped decanter. "Three young gods on Mount Olympus," Billy said. "Oh Zeus, we break bread to thee!"

A temple rubbing hanging in a frame, the four-armed goddess Kali, black matron of generation and destruction, looked down with startled expression, while a bird whispered in her ear.

"And to thee, Bacchus," sighed Hazel, "we dedicate fluid from thy ruptured grapes."

I moaned from sheer pleasure, "I've never enjoyed myself so much. This *must* be Paradise on Earth."

Then long and late, *Don Giovanni* turned low, we chatted about the past, improvised on the present, while our bodies digested the beast, and grape fueled our brains. Three different people in the same room, a sense of total merging.

I asked Hazel, "You've seen God?"

"I have mystic experiences," answered Hazel, "when the universe moves inside me, and when every wave that hits the beach pantomimes the meaning of ultimate reality. How's that for a high?"

"Something like what happened to me once," I said. "When I was hungry."

"When the blood-sugar level in your brain drops," Hazel said, "you're likely to have a mystic experience, when the whole meaning—how did I put it?"

"Before you came to live with us?" Billy asked me.

"Before I got you shot. Deep inside a virgin cave."

"Virgin no more," groaned Hazel. "Not after you clobbered around inside it, brute."

"Mystic experiences deep inside virgin caves," Billy said. "My English adviser would make some inappropriate comment about symbols."

"It didn't mean anything," I said.

"Your romantic past," Hazel commented. "What rubbish!"

"O the golden past!" Billy exclaimed.

"O puberty and pimples, O blind dates, O virgins and virgin caves!" Hazel said, then in an undertone sighed, "Oh, to be a virgin once again."

My golden mood washed suddenly down the drain. I became aware that my bladder was bulging toward rupture. "I ought to tell you," I began.

"What?" she asked.

"That I don't know where the can is."

When I staggered back, pursued by the splash of a flushing john, I told them, "Time to go. Before I pass out."

"Sleep here," Billy offered. "In the living room with Hazel. But you'll have to behave yourself."

"Unfortunately," murmured Hazel.

"Hazel's engaged to a physics prof out in California. Some nuclear nut bulging with I.Q. points. She's getting married in a month."

I collapsed onto the couch.

The morning after my exhibition opened, thunderous knocking lugged me into a monstrous hangover and two telegrams. The first said, "ADVANCE CRIT, SALES INDICATE TREMENDOUS SUCCESS IN STORE. ROBERTS." The second: "BACK IN ONE WEEK. ACHING FOR YOUR BOD. BRING HOME RICHES AND MARRY ME. LOVE, NINA."

Fragments of "opening night" tormented me like horseflies.

How many times had I bent ass for some critic who gabbled of energy, pure form, the holy shape of the human bodies; for rich ladies and gents detailing their déor, the color scheme of their town or country house, wondering if some piece might clash with walls, sofas, paintings they already owned.

"Yes," I said, "I think it's a good investment. But ask ———" the one in black mesh stockings, who said she'd sleep with me anytime she wasn't feeling sick; this evening she felt awful.

"She thinks your stuff swings," the wife said, coming back. "Where's your agent?"

Roberts did not show up at all.

Flashbulbs. "Let's get a shot of you with this one. More to the left, the dailies still aren't up to printing tit."

"I regard my sketches," I told some newspaper critic, "as a sort of battleground for creative inspiration, where I can be irresponsible in a way I really can't be when I'm creating what I consider to be a major work. It's like poetry, you know . . ."

Scamp turned out in force. "We're giving this exhibit an eight-page spread. Yeah, we'd love a shot of this one, too, at the proper angle."

"Well, I'm glad it's art," a woman said, "because it it weren't, the police would arrest everybody here."

"Where's some more bubbly? Where's something else to eat?"

"What on earth did those two girls just finish doing? I didn't know they allowed that sort of thing!"

Billy and Hazel wandered through the crowd. "Hey, man, where've you been?"

"In the can, Billy. I'm sick."

"We're so proud of you!" Hazel cried.

"I want that one, in the bathroom, in the shower with me. Is she guaranteed waterproof?"

"Don't you think you've done your duty for tonight? Come on, honey, come with me."

"You're very gifted in the sack, darling, a real take-charge guy."

"Where's the toilet?" Champagne gave me trots around midnight, after which I remembered nothing . . .

The good reviews came in. Tiny red stars, the sort teachers lick on neat homework, twinkled on my art—citizens buying.

I received Roberts' check for a small fortune, and there could be no doubt: out of the ooze and slime, Prince Elmo Hatcher had emerged a success.

War

•1•

AFTER MY exhibit closed and Billy graduated and Hazel boarded a plane for La Jolla and the lucky bastard she would wed, Billy decided it would be a great good time if we drove together across half the country back to Goldengrove.

"The only tie I still have there is the house," he said, "and it's about time I got it sold off. Renting's a royal pain in the arse. Then I'll drive on to Cal for Hazel's wedding."

"There's not much drawing me back, either. Except Nina," I caught myself. "But once we're married we're liable to settle anywhere."

"Oh?" Billy looked at me quizzically. "By the way, how come she's so anxious to get married this soon after the divorce? I'd want a little time to cool off."

"We both feel like jumping straight into the fire," I said.

"What settlement's she getting from her husband?"

"A fortune probably. His father's rich."

We rented an overpowered flaming-red Buick convertible. And one hot Saturday morning in late June, sun half a flaming orange ball through the haze of industry and infernal combustion engines, we stripped shirts from our backs, whirred down the top, and arrowed south into a bull session half a continent wide. The city still slept. We passed an all-night laundromat, fluorescent ceiling tubes burning, one lone woman hauling wet clothes from a machine into a wicker basket.

"The end of the world!" Billy howled, releasing the wheel to clasp hands above his head in a boxer's victory sign. "A laundromat at six A.M. with one sad divorcee cooking her panties into a broth!"

We rocketed along, eighty-five per, sucking sunlight into our bare flesh, as scrambled eggs, coffee and fresh-frozen orange juice metamorphosed into adrenalin. A machine spat out a computer card, and we swooped over the vast six-lane asphalt desert of the Jersey, behind belching diesel caterpillars, past refineries like vast metal intestines. "Beautiful, gorgeous!" Billy cried. He gushed along at ninety-five. "We consume more gas the faster we drive," he said. "That's why I'm driving so fast. I want to pollute the atmosphere and hasten the end of the world."

By the time we got onto the Pennsylvania Turnpike, and the noon sun in its kiln was baking me red, our bull had thickened. Workingmen were raping the ancient nineteenth-century railroad tunnels through the Pennsylvania mountains. For miles behind each tunnel, traffic piled up. A man lay face down on the roadside in front of his car, hood heaved up. A white handkerchief fluttered from the radio antenna. He pounded gravel with his fists, raked his forehead back and forth, wailed, "God damn this life to holy hell!" Half hidden by roadside shrubbery near the fence, his wife and children watched, horrified. "He takes being alive far too seriously," Billy observed.

Evening cooled when we crossed into Ohio, and it was my turn to drive.

"You really love this girl you're marrying?" Billy asked.

"What's love?"

"Because you know I sometimes wish you and Hazel had meant more to each other."

"You goddamn romantic fool!"

"Ah, Prince Elmo, *you're* the romantic, didn't you know? All the great romantics screwed their sisters."

"Look, Billy—" I ran off into the shoulder, then carefully fought my way back to the asphalt.

"It's out in the open," Billy chortled. "Did you think I'd forgotten? It's a blood bond. To glue it even tighter, I guess we should both screw Hazel."

"Did you?" I shouted.

"No," he insisted, "no, no, no." The longer we drove and the more tired we grew, the more we regressed, though Billy talked for both of us. "The wildest thing, when I was only about five, I had this love-affair with a wind-up alarm clock. We owned a nightstand, sort of box-like with a little door, and I swaddled the clock in every clean handkerchief I could swipe from my father's drawer, and stuffed the whole caboodle inside that nightstand and shut the door, so I could just *think* about it all snug and safe. I was the clock dig? That was me! I'm so stupid I only just now figured it out. . . ."

Then I dozed at the wheel, and Billy dozed, and a truck swelling head on, air horns shrieking over the still Ohio fields, almost squashed us. Sky grayed. Sunday morning. Gas needle hovered on E for miles as we passed one lifeless station after another, then finally found a Shell open twenty-four hours.

Midmorning, we pulled up before my apartment. "Left it a terrible mess," I said, "but maybe there's a place you can sleep."

We helped each other stumble up two flights. In the twilight, I made out a pathetic figure leaning against my door, a poor hunched-up bundle of sleeping woman, head between her knees, suitcase at her feet.

"Nina, Jesus Christ."

"Huh?" asked Billy.

"My fiancée. Honey, wake up."

A drawn, wasted face opened into mine. "Who—?" Energy flowed into her eyes. "Where have you been? I expected you to be here already. Who is that? Oh, God, I can't begin, I'm too ashamed—I had to walk here last night from the train. No place else to go." I helped her stand. "We have to talk."

"This is my—"

"Alone!"

"Have to leave anyway," Billy said, "Hell of a trip to Southern Cal."

"Billy—" I stood ankle-deep in the ghastly clutter and from my window watched him climb into the fattest, reddest Buick in the world, start it, flip the switch which brought the gray top down like a shroud over his head.

In my sunburn, Nina's fingers felt like claws. "Humilia-tion!" she sighed. "His lawyers worked it so I didn't get enough for a plane ride home. The bastard got his revenge. He had my dog put to sleep. You're all that's left." She said it like a declaration of war.

•2•

We spent a grim, foggy two weeks together in that quagmire apartment. Except when she wandered down to the bathroom, Nina stuck to the dirty sheet on the dirty matress. When we weren't screwing, she lay on her side, chin pressed against her knees, naked, staring at the dividing wall. We swilled vast quantities of whiskey, but she couldn't sleep. Once I tried to straighten the apartment. "Don't bother," she said. "When we get married we'll move out."

Roberts' office began mailing copies of magazines, with reviews of my show. *Time* featured it, with two pages of color photos. "Surfaces smooth, taut as a well-packed ski jump, and as icy-cold, the sophisticated woman of the sixties. . . . 'I'm just a lightning rod for the age,' said Hatcher." I made *Newsweek* ("Signals a scandalous decade."). *Life* ran a color photo of my motorcycle girl, strategically concealed by portions of my own vacuous bulk. *Esquire* spoke of the "nuclear woman." One press-release described "the relationship between crime and art, since artists in their work often violate the common precepts of morality. . . ." A playboy wanted his sixth wife in plastic. A coming Italian starlet wanted herself similarly immortalized. The Yale Art Galley suggested I donate a sculpture for a tax deduction.

I was famous. And I couldn't tell where the bullshit began and ended.

The requests by the playboy and the Italian starlet made Nina furious. "You aren't going near one of those naked sluts!"

"But each commission means maybe eight thou."

"The hell with that. If I even so much as suspect that you're alone with some other naked woman, I'll gouge her eyes out."

But her mood soon changed. "What right do *I* have to sound so self-righteous? Just some bossy slut clawing your career to pieces before it's started. Oh, just *listen* to me!"

The midnight before we went for our blood test, as she lay bathed, fragrant in my arms, she said, "Before we get married, you have to know something. I feel too guilty just keeping it trapped inside. And if I don't let it out, it'll ruin our marriage, too."

"You don't owe me any explanations," I said. "I don't *want* to hear any more confessions."

"Well, you'll have to, or we won't get married. You're sensitive, Elmo. If you still want me after this, maybe I'll find it easier to live with myself."

"All right," I sighed.

"That affair I told you about—well, Ivan's not Charlie's real father. *He* is."

"Jesus Christ in heaven."

"Pretty sickening, isn't it?"

"But how can you be sure?"

"There is no doubt."

"Does Ivan know?"

"I'm going to tell him. It's not fair to him, thinking Charlie's his son, when it isn't true."

"No, wait a minute, Nina. Look what you'd destroy!"

"But Charlie and Ivan will just be living a lie."

"So what? You can't suddenly just yank a son and father from each other."

"But it's so important to be honest. I know that now. Do you hate me?"

"No. People just lose control of their lives. But listen, Nina, if you tell Ivan, if you jerk his son away from him this way, then it's my fault, too. I won't let you."

In the yellow light from the street lamp outside, her face seemed to disintegrate. "I wouldn't be that awful," she sobbed. "How could I do a thing like that?"

•3•

The doctor—large and loose-jointed, bald, untidy, a professor of medicine in the university—drilled us with his eyes. "I called the two of you in to discuss a serious matter. I'm speaking with you together, rather than separately, because you'd soon raise this question between yourselves, and a third party might help defuse the situation. You both have syphilis."

I said, "Oh."

Nina looked squarely at him.

"It responds nicely to penicillin and other drugs, but to prevent unnecessary spread, I'll have to ask each of you who else had contact with."

"Can't you get it off a toilet seat?" Nina asked, voice dull, tired.

"Let me put it this way," replied the doctor. "No. It is transferred by contact."

"Maybe I have hereditary syphilis," I said. "My parents were pigs."

Cold and level, Nina said, "Didn't you realize you were giving it to me?"

"Young man," the doctor said, "I can assure you, if it's assuring, that your case is *not* hereditary. It's scarcely gained a foothold."

"Thanks a lot!" Nina said. "Next time I'll go to a woman doctor."

"Ah, can either of you recall having had contact with another party, besides your fiancé?"

"Of course not," Nina snapped. "I detest these insinuations."

"No," I lied.

"No further questions." The doctor examined two lined sheets of paper. "Do you have questions for me?"

"Can we get married?" Nina asked.

"After you're cured. Three weeks, to be sure. If the strain is nonresistant."

"You're assuming we have the same strain," she said.

"I'll keep this off public record," he said.

"Thanks loads," snapped Nina.

"My nurse has your shots ready."

We walked into the blast furnace of a cloudless summer afternoon. Coldly furious, Nina said, "Now I know what you were up to all those weeks we were separated—screwing filthy, diseased women."

"What about you?"

"Bastard! Using what I told you in confidence to attack me. Is that why I put myself at your mercy?"

"No, I don't know, I can't follow anything."

"You've already admitted it, telling the doctor you suspected all along. And it didn't stop you, did it?"

"But he said—"

"What were you doing in Boston, you and that Billy Pickwick? I bet he brought his sister along, didn't he? I know the answer by looking at you, and I know where you bought your little present for me."

"Leave her out!" I grabbed her arm.

"All those years you were living with her, you just picked up where you left off."

"No! There was never anybody else but you, Hazel—God damn it, I mean Nina!"

"That's all I wanted to hear." She seized my arm from the quicksand where she sank. "Now I know."

•4•

We had no friends. A J.P. married us before two strangers in the courthouse hallway, while pigeons crapped all over the monuments out in the sunlight. Even Krishna Singh was gone, traveling with Tarze Roberts in Southeast Asia, where our country indeed appeared to be involved in armed conflict.

During our cure, I'd considered where we should live and finally settled on New Haven—ninety minutes by train from New York, but far enough from that city's howling overstimulation to keep me sane. By phone, I rented a furnished house on Whitney Avenue, an expensive district about a mile from the city's center and from Yale. Rent amounted to four hundred fifty dollars per month for the lease's two years. I secretly took all commissions offered me—we needed cash, the future was too frail. If Nina liked, she could guard me while I worked the naked ladies into clay. Or maybe I could talk them into letting me improvise from photos. Details—work them out later. Only so long as the money lasted could we buy our freedom.

From the courthouse, we drove to the first Holiday Inn and took a room and undressed. "I want to swim," Nina insisted. "The pool looks clean and uncrowded. No, get your hands off me. Don't you ever think about anything besides satisfying your big selfish starving prick? I *mean* it!" So we submerged our hot bodies in a pool which suddenly swarmed with a convention of smashed fraternity boys, who surrounded Nina, splashing and shouting, and when she announced, shrill and chortling, "Leave me alone! I just got married today to that big blond clunk over there!" boxed in the two of us and insisted they would leave us be only after they'd pitched us into the air on a blanket, had dinner with us, got drunk with us, and sung us a serenade which their Founding Fathers had cooked up especially for couples on their wedding night. Half of these boys were blond and disconcertingly resembled me.

"Student at the university, man?" one asked.

"Was."

"What house you a member of?"

"My apartment house."

"Hey, boys, this guy's an independent. Listen—how'd an independent hook up with a gorgeous chick like Nina?"

"Simmer down," Nina told me. "I don't mind a little horsing around once in a while."

"Wanna go to the movies with us tonight, Nina?" one asked. The rest hooted.

"Let me ask my husband."

"Hey, Nina baby, how well do you two newlyweds know each other by now?" Ha ha ha. "Because I mean, if you already know each other that well, what's the big deal about separating a little while to see a movie with us, huh? We could all pile into a couple cars, leave what's-his-name here, of course, and shoot on down to the old finger bowl"—ha ha ha ha—"I mean, the drive-in movie, and eat a little hot buttery popcorn—"

"And other salty stuff!" a gaping pink face hooted from the water. Ha ha ha ha haaaaaa!

"Oh, you boys!" Nina laughed.

"Your husband looks uneasy. He looks downright jealous. Hey, man, we just want to provide a little free entertainment for your wife. Do you a favor, man, give you a little rest!" Ha ha ha ha.

I smashed his mouth so hard he arched into the pool's middle.

"Hey, man, not too cool," somebody said.

The boy floated unconscious. Blood seeped from mouth and nose. A couple of "brothers" rescued him.

"That was really a stupid thing to do," Nina said. "He was just joking."

"If our brother's bad hurt, your new husband won't have anything left but his temper."

"You guys want some more shit kicked loose?" I asked.

"Oh, shut up, Elmo," Nina said. "Sorry, boys, my husband's got a hot temper."

We returned to the motel room. "I hope you're proud of yourself," she said.

"Shut up! It was your fault."

"Like everything else, eh? Look, get your hands off me, don't you have any self-control? Come on, let's go eat. Maybe a drink will loosen me up."

I looked at her naked body, lean and powerful, those jutting breasts; and at the wide, firm mattress, counterpane of red, red dust ruffle flowing to the rug. The mirror opposite doubled her body as she dried.

Over the steak and wine, I asked, "Did you lock the door?"

"Didn't you, dummy?"

A long tableful of fraternity boys murmured silently, leering at us across the motel's fancy dining room until they left, fingering coy little waves at Nina, which she returned. I wanted to beat her up.

When we reached our room, I started in. "You did leave the door unlocked, idiot."

She slammed it shut. "Anybody who burns his fiancée better not complain about petty details, mister."

"Who gave who the syph? I tried to call you once down at that dude ranch. Some guy answered and I heard the leer curling itself clear across his tongue. What am I supposed to think of a woman like you, hey?"

"Son of a bitch," she snarled. "I should've finished you off in the road when we were kids, while I still had the edge in size."

"Maybe I wish the same thing."

"Then maybe you better think twice every night before you sleep. You might not wake up."

"Stop, maybe we've gone too far," I said. I was getting scared.

"Too late to stop now," she said. "I'm going to tell you something."

"No more confessions."

"You'll love this. It'll prove how right you were about the dude ranch, and the great time I was having."

"Stop!"

"About how I played mare to twenty or thirty different riders, all those cowboys—I mean, like paradise!"

Then I went beserk. Oh, I just flung myself onto the bed, opened my mouth, and blurted out the truth about Cerulia and Helen.

With cavernous astonishment looking down on me, she cried, "Hey, you *aren't* lying, are you? I mean, nobody would say that if it wasn't true." Slowly she peeled off her clothes. "Wowie wow," she murmured. "You know, I guess we both got what we deserved. Let's put our whips away now, lover, and forget the past. We'd *better* forget, because if anybody finds out they'll lay us in a sewer pipe and throw a cap over both ends. We've got to stay together now, like the only two people in the world with the same disease. Are you ready for me, lover? Yes. Rip me open. That's that way. How's the war now?"

"Deep penetration on all fronts," I groaned, as the mattress rustled and heaved.

Then we heard scuffling, like a huge rat, from under the bed. Grinning, lips split, left side of his face swollen and blue, the fraternity boy loomed over us. Silently he bowed to our stunned coupled forms, then strolled out, shutting softly the door we forgot to lock.

We repacked. Lugging suitcases, trailing wet bathing suits in out free hands, we staggered to our XKE and found that the air had flown from all its tires.

•5•

Our house, yellow with a green roof, peaked in front like a Swiss chalet. The narrow lawn in front and back formed the landlord's work of art before his wife died and he moved into an apartment. Yellow-green and thick, no dandelion or plantain for blemish, its insane perfection resulted from years of daily care. Requiring biweekly mowing in the rainy season and during its weird October growth spurt, a last convulsion before it slept, this bent grass was so delicate it adhered to a moistened fingertip and came up by the roots. A seven-foot-high box hedge guarded one side of the backyard; a fifteen-foot-high rhododendron bush, viridian and fat-leafed all the year round, guarded the other. For shade, a gigantic oak jutted near the back door.

In September, immediately after we arrived, I redecorated the drab interior—the dust-brown beige, the sickroom green and dead-skin yellow, the wallpaper glued up forty years before. First I rollered antique white onto every wall and ceiling—then spent two frenetic weeks muraling dancers and oboe players, nymphs ankle-deep in streams in virgin forests, children hiding in the shrubbery, moss-covered piles of clothes scattered among the trees.

Nina basked in our green Eden out back, sponging the warm fall into her flesh. Sometimes she wore only sunglasses, rolled languorously, green flecks sticking to her skin. Wandering into the house, she'd clutch me and murmur, "Sweet boy. Lay down your wee brush and make love to me in the back yard."

"But some kid might knock a baseball onto our property and—what's wrong with the couch?"

"Come putt my green," she purred, and we writhed loose the lawn in moist divots. Late rush-hour traffic hissed down Whitney Avenue. Afterward, wandering inside, we stroked mud smears off our shoulders, asses, and flanks.

Late one night, after we'd split a fifth of Johnny Walker Red, Nina became more relaxed and loving than I'd ever known her. We lay on a big new crimson-and-yellow rug in the living room. She smiled at the naked children I'd drawn on the wall, dancing in the chaotic reflections from the fireplace, and said, "My childhood wasn't so bad, I guess. Maybe a lot more like yours than you know." She gouged my rib cage. "Back at the beginning of time, some caveman would just slouch around the fire and keep his women happy and pregnant. Nobody cared if they were related, and the little kiddies just kept appearing." She snuggled closer.

"Let's make a baby now," I said.

"No!" She sat up. "Might be a girl. And I know all about you hill apes, screwing sisters, mothers, daughters. Just like animals! Like my pet Boots. You know."

"We've come a long way since those days," I said.

"Don't you know," Nina went on, "that's how fathers and daughters pass the long hot afternoons in Sicily? For them, fucking's just a fancy way of saying 'hi.' But here, if some big hairy clunk who's always been everything you're supposed to respect suddenly turns into a whining epileptic, tearing your tender young insides apart with his hardware—well, it's pretty awful. And you can take it from me, cause I know." Rolling me onto my back, she nibbled my shoulder. We rolled over and over each other, around the garish rug, gouging, panting, biting, until I was mounting her and she shoved me off.

"Stop! I'm not protected!" She paused, panting. "You think I want to risk something like that happening again?"

"Something like what?" But I was beginning to see. "No more confessions," I pleaded.

"Boob!" Kneeling beside me, she licked my chest's blond pelt. "Don't you understand what I mean yet? That whole awful business when we were kids?" Scratching at one of her nipples, she said brightly, "My own father fucked me."

Strangling in my juices, I could not speak.

"So I wore Boots," she shuddered. "Where people could see. And then, Elmo, you and I, *we* had our revenge."

I remembered her father that gray morning when he came to haul Nina away from school.

"Listen to me. Please." Now she was pleading. "You and I, Elmo, we're even closer than any blood kin."

Hardly breathing, Nina waited so long for me to take her gift. When at last she knew I would not, she sighed, "Good night, Prince Elmo."

Next morning, shaving her legs with a safety razor, Nina peeled away a narrow six-inch strip of flesh. The wound bled an hour. Our idyll had already ended.

I rented a studio one block from Yale's Bridge of Sighs (seventy-five per month, in advance) and began working six days a week.

Our first phone bill came. "Nina, there must be some mistake here. They want one hundred eighty-seven dollars."

"Is that a fact?" she asked. "When are we going to meet some people around here? I'm bored crazy."

"We'll talk about that later. What about the bill?"

"So why bother me with it? Check the phone company, for Christ's sake!" She snorted off.

I dialed. My "representative" at Southern New England Bell asked, "Were there houseguests during September and October?"

"No."

"We will verify the other parties," she said.

The first number rang. "The name of the party is Krishna Singh," said Krishna Singh. "Who wants to know?"

I shouted, "Me, God damn it!"

"Do you wish to place a long-distance call with this party?" the operator asked.

"Is that the only way I can grill the bastard?"

"Please, who is employing language so foul?"

"Connecting yewwwww!" the operator shrilled.

"Me, you s.o.b. Why in Christ's name did my wife make ninety bucks' worth of long-distance calls to you last month?"

"Oh, eat it, Elmo." His phone clanked down.

"Try this other ninety-dollar number," I said.

A woman in Berkeley, California, answered. "Dunno," she told the operator wearily. "I didn't jabber long distance last month. Was it some broad?"

"Yes," I said.

"Then it's probably my husband. I'll call the living doll to the phone. Darling! It's about one of your women."

"For Christ's sake. All right, I just want to know what's going on," a voice caromed off my ear.

"My party," the operator explained, "thinks there has been a mistake on his phone bill. He wonders if you received any phone calls during September from a Mrs. Hatcher."

"So it's Nina's new husband, huh?"

"His wife cried, "Caught up with you, you limp phony!"

"I don't feel like wasting more money across this line," I said. "What's your name and what the hell's going on?"

"In twenty-five words or less, huh?" he shot back. "Go pay your bill, buster. And when you do, think about what you did to Ivan Rhodes, okay?"

"Hypocrite!" yelled his wife. "His name's Dick Fotheringill, mister! and he—" the phone slammed down.

That night, I told Nina, "There wasn't any mistake."

"If you ever spent time talking with me, maybe I wouldn't have to keep calling other people. All I want is some attention."

"But a hundred ninety bucks!"

"Liar! It was a hundred eighty. You don't care about me. All you thought about was redecorating with these damn paintings of naked women, you oversexed bastard, and when you finished you ran off to your goddamn studio and buried your nose in your goddamn work. I don't know anybody! All you want to do with me is screw. I hate my life here!"

"What's so special about Kris that you spend ninety bucks a month of my money talking to him?"

"*Your* money! Don't I have any freedom? What am I supposed to do with my life, sit around the house all day like a good little wife, waiting for you to finish making statues of naked women so you can come home?"

"If I don't get some more money together, we'll be paupers."

"Did you think I didn't know you'd see that bill and find out who I was calling? How dare you imply I was sneaking! Anyway, Dick's all the way across the country—what danger is it to you if I just talk with him?"

"Just who is this Dick?"

"I told you about him."

"Nina, I never heard of him before this afternoon."

"What did you do, act nasty to him over the phone? Believe me, he doesn't deserve it. He's one of the nicest people in the world. When I was more miserable than I've ever been in my life, Dick did me a favor I'll never forget."

"What sort of favor?"

"He made love to me," said my wife. "But you wouldn't understand."

"You never told me about him, Nina."

"Like hell I didn't," she fired back. "He's Charlie's real father."

During this marital spat, we'd been standing at the dining-room window, surrounded by nymphs and satyrs and brooks, while dusk slanted into our lush back yard like a guillotine whacking its block. Now Nina staggered into the living room, pitched herself face down on the couch, and sobbed, "Oh, God, it's that time of the month. The moon's pushing it out of me, and I want to cut myself open. God, I feel so alone! . . . I want my son. Charlie. I want my little boy."

A week later, Nina and I waited inside Idlewild. A three-engined monster sidled in, the four-wheeled ramp glided into place. A tired stewardess appeared holding the hand of an angelic, plump little boy, beautiful sun-blond hair tousled by breezes.

Nina gently cradled Charlie against her in the XKE's tight bucket seat. All the way home she stroked his fine hair. Charlie seemed totally at peace.

"Oh, Mommy, I missed you."

"Mommy missed you, too, Charlie, so so much." Traffic strangled the airport, and I made wrong turns which pinned us a half hour bumper to bumper on the Whitestone Bridge. Then a jackknifed semitrailer which had wiped out two cars trapped us motionless on the Connecticut Turnpike most of an hour. Finally we edged past the flaming wreckage. Ambulances, red lights whirling, clustered near the bonfire.

When we entered our yellow house, Charlie asked, "Where's Daddy?"

"He isn't coming," Nina replied. "We've found you a new daddy."

"I love old Daddy. He reads stories."

"Your new daddy will read you stories, too. He can draw pictures for you."

"You draw pictures?" he asked me, pointing at the walls.

"Yes."

"I don't like pictures."

"Darling, your new room is all fixed up for you," Nina said. "Elmo, take him upstairs."

Charlie reached for my hand. "You smell funny," he said.

A cast-iron dump truck, bought by Nina that morning, sat parked on his new bed. Charlie pushed it off into the floor. "Accident," he said, blandly looking up into my face.

He sat on my lap, on the bed, while I read about Mulberry Street. When I finished, he said, "Now draw pictures."

I pulled a small pad from my jacket, and a felt-tipped pen from my shirt pocket. "That's me coming from the airplane," Charlie said. "Now draw Mommy." I did. "Draw Daddy, too." I drew Ivan. "Daddy looks sad. Make him smile." I drew Ivan smiling.

"What's your real name?" Charlie asked.

"Prince Elmo Hatcher."

"Do you love me?"

I paused. "Yes," I answered. "I do."

"You're my daddy now," he sighed. "Can I have the pictures?" He took them. "Dress me in my jammies." I helped him into his pajamas. "Tell Mommy to kiss me good night," he said from under the covers.

I stepped into the hall, where Nina waited. "Well?" she whispered. "How did it go?"

•6•

Six days a week, I left the XKE with Nina, walked to my studio, and drowned myself in work—wondering why I bothered. I had pursued my daydreams and taken them to bed, only to find strange creatures warming my arms. Maybe there was a moral somewhere, a profundity that I, skipping like a flat stone across the water's surface, couldn't know without sinking. At any rate, I entombed myself in the front portion of a nineteenth-century brick office building four stories high. A life-insurance agency had gone bust in the pair of rooms which formed my studio. Giant sash windows without curtains sucked light from the gray street, and admitted the stares of pedestrians. Nina and Charlie were my sole human contact, while nonhuman ladies crawled cool and whitish from creases in my brain and buried themselves in clay.

Plaster cracked from bare walls and twelve-foot ceilings onto the split and warped floorboards, onto the coffin-vat of wet clay, the large fan, sanded-out molds, compressed air cylinder, waterbuckets, into the bathroom's stained sink and seatless john, onto crushed worms of paint tubes and rabbitglued canvases stacked against the wall, onto the umbilicus which fed the black telephone's belly. And I worked to pour food into that monster's cannibal guts.

Our phone bills climbed to nearly three hundred dollars a month. "I'll call anybody," Nina announced, "anywhere I please. I only do it because you never talk to me."

"I'm not going to pay. I'm letting them shut it off. I'm—"

But I always paid.

The phone would drag me from my clay.

"I'm losing my mind," Nina would complain. "What are *you* doing?"

"Working, God damn it!"

"Can't you even pull yourself away one minute? Charlie's driving me crazy. Hear him shrieking in the background? He's throwing a tantrum because I won't let him write all over the walls with his goddamn Magic Marker."

"For all I care, he can burn down the whole house!"

"Yes, I know. You feel trapped and you want out. That's why you're never home."

"I've got another exhibition coming up. And we're running out of money because of your goddamn phone bills."

"Is there a woman with you?"

"Come see for yourself."

"Sure. By then you'll see to it she's gone."

"If you don't believe what I say, raid me."

"I don't give a fuck what you do, Elmo, except that right now I'm going out of my mind. Look, in five minutes I'm jumping into my car and leaving Charlie here all by himself."

"You wouldn't do that."

"I need help," she said.

By December the house was more chaotic than my studio, and Charlie whirled like a dervish through the clutter. I shouted, "Can't you do something about this goddamn mess, Nina? You're driving me out of my mind!"

"And what do you think you're doing to me?"

Then her mood would change incredibly. I'd shuffle home filthy and the house would gleam, smelling of fresh wax and dinner, and Nina gorgeous and perfumed would embrace me at the door. I'd wash and dress, and we'd eat lobster under candlelight. Charlie would sit so peacefully in his little-man's suit and tie. And afterward, Charlie tucked away, I'd build a fire, and Nina and I would make love languorously on the living-room couch, our shadows tossing among nymphs and satyrs. Then Nina would pull my head into her deep bosom and cry, "Oh, God, I've lost control of my life, I don't deserve you."

But in a day or so, I'd return in the evening to find her lying on the couch, staring at the ceiling, oblivious to Charlie tearing through the overturned lamps and chairs, his Magic Marker leaving a trail on furniture, walls, woodwork, and she'd say, "You were with a woman all day, weren't you? Your phone was busy."

"Must have kicked it off the hook."

"You took it off on purpose."

"Yes," I admitted. "I was working hard."

"See." A dead voice. "You always tell me lies."

Maybe so. The sculptures I pummeled from my clay looked less and less like Nina—and more like Hazel, whose last name I didn't even know.

Inevitably, one of the women finally showed up, a rich man's mistress, whore-blond piece of ass rapping an ivory umbrella handle against the frosty January glass. I wanted to murder her.

"Door's unlocked," I shouted at once, dialing our house, getting the busy signal.

"Do I peel it all off?" she asked.

"Where's your boy friend?"

"Frisco. Hey, Max trusts me, you know? This here's a pure business arrangement—unless you got other ideas."

"Have to call my wife."

She draped her coat over the compressed air machine and began working out of her dress. "Max wants me wearing my garter belt and high heels," she explained.

A citizen checked his haircut in my window and suddenly reeled against a parked car.

"Better paint over that window," she laughed. "You artists are like doctors. A naked broad don't get the old juices flowing any more, huh?"

The phone jangled.

Nina's dead voice asked, "Anything new?"

"Yes. I mean, no."

"You have a woman there."

"One of my, uh, commissions."

"You promised me. She's naked, isn't she?"

"Uh, getting undressed."

"You always lie. She came by the house, trying to find you."

"This is business, Nina, you don't understand—"

"Do what ever you like." She hung up.

"Trouble with wifey?"

"Look, just take any position that feels natural, and hold it." I grabbed sketchbook and charcoal. "I'll make a few drawings right now, and you can be flying back to Max in a couple hours. He should've sent photographs anyway."

"Everybody's in a rush. Okay. I read."

I ran home to find the car gone and Charlie alone, busily smearing peanut butter onto the sofa. "Hello, Daddy. Charlie's painting."

"Come here, honey. Let's wash off those hands."

"Is Mommy ever coming back?"

"Of course."

"Mommy was crying."

Towels soaked in deep tub water.

"What happened here, Charlie?"

"I gave them a bath," he explained. "The ones in the closet, too."

"We'll have to do something about that, Charlie," I said, feeling a chill draft.

"In my room," Charlie said. "read me a story about where the wild things are, Daddy."

Something had been pitched through the glass in one of Charlie's windows. Looking out, I saw in the front yard the new dump truck Nina had bought him.

"Charlie, better tell me. Did you wreck anything else in the house?"

Charlie concentrated. "No."

Near four that morning, the front door slammed and woke me. Someone landed on the couch. "What's this goddamn muck?" Nina cried. She made no further sound, and finally I managed to doze, until the alarm's buzzer knocked me out of my cold bed.

In February, Ivan Rhodes visited his son—that is, Charlie Rhodes.

"You'll have to be here when he comes," Nina said. "I have an appointment."

"Where? Who with?"

"Isn't it a little late for questions like that?"

Ivan had gained at least fifty pounds. The suet of his cheeks swallowed his eyes. But he wore new clothes cut to his ponderosity. He had flown East. The Continental parked at the curb was rented. When he shook my hand, his palm felt soft and wet, the grip forceless. "Hey there, man," he said, "no hard feelings."

"Glad you see it that way."

"Where's Nina?"

"Had some appointment."

Charlie looked up at Ivan and shook his head side to side. "Who are you?" he asked.

"Can I come inside? Or should I just take him in the car?"

"Up to you."

"I'll come in. Where's your john? Little thing I need to do."

He came back beaming like Buddha, pupils contracted to needlepoints.

"Where's my son?" he cried heartily, spreading his arms. "How's my little boy?"

Charlie ran up the stair case out of sight. "How about a drink, Ivan?"

"Naw. Cut out the booze long time ago. You go ahead." He looked about the room. "Nice pictures. Talented guy, Prince Elmo. Listen, though, I'm hungry. Any candy in the house?"

I brought him an unopened heart-shaped red valentine of chocolates from the kitchen. Ripping through the cellophane, Ivan began eating them two at a time. "Better see Charlie before I go," he said.

I went upstairs. Charlie had smeared crimson all over his face. "Your father wants to see you, Charlie."

"You're my father," he said.

I carried him downstairs. "Nina left a lipstick lying loose," I explained.

"Come to Daddy, Charlie."

"I hate you," Charlie insisted.

The front door opened, and in swung Nina. "Hey there, fatso. When did you blow in?"

"Just getting ready to leave," Ivan muttered, still seated on the couch.

"Who painted Charlie's face like a wild Indian? Was that one of your brilliant ideas, Ivan? Think maybe I'd enjoy having to clean it off?"

"He came downstairs like that," Ivan said.

"How'd you get so fat, Ivan? Still hooking down the old hooch? No—I'll say it for you. You're so miserable since our divorce, you're drinking yourself into an early grave. My fault as usual, right?"

"This isn't necessary," I said. Charlie wandered away upstairs.

Struggling off the couch, Ivan mumbled, "Bathroom."

"How is the good old son of a bitch?" Nina asked me.

"We didn't talk much."

"Say, did you remember to tell him Charlie's not really his son?"

"For Christ's sake, he might hear."

"You are such an appalling hypocrite!" she shouted. "It surpasses belief. Cut the guy's throat and suddenly you're his father protector."

Fingers clasped across his paunch, Ivan wandered back beaming. He hoisted his topcoat on. "Tell Charlie goodbye," he wheezed. "Seeing me kind of shocked him."

"If you'd sat on him," Nina said, "you'd have shocked him even more."

"So long, Prince Elmo." We shook hands again.

"That is such a heartwarming goddamned sight," Nina observed. "Next time around, maybe you winners ought to marry each other."

Ivan waddled to his car.

That night, I said, "Nina, we've got to straighten ourselves out before we lose control completely."

"That means you're horny and want to get fucked. No, thanks, mister. I'm spending the evening out. Give one of your models a buzz, screw her in my bed, I don't care."

One night while Nina was out with the car and Charlie had just fallen asleep, the phone rang.

"Yeah, who's this?" a man's voice asked.

"Who is *this*?"

"Does a woman named Nina live there?"

"Who wants to know?"

"I don't see how that's any of your business," the man said. "She didn't say nothing about other men. Now do I get to talk with her or not? I'm liable to pile on over there."

"Come on," I told him. "Nina's gone this evening but I'll wait right here."

"Who are you, anyway?"

"Her husband."

"Aw, come on, buddy, you got to be kidding. Listen, describe something special about her, maybe I'll believe you. Listen, she got big tits, I mean real big, or, say, medium?"

I slammed down the receiver.

That midnight while I writhed sleepless, the bedside phone jangled. "Think I got the wrong number," a second man said.

"Maybe not."

"What's that, a proposition? Maybe she was telling the truth about you."

"Who?"

"What a waste of time!" He hung up.

Near morning a naked body squirming on mine snatched me awake into a zone of pure war. Above me, Nina floated in the dark, eyes and mouth swollen slits for pleasure, hot booze breath moaning, "Oh, move, move!" I shot my angry load, then shoved her off. "Yes, I'm an evil bitch," she groaned, "beat me all you want, I told them to call, I deserve it." My fist split her lips. Blood splotched the sheets. I hit her in the face, right, left. When I quit, my elbows and shoulders ached, bones in my palm and fingers felt splintered, the sheet had scraped my knees raw. "Don't stop now, kill me, please, the only thing I want to do now," blood oozing from her lips, "is die."

I staggered into the bathroom for wet rags to sponge her and saw the rubber snake dangling into the tub, dripping on the yellowed porcelain.

We stopped speaking. She stayed home now, lips swollen, scabbed, eyes blackened, body bruises changing purple to brown to yellow. She never rang me at my studio while I worked, seven days a week now, dawn to midnight. From her perennial resting place on the couch she would reach out silently for me when I passed and if I came close enough, seize clothing, and whimper like a kicked animal when I yanked loose.

In March, I got two letters worth mentioning. One came from Billy Pickwick, saying he was free on bail after his arrest for demonstrating against the House Un-American Activities Committee in San Francisco: "Great and glorious fun, the bull's club thudding against your skull, that familiar smooth guillotine plank in the lockup, friendly guards, and French cuisine—all infusing one with purpose and identity. Hazel, married and gorgeously tanned from afternoons on the beach communing with the Almighty, sends her love."

Addressed and readdressed by postmen, the second letter came from my draft board secretary, informing me that if I did not register my whereabouts soon, serious action would be taken.

I crumpled both letters into the trash.

Nina began vomiting. I'd hear her retching in the bathroom

before I hauled ass out of bed. When I left for the studio, she'd still be at it, never asking for the help I never gave. Charlie told me she vomited during the day, every day; and she wasted to bones on her couch. At first, I thought she'd caught flu, and furiously expected to get it myself and lose the pace of my work. But soon I figured it out. The bitch had gotten herself pregnant.

The more Nina faded, the more Charlie became my last human bond. Mornings, before going to work, I'd prepare Charlie's meals, putting out extra for the bitch, if she wanted to eat. For all I cared, she could munch garbage.

But when I couldn't even force myself to mold clay or spread the deadly glaze, I'd knock off and drive with Charlie into the warming hills where buds studded the laurel bushes; up onto East or West Rock, from whose height we watched the city drowse beneath its blanket of car-and-factory haze. Human beings dwindled to bugs, and Yale's Gothic seemed an elaborate display in the children's museum. Kinship growing between us, Charlie and I strolled the beaches of the Sound, where the tide shrank from black lines of waste, beer cans housing live crabs. The sand would be lonely except for a walker and dog, or teenage lovers arm in arm, shoes dangling from free hands. Sometimes Charlie paused, bent, returned with a gull-broken shell in his palm.

"Throw it away, Charlie."

That year, clams spread hepatitis.

If we stood quiet enough, gulls would settle near us, scavenging, eating the dead. I couldn't believe their enormous size.

"Mommy's going to die," Charlie said one morning on the beach.

"Maybe."

"She never does anything. She never hugs me."

"If she dies," I asked, "will you care?"

"When Mommy dies, I want her sleeping on the couch. I hate you when you go to work, like I hate my old daddy." He watched the gulls before pronouncing sentence: "Everything is going to die."

"It's April Fools' Day," Nina said from the couch, the first time she'd spoken in weeks. "That means it won't be long until your exhibit. Hope you have all your work done in time. You've worked hard, and nothing's gone right, has it? It's mostly my fault. But it's too late in the day for apologies. You're not going to talk with me, are you," she observed sadly.

It was ten at night. I sat tightlipped in an easy chair, the *New Haven Register* clutched in my angry hands.

"Doesn't it mean anything," she continued, "that I haven't made a long-distance call in months? It hasn't been out of goodness, just because I've been so sick. Nothing seems to be worth doing any more. Did you read about how the Navy floated a person in a rubber suit, in water, in a dark and silent chamber, and he lost all sensation of a world outside himself? That's the way I feel now. Please talk with me again."

I read where a truck on the Jersey wiped out a rabbi and his vacationing family in the fog. In some foreign country whose name I'd never heard before, a land mine dismembered two American soldiers.

"I haven't felt anything since you beat me up," Nina said. "I deserved that. I'm not putting you down. Please say something to me."

On page three, the girl whose ponytail had caught in a cornpicker, and whose face had been pulled off, and who'd lain in a hospital since, eyebrows, eyelids, lips, and ears grafted to her belly until doctors could begin remaking her, died for reasons unknown. This spring, a new stratospheric hemline was expected to hit strange heights. A Southeast Asian terrorist organization, led (it was rumored) by a woman educated at Radcliffe, decapitated the teenage daughter of a village official, and thus demonstrated the consequences of cooperating with foreign powers.

Nina was saying, "I feel terrible about Charlie. All that energy. I keep remembering my parents, my bitchy mother. Take after her, I guess. My father's a skinny little guy, all eaten up, furious eyes, oh, Christ. He loves guns. I think that's why he owned a hardware store, until they retired to Fort Lauderdale. You really aren't going to talk, are you? I remember the way his socks'd gradually get eaten inside his shoes, until the bare back of his heel stuck up from the leather like an ostrich neck. Ha. Oh wow, I married Ivan to get away from Mother, and—I can't seem to get rid of this furious grudge against you. Life can be wrecked awful young. Look at poor Charlie, what chance does he have? You know, I think Ivan's hooked on dope. Well, husband, what's your opinion about this marriage? Hadn't Charlie and I just better cut out? No answer. Well. I'm pretty far into a new brat, you must have figured it out some time ago. Did you? Well. I hoped it was yours, but I guess there's no way of being sure. Does it make any difference to you?"

Dick Tracy drilled some deformed specimen of humanity right between the eyes. "*Have a taste of this magnum, you little rat!*" Al Capp's round-rumped belles bent to be buggered by the eyes of American citizens.

"Come sit beside me on the couch, honey?" she pleaded mildly. "I used you in some pretty unfair ways. I feel guilty about lots of things, but most of all I feel guilty about Charlie, and you. Come on, Prince Elmo, we've both done some terrible things in our lives, and some of them we've done to each other, and we've always been able to forgive. Well, I haven't. No. But you have, up until now. I just want you to know how I appreciate it, really. Not very many men could have forgiven so many things. My throat's sore from talking so much. You aren't going to sit beside me, are you?"

Rapes, burglaries, murders, suicides, and scandalous divorces filled the newspaper's back page. Rudolph Stayne's most recent wife accused him of having affairs with two hundred seventy different women during their marriage.

I crumpled the paper, threw it at the rug, and stalked to the door.

"Please don't leave us alone tonight," she begged.

I wanted to spend the night painting away at some gargantuan canvas which would pull everything together once and for all. Another Guernica, controlling the chaos it depicted.

"This is the last night I'm going to be here," she said. "If you care about me and Charlie, stay, because if you don't, I'm going to leave. I'll take Charlie with me, even though he thinks he belongs with you. I'm an awful person, but I've suffered a lot, too. Don't go, honey. Maybe there's still a chance."

I slammed out the front door.

At the car, I thought a moment, then shoved the keys back into my pocket. I could walk.

But I didn't reach the studio until eleven, and felt too tired and depressed to work. No unity tonight; I couldn't see the forest for the trees—it was all her fault, the bitch—and damned if I felt like going back. I took off up Chapel Street, just walking, feeling sweat begin to flow under my plaid shirt, smelling fumes from pizza parlors, and the diner across from the YMCA. Passing the twinkling shadow of St. Raphael's Hospital, I branched down Derby, past the Yale Bowl's dark shoulder, the arch commemorating some dead coach. At a crossroad, where service stations and auto dealers faced each other, the road turned four-lane highway, and I took off running, sticking to shoulder grass because every minute the stoplight released great packs of cars down the asphalt, racing two abreast at my heels, red asses winking out of sight. Then a minute's quiet, northeast traffic separated from me by a forested divider. To my right over a barbed-wire fence I sniffed the great wooded peace of a public watershed (NO TRESPASSING), and at last, reflecting a full moon, saw the twin lakes split by a single dam.

I ripped a pants leg scrambling over the wobbly fence, tumbled down the embankment as headlights burned the air above, then raced for a black copse, stripped, tiptoed over sharp rocks down where the water deepened, and for long moments floated in the icy lake, drank, spouted like a whale, brainlessly watched cars hiss past and cloudwisps melt red across the moon and the man in the moon scowl down into my own white face—

A sudden thought sent me freestyling rapidly to the bank, racing through the barbed shallows, flinging on my clothes, and sprinting to the fence, vaulting it in the very face of traffic, marathoning back the way I'd come with no thought for heart or lungs.

The Jaguar slept in the moonlight when I stumbled up the front steps, through the unlocked doorway of the house. I staggered wildly through the rooms, calling, searching, wanting the sound of life. Then finally, in the dining room, I found them. Charlie lay on the table's altar, Nina on the floor. A gaping wound grinned hideously from each throat—two razored-open floodgates, painting the world red.

Family

•1•

THE POLICE questioned me all that night and through the next evening, when they plugged a polygraph into my flesh. "You're the killer," snarled the chief detective. "You probably drove her to it. This machine isn't giving you a clean bill of health." Only the mincemeat Nina made of her fingertips cleared me, and with reluctance the police let me go.

Nina's parents were notified by telegram. Their response came just before burial—a bouquet of yellow roses for Nina, and a miniature duplicate for Charlie, sent through FTA. They had disowned their daughter after our marriage, and must also have disowned Charlie when they chucked him into the airplane. A second telegram brought no reply from Ivan or his parents.

I selected a single king-sized pine coffin, sheets of fuzzy gray felt disguising its outside.

"What sort of ceremony would you like?" asked the funeral director.

Pick and shovel."

"But the others, besides yourself—"

"Nobody else coming."

I was wrong. At the brink of that machine-dug hole, under a gentle spring shower washing dirt onto the coffintop while a crane lowered the concrete vault, a touch on my elbow. I turned to face Krishna Singh, in black topcoat, sheltered by a black umbrella, blending into the somber air like a chameleon.

"What does anyone need," I asked, "with a bastard like you?"

"Let's forget the compliments out of respect for the dead," he said. "Besides, there are strangers around."

"You're the last son of a bitch I ever wanted to see." Mist rose from the soggy earth.

"Couldn't put my own feelings any better. For some half-assed reason, Roberts keeps a close watch on you, and the funeral parlor's part of a chain he owns. This is my last business trip for him. Because he likes to rub things in." His breath smelled of cinnamon.

Workmen maneuvered the vault into position as it dangled from their motorized crane. Water trickled over my forehead and nose.

"Thought you were being trained to take over when the old fart conked out."

"Yeah, so did I," he said quietly. "And I really threw myself into the role. But all I get's some useful training in hand-to-hand combat."

"You're a jerk, Kris. Just say why you're here and go crawl back under your rock."

"To finish arranging your exhibition." He looked distractedly into the grave, while loathing wrinkled his eyes and mouth.

The vault disappeared beneath ground level, shielding two waxen bodies against worms. "Glad to see even Roberts can flush a creep," I said.

"Don't push too hard, brother. I'm not feeling friendly."

"And what about you and my wife, you black bastard? What about that?"

"Yeah," Kris mused. "I pretty well beat your ass there." Strangely, he looked miserable. "Before you got married. I think maybe she was trying us both out, just like Roberts. Hey? Then you forced the issue."

"Huh?" A machine began plowing thick batter into the grave.

"Dumbass." He shook his head slowly, looking at me. "Why anybody'd choose a simple fuckhead like you— But then we both know why. Even you've figured that out by now. Ise jes a local boy," he aped. "A little Shawnee blood maybe mixed in, and a little of your own sweet white, brother. But it's the black blood that makes those delicate creatures burn, isn't that what all you honkeys think, huh?" He pointed angrily into the hole, collapsed the umbrella, and rammed its silver tip in the dirt. "I had that woman a hundred times, man, every way, don't you think?"

I saw myself seize his nose, yank his tongue loose by the roots, gouge his eyes, and while he lay near the whining machinery, ram his umbrella tip into the empty, bleeding sockets.

But I lay looking up at him, rain pelting my eyes, right hand numbed. "Motherfucker!" he cried. "Aren't we on the same side? We should have been friends!"

"Hey, look, wouldja believe them two guys fighting? What the hell's the white one got to laugh about?" I heard a gravedigger say.

Krishna Singh, whatever his real name was, Errol Flynn this, Rudolph Stayne that, forced his umbrella tip between my teeth.

Gravediggers clustered around grinning. "Hey, buddy, don't kill that joker."

Tongue against steel, I laughed, "Kill me, pleathe."

"No such luck. I'll just water you, ha ha." Ballooning his cheeks a couple of times, he spat juicily into my face. "Oh, hello, only a small personal account being settled here," Krishna Singh charmingly assured the spectators; in that second he had resumed the phony act. Winking, he yanked his umbrella from my mouth, and flashed his brittle theatrical mask down upon me. "One more small blow, and I am on my way." The mask instantly dissolved. "You won't feel nothin', brother." Clenching his jaw, he flicked his shoe toe with a hollow thud into my balls. And I felt only a prickle at the base of my skull.

•2•

Staggered along a Wyoming road. Downpour pounding the rolling khaki hills. A woman carting five young children in a station wagon offered me a lift into town. "Drifting?" she asked.

"My good woman," I announced, "my name is Prince Elmo Hatcher, heir to the throne of America."

"Children, did you hear that?"

In a squealing tangle, they wrestled and fought all over the back.

"When I assume my rightful place, madam, I will grant interest-free loans to artists, creative writers, and the indigent. I will open a chain of supermarkets selling an endless supply of free food."

"Hey, you're crazy. But you sound harmless."

"And I will establish jobs, with salaries beginning at fifteen thousand per year and on-job training—"

"Tell my husband."

"—with people learning how to enjoy themselves, eating the best food, drinking the best booze, traveling to exotic ports and getting along with the natives, and . . ."

Lay in a Nebraska field of tall grass near the roadside, at night, wishing gophers, like Shmoos, were edible. In a Reno alley, my nose scraped between paving bricks. Shoes thwocked the soft portions of my body, the world behind my eyelids reddened. Two police towering above me, I awaited midnight emergency treatment in a St. Louis hospital. The corridor swarmed with cops, with citizens moaning. One lone intern stitched in a little room. Three black girls who claimed the same man raped each of them at pistol point, tearily awaited examination. A motorcycle Viking protested an orderly's cutting away his bloody T-shirt, uncovering neat stab wounds: "Hey, Doc, that there's a two-dollar shirt!"

Outside Denver, after dark, a couple picked me up in their Land-Rover, fed me, bedded me overnight in their mountain camp for autistic children.

Slept on a beach off Route 1 near San Francisco, sand warm and soft when I first lay down, hard brick by the time I slept, and woke to teenagers body-surfing in water touching my fingers.

Deputy toed me awake on the cement cell floor. "Okay, buddy. We traced you back to Goldengrove, Indiana. Your draft board's a-wonderin' where you're at."

•3•

The kid's ears thrust out like jug handles. He wore blue overalls and a T-shirt, and pleaded with the black Army sergeant at the desk, "Please, sir, you just got to take me. I can't stand it. Let me at them bastards, you got to let me pertect my country."

I stuffed my clothes into a swimming-pool basket and

clutched the safety-pin tag. "Hey, you got to wear underpants. Ain't you got ears?"

"Don't have underpants."

"Well, mister, nobody here wants to look at your thing. Put your goddamn pants back on."

I handed the man the empty jar. "You was supposed to provide a sample," he said. "How come there ain't any piss in here?"

"Can't get it to come out," I told him.

"Get your ass back there, mister, and stay until you can squeeze some piss into that jar."

"He can't order you around that way," said a young man with shoulder-length hair. "You're not in the Army yet."

"You shut your goddamn mouth."

"Don't you dare lay a single finger on me, buster," the young man said calmly, "or I'll sue for assault and battery."

"Get that man out of here!"

"Check that you're neurotic and homosexual," the young man persisted. "Don't sign the attorney general's form—"

"Can't seem to get any piss out," I told the soldier. "Must be nervous."

"You can't leave here, mister, until you piss. Now *piss!*"

Finally I squeezed an eighth of an inch onto the bottom. "Fine fine fine," he muttered.

"No, you can't take my blood. Get your hands off me!" Back against the wall, the young man with long hair fought off several soldiers and doctors.

"Come on now, John, you're a brave lad, aren't you? It won't hurt. You can do it. I know your head's in the right place."

"He's holding things up," someone complained. "Bring him back later, we'll work on him then."

As the young man passed me, he whispered, "Don't give them any blood."

"Get that bastard out of here quick," a soldier said, "before he fucks everything up!"

"Fascist pigs!" shouted the young man as they led him out. "Nazi cocksuckers! Right-wing Republican queers!"

"You can't take my blood," I told them.

"Aw, come on, buddy, not you, too."

"I'm not going to let you stick that needle into my arm. No, get that rubber tube away! You'll strangle me. Get away, goddamn it!"

"He's just copying John," a soldier said. "Come on—Prince? You look like a brave, strong fellow. This shouldn't give you a bit of trouble."

"Fuck that stuff!" I shouted. "I'm not giving you any blood!"

The doctor soothed me down. "Listen, Prince, we don't want to hurt you. We just want a chance to do our job so we can all go home for the night. But if you don't let us do our job, did John tell you that we can keep you here for a full three days, or until you finally do cooperate?"

"Is that a fact?"

"It certainly is," said the doctor. "Now let's just hold out our arm, and put on this little tourniquet, there, that's right—"

"I'm not going to let you take my blood!" I screamed, pulling away.

"The hell with this," the doctor said. "I don't have to tolerate two in a row. A couple you guys, hold him down. Somebody shut the door. Fine."

Up in front of an emormous room full of people, a soldier was saying, "Now, sign the next form at the—"

"Listen, men, don't sign this form. If you don't sign it—"

"Get that man out of here!" the soldier shouted.

It was the young man with shoulder-length hair. "—it'll be another six months before they can—"

A khaki phalanx hoisted him and carted him off.

A soldier walking up and down the aisles looked over my shoulder and said, "You haven't signed yet."

A doctor looked up my rectum and felt my balls. "Looks like you've been knocked around a little, mister," he observed. At some point, I took a multiple-choice examination. A young man rested his hand on my ass, whereupon a pair of soldiers hustled him away. A soldier hauled me out of line into a room, where he sat me on a bench with two other bare-chested men before an old sergeant sitting at a desk. At five-minute intervals, he called out the names of my companions, who rose and disappeared into a backroom.

"Prince Elmo Hatcher."

"Yes!" I cried, staggering toward him.

"Easy, lad, it's only a headshrinker."

The psychiatrist was small and roly-poly, with owlish glasses and bright, brown eyes. Hair fell carelessly across his forehead, his collar flopped open two buttons, and he wore no tie.

"I screwed my own sister," I told him.

"Was she any good?" he grinned.

"My mother, too."

"Sounds like you had a rich old time. Ever fuck any goats?"

"I had syphilis."

"Not my department. I'm just here to see if you're crazy enough to shoot people." He looked down at a form. "You say here you're homosexual. Are you a practicing homosexual?"

"I don't like the word practicing," I told him.

"You interest me for another reason," he continued. "On your record, it says you were raised several years in the home of Robert Pickwick. He was a friend of mine in college. Now, Prince, tell me, do you think he'd be proud of you today?"

I began crying.

"There there, now," he said, coming around the desk and patting my shoulder. "Have a Kleenex."

"I'm not really a homosexual," I sobbed. "I was just lying."

"Well, cheer up, fellow. Your life's obviously in such an incredible state of disarray, maybe the Army's just the ticket. Slap order onto things in no time flat!"

I went out and signed the papers.

When I was leaving the building, I passed the same black sergeant with the same jug-eared supplicant before him, kneeling this time on the concrete floor, on its thick brown wax armor. "Please, Mr. Sergeant," he was saying with clasped hands, "you ain't got no right to turn me away."

I don't know whether Uncle Sam accepted the boy with jug ears. But he accepted me.

•4•

I learned to operate several amazing weapons—a small grenade launcher which fired a projectile the size of an egg, fertilizing itself after whirling some thirty feet from the trigger man, and hatching a wire coil into myriad seething fragments; a machine gun like the ones in those Rudolph Stayne-Ronald Reagan films, with its Buck Rogers shock absorber at the barrel's base, and a plastic shoulder stock like a drugstore toy; a small rifle, also with toy plastic stock, which fired small bullets so rapidly it ate through the seventeen-shot clip before the first ejected casing reached the ground. Our training manual was a comic book: a hard-eyed chick, chorus-line figure squeezed into short-shorts and halter, word-ballooned instructions like "Keep her sweet piece clean and lubed-up slick, and you'll score sure and deep every single squeeze!"

John and I arrived together in basic training, scalps shaved to the bone. After three days of coercion, he told me, the Army had persuaded even John that life might be simpler if he submitted to the draft. One of his tormenters, a captain, scarred, grizzled veteran of World War II and Korea, had mused, "I understand you have a little sister, John." "So what?" "Humm . . ." "What the hell does she have to do with this?" "Very interesting." "Goddamn it, what are you freaks doing to my sister?" And so on.

Now I whispered, "Where the hell are we fighting?"

"Don't worry," he replied. "We'll find out."

•5•

During my last week of training, base headquarters ordered me to the brigadier's office. There I found Tarze Roberts.

"Haircut improves your looks," he said. "Like a man all primped up for electrocution."

"Yes, sir."

"Don't stand at attention for me. Sit down. Your general's my friend. I also know the Secretary of Defense. Say the word, I'll buy you out of this."

"I don't like owing you, Roberts. It's too goddamned expensive."

"Nonsense. Your last exhibition sold out. That mysterious

disappearance helped, and surfacing in the armed forces of our country—great romantic flack. Your brother sends regards, by the way."

"Which brother?"

"What's that?" He almost cracked a grin. "Why, Duke. Lots of nasty aggressive vigor there. But he's reached his ceiling." Roberts paused; he fiddled with an empty six-cigar container on the general's desk. "Prince Elmo, if we lose this war, I could drop more, buck for buck, than our government. How does that grab you?"

"Doesn't."

"That marriage of yours, you suffered quite a bit, eh?"

"Not like my wife and kid."

"But *you* survived."

I looked at my watch. "Twenty-mile hike leaving in ten minutes."

"You haven't let me down yet, Prince Elmo. But I must have further proof of character, and above all, the ability to survive!" He waved one hand above his barren scalp. His face was crumbling like a rotten sponge. "I don't have many more years to survive in person," he said. "Three, maybe less. Let's call this your final test, Prince Elmo. Imagine owning a world—speaking metaphorically." He lifted the torn six-cigar container. "This box is mine. All boxes are mine." Suddenly his face split into a nasty, slobbering cackle. "I also"—he choked on phlegm, it was so funny he could hardly hack it loose—"sell the Army its"—wheeze!—"coffins!"

•6•

I began as rifleman in the second platoon, Company B, 3rd Battalion of the 22nd Infantry Regiment. John, also in my platoon, had been trained as radio telephone operator, and now answered to the call "RTO." Our platoon leader was another combat virgin, Second Lieutenant Anthony Wayne Shelley—tall, built like a boxer, red-haired, freckled, dimpled, and snub-nosed. It turned out that the only platoon member who'd fought was our machine-gunner, a nervous, bespectacled corporal named Henry, just beginning his third tour of combat.

February 12, balls tingling, I penetrated the war zone in a jet which plummeted onto the landing strip like a free-fall elevator. Since the enemy controlled half the base's periphery and sniped us in the air with American fifty-caliber machine guns, takeoffs and landings had to be quick. Talcumed with golden dust, the hot air hung humid. Scattered persons in uniform, including a newsreel crew, observed from behind barbed wire while we poured from the plane. When my feet touched earth, an observer exploded in a puff of amber smoke, followed by a dull thud.

The newsreel crew rushed into action, cameraman rotating his trinity of lenses.

"Take cover, men!" an officer cried, and we ran toward the nearest barracks.

Behind the barbed wire, men scrambled and shouted. The air reeked of jet exhaust, excrement, and burned meat.

I swam in my own sweat, in a camouflaged bus, down a red-dust road lined with barbed wire, to a gigantic housing development of tents pitched on wooden platforms. We first visited the armorer, who gave me a rifle and bandolier of ammo, which I signed for. John and I were assigned bunks in the same wood-floored tent, where we met Corporal Henry sitting under the rolled-up tent wall cleaning his machine gun.

"We saw a man blow up at the airport," John said.

"White man or gook?" the corporal asked.

"Notice, Elmo?"

"Wasn't close enough," I said.

"Some of the best fighters on our team are gooks," the corporal said. "Asians aren't raised to respect human life like Americans. One shot from a village, and in go our gooks and cut the throats of everything that moves."

"Ever used that?" I asked, nodding toward the machine gun.

"Matter of fact, I got one hundred twenty-four sure kills, plus some I kissed off with other guys. When everybody's shooting, you can't always tell who put the first few holes through a guy. And if artillery or airstrike chews them up, forget it."

Nobody claimed the fourth cot. That night the temperature dropped near freezing. I awoke next morning to find my razor blades missing, not to mention my soap, my watch, a mechanical pencil, and two clips of ammo.

"Some of our gooks sneak around stealing things to sell on the black market," the corporal explained.

Lieutenant Shelley met us at the bus door, like a Greyhound driver taking tickets, and greeted us individually, clinging to my hand while he said, "Glad to have you aboard, Private Hatcher, yes. And you—" The "platoon" was short twenty-five bodies—a platoon only on paper. We had less than two squads, just one sergeant and one corporal, fifteen men total.

For a mile or so, the landscape lay barren—red and eroded clay punctuated with bomb and artillery craters, and sudden swaths charred black, all gradually spilling dust into the cloudless red day. But suddenly the road slid into lush plantation on both sides, trees lined neatly in endless rows, rolling hills, a lazy brown canal, green vines, grass plush and waist-high, and clear sweet air.

The bus dropped us on a semicircular drive before a seventeenth-century French chateau shaded by oak and elm: Battalion headquarters, where we'd get briefed. We entered by an elaborate double staircase of sandstone. Distant artillery thudded. In the foyer, we passed an antique table, elaborate hand carving on its legs, mother of pearl inlaid flower and landscape designs on the sides, a royal-purple marble top. Nudging me, John said, "Sixteenth-century French. Worth at least three thou in the States."

The briefing room must have been a boudoir. Mirrors covered the ceiling, and gilt figureheads, female, jutted naked from the corners. We sat in folding chairs, the sort rented out by funeral homes for Thanksgiving dinners. Wide-gaping French doors sucked warm sunny air inside. Shelley positioned himself before a bulletin board, unrolled a fresh topographical map, pinned it up, consulted notes, and said, "Men, for those who smoke, the smoking fire is lit. We proceed five hundred meters from battalion headquarters across a no-fire zone two hundred fifty meters wide. At this point, we reach a village of friendlies. The guide and interpreter meets us, and we proceed roughly twelve hundred meters further through the second village. Intelligence indicates enemy there. We smoke them out. Moving from this village west five hundred meters, we cross three canals, two hundred fifty meters apart across open terrain, into this wooded area here, where the enemy may have a bunker complex dug in. Orders are, if the darned thing exists, waste it." He paused. "In my opinion, men, we shouldn't face much in the way of enemy action. Most of the war's being fought by the newspapers back home. Nevertheless, people who know much more about the situation than we do have placed us here to do a job, and, by golly, if anybody gets in our way, we'll make them darned sorry."

A gravel foot path halved the mansion's rear lawn, vast green gently down-sloping a full half mile. From identical fountains on either side of the walk, marble dolphins spouted water. Rainbows shimmered in the spray. At lawn's edge we entered a field of sugarcane which towered above our heads, rustling in the breeze. I remembered similar fields within a few miles of the shack when I was a child, and a swaybacked one-story mill which cooked sorghum molasses: mule walking his slow, steady circle about the stone. Abruptly we stepped into the open again and picked up a ten-foot-wide dirt road, yard-deep ditches running on either side. Beyond waved fields of waist-high brown grass. Excrement, studded with buzzing emerald flies, coiled in the ditches. The air reeked so powerfully it cleared my stuffy head.

A crowd of tiny naked children met us at the village, crying, grinning, waving their arms—as a group, the most beautiful children I'd ever seen. "Chewing gum." "Boom boom." "Chocolate." Pigs grunted softly among the trees.

Shelley scrounged in his pocket. The corporal said, "Sir, in my opinion, we shouldn't give these little bastards anything"—patting his weapon—"except maybe a good healthy taste of hot lead."

"These are friendlies," Shelley replied.

"Fuck that, sir. Let them catch you in the dark in their black peejays, and they'll trim your balls off."

This naked party danced about us while we entered a large dirt clearing rimmed by thatched shacks. Beyond the clearing and the shacks, a forest gloomed. "We're supposed to pick up our guide," Shelley said.

A small group of adults, scantily dressed men and women, all exceedingly clean and well groomed, advanced toward us. In their midst, a woman, crying, carried a small girl in her arms. A cloth, heavily bloodstained, swaddled the child's left forearm. "Medic!" Shelley cried. "Do something about that child!"

Our interpreter-guide emerged from these adults and explained to Shelley and me what had transpired just before our arrival. A squad of guerrilla terrorists, led by one "Susie Q.," or so the name sounded in the interpreter's pronunciation, had arrived in the village to collect taxes and recruit fresh troops among the villagers. To neutralize any reluctance in this village of "American sympathizers," they herded all villagers together, forced the "mayor" to kneel, then shoved his seven children before him in a clump. "Which of your children," asked Susie Q., "do you select to be made a punitive example before your villagers?" The mayor replied that he himself wished to be the example, and please, would Susie Q. not harm his children. But Susie Q. informed the mayor that if he did not select one child from the lot, all his children would be shot dead without further ceremony. But that the one child he himself selected would not be killed. After this coercion, the mayor selected his second youngest child, a daughter, to be made example of. Susie Q. then laid another choice at the mayor's doorstep. "We are going to mutilate your child. Which part of her body do you select for mutiliation?" When the mayor said it was impossible for him to answer, Susie Q. informed him that she would order the child decapitated if he did not immediately comply. The mayor asked if perhaps Susie Q. might be satisfied to mutilate the little finger of the child's left hand. Meanwhile, the child, seven years old, sobbing in terror, heard this deliberation pinioned by a member of Susie Q.'s squad between Susie

Q. and the mayor. "Not high enough payment for your sins against the People's Movement for Independence," explained Susie Q. The bargaining continued, one finger at a time, while villagers quaked and wailed, until Susie Q. settled for the child's entire left hand, to be hacked off just above her wrist. This Susie Q. accomplished with one machete stroke. But just then a sentry announced our arrival, and the terrorists, not lingering for money or men, fled to the west.

"Oh, my God!" Shelley exclaimed. "I've heard of things like this happening, but I just didn't believe it!"

The corporal said, "If we hustle, maybe we can catch up with the dirty bastards."

"Who is Susie Q.?" I asked.

The interpreter explained that this was the name by which the most effective terrorist guerrilla was known. Was Susie Q. a woman? The interpreter didn't know. Either a woman or a man of extraordinary beauty and grace, as well as bravery.

After the medic had done what little he could, and Shelley radioed battalion headquarters ("Sir, there's a child here, a seven-year-old girl . . . Yes, sir, terrorist victim. Positive, sir . . . . Susie Q., sir. Amputated left hand, needs medical attention badly, sir, could she come to headquarters immediately and be looked after? . . . What? She doesn't need a photographer, sir, she needs a doctor, sir! . . ." and muttered and shook his head, the platoon plus guide moved gingerly through the village, to the west. "Chamber a round," Shelley ordered. "Spread out, men, prepare for enemy ambush. We're not dealing with ordinary human beings here."

"Maybe we could walk a little artillery in front of us, sir," the corporal suggested. A private kept pace beside him now, holding a hundred-bullet web like a bridal train.

"Negative, Corporal. Only twelve hundred meters to the second village."

"But, sir, that village's full of commie sympathizers."

"Negative, Corporal. Now, spread out. You and me, Corporal, share the point. RTO here with me. Sergeant, fall back about thirty feet. For heaven's sake, men, move out!"

We slunk through a forest, which opened into another cane field, veined, this time, with irrigation ditches: yellow water, floating clumps of excrement. A single-engine Cessna, forward observer to direct artillery and air strikes, circled overhead.

Then out of the cane into an open field again, some three hundred yards of waist-high grass bending slightly in the breeze. Smoke wisps rose beyond a clump of forest at the field's verge. The whole scene appeared pastoral, still, at peace with the juices of natural process. "Spread out, men!" called Shelley, looking back, motioning us onward.

"Don't straggle!" The Cessna droned, red light winking beneath its tail. We ran for the woods' cover: Susie Q. could scarcely have found a better place to ambush us. But nothing happened—except that, passing through the forest into the second village, we discovered that no village remained.

"What in God's name is *this*?" Shelley wondered. We grouped at the clearing's edge. "Some sort of trick?"

The entire area, roughly football-field size, lay annihilated, an acne-blasted face. Charred and smoking patches remained of some huts. For the rest: shell craters six feet deep, fresh, smoking; and bodies; and parts of bodies, disjecta membra, cooked limbs and chunks of limbs, pieces of torso, smashed internal organs, heads, like a thousand sex murders in a single block. Among the human fragments, I identified a few raw hunks of blown-apart pig.

"That incredible, inhuman, unbelievable creature!" gasped Shelley.

"Who's that, sir?" asked the corporal.

"Susie Q., for God's sake!"

"Oh, hell, sir, Susie Q. didn't do all this." He pointed upward at the winking Cessna. "Our boys walked some artillery through here to soften 'er up."

"I thought they were hitting those bunkers further on." Shelley unfurled his map. "Look. It's not for another fifteen hundred meters."

"Well, sir, maybe it's some sort of mistake. Whyn't you ask the guy up there?" The Cessna droned out of sight beyond the trees.

"Let's beat it, men," Shelley said. "Come on, move out."

We'd been told to expect three parallel canals on a wide-open field of grass. Water flowed sluggish and thick in the first. I submerged to my neck, then the bottom gave out, and I sank to my forehead in the foul yellow soup, regained balance, floated pack and weapon to the other side. Clambering up the embankment, I saw two black-clad figures running beyond the second canal. The corporal fired a burst, then commented, "Fuckers way out of range."

Shelley phoned in more artillery. In a few seconds, silent smoke geysered from the tree line several hundred meters away. Soon, a chopper sputtered overhead and proceeded to circle the forest, hyphening tracers downward. Dull thuds. The earth tremored. After we crossed the second canal and spread out over the open field, we could hear a short artillery round. I hit the ground in time, but one rifleman, caught standing, was suddenly a circus dwarf asleep with bloodless face, his lower half a pudding of blood and bones.

Shelley yanked the telephone off its pack and screamed, "You idiots dropped a round right on top of us! . . . I don't give a damn if you didn't know the round was defective, you killed one of my men!"

The corporal whispered to me, "Two wasted G.I.'s his first time in the field wouldn't look good on his record."

Then the chopper floated slowly down out of sight beneath the tree line, where artillery rounds still exploded.

"Just a minute," Shelley was saying over the phone. "That chopper just landed in the area you guys are lobbing shells into . . . What? Well, quit a minute, will you, and find out! . . . Oh, my God, they're what?" Looking at me, Shelley said, "Those men were shot down. They're screaming for help." He listened a minute. "Their radio just went dead."

The artillery stopped its pounding. Smoke drifted peacefully above the silent forest, a factory after the closing whistle. "Come on, we've got to rescue those boys in the chopper," Shelley cried. "Where the heck's our guide?"

The man had disappeared.

"Only good gook's a dusted gook," the corporal said, "whichever fucking side he's on." Had he killed our guide?

The map's third canal turned out to be a deep, wide, rapidly flowing natural river. From just above the trees, streaming sun ricocheted off the fresh, clear water.

"Float your packs across, men, keep your weapons dry," Shelley said.

Water sweet enough to drink. Stinking yellow goo from the canals melted off me as I swam out midstream, cutting diagonally against the strong current, immersing my head to clean it, too. Pulling hands one at a time from my pack, I swished them beneath the water. Oh to swim this river naked like the Gorge!

Only thirteen of us reached the other bank. "What happened?" Shelley asked. "Anybody see him sink?"

The vanished rifleman had presumably drowned crossing. Nobody knew.

We thirteen survivors crouched beneath the embankment at the river's edge to dry and reload our weapons.

"Okay, men, move out!"

Shelley, John, Henry, and I stomached ourselves into the wait-high grass twenty meters from the smoking forest where bunkers were reputed to lie. The remaining nine men stayed put, examining fingers, boots, and knees.

"I swear," Shelley said, "you yellow chickens move or you'll end up in the guardhouse."

"So what?" one muttered.

"Sir, I have an idea," whispered the corporal. "Maybe if you ordered me to waste a few of them, they'd haul ass."

"You're out of your mind," Shelley retorted. "Come on, if we set a good example, they'll follow."

The four of us moved crouching, eyes and steel pots periscoped above the grass.

"Sir," the corporal whispered, "there's a bunker over there."

I heard John ask, "What the fuck am I doing here?"

While Shelley phoned the C.O., I kept squinting for the bunker—and finally spotted, at the base of a large tree about fifteen meters away, a mound, like a huge anthill except for the firing slit. We crept up closer.

"C.O. says clear it," Shelley whispered. Yanking a pin from a grenade, threw it at the bunker's fireport. But in his haste, he missed. The grenade rolled down the bunker's sloping side and into the face of John, who had stumbled in a dash to grab it. "Never should have—" he screamed. I fell flat, and the grenade blew. A scrap scalded my right thigh.

Whereupon I thought I saw Krishna Singh, fully armed, leap from a bunker not twelve feet away. I rattled off a clip and watched him drop to the ground.

Shelley rushed the second bunker. Loading another clip, I followed. The rest of the platoon had finally unstuck themselves from cover and were moving up. I reached Shelley at the bunker, a mound four feet high, and we rested against it, on either side of the fireport. Suddenly a tongue of flame roared from between us, crumpling three of the latecomers. Shelley raced behind the bunker and fired off a clip, spent casings clinking against his pot. "Dirty son of a bitch!" he cried.

Silence.

Henry hunkered over the man I'd shot and stripped away his weapons and equipment, including the American grenades. "This gook looks like an officer," he shouted, waving a sheaf of papers at us. "Pretty good, Hatcher, for your first kill."

"It was nothing," I mumbled. "Thought he was somebody else."

"Bring me that radio pack, Hatcher," Shelley ordered.

I couldn't bring myself to look at John. Eyes averted, I hauled the radio off his corpse. Miraculously, it still worked. Shelley told the C.O. what had happened, omitting one detail—that he himself had blown off his RTO's head.

Our original force of fifteen had already been knocked down to nine. Shelley ordered a private to hoist the radio; then we spread out in line along the forest rim, and slunk stealthily north, forest to our left. To our right, the river now lay in shadow.

Red light blinking, the Cessna passed above us. From the forest edge, Shelley waved his rifle; the Cessna dipped its wings. Its reflection swam the water. "Plenty of jets up there," Shelley said, "circling like vultures, waiting to be called down if we need them. Now let's see about that chopper!"

We moved through eerie twilight among the trees, cool and still. Some freshly split tops had fallen only part way, attached to their tall, jagged stumps like cracked wishbones. But the forest roof remained whole; neighbor trees had mushroomed suddenly and healed any gaps. We skirted fresh craters from today's bombardment, and old craters half filled with water, leaves drifting on the surface.

The ragged helicopter rested on its side, rotor bent like a knife caught in a garbage-disposal unit. One pencil-thin wisp of smoke rose from somewhere in the engine. On the leaf-thick turf beside the machine three white women, nude from the waist down, lay unmoving on their backs in a neat row. Their legs had been spread apart knees up, footsoles on the ground, in position to make love.

The corporal and Shelley walked over to examine them. Shelley leaned against the machine and clapped his palm across his mouth. Corporal Henry exclaimed, "Come here, you guys have a look at this."

The rest of us hung back.

The corporal, leaning his machine gun against the fallen chopper, said, "Susie Q. must of passed this way all right."

Shelley reeled toward me, freckles rubies against emerald. "We got to cover them." He looked back and shuddered. "Pilot and two gunners," he choked. "Somebody emasculated them."

"And shoved the whole wad into their mouths, sir," the corporal added, bending for a close look.

"Shut up, Henry," Shelley ordered, "and cover them with your tarp, for the sake of God!" He pressed the green receiver to his ear and contacted the C.O. "We stay here tonight and keep the area secure. Also keep our eyes open for enemy activity, so maybe we can call in another air strike."

On a cushion a few yards back from the chopper, amid trees and brush, I contemplated by penlight unopened tins of beef and peaches. I couldn't eat. Lips smacked wetly nearby. I heard the rhythm of insects, the irregular shrill of large animals prowling. Ten feet away came rumbling noises of a soldier defecating. "Man, you sure miss the comforts of home out here," Shelley whispered. Trousers rustled into place. A belt clacked. He sat beside me in the dark. "Hey there, Hatcher. Eating?"

"No."

"That really makes me feel ashamed," Shelley whispered.

"I was so hungry, I ate in spite of everything. Oh, how could I eat after John?"

"You didn't mean for it to happen, sir."

Shelley was quiet awhile, then said, "Remember those American grenades we found on your gook? There are actually people in the U.S. who supply the enemy. They might as well be over here with guns in their hands killing their own brothers. One thing I'm defending is freedom of speech. But by golly that's too precious a right to be perverted by radicals."

"John was a radical before they finally drafted him."

"I know. What they did with him, they ought to do with the rest of those protestors—put them over here in the front line, set all their heads straight. John didn't really want to serve his country." Shelley paused, then added, "Maybe that's why he got killed."

I heard insects.

"Cougar in this jungle," Shelley whispered. "Hear it? C.O. told me next month they dump this whole area with herbicides, kill off vegetation for fifty years. Wish there was some other way. Too much gook enemy activity hidden under the trees. I remember when elm blight killed half the trees in my hometown. Couldn't believe how bare the place looked." He paused. "Where you from?"

I told him.

"Rich home?" he asked.

"So poor we had to crap in the woods. You a rich kid?"

"Naw, dropped out of college middle of my senior year. Not much of a student, except an English teacher once told me my writing was sort of poetic. Went to ranger school, because I figured if you're going to do a thing, you ought to do it right. You and me, C.O. told me, going to be decorated for what happened today, speaking of doing things right." He fumbled in his pocket, then snapped his penlight on. "Feast your eyes." The circle of yellow haloed a girl with a beaklike nose and brown hair in a beehive, full lips, hollow cheeks, face decidedly boyish. "Fiancée."

"Nice-looking."

"Bet she is. Look at this one." Skin-tight short-shorts, hands on hips, twisting around Betty Grable style. Almost breastless. "Isn't that one beautiful ass?"

"Fantastic."

"We're getting married in Hawaii six months from now during R and R. I promised not to touch another woman while I was over here. Country's crawling with clap. I don't have to worry about her. She's a virgin."

"Lucky guy."

"There've been times when it got pretty hard, saving ourselves for marriage. She'd want to even more than me, understand? One night I spent in her parents' house, and around 2 A.M. she glides into my room naked except for this filmy little peignoir. We spent about an hour together in the sack, just trying to keep ourselves from going all the way. I put it in till I touched her cherry."

"How come you're telling me these things?"

"Don't know," Shelley whispered. "Just feel like talking, I guess. I don't want you to think *I'm* a virgin. Screwed five different girls. But I only screwed each of them once."

"Doesn't that bother your conscience?"

"Nope. While I was screwing them, I was really in love. I didn't even use a rubber."

Later, after I'd done my turn at guard and slept, I woke up bootless in my bag, stomach snarling. And with my fingers stuffed several tinfuls of food down into my guts. War digested easily, as if I'd been eating it all my life.

The alarm rang: Henry's machine gun. I shoved the sides of my sleeping bag, snatched my weapon, and seconds out of sleep, blasted at somebody running with astonishing grace about twenty feet from me. Movement in a clump of brush. I threw a grenade, dropped, heard it go off. Automatic rifles blazed from the forest around our whole perimeter. Black force landed on me, I struggled against a lithe muscular form wielding a knife. I stared up into a woman's fiery eyes, and past her, saw a gushing green plume blasting up through the forest roof. Then the whole green mass, smoke and leaves, blew downward, lifting my attacker yelling away in the sudden blue sky. Black swept-wing fighters sent black ovals end-over-ending from their bellies down to where I lay deafened, flaming particles raining on my forehead and cheeks.

Calm.

"Anybody here?" A figure crawled slowly past. I shifted my scorching rifle to kill. Shelley's blackened face peered into mine. "Hey there, Prince Elmo. How's it going?"

Somebody was screaming.

The hole above me filled, and lo! a U.S. helicopter hovered overhead. Its ladder unrolled, green angels clambering to where we lay.

"Shelley, what did you do?" I asked.

"Called air strike down on top of our position," he replied.

I managed to sit. "Anybody else alive?"

"Maybe Henry made it. He's out cold, though. If you want an uneducated opinion, I think we're about it. Me, you, and Henry."

"Who's screaming?"

"Just crawling over to have a look," Shelley replied. Ten feet off, smoke fumed from a blackened shape.

"Who's in charge around here?" asked a fatigue hat, an automatic pistol.

Shelley stood saluting our captain.

"Gooks all took off, eh, Lieutenant? Any kills?"

I stood. The sergeant who came with the C.O. leaned over the smoking, writhing shape. "Wounded gook over here, sir," he announced.

The captain strode over, helicopter hovering above, ladder dangling. He examined the shape, placed his pistol against its temple, and fired. The head bounced like a ball. In the camera-snap opening between head and ground, leaves and dirt jumped.

A medic rapidly checked one body, then scurried to another.

"What's the score?" the captain asked.

"Everybody dead, sir," the medic replied.

"That was one hell of a gutsy thing you did, Lieutenant," the captain told Shelley.

"Sir, there just didn't seem to be any other alternative. We were outnumbered ten to one."

"Machine-gunner's alive, sir," the medic said.

"Good!" the captain exclaimed. "I know him. He's a good man."

"Well, he seems to be coming around, sir. I'm checking him for wounds. Negative so far."

"Don't let that man die from shock," the captain ordered. "Prop his feet above his head. He's too good a man to lose."

"Yes, sir."

"It's gutsy actions like yours, Lieutenant, that make the Army what it is today." The captain knocked a pack of Luckies loose and extended it to Shelley and me.

"Wounded gook over here, sir," the medic called out.

"You take this one," the captain said to me.

"Don't smoke, sir." I knew what he meant.

The captain laughed through his nose. "How's your attitude toward gooks, Lieutenant?"

"You don't have to ask me that, sir," Shelley replied. "They mutilated those chopper boys."

"*You* take this one," the captain said, extending his forty-five to Shelley. "After what your platoon's been through the last twenty-four hours, Lieutenant, you'll feel much better."

Shelley shuffled over to the prostrate figure.

"Best spot's his head," the captain instructed.

"Sir, might be a woman," I said. "A woman jumped me in my hole, just seconds before the strike."

"Wet dream, Sergeant," the captain laughed. "Lieutenant, we don't have all morning." Shelley bent, propped the muzzle against the figure's temple, turned his face aside, closed his eyes, and blasted brains all over his pants. Urine streamed down my legs.

"Bet they didn't let you do that back in ranger school," the captain remarked. Shelley lowered the hammer against his palm and returned the captain's steaming pistol.

Laddered from the hovering chopper, men loaded scorched and bloody American corpses into individual zipper bags manufactured from opaque plastic. Then the chopper lowered a grappling hook.

"Leave the gooks for jungle bait," the captain said. "Let's see that downed chopper."

During the night, we discovered, hyenas had feasted on all three bodies. "Maybe it was gooks that ate them," the captain laughed. "They sometimes roast a man's liver on a stick and eat it to frighten a guy's buddy into talking."

Shelley got the Congressional Medal of Honor, and I the Distinguished Service Medal, as if I had actually become the equal of Grampa. I was also promoted to sergeant. A patriotic article on the maneuver, complete with photos, appeared in *Life*.

I had already gotten Hazel's letter telling me of Billy Pickwick's death for public agitation against segregated schools. "The sheriff arrested Billy for inciting to riot. Sometime after midnight, apparently, a select group of whites from the community removed Billy from his cell and drove him to a pine forest and lynched him with chains, gasoline, and shotguns. Nobody has been arrested. A Negro leader in the North made a statement, shortly after the body was discovered, in which he affirmed that liberal white do-gooders like Billy had no business meddling in the black man's struggle."

In a P.S., Hazel told me that she had separated from her husband and would be moving to Paris.

Did that mean she was free?

•7•

For the next eight months, more soldiers smoked dope than drank beer. At the request of news cameramen, G.I.'s sliced ears, noses, and testes off enemy corpses. Soldiers rested up by swimming in the South China Sea; sharks ate them. Men awoke in their bunks to a keen tickling of the throat; a form the size of a half-gallon milk carton rested lightly on their collarbones; tar-drop eyes glared into theirs; when they finally stirred and howled, a bat with a one-foot wingspread flapped silently away. Vampires crowded the caves of this country. And though they couldn't lap enough blood to kill a man, the nightmare shock caused death and insanity. The bats had rabies. In base hospitals, men bit nurses, refused water, writhed, collapsed into coma, and died.

After a day in the hospital, Henry emerged from the Susie Q. encounter caressing and oiling and stroking his machine gun. "How the hell many *did* I get the other day? Six? Seven? Let's say I've got one thirty-one total. On the lean side, but it sounds fair enough, doesn't it, Elmo?"

The very evening of his return, however, Henry, high on marijuana, riddled a fellow G.I. he claimed "just sidled over and gave my ass a good feel." He funneled at least seventeen bullets into the fellow. Authorities took Henry into custody for psychiatric observation. As his lieutenant, Shelley was called in. A psychiatrist soon flushed out Henry's past, and Shelley returned bewildered by a weird story.

Before joining the Army, it seemed Henry had been a housebreaker. "He'd bust into a home when people were out," Shelley explained, "but he'd only steal a pair of panties." He'd leave little traces of himself so the family would know somebody had called—a black spot on the mirror, a four-letter word scrawled in pencil above the bed. Sometimes he'd crap in their toilet, then not flush. Or maybe he'd masturbate into a dress belonging to the lady of the house. Expert with tools, sometimes he'd even repair things. He stole cars, too. Henry told the shrink he once repaired a stolen car's transmission before returning it. "What do you do with a guy like that?" asked Shelley. "He isn't all bad. That's clear."

Henry had also been an expert Peeping Tom. "By his own count," Shelley said, "he watched a hundred eleven women undress and never got caught. My guess is they'll send him to some post back in the U.S. for observation." Which happened.

In July, Shelley boarded an airplane for Hawaii, to don his Medal of Honor and bed his virgin. The Army granted its hero one week's leave. He shook my hand before parting.

When he got back, he seemed depressed. "Old buddy," he asked, "ever screw a virgin?"

Two mornings later, reveille blew me awake, and passing Shelley's tent I saw him still sitting at his bunk's edge staring at a large, roundish splotch of wetness in the crotch of his shorts.

That afternoon, he returned bewildered from the base hospital. "Just don't understand what happened. Doc said it was a solid dose of clap and had the nurse shoot me full of penicillin."

"Where'd you get it?" I asked.

"That's the darndest thing. You know how I've been the whole six months we've been here. I never even looked at another woman." He thought awhile. "Couldn't possibly be the wife, could it?"

I just looked at him.

Susie Q. was a myth on the rampage. Because I had seen her, had wrestled her, I believed Susie Q. was a woman. But when I told Shelley, he exclaimed, "No woman could do those things!" Sometimes she just staged an ambush, simple combat with knives and rifles, leaving dead and wounded from both sides, though her own wounded always committed suicide before capture. Her areas of specialization, however, were more fanciful: castration, mutilation of children, tearing the fetus from the womb. Witnesses reported her wearing a necklace of dried phalluses and testes. To me, she was Mother of Death, and Father, destroying life at its source: child, genitals, womb.

After returning from his honeymoon, Shelley came around to my theory about Susie Q.'s sex. "That goddamn filthy bitch Susie Q." he'd say. "If I catch her, so help me, I'm going to chop off her fucking tits."

His heroism earned him the nickname "Mad Tony." "I'm going to get killed just living up to my reputation," he boasted. Whenever Mad Tony went someplace now, he'd hear G.I.'s talking about how he "cheated death and dealt hell back on the gooks." And after I'd helped save his life a time or two, we became a *pair* of heroes—Achilles and Patroclus, Mutt and Jeff. "By golly, there they *go*!"

In October, near the end of the monsoon, the Third Battalion moved within one mile of the shark-studded South China Sea. One evening Shelley charged into my tent dripping, waving his arms, chortling, "My God, man, guess who's paying us a visit? Guess who's getting our platoon for his guard of honor?"

I just let my mouth gape. Rain clobbered the world outside.

"Rudolph Stayne!" he cried. "The real thing, in person, Rudolph Stayne!"

"Isn't he a movie actor?"

"*A* movie actor? My God, man, where've you been all these years? He's *the* movie actor. I love him. He's an inspiration."

"I heard he was a raving fairy."

Shelley rose glowering above my cot, gripping his knife handle. Rain thundered against canvas. "Stayne's like a second father to me."

"Look, I apologize. That's the first thing everybody says about all movie actors. It's probably never true."

"You can bet your ass it isn't true about Rudolph Stayne. Man, I know all his movies by heart. He's tough, cool, brave, clever—he always knows what to do. Remember in *They Wore Our Country's Wings,* when he deliberately crash-landed his plane on a Jap island, and his wing circling around up there leaderless said, 'Wow, the old man's really gone bats this time.' But he had it all psyched out way in advance. He knew that all Japs love mechanical gadgets more than life itself, and that all of them would go apeshit because when he was going down he tossed what looked like the newest model of the American all-weather bombsight out of the plane in a clearing, but it was really a combination high-power fragmentation device and—"

"I saw that when I was a kid sneaking into the movies."

"Remember the one where he set a new world's altitude record, and flew so fast the wings fell off his plane, and he almost didn't get a chance to bail out, until a couple of hundred feet over the water, he wrenched the cockpit open and—"

"He died in that one."

"Yeah," sighed Shelley. "But you always knew he'd be back again in three months."

"So what's he doing over here?"

"Producing, directing, and starring in a movie about this war, his last before he goes into politics. But here's the fantastic part—he wants us to take him and his crew out on patrol with us in a couple days, you know, and get a little actual battle footage with him and us in it."

"You're kidding."

"Why? Look, our boys dusted a slope yesterday, and the

info that bastard was carrying—man oh man! We're laying a real sure-thing ambush onto the slopes, and I thought maybe this would be the ideal situation for Stayne. Give him a real rifle, you know? Let him dump a few real live slopes for the film."

"Jesus Christ."

"Somebody's got to do it, why not give Rudolph Stayne a crack?"

"That asshole ever been in a real war?"

"What difference does that make? Do you have any idea how famous we've become back home, you and me? It's like moving out of one dream into another, where you suddenly get all you ever wanted." And then Shelley began telling me that he'd grown up stretched before the television. It was as if his whole sense of reality had grown out of screen and tube.

"After school when I was small," he reminisced, "there was always Captain Video. Remember all those miniature landscapes like something inside paperweights you turn upside down and it snows? And Godfrey on summer mornings. He had an innocent sweet young girl, Barbie Something-or-other. She'd tell Godfrey, "I got engaged," and he'd say how nice, then she got married and pregnant. She was a big whore in real life, but it never showed on TV."

The rain seemed to be dying. I heard the trickle of small rivulets under the tent's board floor. "Would you believe I was really small, till I turned sixteen?" Shelley rambled on. "Then I shot up like a weed. Too late for dating or athletics in high school, but I landed a lead in the senior play. They needed a basketball hero, but all the real basketball players were too busy playing basketball.

"Got to like this girl in college, first one I ever dated. Decided I'd bust her to satisfy my curiosity, so I psyched her out, figured exactly how far I should go each date, like a script. The piece of ass went off on schedule. She cried, wanted me to marry her, called me names, finally broke everything off. After that, she became the campus whore. Never messed with whores in my life, and I wasn't about to get started with her."

Except for an occasional pick-pock, the rain had died. A chill wind breathed between the tent flaps.

A long pause, during which, for some reason, I felt very edgy. Finally I asked, "Stayne married?"

"Sometimes get his life mixed up with Marlon Brando's," Shelley replied.

"Wait, I remember reading a long time ago, his wife divorced him for committing adultery with more than a hundred women."

"All I know," Shelley groaned, "is that *I'm* fucking well married."

Silence.

"Wife writes she's seeing an old boyfriend."

"Rough."

"Claims she never actually screwed him, just—I don't know how to say it."

"Don't, then."

"Oh, what the hell, that they just sort of use their mouths."

"For Christ's sake!"

"Maybe she means kissing," Shelley said.

"Probably."

"Then why doesn't she say so? Man, all those months! And I'm still faithful to her. What about that?"

"Go get laid if it'll make you feel better."

We lay on bunks, on our backs, heads propped in our palms. "It just wouldn't seem right," Shelley said. "If we were divorced, I'd be free again. But when I got married, I took an *oath*! And shoving the moral issues aside, if I do screw some gook female, I'm liable to catch V.D. again. But man let me tell you! Sometimes I get horny as hell. It's becoming a real problem."

"Beat off."

"Are you kidding? I've *never* done that in my life, and I'm not about to start up solitary now."

"What are you driving at, Shelley?"

"Queers are absolutely scum of the earth. Ever see a queer throw a baseball? Like a fucking girl, repulsive."

"Yeah?"

"Of course," the voice grew introspective, "sometimes men, real men, you know, just out of curiosity or necessity, do things queers do, but it doesn't mean they're queer. It's just experimenting. Being a fairy's a state of mind. Like what they say about alcoholics. One guy can drink two quarts of booze a day and he's not an alcoholic, and some guy who never touches the stuff *is,* because he's got the mind of an alcoholic. See? Have you ever—"

"No."

"Well, if you had, it wouldn't mean you were queer. Sometimes I think maybe if some married man, say, did it with another man, it couldn't really be called unfaithful, especially if you weren't queer. And the other fellow, who was letting himself—he could just bend over and think something else, and it wouldn't *really* be happening at all, understand? A woman could be perfectly faithful to her husband in her mind, and let some other guy screw her, because he was only doing it to her *body,* and that's not really her."

It was coming at me like an animal from the dark corner of its cage. I got up and started outside the tent. "Fuck you," I said.

"Sir," a whisper from the bunk.

"Fuck you, sir."

I wandered into a fog that hid me from sentries. Through the mist seeped a urinous glow, the moon slowly growing visible as I reached the barbed wire perimeter, found a dip in the earth and stomached under the bottom strand.

For weeks I had slept and fought a walk from the South China Sea, yet had never been there. Enemy swarmed about the camp. Stray GIs met hideous ends. Alone, unarmed, I offered human sacrifice to "savages." Hell with it. Why hadn't they gobbled me long before now? Why, for that matter, hadn't I just let Shelley go ahead and gobble me? "You're such a good, kind, understanding person, Prince Elmo," Hazel had said years ago as I lay like a limp carrot. Oh yes indeed.

I bumped into treetrunks like a sleepwalker. Yet in this seemingly dense forest only a few bare twigs crossed the light above. Foliage crackled underfoot, the bleached skeletons of birds, and I realized that the whole forest had died. Some pestilential herbicide? I toppled down a fog-obscured embankment. Trees vanished. The ocean crashed loudly against its shore.

I stood on a gentle downward slope in a ruined bivouac. Here lay board tentfloors like I'd left an hour before. But the canvas had burned or rotted away, the boards rotted to splinters. I spotted a waterfilled bombcrater in time to leap across. The scorched shell of a quonset hut arched through the fog which moonshine was burning away. No animal sounds, no human grunts. Only the ocean's crescendo as I neared it, and the splat of bootsoles in dead muck.

One step plunged me into a deep quagmire. Arms flapping like a sluggish bird to keep afloat, I kicked helplessly over a semiliquid void. I had fallen too suddenly to catch breath, and the bog closed above my head. Black porridge filled my nostrils and ears, coated my eyeballs, seeped between my lips, penetrated my brain with the sudden, fierce recognition that I had tumbled into the area's privy, all warnings removed when human life fled the place, and that I struggled over my scalp in a quicksand of human shit.

My face surfaced, black leaf on a black bog, devouring breath before this ooze sucked me under once more. Down I floated, thick sluggish bubbles, marbles from my lips, down and down, until my bootsoles sank into firmer substance. Bending knees I jumped, and this time cleared the surface to my shoulders, leaning toward where, instinctively, I sensed the ocean, and sank fingers at last into the hole's greasy lip.

The smell cleared my mind like a welder's torch. I wriggled upward until my right hand clutched a clump of dry, cadavered grass whose roots still held a death-grip in the earth. The ocean's voice shouted like a lunatic under the gaping moon. Why would the horror be so much less if this were horseshit, crocodile shit, anything except human shit?

I snaked out gradually on my belly onto the clay, and visions more real than the world itself flamed inside my head. Dick floated on his belly in the Gorge. The naked lady shook herself dry on the ledge like a dog in the bright summer sunlight. I crawled panting, dripping toward the ocean's belch and cough, fighting Nina Never in our guise as children, razoring the tip off my nose, re-entering Helen's belly. Out there, sharks with soulless cufflinks for eyes gorged on tincans, moray eels, and slaves cast overboard. I peered up from the water between

Cerulia's bare thighs. Nina Never's saltwater blood mingled with her son's. Undertow gripped me, gravel sandpapered my face clean, the South China Sea laundered me in its swirling Bendix like a pair of filthy drawers. A French whore blew the wax out of Grampa's old ears; brown clumps melted like butter down the walls. I broke from the undertow, surfaced in the wake of the moon, fought the current sucking me under.

Clawing gravel at the maw's edge, I inched gasping up the stony beach.

•8•

Rudolph Stayne looked like a Great Man: a tall, lean wedge, wide-mouthed, lantern-jawed, thin-lipped, hawk-nosed. Minute white lines seamed his dark tan, scars from face jobs he must have suffered to make the bed of his countenance.

"When I finish up with this here picture," he told assembled reporters, soldiers, officers, and film crew, "I'm a-headin' right back home and run for public office." Governor? Senator? "Why, heck, boys, I'm just liable to run for President of the United States."

"My God, Mr. Stayne, that's fantastic!" Shelley yelled. Others applauded. I felt sick.

"You fellas clear off now while I confab with these boys here," Stayne told his audience, assembled before the double staircase of the chateau, batalion headquarters. "These boys" were Shelley and I, who would explain the next morning's maneuvers to him.

"Stayne, have you ever been in a real war?" I asked as we entered the briefing room.

"Heck, I know all about the business of shootin' guns. Boy, I was a weapons expert before you were even born, hey, Mad Tony? Says he watched me couple year back on *American Sportsman,* on TV, bring down that prizewinnin' kodiak—what was I usin' that day?"

"Five-oh-five magnum," Shelley blushed, "cut-down barrel, hollow points."

"Brute of a weapon," Stayne mumbled. "Man, that beauty had a recoil like my first wife's ass, haw haw! When the boys come along and stripped that big mother's hide off, half his insides were jellied meat. Army? Battles? There ain't a thing I don't know about 'em. After D-Day, Roosevelt gave me a decoration for boostin' morale back home."

"For *They Wore Our Country's Wings,* right, sir?" Shelley beamed.

"Mad Tony here's my old buddy." Stayne draped a heavy arm across Shelley's shoulder. "I love and respect the gun," he went on, "like I respect the body of a beautiful woman. And I love the Army," his voice grew husky, "cause I love my country. I'm tryin' to say a lot in this movie of mine. Want to show the rest of the world an' maybe a few ignorant folks back home what it means to be a real American man."

"Better brief this character," I told Shelley. "People might shoot back."

"Hey there." Stayne released Shelley from the one-armed embrace and rotated his gruff, pleasant face toward me. "What's all this hostility I feel comin' at me?" He extended a big, hairy paw and cuffed me on the ribs. "Don't let everything get on your nerves. Take a tip from the old warhorse here. I been a lot of different people durin' my life—been Daniel Boone and Davy Crockett, George Washington and Teddy Roosevelt. Remember playin' Andy Jackson, only president who ever killed his man duelin' over a woman." He moved his gruff, furry whisper near my ear. "Strictest confidence, boy, I killed my man, too." He peered into my face, eyeballs like blue bloodshot marbles. "Yeah"—he groaned a deep breath, the hot oven-stench of old lungs—"sometimes sorry I had the story hushed up. One time, when I was a whole lot younger, down on the waterfront, I got me a sailor boy with a knife." His fist suddenly shumped my kidney. "Haw! Gotcha, boy!" He whirled from me, made a sudden grab for Shelley's crotch. "Gotcha!" he cried, gargantuan authority disintegrating into playfulness.

Bewildered, Shelley began explaining how we'd conduct the ambush. Captured information indicated that enemy guerrillas, maybe those led by the notorious Susie Q., intended to attack an American patrol, which routinely followed a certain route and passed "this particular point at the rim of this forest." Shelley marked an X on the map.

"Heard those little gooks had women along sometimes," Stayne said. "But I thought it was cause ever now and then they might want a little taste of nooky back there in the woods. This gal actually leadin' them?"

"We don't know for sure she's a woman," Shelley said.

"She's a woman," I said. "I fought her, knee to knee."

"Hey, Sarge, didja get a little pussy there?" Stayne guffawed.

"She's cold-blooded," I said, "and smart. If she captures you, she'll work you over awhile before you die."

"Squat on the old spit, hey? Boy, I never yet run across any woman I couldn't split a hundred different ways to Sunday." He suddenly unzipped his pants, reached in, hauled it out, and whirled it around in the room. White cloth—lace?—foamed in his fly. "She takes one squint at this here, boys, and she'll flop on her back beggin' like a hungry dog. Won't have to shoot off her head, I'll fuck it off."

Shelley kept glancing nervously out the window, then at Stayne's exhibit, then out the window again.

"Hell, boy, let 'em see. Everybody ought to know what a real man looks like. Anyway, Sarge, this is mainly for your benefit." Stayne stuffed it back into his pants. "I sort of got the feeling a few minutes back, you weren't too impressed with my manly abilities."

"Maybe they'll pickle it in the Smithsonian," I suggested, "like Dillinger's."

"That story about Dillinger is just a myth," Shelley said.

"Hell, Mad Tony," Stayne said, "Sarge here knows everything, right, Sarge? You and me, boy, we're just ignorant country folk compared to what's-his-name here"—he squinted at the name stitched above my pocket—"Hatcher?" Where'd you get this asshole anyhow, Mad Tony? He looks like one of them Forty-second Street hustlers."

Shelley, who had scarcely looked at me since the night I had slogged out of the compound, said, "Just say the word, sir, and we'll cut him off the patrol."

"Naw," Stayne snorted. "Might make a mistake, being so unused to shooting guns. Nice big target like Sarge here—"

The C.O. strode into the room and crisply saluted Stayne, as if Stayne were Commander-in-Chief. "Sir, this is definitely a great honor," he snapped.

"Hear you're one tough fella," Stayne said. "General says you don't take shit from prisoners."

"No, *sir*!" The captain's rugged features blushed with pleasure at Stayne's compliment. "Sir, the general's concerned for your safety and sent me to assure you—all possible backup, air assistance, choppers, jets, extra troops ringing point zero."

"Don't tighten things up so much the slopes get scared off," Stayne said. "I run my cameras on a whole patch of nothin', I waste a bundle. So let's keep the operation real small, hey? Me and Mad Tony here, we'll pulverize every gook in the territory."

The captain shuffled nervously before Stayne's awesome presence, while the actor held Shelley in his fatherly embrace. "Sir," the captain said, "when that sneaky Jap blasted you after you'd taken Suribachi, I was shattered. I mean, I just wanted to go up there myself and blast that gook to smithereens."

"Yeah, Cap, that's exactly the emotion we wanted to arouse in every real man in the house. A kind of warm sense of brotherhood. You can respect a man and be friendly with him, ya know, in a way no woman'll ever understand."

The captain and Shelley nodded knowingly.

"Hey there, Mad Tony, old buddy," Stayne said, "let's go get in a little target practice before we shoot that old script tomorrow."

When I reported at 6 A.M., camera and sound men had already gathered, along with the rest of the platoon. Shelley and Stayne appeared a half hour late, arm in arm, smoking; Shelley limped slightly. "Hey there, Prince Elmo!" he cried.

"Me and Mad Tony had a rip-roarin' time last night," Stayne rumbled. "Popped us a virgin, right, boy? Smokes all around!" He extended a battered pack of homemades.

I was about to say "No, thanks," but Stayne passed me by.

"Now, me and Mad Tony here discussed this maneuver," Stayne said, "and we decided that I got one hell of a lot more at stake here than the U.S. Army, and therefore I ought to have at least equal say in calling the shots."

"Right, King!"

"Actually, the Army's cooperating fully with me. They already gave me a little present." He unshouldered and waved above his head a gleaming new weapon—like mine cut to smaller scale, more machine pistol than rifle, with a collapsible stock. "Best little weapon I ever hefted."

"The King sure is one wild man with a rifle," Shelley chortled, sucking smoke into his lungs. The camera crew had lit up. So had most soldiers.

A khaki schoolbus pulled up for platoon and movie crew. Piling into the bus, Shelley said, "Man, I remember when I was nine, that movie you made about the M-1 rifle." He and Stayne filled the same seat toward the front of the bus as we jostled down the road through a familiar wasteland, dead clay punctuated by scorched stumps, erosion, ditches, shellholes, bomb craters reflecting the gray sky like eyesockets of muck. I slumped directly behind them.

"Old buddy," Stayne replied, "I think that movie was about the Springfield ought three."

"Gotcha there, King! The M-1's gas-operated auto, isn't it? But the ought-three—"

"Beautiful weapon," Stayne gloated, "trim, beautiful lines on that little baby."

"Little baby," I said to Stayne.

"You ain't gonna last through the day, boy," Stayne growled.

The schoolbus halted at a canal's edge, water running high from recent rains. Currents swirled in its yellow muck, and the sky was melted plumber's lead. Across the canal, a cane field rustled and shivered. A few workers at its fringe ran when we approached. Along the canal's edge, the platoon and camera crew fumbled like children. A chopper sputtered high over the canebrake.

Breeze in my face bore the reek of dope and human waste. "Shelley," I said, "let's see the map."

"Don't crowd, buddy," Stayne elbowed me away. "Mad Tony,

how 'bout some shots of you and me going along the cane over there, you know, local color. Hey, Giorgio!" A cameraman scurried up, shoulder-mounted rig bobbing. "Follow me and Mad Tony along here a ways.

A woman emerged from the cane on the opposite bank, toting a bundle in her arms.

"Enemy," Stayne said. "Get this shot, Giorgio, fast!"

Stayne raised his machine pistol. The woman froze, mouth dropped open.

"What's wrong with this thing?" Stayne asked.

"You got the safety catch on," whispered Shelley.

I moved up behind Stayne, reaching for his arm too late to stop the burst of fire.

"Hey, King! That was a woman!" Giorgio cried.

"Fucking gook female impersonator!" Stayne roared. "She was carrying enough stuff to blow up the whole platoon. Keep the camera running." An indentation, like a cathedral niche, had formed in the wall of cane. Red fragments glistened against green. For the first time, I noticed that Stayne was in costume for the role of soldier, a major's gold cluster on his shirt collar. Greasepaint and powder layered his face.

"King, can I cut now?" Giorgio asked.

"Zoom in and hold a few seconds. Nice color shot."

"I think," Giorgio said, "she was carrying a baby."

"Fucking idiot! Look how she blew up when the bullets hit!"

"Your rifle did that," I told him.

"Who asked you?" Stayne yelled.

I reached for Shelley's map case, but he whirled out of reach and leveled the rifle at my gut.

"What? Tryin' to touch your ass?" Stayne asked. "Look, Sarge, this ain't the time for queer games."

We followed the canal another half hour, to the edge of a bombed-out field. "Godda cross the water here," Shelley slurred. "Ged on other side."

"Shit on that," snapped Stayne. "I'm not gonna get the cameras all gummed up. Ain't there a goddamn bridge someplace?"

Shelley shrugged. We kept wandering along the canal till

we hit weeds and brush at the edge of a thick forest, like the jungle where we'd lost most of the platoon during my first patrol. Were we entering the same vastness from a different point?

"Whad now?" Shelley asked.

"Hell, you know where we're supposed to be," Stayne said. "Georgio, take a light reading there in the shade."

Camera balanced gingerly on his shoulder, Georgio penetrated the deep shadow, and an automatic weapon crumpled him onto his face. "Back up!" Stayne screamed. "Hit the dirt, men! Hey, you, get the film rolling."

The second cameraman crawled over and said, "King, I think Georgio's shot."

"Of course he's shot," Stayne said. "Mad Tony here fucked up."

Leaves, twigs, dirt exploded through the air; the weapon rattled. A rifleman stomached forward, pitched a grenade into the woods. It clunked a tree and went off, showering hot fragments back on top of us.

I lay waiting.

Rifle fire from the woods ceased. "Maybe the boom got him," Stayne said. "One of you boys find out. Whassa matter with you, Mad Tony, dead or something?" Shelley appeared to have fallen asleep face down in the dirt.

"Fix bayonets," Shelley muttered. A few men fumbled short black knives onto the ends of their rifles. "Charge," Shelley said more boldly, and four or five soldiers rushed crouching into the woods. An automatic weapon rattled.

Silence.

Finally, one of the soldiers crawled out backward. "Hey—" he stage-whispered over his shoulder.

"Getting this on film?" Stayne growled.

"—I think he's out of ammo."

"Well, shoot the bastard," Shelley said.

"Can't," whispered the private. "Weapon's jammed."

"Tell the other guys to."

"All down."

"Look, let's just go in and take the bastard," Stayne said. "Come on, men." He edged forward, heavy hams riding near the ground. The rest followed. I stayed behind the back-up camera into the forest, where a little man was running from us, crashing through briars and foliage. The quarry's feet tangled in a vine; he fell, rose, whirled to face us in the cool twilight, knife clamped to his blunt weapon's muzzle.

"Hold on a minute, guys. Don't shoot the little freak," Stayne ordered. "Catch up here with the camera. I got an idea."

The trapped man faced our half circle, pivoting slowly back and forth, bayonet at ready.

"This's got the makings of a real scene," Stayne mused. "Looks like that slope feels like working out a little with the blade."

The quarry lunged like a baited bear. We jumped back.

"Bedder do something aboud this guy," Shelley said.

"Hey, camera, stand about here." Stayne marked the spot with his big foot. "Look, Mad Tony, this guy ain't letting us take him alive, that's clear." The little man half lunged again at the circle, then fell back, tense, waiting. "And we can't just dust him, can we? That wouldn't be sporting. The honorable thing to do is, we take him on his own turf, with bayonet, one G.I. at a time."

"Please let me waste the bastard, sir," whined the one rifleman left from the original charge.

"Shiddup," Shelley ordered. "This is King's show."

I asked, "Where's our medic?"

"Back with the guys this slope just shot," someone answered.

"All right, I'm in command!" I cried. "The lieutenant's stoned out of his mind, like most of you. This fairy"—I pointed at Stayne—"has no authority. If he doesn't drop his rifle, I'll shoot it out of his hands. Then we scratch this half-assed operation."

Something hit me—hard—and I found myself on the forest floor, breathless, clutching crotch and belly, rifle kicked beyond reach by the same big boot that felled me. "Lemme blast this sonbitch mutineer right now, Mad Tony," Stayne gruffed, looming above me. "Just give the word."

Shelley's eyes looked like pissholes in the snow. He kept shaking his head. "Keep him guarded," he said.

"Shee-it," Stayne snorted. "Who volunteers to go in first?

Come on, there's got to be a hero around. If you men can't handle this dinky slope, I will."

Shelley walked behind a private and told him to "spear the gook."

"Sir?"

Positioning his riflestock between the private's shoulders, Shelley poked him. The G.I. lumbered timidly into the clearing.

"Easy there," Stayne cautioned. "Watch out, fella, he's moving in to your right."

Fierce and delicate, the oriental dance-stepped, feinted twice, lunged, struck like a viper, and slipped his blade into the man's ribcage. The G.I. tumbled, spewing a thick rope of blood.

Several of the men yelled in anger.

"That's a real gutsy little battler there," Stayne said. "Hey"—turning to the cameraman—"getting all this color?"

A soldier lunged furiously at the enemy. Blades whetted each other, thin hiss and clank. The quarry whirled up his weapon like a scythe, half-beheading the American, who fell spinning. Then the bewildered prey feinted backward, gasping, furious, terrified, eyes dilated black like a cat's, awaiting the next attacker.

"This has gone on long enough," Shelley announced, stepping in. All fell silent. The forest roof whooshed in a light wind, bird sounds far away, the peck of rain against sheltering leaves. I braced myself on the cold ground. Shelley deflected his antagonist's thrust—metal clacked plastic—and Shelley's left foot lunged forward, the blade of his bayonet penetrating the small man's abdomen, then fired a shot into him, the recoil releasing the blade, which he plunged again into the kicking gutted animal.

"How'd that feel, old boy?" asked Stayne, impatiently waving the mike man forward.

"Aahhh, it was good to kill him," sighed Anthony Wayne Shelley.

A soldier remarked, "He ain't dead yet, sir."

"Only one way to handle dirty commie pigs like this," Stayne announced, strolling to the fallen man and firing at point-blank range. "Wonder how much footage we can clear past the censors," he mused, ejecting a clip.

I edged painfully toward my weapon, and a vision formed of Rudolph Stayne in bleeding hunks, each chunk alive transmitting pain to the head. Rain drizzled through the leaves.

"Let's do a ball job on him," Stayne said. "Cram 'em down his throat to teach his comrades. You do the honors, Mad Tony."

Shelley hesitated.

"Think of it like a Thanksgiving turkey," Stayne prodded. "Give him a taste of his own medicine."

Reluctantly Shelley detached the bayonet from his rifle and bent to the work.

But just then weapons fired. Creatures howled in agony, branches and blood and twigs and dirt sprayed the air red. Fiery shadows, arms and shoulders, faces, a foot, a thigh, clawing fingers, sky raining fire—a world churning to obscure laws, flinging itself apart.

I awoke in a dry narrow cave, inflamed by Coleman lanterns, like two blinding white flashbulbs staining the retina with odd and unnatural shapes. Tangled film coiled all about. Rifles stood neatly stacked. Earth floor, jagged rock walls, shadows—my shadow, the shadow of Rudolph Stayne lying trussed naked beside me, and the shadow of a lean attractive oriental standing over us, grim-lipped, wearing black peejays and an intricately twined necklace of dried vegetables. A silk cloth tightly bound the scalp. We lay near the cavern mouth; I heard the steady roar of monsoon rain behind me, flooding the world outside.

"Hey there, American." said the oriental, soothing, melodious. "Awake now? Blond, pretty sweetheart."

"Mmmmmmf," Stayne grunted. "Ooooogh, need some coffee bad."

"Got any coffee lying around, Susie?" I asked.

"Sure, bubbling away in my little electric percolator. What makes you think I'm Susie?"

"Saw you before."

"But what made you think I was Susie then? Has the capitalist press circulated my picture?"

"Where'm I?" Stayne grumbled. "Some asshole busted me over the head."

"This really is a tremendous honor, Mr. Stayne," said Susie Q. "The kids sponsored a Rudolph Stayne film festival while I was in college. We had a Bogart festival and a William Boyd festival, too. Great fun. Seeing you sure does bring back memories."

"Hey, Susie Q., where'd you go to college?" I asked.

"I'm a Cliffie," she announced brightly. "Graduated two years ago, then returned to help free my people from white racist pigs like you." Wrinkles puckered around two small, mad flares, her eyes.

"Did you by any chance know an old buddy of mine, Billy Pickwick? He was in Cambridge around the same time."

Thought screwed up her face. "No," she answered.

"Hey, what the fuck?" Stayne bellowed. "Is that my film scattered all over the place, for Christ's sake?"

"Yes, darling."

"Well, God damn it! *There's* a few thou down the drain."

Susie reached behind a rock, waved a pair of fancy lace panties like a flag, and giggled. "Big tough man, do you always do battle in underpants like these?"

Stayne could only groan.

Commotion behind. Shadows flowed across the wall: suspension bridge. Two men lugged Anthony Wayne Shelley into my vision and dropped him beside me, so I lay between him and the actor. "I'm wounded," Shelley moaned, as the men shuffled into the hiss of rain.

"Hey there, Mad Tony, boy!"

"Where?" I asked.

"I think in the ass," Shelley said. "Numb from the waist down. These damn slopes slaughtered everybody else."

"They fucked up all that good film, too," Stayne said.

"You have a very odd sense of values, Mr. Stayne," Susie Q. observed. "Right now you should be trembling in fear for your life." She fingered the organic decoration twining her neck. Then she unbound the cloth which held her hair. A black, thick cascade tumbled over her shoulders.

Shelley whispered, "Pretty. You must've captured a supply of American shampoo."

Susie leaned above us, smiling. "Would you enjoy taking me in the act of love?" Her sable brush tickled my bare stomach above the groin. I noticed she was chewing something, and that her eyes looked doped.

Stayne rumbled, "Shee-it, baby, I'd do it, except you'd be spoiled the rest of your life. You'd never want to let me go. And I sure as hell don't feel like being locked up till Doomsday in this lousy cave."

"Count me out," said Shelley. "I got us into this mess, and you can't do anything to me I don't deserve. But I wish you'd cut the horseshit and blow my brains out. Or else have the common decency to let me bleed to death in peace."

"Why doesn't somebody call in the Marines?" I groaned.

"Already did," Shelley whispered.

Susie whipped the peejay top over her head and off. In place still, the necklace jostled her tight hard breasts, right nipple missing like a bite swallowed from an apple. "You," Susie aimed her lean front down at me, "did this. You will therefore receive a special treat."

"Shit, baby, don't worry about a thing," Stayne said. A good old cosmetic repair job on that poor damaged little tit—you could make it part of my ransom. The studio'll ship a really super doc all the way out here in the jungle. For free!

"I spit on your superficial show of bravery." A thin black stream jetted between her front teeth. "When the time comes, you will all three prove cowards like everybody else." Reaching behind the same rock from which like a Rotary Club magician she had produced Stayne's lace underwear, Susie flashed a dagger with a wavy-edged blade. "I am no ordinary mortal," she sighed, swaying with the knife. "In my eyes, and in the eyes of God, you are lumps of matter. I will torture you with the same compassion I'd feel cutting into a chicken or a radish." She dropped her pajama bottoms and stood naked, graceful, a goddess, forked root swaying as if before an altar, murmuring, "No man has ever soiled me in the act of love." Her body gleamed gold in the blazing lantern.

Stayne shuddered beside me. "Lady, I'm not even here in real life. I mean, I'm not a soldier or *anything.* I'm a famous man"—voice a croaking puddle in his neck—"I'm worth a mint to the right people."

"All things are equal," Susie chanted, passing the blade back and forth above us in ceremonial gesture, "all the same in the eyes of God."

"They sure must teach kids a lot of bullshit in those Eastern universities," I groaned.

"Look, all I ever wanted to do was finish this movie and run for president," Stayne pleaded. "I mean, if I was elected, look at all the things I could do to help out over here. I could make everybody support *your* side, just twist a few arms. It's the chance of a lifetime. Look, if being a commie ain't all that important to you, think about women a second. There's at least six women back in the States'd starve to death if I wasn't around to pay them alimony. I mean, stop being such a goddamn brick wall! Just say what the fuck's *important* to you, and I promise on a stack of Bibles, it's yours. Just get that goddamn blade away from me!"

"Leave him alone," I told Susie. "Do that shit on me, it doesn't make any difference. I've been dead so long now I can't remember."

"Don't waste your breath," Shelley said. "These commies'll do anything in the name of their cause."

Stayne squealed like a stuck pig.

"Cut that out!" I shouted. "That's a goddamn stupid unnecessary thing to do!"

But it was done. Stayne groaned, rocking gently back and forth like a babe in an antique cradle, beneath a fount of blood.

"She's as bad as I am," Shelley murmured. "How the hell did people ever come into being? What a fucking error!"

"My eunuch," she whispered, bending, tenderly stroking my bared loins. Ankles struggled against their cords.

An inhuman howl—mine?—and sympathetic reverberations in nature, earth- and sky-splitting, feckless moan of extras as a Cecil B. DeMille temple crumbled about their ears, harsh, brightness like a thousand footlights.

"It's the cavalry!" screamed Shelley.

Susie flung her knife between us and rushed toward the noise.

"Hey, old buddy, roll over on your side," Shelley counseled. He had the knife. I looked at Stayne floating asleep on his back, dead eyes bulging. A keen, bright edge nicked my palms, my wrists. Then my hands separated.

"Quick, get one of those damn guns!"

Hobbled forward on my knees, falling all apart below—couldn't look. Fumbled from the pile a squat enemy weapon and trained its muzzle on Susie Q. racing lithe out of a sudden lightburst, out of the hot thunderous clamor, inhumanly, a white scimitar. Couldn't locate the safety, the trigger, the weapon. It softened to rubber in my hands, barrel dropped, ping-pong balls clicked against the cavern floor.

"Kill the bitch," Shelley wailed.

She swooped past like a hawk, lifted the Coleman lantern by its arched wire, faced me, nonhuman, slowly turned her back, hovered with tiny wings blurring like hummingbirds' and a thick tail, dart at its tip, dangled between her scaly buttocks. A nimbus of white light framed her flight down the black rock throat. "Why didn't you shoot?"

"Must be another exit from this joint," I realized, passing out in blackness.

Home

•1•

FROM HIS deathbed, Shelley scratched off this note to me: "Just now an RTO with both his legs gone pointed out a startingly beautiful sight. 'Look there, sir, a golden dustoff!' Sure enough, there in the evening sky was a gleaming DC-7 climbing high for its flight to the U.S.A., and I thought maybe you were inside it. Truly it was golden from the setting sun reflecting from its silver surface as well as in its connotation of returning to the final safety of *home.* Elmo, if only I could capture the deep feeling and tenderness I felt at the moment—tense and ready for the enemy to strike us dead at any moment—for the little bastards are hitting the base with rockets every day—and now for a second there was a symbol of safety and security, a Golden Angel climbing to heaven. The warm purr of the jet engine was added background music—representative of American power and ingenuity. That golden moment made the whole day! If every man, woman, and child could experience that same feeling just once—there would never be cause to fight communism in the U.S.A.—it's so evident here that America is 'the world' all in itself—the finest, the greatest, the purest things that contribute to a good life. Nowhere else. Perhaps we could collaborate on a novel if I ever get well and come home."

If, however, the "golden dustoff" held my carcass, its destination wasn't the U.S.A. but an Army hospital in Japan where, between elaborate and complicated operations, I finally got Shelley's note. After he had died.

Before kicking off, perhaps in a fit of remorse, Shelley had also lauded my "bravery"; I'd also receive a Medal of Honor, said a letter typed on twenty-four-weight bond, when I was well enough to return "home" and stand for the ceremony. So once again I surfaced in the press. One article, "An American Hero," got sandwiched between pictures of a twelve-year-old rape victim pregnant by her rapist, and an essay on the deterioration of American youth. In *Scamp,* Duke's name was stuck to an essay extolling his younger brother. A producer offered me fifty thou, for the rights to a motion picture based on my life. Accepting, I wrote that he could attach my name to any story; his fantasy would be as good as mine. I lay emasculated in my hospital bed and everything was all right with me.

Well, not quite emasculated. Susie had needed a few seconds more when the cavalry burst into the operating room and pursued her deep into the cave. Discovering finally a vast subterranean lake from which no escape seemed possible, they consoled themselves by murdering most of her followers. Rumblings of an apotheosis for Rudolph Stayne sounded from his country. Congressmen threatened a national holiday, petitions circulated to erect a monument—a more dignified reminder, perhaps, than pickling his privates in the Smithsonian. Though my own still appeared to be attached, the doctors were astonished that I didn't care.

When pain ground my teeth together, nurses shot dope into my arms. Snakes clustered under my mattress. Moray eels floated among the dust motes, gleaming like tiny coals when sunlight poured into my room. On long green lawns outside, the girls lounged naked, sponging sunlight into warm flesh; it was snowing; touching their bodies, white flakes melted into sparkling sweatbeads.

Surgeons operated twice in January. And in February, one last time.

"Maybe you'll be all right," said the chief of the operating team after it was over. "Then again, maybe you won't."

"So who gives a fuck?" I murmured.

Then I heard from Roberts, a telegram reading, "ARRIVING LATE TOMORROW BY JET STOP YOU ARE MY HEIR."

The face had crumbled to a palmful of debris beneath the glistening skull. "My boy," he wheezed, sitting at my bedside. Burdened with leather attaché cases, two aides hovered behind.

"Hey."

"All this must be a tremendous shock. But—forgive me—you don't seem excited."

"Drugs," I lied. "For pain."

"But you're going to be fine, just fine!" he gasped. "The

doctors say"—expensive powder-blue cloth clung to his meatless bones, and he clutched my shoulder with a veined, withered paw—"you have *survived*!" He motioned to one of his aides, who stepped forward, placed an attaché case on the bed beside me, popped its latches, stepped back. Roberts fingered some documents. "First step is adoption," he said. "To simplify your future."

"Been my own father since Mr. Pickwick died."

"Wrong, Prince Elmo." False teeth clicked; his Adam's apple bobbed as he nervously swallowed spit. "You have never in your life been without a father. *I* am your real father." He watched for my face to register what I'd known for years he was someday going to tell me. "You must be astounded."

"What really astounds me," I said, "is that you're sure."

He nodded. "The father of twins." He coughed out a small sob. "Helen was the mother."

"That's what I mean."

He trembled a little; rocks grew beneath the flesh of his cheeks. "The shock of being launched suddenly into a strange new universe," he muttered.

Patting the mattress with both palms, I said, "Man, it's the same old shithole, no mistake about that."

Pivoting his head on the buzzard's neck, he snarled, "You guys leave your briefcases and git! Got a few confessions to make to my son."

As they padded out, the old bastard leaned forward to push a heavy burden of sins off his chest—and onto mine. He felt guilty. He had used the world poorly to gain his ends, but only now could feel bad. The sons of rich men were hideous disappointments. They never had to fight for survival the way he had. Only somebody who started with nothing could appreciate the meaning of his empire. I was all he cared about now. He wanted an heir with proven character, somebody who could not only survive but excel. He had no morals. Helen: one among a thousand women he'd screwed. He had committed homosexual acts. He'd contracted murders. He had taken Cerulia's virginity when she was twelve. But wait a minute, now that he thought about it, maybe someone had already gotten to her. Anyhow, it seemed like a form of incest. Oh, he was a dirty old sinner, all right! He even paid poorly for her services. He had governed his life as if the whole world were his own private whorehouse. One of his best offspring was nothing but a cross between injun and nigger. He had done more for me than for anybody else his entire life through and hoped I appreciated it, that if I harbored any resentment, I'd forgive him. He had malignancy of the intestines, cellular anarchy, and shot morphine to kill the pain. Rotting innards made his breath stink. He'd enjoyed debasing people to see them grovel. He was sorry now. But people for the most part were assholes. Use your wealth for self-improvement, he directed. He himself, too busy amassing it, had never taken time off for making himself a "better human being." Maybe he should join the church and die Christian. The disease, he admitted, was affecting his mind.

As for advice: sodomy, he felt, gave more trouble than pleasure. Sex in general was vastly overrated, and he wished he'd spent less time screwing other people. Maybe I could just hole up in the mansion and run my world from there. Communicate only by telephone. Stay in boxes: sooner or later, everything gets packaged. Don't grow a beard; but a mustache lent dignity. He was uncertain what should be done with his body. Might have it cremated. But he also considered mummification: did I know that Jeremy Bentham's corpse still presided at trustees' meetings at the University of London? Steer clear of the space industry; it would fold when man reached the moon, or soon after. Be sure to eat well: a rich man's one sound pleasure. Munitions formed a solid investment. Don't pooh-pooh flying saucers. Maintain American citizenship, being American was the essential first step toward an orderly life. But make sure the FBI and Internal Revenue don't bug your offices. Keep a cold, hard eye on reality. Squeeze all you can out of life: you only pass this way once.

I agreed to the adoption only if I could keep my real name, Hatcher. Then, recommending cremation, I promised the reverence due his ashes.

•2•

April. Hazel and I in lawn chairs, at dusk, sipping brandy in the yard of her home five miles outside Paris. Two plane trees threw a roof across most of a blue sky melting into yellow. Michelangelo's *David,* miniature limestone replica, scowled from its marble pedestal near the bushes which hid us from the road. Built in 1800, Hazel's home resembled a miniature chateau: stone, three floors, cool basement where the landlord sealed off with steel gate and padlock his well-stocked wine cellar.

We'd scarcely recognized each other when she'd met me at Orly that morning. I resembled a man in his forties poorly cared for over the years—stooped and pale semi-invalid leaning on a cane, teeth chipped, hair already dull and graying at the temples. And Hazel had minimized her gorgeous bloom: evil, criminal garment, the loose white blouse disguised her breasts. Hair yanked back tightly and fastened in a bun, eyes crinkled by concentration and worry, and shielded by glasses, she showed her past in her face: this woman was a Ph.D. and divorced, she performed difficult research, produced important papers, lectured in French, German, and English. Thank God for the short skirt, those sleek, magnificent legs. Well. And I had grown a small paunch those months in hospital beds. We politely almost concealed alarm, hugged like brother and sister, and Hazel said, "Why don't I show you where I work."

"Fine. And then why don't we go somewhere and get drunk?"

"We can do it there," Hazel said and drove us, in a cigarette-pack car, to an ancient building recently gutted and filled with chrome, steel, and concrete glazed pastel blue. In her twilit lab, we drank tinned orange juice mixed with grain alcohol, and studied the intricate lacework on her microscope video screen.

"Who's the painter?" I asked.

"Nature. She'll shame you artists every time."

The pattern moved, a kaleidoscope changing in patterned and orderly fashion. Hazel turned a knob at her machine's base, increasing magnification. The design neared, collapsed into a weird colony of discrete, roundish organisms. "Viruses," she explained, "inhabiting a hunk of tissue."

"Home again," I sighed. "You know how we artists love to impose order on chaos."

"So where's the chaos?" Hazel laughed, increasing magnification till only one organism glowed on the screen, one cut-diamond crystal, a single tiny hair centered in each of its triangular facets.

"Why's *my* life such a mess?" I wailed.

"Order depends on magnification." Hazel twisted the knob, the diamond dissolved, a shapeless gray blob filled the screen, she snapped the instrument off. "With a later-model microscope, who knows?"

In the next room, a horizontal bronze-gold tube, three feet long by a foot wide, spat prongs and wires out one end, while a camera peered into the other. "Photographs living brain tissue," Hazel said, motioning me to a table slide-viewer. "Speaking of patterns." The screen glowed with a slimy, oozing grid of interlacing connections, maze of black wires. "Last anatomical frontier."

"If you photographed my brain," I said, "those circuits'd be broken. You ought to hear old Roberts go on about boxes. *Everything* fits into a box. Poor Billy had advanced political opinions. Dick, poor bastard, dreamed up a cemetery to make himself rich. They all had some half-assed sense of order anyway."

"You're a sculptor."

"Something that happened to happen, like salivating."

"Poor old Prince Elmo."

"There you were, wiring dead beasts back together. Helen had some fix on romantic love. Your father had his chinchillas. You mother wanted to explode back into the Garden. Nina . . . What happened to your marriage?"

"Not much." Hazel's forefinger absently flicked the bronze tube. "Argued about who made coffee. Nonsense." Flick. "He was hung up on manhood, and—I guess we didn't like each other much. Let's talk about other things."

She drove me around the city. "Love the place. But it's liable to blow up. Wanted to show you—" Easing past a drugstore, she pointed where sawhorses and blinking electric lanterns blocked off a debris-piled section of sidewalk: smashed tables and chairs, glass shards, plaster, cement, the gutted first story of a restaurant. "Terrorists bombed it two days ago," she explained. "All the tables were filled. Plastique charge, wrapped in newspaper. Dozen killed, twenty maimed, women, children." Black mouth gaping toothless. Slant of splintered beams. My uniform sheathed me, my sergeant's stripes, my Distinguished Service Cross . . .

Now I sat in the lawn chair, sipping Napoleon brandy, ambrosia poured from a black bottle. Cultivating a golden buzz. And Hazel unpinned her hair, which flopped, curled, twined over her shoulders, long, thick hair. Pressured by her tits, a blouse button popped open. The crescent moon hung gold splotches through interstices of a plane tree. The stripling beheader's scowl darkened, and Hazel suggested eating dinner somewhere, or we'd pass out. I indicated a charcoal grill rusting against the house wall. No, she insisted on a restaurant.

In my small room, which filled the top floor, I glanced into the full-length mirror which moved on rollers, at my diapered self. Flies hummed about the ceiling. The windows were door-size glassless steel shutters thrown wide. Across the road, roofs darkened. I changed laboriously into dress uniform.

Floating white balloons of Sacre Coeur. Hazel wanted to drive us onto Montmartre, but I insisted on walking up the long, pale series of steps. Hazel and my cane assisted. "You all have to prove what strong, manly creatures you are," she taunted. "If they'd shot off your legs, you'd walk on your hands. Jesus!"

"They said I should exercise."

"That wretch of a female, why didn't you shoot her?"

"Hallucinated, like one of those nightmares. Probably just couldn't harm a Radcliffe girl."

We crested the hill. "Never thought I could bring myself to hate anybody," Hazel panted, "until they murdered Billy." She'd left her glasses off. Suspended from her shoulders by slender straps and dropping loose to mid-thigh, her white dress exposed the wide roots of her bosom. Young matron now, she reminded me of her mother that July Fourth at Roberts' lawn party, fireworks from the stadium burning the sky. I gasped for breath like an old man.

In a closetlike cafe which held fewer than a dozen, we sat

beside two women, one young and pregnant, the other perhaps fifty. Both were full-lipped, full-bosomed, had protruberant teeth, black eyes, smooth flawless skin. Their soprano voices were the same. All energy and good spirits, they made the same animated gestures when they talked, mother and daughter. Hazel and I ordered braised pork chops. White St.-Emilion came in an ice-filed zinc bucket. The cafe grew crowded. Wearing a red jacket like a cartoon organ-grinder's monkey, a man played accordion and sang, and we sang along—

"vec les pieds
Contre la muraille,
Et la bouche
sous le rabiner . . ."

A gap-toothed West German film producer asked Hazel to dance. While he flung her about the narrow space between tables and singer, the ladies with flawless skin tried to talk with me—difficult at first because of their small English and my time-dissolved college French. The German graciously returned Hazel, and sat beside her. She was beautiful, he said; she spoke German; he would star her in his next film. The five of us talked, Hazel translating, and suddenly nobody needed to translate and I remembered supplying a word *in French* for the older lady, who was praising her son-in-law, an ocean-liner captain presently mid-Atlantic, much loved (the pregnant daughter blushes, clamping her plush lower lip charmingly under her buck teeth), waving a slender hand for the word—"*très . . . très*–"

"*Sensible*!" I cried.

"*Oui! Très sensible! Oh, monsieur! Tu parles bien la français!*"

"Sensitive, very sensitive!" burbled Hazel.

The daughter nodded and blushed.

"Sen-*sible*!" thundered the German. "Dot's de vord, all right!"

The mother stroked my hand. "*Très sensible,*" she crooned. "*Oui, monsieur, tu es sensible, tu . . .*" She shook her face near the empty glass, which I filled with the last of our bottle, and a red-faced beaming woman, reaching across our glassed-in candle, swooped the empty from my grip and handed me a full one, fresh and cold.

The mother smiled down at her daughter's condition. As only child, the first grandchild. The future grandmother dreamed nightly, she said, of children tumbling about her house, tumbling under Jacques' poor feet, on the couches and beds. A little girl stumbled feet first into a posthole; only her golden curls shone when you looked down, but the dreamer reached in and rescued the child by her hair. *"Quelle rève!"* she cried. An old, hairy man, unwashed, garments clinging in shreds to his bony frame, appeared in the dream and tried to kiss the terrified woman on *la bouche.* Eyes sparkling, the daughter cried "Ooooooo!" The mother applauded. She wept. She laughed.

Hazel and I staggered down the steps from Sacre Coeur, a white flame. We sang, " *'vec les pieds . . .*" I peered through the windshield's golden fog at a squarish moon, semicircular bite gone from its underside.

". . . where they planted their unknown soldier," Hazel slurred, daredeviling through traffic, taking us home. "Wunnerful, real civ'lized place, heart of the whole worl' . . ." I remembered pictures of Victor Hugo's funeral, catafalque resting beneath the Arc de Triomphe.

I'd been sleeping dreamlessly for hours, in uniform—tie loosened, collar and tunic unbuttoned—in my top-floor room. Noon air blew clean and fresh across my face. Flies slowly stalked the ceiling's yellow plaster. I blinked my eyes, explored mouth with tongue, and in spite of how blasted I was the night before, tasted no hangover.

When I got downstairs, Hazel was frying bacon.

"Takes a while getting used to a foreign country," she said. "For instance, do you know the French for washer?"

"What is it?"

"*Rondel.* I had to get hold of one once and didn't have the slightest idea how to ask."

"Good life here?"

"You've seen it. What I want, I guess." She bit her lip. "I'm expected this afternoon at the lab."

"And I have a flight to the States."

"Run you to the airport?" Her eyes were moist, and she wouldn't look up.

"I'll take a cab."

"I wish you could have stayed longer."

"I'll come back."

"Are you really going to be *so* rich?"

"Whatever happens, I don't expect it'll last long. Next time you see me, expect a pauper, or maybe a gibbon ape."

"We didn't have time to talk. There's so much."

"Look, I will be back. Just don't disappear on me."

I was still waiting for the taxi when she had to leave. We kissed. Her mouth tasted tart, sweet, salty from our late breakfast.

She started her minuscule car, then rolled down the window. "Get well!" she called. "That's the most important thing."

"Yes."

"This time let's not change too much!"

Let's not do that.

•3•

Roberts died like Socrates, that is, from the soles of his feet up, while I sat beside his New York hospital bed. He weighed less than seventy pounds. When the cold reached his upper thighs and groin, he gripped my hand, shed tears from old bloodshot eyes, and pleaded, "Gimme that piece of bread, that was *my* bread, mister."

"He's dead," I told the physician.

"Yessir," the physician acquiesced.

"Hadn't you better make sure?"

"If you say so, sir."

"Jesus H. Christ!"

Then I visited Duke, who'd established lavish new headquarters in Chicago. During the few years since I'd last seen him, he'd aged at least twenty.

"Really am fantastically hungry," Duke said. The old engine's always running, enough energy for a city. Take you to the workout room some evening when your wound heals up."

"Right now it looks like I'm wearing diapers."

"Maybe you can't run or fuck," Duke laughed, "but you can still eat. That's all you really gotta be able to do in this goddamn world, be able to eat back. Hey, kid"—he gave my hip an intimate little pat—"tell your own blood a secret. Did those little bastards shoot off your thing?"

Through a floor-to-ceiling window—two thick slabs of glass sandwiching a vacuum—I watched Lake Michigan glimmer fifty stories down through its shawl of smog. Duke gestured at the window with my cane: "Paint us a big mural right there, old buddy," he said, meaning the bare blank wall behind us. "I want our shack and hill, the woods, the Gorge. Cram the water top to bottom with swimmers, deep as this building if it was all glass, people getting smaller and smaller toward the bottom, screwing up a storm."

"Screwing?"

"Buddy, you don't have to use your imagination. Think of Cerulia, Helen, Big Dick, and Fern Hill swarming with hot bodies. Remember the bread man who didn't look like he had enough energy to climb the path, getting it off half the women on his route?"

"I'm hysterical with nostalgia."

"Remember what hunger was and hooking lunch from Kroger? Hey—down at the bottom, stick the white fish Grampa and our old man talked about."

Just as the food came, Duke commented nervously, "Guess you're the boss now, old buddy."

"I'm giving you the magazine," I said, buttering a roll and eyeing without hunger the mound of lamb curry on my plate.

He blinked. "Will you sign a contract?"

"I'll have some of my new flunkies draw one up."

Duke whacked me across the shoulders. "That's the Elmo I used to know. Say, buddy, could you maybe loan me five hundred?"

"Five hundred what?"

"Thou," he beamed, "Five hundred thou."

From my Palmer House suite next morning, the shrieking El muted by the hum of my air conditioners, I "conveyed my intentions" to the head of the New York law firm which for years had devoted itself to managing Roberts' holdings.

"That'll have to go through channels, sir," he told me over the phone.

"Fuck channels."

"I'm afraid, sir, it's not so easy. Months ago, when we tried to explain—"

"It *is* that easy!" And I hung up.

Not knowing what to do next, I stayed in the Palmer House several weeks without leaving my suite. Requests for appointments gushed in at two or three hundred an hour. Secretaries to handle this mess populated a separate suite. Two lawyers, working full time with four assistants, buffered and filtered. Characters with "ideas for sound investments" attacked me at fifteen-minute intervals. One fellow said, "What you oughta do, is draw this fantastic comic strip I got in mind and syndicate it. See, it's along the lines of Superman, only—"

"Time's up," a secretary announced over my intercom.

Another wanted me for a rock album.

"I can't sing."

"Even better," he said. "We made a record by this mass murderer. Rhythm section beat on a chopping block. You can do fantastic things with a steel wastebasket over your head."

Both Democrats and Republicans wanted me for Congress. "You're an interesting guy, war hero, and rich. You look kind of beat up, but you could get your teeth capped." I killed these feelers during a TV interview in my office.

"President wonders, sir, when you'll have time to attend the White House ceremony."

"Why?"

"He wants to present your Medal of Honor."

"Tell him to shove it up his"—broadcast nationwide as—"beep."

At that point, my U.S. Government troubles began. Agents bugged every outfit connected with me in any way and tapped all my phones. Staff members began quitting. An employee of mine, a total stranger to me, embezzled two million dollars and flew to Rio. An agent from Internal Revenue got my lawyer: "Our audit shows Hatcher owes eleven million four hundred thousand in back taxes on his Southeast Asian holding company."

"They're harassing you," my lawyer told me. "But you may end up behind bars."

I told him to donate all my Southeast Asian proceeds to Fern Hill.

"What? A charity?"

"It's a nudist camp," I said. "Also, while you're at it, get my mother paroled and set her up a trust fund for twenty thou a year, on condition she never sees me again. And track down my sister. And look—I have a daughter . . ."

Helen was paroled, and I hope she's enjoying herself. To this day, Cerulia has not been found, and all attempts to trace my daughter and Helen's have failed. Nor, for that matter, do I have any information about my "black brother" Kris—though on a recent newsclip I'm sure I spotted his lean form stalking alongside a Caribbean dictator, just come to power following the murder of his father.

Roberts' mansion now belonged to me. I announced to the news media a brief return to art—to a basic form which freed the true and essential chaos from humbug order—and that they should assemble reporters and cameras on the mansion grounds on July Fourth. An enormous mob gathered to gape at what the "Mad Millionaire," as the press now labeled me, might do next. One of my helicopters settled me onto the estate, crumbling to dust, which I toured alone. Before dying, Roberts had removed all art works; even the pseudo Bosch was gone from the bedroom. I carried a cigarboxful of ashes, scrap or two identifiable as tooth, half-incinerated bone, and before leaving the mansion's master bedroom, I dumped them down the toilet.

My minions busily saturated floors, woodwork, and funiture with mineral spirits, which we ignited. A newspaperman on the spot asked what I intended this act to symbolize. "Oh, lots of things," I told him. Hovering high above the earth, I enjoyed the swirling tornado of black smoke. A week later the ruins still glowed and fumed.

Deciding to settle where I was born, I explored ownership of hill and Gorge. Roberts had owned the Gorge, so now it became mine by inheritance, but the county had confiscated the hill for nonpayment of a new property tax. I bought it back. The shack had rotted to a sodden mass of splinters. Debris floated in the Gorge—beer cans, soggy paper cartons, condoms, oil slick from sunken cars. I ordered a dredging and cleaning operation. On the hilltop, men worked day and night constructing a barn-size house of my design: vast, open loft, windows and skylights of bulletproof glass.

Anonymous threats on my life occurred constantly, and I lived surrounded by bodyguards. Rumor whispered of a CIA plot to assassinate me. In late September, I moved to my new home and drowsed all the next year slumped drunk before a blaring color television. An electrified fence barricaded quarry and hill. The woods outside my windows turned gold and blackened, the Gorge froze, a thick white snowfall covered it. On TV, amid stories of murders, drownings, suicides, wars, mass executions, and starvation, I became conscious of newsreels shot through my windows, of me slouching aimlessly about my loft, picking my nose, scratching my ass. "Exclusive films taken by airplane of the reclusive billionaire in his retreat. Questions have been raised whether or not the mysterious hermit is really alive." Students picketed outside my fence: apparently I'd become to them one among many symbols of a capricious, idiot establishment which threatened their very existence. At best, I'd failed in responsibility; I was so sinfully and stupidly rich, and the world remained . . . what the world remained. And I couldn't even get an erection.

I bought a full-page advertisement which *The New York Times* ran daily for a month, offering two million-buck prizes: one for discovering a panacea, the other for discovering a total explanation of the universe—and a grand prize of ten million if both proved to be the same. My law firm dropped me. Embezzlers so pillaged my holdings I'm not sure I still had ten million bucks when I offered the prizes.

By telephone from my retreat, I hired lawyers and accountants to investigate converting my vast land holdings in Brazil to a free cemetery, with free embalming, free transportation, free cremation, free tombstones—free to any corpse in the world. They learned that a month earlier a new military dictatorship had confiscated all my land.

I projected a Whorehouse Hilton in Juárez. Or a vast temperate paradise somewhere in somewhere, applications open now. I donated vast sums to any charity which put the bite on me. I spoke directly with no one, however, communicating through the single telephone I permitted inside my retreat. My helicopters! Take me— A loan company had eaten them. The bank account in Switzerland—but nobody could supply its number. My bodyguards were slinking off, copulating stealthily with one another in the underbrush. Internal Revenue eyed me through binoculars. Maniacs and process servers pitched tents outside my fence, waiting for a chance to pounce. Comets, meteors, tornadoes, and lightning threatened. Down in the Gorge, the white fish licked its lips, belly rumbling.

I imagined turning my childhood cave into a free tourist attraction. But no employee could find it—no matter how detailed my instructions. Had I only sleepwalked through my past? My mail was opened and searched. Each day my holdings diminished. I became terrified, finally, of running out of money altogether, but more terrified still of running out of life. Switching off the TV and yanking its plug, I stopped boozing. Enemy agents prowled the bushes. Factory smoke drank the sky. Galaxies swirled and faded. I dreamed of a quilt, its design a flickering, moving flame, and an album of copperplates, faces fixed against death.

Then one April evening I stood looking through my tall window at the Gorge black and still, and I closed my eyes. Living, dead, missing in action, the people in my life floated to the water's surface, peaceful, whispering their names—Dick and Helen, Cerulia, Grampa, Granma searching my face like a bit of colored cloth, Duke and Billy Buck, Mr. and Mrs. Pickwick holding hands, Nina (her starved look gone), with Charlie and Ivan, together as if one family, Kris keen as a knife blade, Tarze Roberts, Mad Tony, and Hazel at last—flames about my body, bright fragments swimming through a fissure in my brain, all whispering, "Remember us." Tears pierced my eyes and threaded my face. Taste of salt, odor of cleansed flesh. All that I'd given up, almost close enough to touch. I sat down to meet them—to meet the story of my life.